"LET'S JUST FORGET IT, OKAY?"

Nick ignored her. "I was just trying to apologize for my family. Sometimes they don't know when to stop."

"Thank you." *Okay, now let's be done.*

"It's not as if . . . as though . . . you and I . . . we don't even . . ."

That was it. "I think I know what you're trying to say." Alex took a deep breath, straightened her shoulders, and stared at his face, half hidden in darkness and shadow. "You and I are not interested in one another in any capacity other than a strictly business one, in which you will act as a guide while I conduct my research in this town. There is not, nor will there ever be, even the merest hint of attraction to one another, and any attempt to enhance the relationship will be done so merely in the name of politeness." *There. Let him think about that.*

He did not respond at first, and she wondered if her words had been too harsh, too cruel. She'd spent so many years cocooning herself against others, burrowing under layers of aloofness that she didn't stop to consider whether the very thing that protected her injured others. "I . . . I'm sorry."

The kiss came from nowhere—hard, powerful, consuming. He pulled her to him, his arms strong, protective, pressing her against his chest, hard planes to soft. She opened her mouth, let the feel of his tongue move over her, into her, through her. Heat pulsed deep inside, hot and wanting. Closer, she wanted to get closer. . . .

Also by Mary Campisi

PARADISE FOUND

Coming in January 2003
THE BUTTERFLY GARDEN

SIMPLE RICHES

Mary Campisi

ZEBRA BOOKS
KENSINGTON PUBLISHING CORP.

http://www.kensingtonbooks.com

This book is dedicated to my husband, Jim.
Thank you.

Prologue

She stared out the window, waiting. They would be back soon, wet and dripping from the water, and then it would be time for breakfast. Oatmeal with yellow raisins, two sprinkles of brown sugar. Her stomach grumbled. She leaned forward, pressed her nose against the glass. The water was dark today, the waves loud and mean-looking, like a lion roaring when they hit the rocks and burst apart. She wished she could run outside right now, in her nightgown, fast, all the way down to the beach, with the sand between her toes, the salt stinging her face as she flung herself into the water. But she'd promised them she wouldn't. *Next year,* Daddy had told her. *Next year you can come with us, and I'll show you what heaven looks like.*

She couldn't wait until she was nine; then she could go with them, see what they saw, see Daddy's heaven. Just the three of them. It had always been that way, unless she

counted Chessie next door. She guessed she was as close
to a relative as she had. Chessie was like an aunt, kind of
big, with a soft voice and a shiny black braid. She'd miss
her when they left next week. But Chessie said she'd save
all the best seashells for when they came back next summer.

Her stomach growled again. She squinted out the window.
Nothing. Maybe she should go to Chessie's, bring over the
oatmeal and raisins, see if she'd fix them, maybe give her
an extra sprinkle of brown sugar. Maybe . . . no, she'd wait.

She picked up the mirror Mommy and Daddy had given
her yesterday. It was blue and green with a long handle and
the most beautiful jewels all around: red, green, blue, yellow,
all sparkly and bright. She turned it from side to side, stared
into it, blew her breath onto it. *The true jewel is in the
mirror,* her father had said. *Look into it, child. Look into it
and see the jewel.* Where? Where was it? Where?

The red numbers on the clock moved forward, one click
at a time . . . 8:24 . . . 8:32 . . . 8:51. She put the mirror
down, got up and went into the kitchen, grabbed a graham
cracker from the cupboard. 9:11 . . . 9:15. Nibble, nibble,
nibble. 9:38 . . . 9:59 . . . 10:00. She brushed her hands
one against the other, watched the sugary crumbs fall in
her lap.

Maybe she should go down to the beach, dig for sand
crabs, look for her parents. Maybe . . . no, she'd wait.

10:05 . . . 10:07 . . . 10:13. She pressed her nose against
the glass again, harder this time. Her eyes were starting to
burn, like they did when she got suntan lotion in them.
Mommy knew how to take care of that . . . she put drops
in and told her to blink, blink, blink. Daddy told her to cry
and it would wash everything away. She swiped a hand
across her nose. *I'm crying now, Daddy. See? I'm crying
now and it still hurts.*

Maybe something was wrong . . . wrong, wrong . . . *very*

wrong. Very, very wrong. At 10:29, she jumped up and ran out of the house.

"Look at her." The woman with the shiny necklace and smelly perfume shook her head. "That blond hair all knotted up ... and those feet. They're filthy. She looks like an urchin, Walter."

The man, tall with a deep voice, said, "Not in front of the child, Helen."

"Oh, Walter, for heaven's sake, she hasn't spoken a word since we got here. For all we know there's something wrong with her. A genetic malformation ..." The woman patted her big, yellow-white hair in place. "Who knows ... between that brother of yours and that Russian woman," her voice dropped, "she could be retarded."

"Peter had the IQ of a genius," the man said. "And Nadia certainly was more than borderline functional."

"You know what I mean."

The man pinched the top of his nose, let out a long breath. "What I know is that my brother and his wife are dead and this child is headed for the orphanage if we don't take her in."

The woman named Helen sniffed, her blue eyes darting to the corner where the girl sat hugging her knees, staring at them, eyes half closed, mouth open. "I don't think we should rush things. Couldn't we at least have her tested? Just to be certain there isn't ... a defect of some sort."

"There's no defect," the man said, his voice stiff. "She's just lost her parents, for God's sake. She doesn't know us from a stranger on the street. How do you expect her to act?"

The woman pinched her red lips together. "I'm sure I have no idea. I never had a brother who slept under the stars and believed in Karma. For all we know, she's been weaned on magic mushrooms and has no brain cells left.''

"Peter was an artist, not a junkie.''

The woman laughed. ''Walter, this self-righteous attitude does not become you.'' Pause. ''Or is that guilt I hear?''

"That's enough.''

She ignored him, laughed again. ''It *is* guilt. I think I'll bask in the glory of it—I don't see it too often. The great Walter Chamberlain in a moment of guilt. How utterly . . . unique.''

"I said that's enough.''

"I'm not going to be stuck with this little piece of baggage because you feel guilty about cutting off your brother from the family purse strings. And neither should you. You gave him a choice and he took it.''

"I thought he'd come back.'' The man ran his hands over his face; his voice drifted away. ''After a month, maybe two . . .''

"He didn't want the money, Walter.''

"But he could have had anything, anything. Instead, he chose *this*?'' He swept a hand around the room. There was a red-and-gold couch, three folding chairs, and an easel. *''This* is what he wanted?''

The woman walked up to him, raised her face to meet his. ''He wanted freedom, Walter. The one thing you couldn't give him . . . or take away from him.'' She stepped back, opened her purse. ''Now, I'm going outside for a cigarette, while you decide what to do about her.''

The girl hugged her knees closer, her eyes following the lady's yellowish-white head out the door. They'd been talking about her. The tall man named Walter looked like Daddy in an old kind of way. Uncle Walter and Aunt Helen. That's what they'd called themselves. How could they be her aunt and uncle? She didn't have any relatives. Just

Mommy and Daddy and herself. Just the three of them. That's all it had ever been. *Mommy! Daddy! Come back!*

"Alexandra?" The man, Uncle Walter, was looking down at her.

She lifted her head, stared back at him. Maybe the policeman was wrong. Maybe the man and woman they found washed up on the beach three days ago weren't really her parents after all. Maybe they just looked like them . . . Maybe . . .

"Alexandra?" he said again. "Do you hear me? Can you understand me?"

Uncle Walter had said something about losing somebody. Maybe Mommy and Daddy were just lost. Maybe he was going to help find them.

"Aunt Helen and I are going to take you back with us . . . to Virginia."

She opened her mouth. "Mommy . . ." She sucked in a gulp of air. "Daddy . . ."

He shook his head. His hair was the same brown as Daddy's. "I'm sorry, Alexandra. They're gone."

Gone. "Can you . . . find them?"

"No. I can't." He looked out the window, toward the ocean. "They're in heaven now."

She bit her lip, hard, harder. *They're in heaven now . . .* The sound of the waves beat in her ears . . . *heaven. . . heaven . . . heaven.*

"I promise you, Alexandra, I'll make it up to you," her uncle's voice reached her from far away. "I'll give you everything that should have been your father's. He didn't want it, but you will. You'll see . . ."

Chapter 1

Arlington, VA
Twenty-six years later

"You'll save the maple tree, won't you?" The man rested his hands on the desk. His fingers were gnarled and weather-beaten, the nails thick with yellow deposits. "You know," he said, his faded blue eyes on Alex, "the one I showed you yesterday."

Alex looked away, rifled through the papers in front of her. This was the part she hated the most—looking into their eyes, seeing the loss, the pain of leaving, the agony of knowing their homes, their land, would be bulldozed, plowed under. Gone. All gone. Nothing left but snapshots, bunches of them, stuffed in shoe boxes or photo albums in a vain attempt to hold on to a feeling, a moment in time that would prove as elusive as a grain of sand. Some left the

remembering inside their head, buried under layers of inconsequential nothingness, crowded between mounds of garbled
data. Underneath it all, crammed together, was a history, a
life, a remembering that faded, disintegrated with time. That
was it.

Was it really so much to ask that a tree be saved? At least
it could serve as a landmark for what had been before, a
compass of sorts to lead generations of families back to their
ancestral homes. A simple tree. "I made note of it," Alex
said. "And we'll certainly try—"

"Mr. Oshanski," her associate, Eric Haines, cut her off
in his typical lawyer style. "We'll make every attempt to
save your tree"—he smiled, a quick flash of white—"and
hundreds of others like it."

The old man leaned back in his chair, blew out a long
breath. "My father planted that tree when my sister Emma
died. She was only two. Scarlet fever, they said." He stared
at his hands, clasped them together. "He told us it was
Emma's tree and every time we looked at it, we should think
of her."

One tree. They could promise to save one tree, couldn't
they? Alex looked at Eric, waited for him to say more, to
tell Mr. Oshanski that he'd make certain the tree stayed. For
Emma. But Eric was already shuffling through the documents in front of him, reaching for his pen.

"We'll see what we can do. Now, let's get the rest of
this paperwork out of the way and we'll be all set."

The old man smiled at them. "Thank you." His eyes
were wet. "Thank you for doing this for me. For Emma."
He reached into his pants pocket, pulled out a handkerchief,
and blew his nose. Twenty minutes later, Mr. Oshanski
shuffled out of Alex's office, a cane in one hand, a check
in the other.

"We just made Leonard Oshanski one rich old man."

Eric tossed his pen on the desk, leaned back, and clasped his hands behind his head.

Alex fiddled with her own pen, a Montblanc, black with gold. "You did mean what you said to him, didn't you? About saving the tree?"

"Why do you always doubt me, Alex? Of course, I meant it."

She nodded. "Good."

"It'll never happen, though. You can't bulldoze *around* one tree. Think of the time and money it would cost." He shrugged. "Even if that weren't an issue, the heavy equipment would kill the roots. The tree would never make it and then, somewhere along the line, you'd have to come back in and dig it out. More time and even more expense."

Alex stared at him, wondering how she'd ever thought there was a soft side to this man. How could she not have noticed the pauses, so calculated, the way he played with words, spoken and unspoken, twisting, massaging them to create his own justifications, state his own case? He was a lawyer, after all, and a damn good one. Negotiation, that was his forte. That's why WEC Management employed him as legal counsel and that's why it was one of the premier developers of exclusive vacation resorts in the country. Eric Haines knew how to negotiate, knew how to make his words all sincere and warm-sounding, knew how to make them come out in a voice that wrapped itself around the listener, soothing, calming, lulling. There was something about the way he looked at a person, as though they really mattered, as though *he* really cared. He could convince them that signing over their property was the right choice, the noble choice, for the betterment of family and personal interests. And it all seemed so genuine, so damn real, that people believed him. Even people who knew better.

"So, basically, you had no intention of saving that tree?"

Eric sat up, rifled a hand through his hair. It was a pale

gold color, like wheat in a field. "Why is it that every time we finish a deal, you go through this thirty-second guilt trip, which, by the way, only lasts until Walter gives you his 'well done' nod and you see your name in the *Wall Street Journal*?"

"It's not a guilt trip." She paused, stared down at Leonard Oshanski's signature. Each letter was well formed, written with great care, with pride, with confidence that right would be done. "The man just signed over thirty-three acres of land and all he's asking is that you save one tree."

"Wait a minute, Alex." Eric slid his wire-rimmed glasses to the bridge of his nose. "He received a chunk of money for those thirty-three acres. Let's not pretend it was a charitable donation."

"I know that." Money. It was always about money.

'And you heard me say I'd try." He shrugged. "So I will. But I'm telling you the architect is going to laugh in my face." His voice softened. "I'll buy the old man a new tree. You can pick it out. What kind did he say it was, again?"

"Maple. And it wouldn't be the same."

"Says who? We'll get the same size, plant it in the same spot, who'd be the wiser?"

She stared at him. "Well, we would be, for one."

"Jesus, Alex, it's just a damn tree. Next, people will be asking us to leave their flower patches or mark off the spot where they buried Fido." He reached out, touched her hand. "This is business. We make deals. Both sides get what they want, but neither side gets everything. That's what makes a good deal. Compromise, so nobody feels like they're getting screwed."

Alex sighed. "I know. It's just that the look on his face . . . it was so sad."

"I'd like to see how sad he is when he takes that check to the bank."

She sat there, watching his tanned fingers lightly stroke the back of her hand, and felt nothing. It had been a long time, sixteen months to be exact, since she'd had any emotions where Eric Haines was concerned. She pulled her hand away, slid it into her lap.

He pretended not to notice. "Just wait until Walter hears the deal is final. Then I'll have to listen to how his niece once again exercised brilliance and strategy in the selection of a WEC resort."

Alex smiled, thinking of her uncle. He would be proud, though he'd never come right out and say it. She could expect a hefty bonus and a handful of prospectus regarding mutual funds, as well as annual reports on his latest stock picks. Uncle Walter spread charts and other investment data in front of her like a grandfather showing off pictures of his grandchildren, with a warm gentleness and overriding concern, and she would never dream of telling him that at thirty-four, with an M.B.A. from Wharton, she didn't need his recommendations.

"So let's go find Walter and tell him the news," Eric said.

"Sure." No sense mentioning Mr. Oshanski's tree. She already knew what he'd say. *There's no room in business for sentiment, Alex. None. Once you start letting your heart rule your decisions instead of your head, you might as well close up shop, because you're as good as done. Bankruptcy court will be waiting with your name on the docket.*

"Then maybe you and I can go celebrate," Eric said, his voice falling to a low timbre. "Pop open a bottle of champagne, go to Emilio's for fettuccine primavera . . ."

"Eric—"

"Come on, Alex." The softness was gone. "How long are you going to punish me for one stupid mistake?"

She met his blue gaze. "I'm not punishing you, Eric. I'm just not interested." And it was true; finally, after all of these months it had become more than just a handful of rote sentences. It had become the truth.

"Christ, Alex, I made a mistake." He leaned forward, splayed his tanned fingers across her desk. "I want to be with you. . . . I love you."

Love? What did he know about love? For that matter, what did she know about it? Alex shook her head, priding herself on how well she maintained control, how she had come to terms with the whole situation without the aid of anyone: therapist, family, friend. "I'm sorry, Eric."

"She didn't mean anything, I told you that." Frustration crept into his voice. "Why won't you believe me?"

"I do believe you. But it doesn't matter now. It only mattered before—before you hopped into bed with Miss September."

"Christ."

"Why can't we just let go of the past, all of it? I respect you as a lawyer, and you're a valuable asset to the company, but you're not a part of my personal life, not anymore."

"But I could be if you'd only let me." He turned his hands over, palm side facing up. "We could take it slow. I wouldn't even press you to get married again, not right away."

"I don't love you anymore, Eric." Why couldn't he just let it go?

"That could come back, given time." His voice dipped, low, persuasive. "Even Walter thinks so."

Alex clenched her hands in her lap, sucked in a deep breath. "Don't you dare get him started again."

He raised his hands, gave her an innocent look. "Take it easy, okay? I didn't say anything." He shrugged. "Can I help it if he thinks you made a huge mistake when you divorced me?"

"He wouldn't think so if he knew the truth." If Uncle Walter knew about Eric and his Playboy Bunny, he'd fire him, no questions asked. Done. He would, wouldn't he? No matter how important Eric was to WEC Management, family still came first. Didn't it? *Well, didn't it?*

"Then I guess I'll count myself lucky that your loyalty to the company overrides your personal feelings."

"Uncle Walter depends on you. Why disrupt the infrastructure of the company because of our''—she searched for the right words—"personal differences?" Besides, just the thought of confiding the truth to her uncle turned her stomach. *Eric chose a silicone-enhanced woman with collagen-injected lips and a 1.8 GPA over me, Uncle Walter, over me!* It was too humiliating, too degrading to even consider. Alex knew all about Miss September, Tanya Wolls. He had studied her as though he were preparing to present his master's thesis. Born Tanya Lynnette Wolleshanko in Tulsa, Oklahoma, age: 23, height: 5' 9", weight: 108 lbs., college: attended OSU three years, majoring in Communications. Currently employed as a hostess at Outback Steakhouse in Tulsa. Participated in Playboy's College Search during her sophomore year, selected for September issue. Favorite color: pale pink. Favorite food: McDonald's french fries dipped in a chocolate milkshake. *Gag!*

And then there was the other reason, the one that even she didn't like to think about. What if she told Uncle Walter the truth and he *didn't* fire Eric? What if he decided that Eric's little indiscretion shouldn't interfere with the company, and continued on as though nothing had happened? Uncle Walter loved her; she knew he did, even though he never said it. *But the company was his whole life.* The company meant everything to him, everything, and Alex did not want to be pitted against it for his allegiance, mostly because, deep down, she feared she might lose.

So she pretended her divorce fell under the blanket of "irreconcilable differences" ranging from *I didn't like the way he squeezed the toothpaste* to *Marriage was too intimate a relationship for me.*

"Alex?"

"What?" She looked up, pushed the past away. "What?"

He was studying her, his blue eyes intent behind his glasses. "I know I screwed up. But I'm not giving up on us. I won't quit, Alex. Not until I have you back."

"Eric—"

A knock on the door cut her off. Walter Eugene Chamberlain, CEO of WEC Management, poked his head in and said, "Well, should I call Armand and tell him to chill the champagne?"

"Tell him two bottles," Eric said, laughing.

"He agreed to everything?"

"Yes," Alex said. Eric met her gaze, smiled. They both knew her uncle wasn't interested in anything as inconsequential as an old man's sentimental fondness for a tree. He was a bottom-line man, period.

"Good. Very good." He smiled, a sliver of upturned lips, and settled himself in the chair next to Eric. "This is going to be a phenomenal addition to Krystal Springs."

"Preliminary projections indicate revenue will almost double once the ski lodge is in place," Alex said. "Krystal Springs could be our most profitable venture yet."

She watched her uncle's smile spread, bit by bit. Talk about development and rate of return could do that to him. When he smiled, which wasn't often, his thin lips pulled across his face in a slow, calculated manner, as though at sixty-four years of age, he still wasn't comfortable with the exercise. He was a handsome man, his skin golden from hours spent on the green, his pale blue eyes sharp, his silver hair neat and tapered from weekly trims, his nose long and straight, his body tall and erect. Walter Chamberlain was like a father to Alex, fitting the role with more ease and right than her real father, who, with each passing year became less reality and more of a scattered memory, torn with gaping holes. She had nothing, not even a picture to remember him or her mother by. Only memories that had faded and an old chipped mirror they'd given her when she was eight, the day before they died.

"I want you to run the numbers again. Use a twenty-four percent rate of return, see what that does," he said.

Alex jotted a note to herself. "I'll get it to you this afternoon."

"And I think I'll go have Sylvia make lunch reservations at Emilio's," Eric said, standing. "And, order two bottles of Dom Perignon."

When he left, Uncle Walter stretched out his legs and sighed. "Ah, Alex, there's nothing like the thrill of a good deal pulsing through your veins to keep you going."

She smiled. "I think *any* deal, good or bad, would keep you going, Uncle Walter."

His mouth twitched. "True. But you aren't much different than me, young lady. You love the chase just as much as I do."

He was right, of course. She did enjoy the challenge of finding locations for WEC resorts. It was like putting together a thousand-piece puzzle of an ocean where three quarters of the pieces were blue, a slightly different shade perhaps, but still blue. Selecting the ideal site was a lot like that, at least initially. There was only one major criterion, the same one for every project: the location needed to be within a one-hour proximity to a metropolitan area. Once Alex established those boundaries, she gathered charts, maps, graphs, studied water tables, terrain, climate, and depending on the type of resort they were considering, summer, winter, or summer/winter, she made her initial recommendations and then went to scout out the place.

That's where it got interesting, living in the town for two or three months, finding out who was in charge—and it was never the mayor—who had an alliance or a relationship to whom, who could be persuaded, who needed money. These were things you couldn't find out from studying a piece of paper. You had to get in the trenches, imbed yourself among them, kind of like a computer virus, absorbing information and collecting data without anyone's knowledge. But unlike the virus that corrupts and destroys, Alex thought of her methods as a way to help those who couldn't—or didn't know how to—help themselves. Consider the widowed part-time Super Duper cashier who'd never been farther than an hour from her home. Buying up her property enabled her to go on a cruise with her women friends and purchase a condo near her son in North Carolina. Or the fifty-year-old man who'd been laboring in the same factory for thirty-two years. He sold his land, moved his family to a suburb outside of Jacksonville, Florida, and opened up a video store.

With research, care, and timing, everybody got what they wanted. It was a win/win situation. In the seven years she'd been involved with the property research division of WEC Management, there'd only been two times when an individual had refused to sell. The first happened years ago, when Alex had just taken over the division. There was a farmer in Roanoke, Virginia, Leon "Rusty" Dade, who owned fifty acres of land. He farmed some, rented out some, and kept the biggest section for his most prized possessions, his Black Angus cattle. And no amount of cash incentives could persuade Rusty to sell. The land was his legacy, could be traced all the way back to his great-granddaddy's granddaddy, and would be his five children's legacy, too. The last Alex inquired, a year ago, Rusty was still farming and ranching and living out his legacy.

The only other time anyone had refused a WEC Management offer was two years ago when its chief competitor, Cora Ltd., slid in and bought up a tract of land an hour from Portland, Oregon. Alex had been sure WEC would get the deal, had been shocked when they didn't. Until she heard that the CEO's son, Sam Cora, was keeping very close company with Lilly Arbogast, whose father, Jed, owned thirty-five of the fifty acres in question. And it didn't surprise anyone, except maybe Lilly, that once the deal was done, so was Lilly.

"So do you want to tell me about the next venture?" Uncle Walter asked, straightening his gray silk tie.

Alex smiled. This was when she felt the closest to her uncle, here, in this room, poring over charts and graphs, watching his eyes spark with interest as she drew him into the planning stages of a certain piece of property, considering and discussing all of its possibilities. The usual stern expression on his face smoothed out, the brackets around his mouth faded, and he seemed almost . . . relaxed. If you could call a man who spent six and a half days at the office, had his hair trimmed every five days, and never went anywhere without at least a sport coat, relaxed. There was a oneness here, a unity, intangible yet real, that bound them to each other when they were planning a project. Alex felt it; he had to feel it, too. So, maybe her uncle didn't say the words, but he cared. She knew he cared. And when he nodded his silver head in agreement, she felt like a child on a hot summer's day, who'd just been given an ice-cream cone. Delight. Pure delight.

"Alex? Plan on keeping it all to yourself?"

"No." She laughed, ran a hand through her hair. "Actually, I think I may have found the ideal location for our next project.'' She met his gaze, tried to control her excitement. ''A *year-round* resort.''

''That's quite a statement, young lady.''

''I know. But it looks perfect . . . at least the specs do. It's an area in the northwestern section of Pennsylvania, about an hour from Pittsburgh. Lots of trees, birds, deer, a lake, even . . . the whole nature bit.'' She waved a hand in front of her. ''The kind of landscape tourists love. And, get this''—she leaned forward, rested her elbows on the top of her cherry desk—''the first snowfall last year was October twenty-second.''

His pale blue eyes lit up. ''Mix it with a little powder . . .''

''. . . and by mid-November the slopes would be ideal.'' She swiveled her chair around, pulled a large portfolio off the credenza, and spread the contents on the desk. Here, we've got a map of the area. There's the Allegheny River, running west, which seems to be right in the town's back-yard.'' She traced a thin blue line. ''And over here''—she pointed to a small blue shape—''is Sapphire Lake. The water alone is enough to get excited about. But they've got mountains, and steep hills, too. I can just picture them with lights and ski lifts.''

Her uncle picked up the map, studied it, rubbed his jaw. ''I don't want another piecemeal project, Alex. This time, I want the whole thing. One deal, period.''

''I agree.'' She shifted in her chair. ''I know you were disappointed that Mr. Oshanski didn't sell out sooner.'' Her voice dipped. ''He had a lot of issues to deal with. . . .''

''We can't afford to fall prey to another person's senti-mental wanderings. If we can't get the package this time, we don't do the deal.''

''I'll get the package, Uncle Walter.'' There was a firm-ness to his voice that hinted at disappointment. Even though he'd told her he didn't hold her responsible for Mr. Oshanski's thirteen-month delayed response, she *felt* responsible. She should have been able to close the deal, persuade him to sell off his land and buy a condo in the suburbs. But looking at him, sitting in his rocker on the front porch of the old farmhouse where he and his deceased wife, Lena, had raised seven children, it hadn't seemed appropriate or plausible to mention. He wasn't the type who would look forward to central air-conditioning or maintenance-free lawns. His children were scattered all over the country, busy with lives of their own, and all he had left were memories . . . and a tree. Uncle Walter would never understand about the tree, or the memories, for that matter.

"What else do you know about the area?"

"Well, it looks like there are two families who run the place." She slid her reading glasses on, scanned her notes. "The Kraziaks . . . and the Androvichs. A Mr. Norman Kraziak owns a sawmill company and a furniture manufacturing plant. They make specialty rocking chairs. And the Androvichs, looks like a Nicholas, own thirteen hundred fifty acres and a logging business."

"Interesting."

Alex glanced up. "How so?"

Uncle Walter's lips pulled ever so slowly into a semblance of a smile. "It's obvious that the businesses are interdependent. They may even have relatives on both sides, through marriage and whatnot. One can't survive without the other. All you have to do is win one of them over . . ."

". . . and the other won't be able to survive."

"Or at the very least, surviving would prove very difficult. That's where we come in and offer them a way out."

"Sounds like a plan." Alex jotted down a few notes. *Meet Mr. Kraziak/Mr. Androvich, ASAP.* "I thought I'd leave in a couple of days. Get myself settled." *Show you*

*that I haven't lost my touch. I can do this, I can get the
whole package.*

"What? Not even a buying trip to New York?"

"No." She gave him a sheepish look. "I hate to admit
it, but I've got half a closet stuffed with clothes that still
have Bloomingdale's and Neiman Marcus tags on them. I
really think I should pass."

"Eric said something about Maui."

Here it comes. "Good. He should take a vacation. He's
been working hard."

Uncle Walter cleared his throat. "Actually, he said the
same thing about you, Alex. He thinks you've been working
very hard and need a break." He paused, cleared his throat
again. "I think he was intending to ask you to go to Maui
with him."

Silence.

Alex underlined the names Kraziak and Androvich three
times. "Sorry." She looked up, gave him a half smile. "I
really want to get started on this project. It's already May
and I want to see the area in the summer. I figure two months
for research"—she tapped her pen against her chin—"that
should put us well into July."

"I'll expect to hear from you at least once a week," Uncle
Walter said. "And monthly visits. You're not that far from
home that you can't make the trip once a month." He crossed
his arms over his chest like a dictator issuing an edict.

"Of course," Alex said, dipping her head to hide a smile.
He got like this every time she told him she was going away
somewhere. *Call. Visit. Don't forget to . . .* "Of course I'll
come home."

Uncle Walter nodded. "Good." He picked at a piece of
lint on the sleeve of his gray suit. "I want to be kept
informed." He looked up, met her gaze. "Remember, it's
a package deal. All or nothing."

Oh, God, not again. "I'll remember." How could she

ever forget? His words were pounding in her skull right now. He was never going to let her forget, never, not unless she redeemed herself with this next project.

He stood up then, brushed a hand over his slacks, and said, "This place you're going to, does it have a name?"

"Restalline. It's called Restalline."

Chapter 2

"What was it this time, Harry?" Nick Androvich looked up from the chart in his hand. "Peanut Buster Parfait? Cheeseburger from Hot Ed's?"

The man on the exam table rubbed his stomach, groaned. "Sausage sub, peppers, and onions."

"From Hot Ed's?"

Harry nodded. "Don't tell Tilly, Doc. She'll shoot me if she finds out."

Nick set the chart on the counter beside him. "I'm not going to tell Tilly anything. I won't have to, Harry. One look at you and she'll know what you've been doing."

"Ah, Doc." He moved his hand up and down from just below his belly button to the top of his groin. "I couldn't help it. I didn't mean to, honest. I just went in to give Bernie his mail. That's it. But I had to get his signature on a certified piece and he was back in the kitchen, frying up peppers and onions.'' He groaned again, let out a belch. "I couldn't stand it. The sausage was just sitting there, all shiny and plump. And that smell . . . After three weeks of broth and boiled chicken, I just went crazy. Bernie and I figured one sub would be okay.''

"Well, now you know it isn't.''

Harry lowered his head. Nick could see the top of his head, shaved to less than half an inch, gray speckled with brown. "No. I think it was the other ones that did me in.''

"The other ones?'' Nick raised a brow, waited. Harry wasn't going to stop until he landed in the operating room. "How many 'other ones' would that be, Harry?''

Harry's shoulders slumped forward. "I don't know what came over me.'' He inched up his eyes to meet Nick's. "I tell you, it was like I was an addict, and that sausage sub was my drug.''

"How many, Harry?'' The man was going to eat himself right into his grave.

"Three.'' The word came out low, barely above a whisper.

"Three,'' Nick repeated. "Three.''

"I'm sorry, Doc.''

"Damn it, Harry, you know better. You were in here three weeks ago because Tilly's chicken paprikash finally caught up with you. Remember telling me it felt like somebody was running a hot poker along your insides?''

"I know, I know.'' He clutched his stomach with both hands, leaned forward.

Nick rested his hand on the other man's shoulder. Harry Lendergin had been delivering mail to the residents of Restalline for thirty-four years. He knew every route, every street number and name, had been assigned to most at one time or another. Over the years, he'd stuffed hundreds of thousands, maybe millions, of pieces of information into mailboxes: bills, letters, junk mail, magazines, good news and bad, hoped for and dreaded, in small white envelopes

and long manila squares. He'd carried Nick his MCAT
scores, then his admission letter to Hahnemann, and later
yet, a certificate from the State of Pennsylvania with his
name on it—Nicholas Anthony Androvich, Board Certified
in Family Practice. Harry was a simple man, honest, hardworking, with a wife, two grown daughters, and an affinity
for food packed with fat.

"I'm from the old school, Doc." Harry shifted around
on the exam table, settled both hands over his stomach,
started rubbing up and down. "When Tilly gives me a piece
of cake, I want it to taste like cake, not that god-awful yogurt
stuff she puts in there. Substitute. That's what she says."
He heaved a big sigh. "She's driving me nuts, you know
that?"

"Harry," Nick said in a gentler tone. "This isn't about
Tilly, she's only trying to help. It's up to you. I know you
know, and I know it's tough. You were raised on bacon and
gravy, you and three quarters of the residents of Restalline
over fifty. Everybody was back then, but your body can't
take it anymore and it's fighting back. You're only fifty-
four years old, Harry. You've got a lot of good years left,
if you take care of yourself."

"I will, Doc, I will."

"Listen to me, Harry. Aside from the way this food is
tearing up your gallbladder, what do you think it's doing to
your arteries? Do you want to end up like my dad?"

Harry shook his head, made a hasty sign of the cross.
"Poor Nick Senior."

"He was less than fifty feet from his men and he couldn't
call for help—not that anybody could've done anything for
him. But at least he wouldn't have died alone."

Even now, after all this time, Nick still cringed at the
thought of his father, lying in the snow, half frozen, dead
from a massive heart attack. He still remembered the pick-
ups, traveling down the long gravel driveway, inching for-

ward, headlights dim, like a funeral procession, converging on the old white farmhouse where Nicholas Androvich Sr. and his wife Stella lived with their three children. His mother had run outside, wiping her hands on the printed apron she always wore. *He's hurt, isn't he? He tried to take down a tree by himself and got hurt, didn't he? Is it his leg? His arm?* Her words got louder, the pitch more hysterical. *Where is he? Where? Nick! Nick! Goddamn you, Nick, for taking foolish chances! We've got three kids to raise, damn you!* Uncle Frank, Nick Sr.'s brother, got out of the first truck, pulled her away, and said something to her. Nick Jr. watched from the top step of the wraparound porch as his mother's legs buckled and she fell into Uncle Frank's arms like a rag doll that's had the stuffing pulled out of it.

Nick knew then, didn't have to hear the words swirling around him in hushed whispers to confirm it. His father was dead. Nicholas Androvich Sr., second-generation son of a Czechoslovakian immigrant and his wife, was dead. Nick Jr. thought of his father lying somewhere amid the acres of land he'd bought years ago, piece by piece, shrouded in maple, pine, poplar, ash, and the elusive cherry. He'd forged a logging company through brawn, sheer will, and a desire to provide a better life for his family, and then, when the dream was just within his reach, he'd toppled over and drawn his last breath among the trees he knew so well. People said Nick Sr. was like his trees, tall, sturdy, formidable, a man who bowed to no one, no one but his own body that gave out at forty-nine. Everyone wondered about his death. Was it the two shots of Smirnoff he had every morning before pulling out that weakened his heart, did him in? Or maybe Stella's mashed potatoes and gravy or her stuffed dumplings? Some said it was his temper, all bottled up like aged whiskey, ready to explode any second. And still others wondered about his family history, his father and his father's father. Genetics. Nick, at fifteen, hadn't known what to think, so he'd thought about all of it, all of the time. Could it have been detected, maybe prevented? Could his father still be alive today? The questions wouldn't go away. If a doctor had examined his father, identified a problem, a blockage maybe, then maybe the outcome would have been different. Maybe . . .

Restalline had two general practitioners back then, Dr. Montolowski and Dr. Heinen. Stanley Montolowski treated everyone with a dose of castor oil and a tablespoon of Brioschi. If that didn't do the trick, he sent them to Dr. Heinen. Charles Heinen was originally from Pittsburgh, a "city-boy," the townspeople called him. He'd moved here with his wife and two small children to get away from the city and enjoy country life. People laughed at his bow ties and shiny wing-tip shoes, so different from Dr. Montolowski's red-and-blue striped tie and scuffed oxfords. Many thought his ways were too different, too bizarre. Whoever heard of sitting in a dark room and counting your breaths? That wasn't relaxing, that was downright crazy! And the tests the man ordered, blood test for this and that, getting poked like a pincushion. Nick Androvich Sr. refused to see Dr. Heinen, even after Dr. Montolowski's castor oil/Brioschi treatment failed. *It's a pulled muscle is all, from lifting logs all day. That pansy doctor wouldn't know the first thing about hard work or real pain. He's a city boy, not like us, not Restalline born and bred.*

Two weeks later, Nick's father suffered a massive heart attack and died. If he'd let Dr. Heinen examine him, would the outcome have been different? Would he have lived? Nick vowed to find a way to educate the townspeople, help them to overcome their prejudices, their ignorance about health care. He'd become a doctor of family medicine because his father had fought illness with blind denial and died because of it.

Nick was not going to let Harry Lendergin be a victim,

even if he had to barricade Hot Ed's to do it. "Right now your gallbladder's inflamed and the attacks are your body's way of telling you it can't handle the food you're giving it."

"I don't want the surgery yet, Doc." Harry's dark eyes filled with panic. "Not until after Marie's wedding."

"No doctor would do the surgery now, not with the inflammation. We've got to get that under control with antibiotics, and then we'll talk about having you see a surgeon. I'll give you a few names."

Harry waved a hand in the air. "Just one name, the one you think would be best for me."

"Fine. Now, can I tell you what I think would be best for you right now?"

"Sure, Doc. Whatever you say."

"Okay. You need something for pain and you need rest."

"Thanks, Doc. I'm grateful, truly grateful."

"I'm not finished yet, Harry. No more sausage subs, no more chicken paprikash, chicken and dumplings, hamburgers, or peanuts."

"Okay, Doc." He nodded his crew-cut head.

"Just wait a minute. No ice cream, peanut butter, doughnuts, Twinkies, or pizza. Nothing loaded with fat."

"Anything you say, Doc. I promise."

"I mean it, Harry. If it happens again, you won't make it a month to Marie's wedding. You'll be in the hospital, period."

Harry's face turned white beneath his tan. "I gotta make Marie's wedding, Doc. I'll eat Tilly's broth and boiled chicken." He shook his head, muttering, "That's probably what'll do me in, but I'll eat it."

Nick smiled, shook Harry's hand. "Call me if you have any other problems. Sometimes the gallbladder acts up even when all you're eating *is* broth and boiled chicken."

"Thanks, Doc." Harry nodded. "Thanks for everything."

Ten minutes later, Harry Lendergin left the doctor's office with a prescription in one hand and his empty mailbag in the other.

"Well, whose kitchen has Harry been raiding this time?" Elise Pentani looked up from the stack of charts in front of her.

"Hot Ed's," Nick said, handing her Harry's chart. "Sausage sub. Three of them."

"Good Lord, no wonder he came in doubled over."

"I told him if he wants to walk Marie down the aisle next month, he'd better stay away from all that junk he's been sneaking." Nick unbuttoned his lab coat, pulled it off. "I've got to stop by and check on Mrs. Graeber." He glanced at his watch. "I told her I'd be there by six."

"Speaking of fat, I bet she'll have a cherry pie waiting for you," Elise said, her lips pulling into a broad smile.

Nick grinned. "I'm counting on it."

"Most doctors want cash." She laughed. "But you, you want cherry pies, chocolate chip cookies, banana nut bread. You have some nerve lecturing Harry."

"The difference is that I can eat a piece and stop. Harry doesn't call it quits until the whole thing's done." He patted his stomach. "But one of these days it's all going to show up, right here."

She shook her head. "I doubt it. Some people are just blessed."

"Yeah, that's me all right. Blessed. A regular *GQ* kind of guy." He ran both hands through his hair, tried to smooth down the flip in the back. He needed a trim. "That's why I'm wearing a red polo from Penney's and a pair of Levi's, relaxed fit, mind you. And docksiders with a stain on the left shoe thanks to Mrs. Graeber's Chihuahua with the irritable bladder."

"And the really sick thing is you still look like you just walked off the cover of a magazine."

"Right. *Zoo World*, maybe."

"Hardly, Nick."

He laughed. "You need to get a husband, tell him all this flattery stuff. He'd eat it right up. Great for the marriage."

Elise scrunched up her nose. "Uh, thanks, but I'm a little light in the male department right now." She held up both hands. "Not that I'm looking."

"You should be. You're what? Twenty-eight? Twenty-nine?"

"Thirty."

"All the more reason. You've been on three dates in the two years you've been working for me. That's crazy."

"Five. I've been on five. Six if you count the cholesterol screening with Dr. Crawford. We went out for coffee afterward."

"Okay, six. You're beautiful, Elise, really, *and* you've got a great personality."

She let out a little laugh. "So what kind of man could match a compliment like that?"

He ignored her. "And you're one hell of a nurse, great with the patients, easy to talk to. Any man in his right mind would jump at the chance to be with you."

"They're all lined up outside, aren't they?" She tapped her fingernails on the Formica desk, looked at him.

"Maybe I'm working you too much. Maybe you need more time to get out, socialize." She was at his office all the time, early in the morning until late at night.

"Thanks, but no thanks."

Now she sounded just like him. *Thanks, but no thanks.* He had a reason to be that way. Elise didn't. She'd never been married, had never even had a serious relationship, not that he knew of, and he'd known her since she was five. So, what was she afraid of? Caring about someone enough to get hurt? Baring her soul and then being rejected? Loving someone and then losing him? What was it? She'd make a

great wife, a great mother. Any man would be lucky to have
a woman like Elise . . . any man . . . even his lamebrained,
stubborn brother.

The idea hit him square between the eyes, so fast that he
had to slow it down and replay it all over again. Elise
and Michael . . . Elise and Michael . . . Maybe she could
straighten him out, knock that chip off his shoulder, show
him how to love, give him hope. Maybe . . . just maybe.
"Elise, what are you doing Saturday night?"

"W-w-what did you say?"

"I said what are you doing Saturday night?" He watched
her cheeks turn a dull red. Pretty, very pretty. Michael liked
dark-haired women, didn't he?

Elise patted her hair, fanned her hand in front of her face.
"It's awful hot in here, don't you think?"

Had she guessed what he was planning? Is that why she
seemed suddenly off-kilter? "We're having a birthday party
at the house for Uncle Frank. He'll be sixty-four. Mom's
making stuffed cabbage and lasagna. Why don't you come?"

She looked away, looked back, looked away again.

"Unless you have other plans? . . ."

"What time?"

"Eight."

"I'll . . . I'll be there." Her voice dipped. "I'm looking
forward to it."

"Good." *Good.* "So am I." *Have I got a surprise for
you.* . . . He glanced at his watch. "Gotta go. Mrs. Graeber's
pie's waiting." Nick grabbed his bag, waved a hand in the
air, and ran out the back door.

Nick flipped on his blinker and turned the silver Navigator
onto the long gravel drive leading to his parents' home.
Twenty-three years since his father's death and he still
thought of the old farmhouse as his mother and father's.

Stella and Nick's. Maybe because his mother had kept almost everything the same as when the old man was alive: the big maple table with four side chairs and one captain's chair, the faded, green-plaid fiberglass curtains pulled back over three windows, those god-awful wrought iron roosters, all shapes and sizes covering the walls, a wrought-iron rooster clock, too. The old linoleum floor, a brownish-tan-square mix, scuffed and cracked along the edges, and his father's most prized possessions—the cherry cupboards he and Uncle Frank had made, hand picked from Androvich Lumber. The only real changes to the kitchen were the appliances. The avocado refrigerator had died two years ago and the Androvich children convinced their mother that the new white refrigerator she'd ordered made the old stove look like an eyesore, and would she please get rid of it? It took some work, and a lot of persuasion, but Stella finally relented and had a white flat-top model from GE installed. There still wasn't a garbage disposal or a dishwasher. *Garbage is garbage. I'm not going to sort it all out.* And, *If I have to scrape and rinse all the food off, I might as well wash it and be done.*

She did accept Uncle Frank's gift, two Christmases ago, much to everyone's surprise. It was a microwave oven, and though she swore she'd never use it for more than reheating her coffee, as the months passed, she learned how to defrost hamburger, bake a potato, fry bacon, and even pop popcorn for her grandchildren. Stella Androvich, old-fashioned, make-it-from-scratch woman, was inching her way into the twenty-first century!

But the rest of the house had stopped breathing new life twenty-three years ago, when Nick Androvich Sr. died. Sometimes Nick thought his mother tried harder to preserve his father's memory than she did to forge on and live her own life. Would Nick Sr. have wanted it that way? Would the old man really have wanted her to keep the red plastic currycomb he used to brush over his crew cut on top of his dresser? Couldn't she at least put it in a drawer, tucked away, maybe take it out every now and then if she felt the need? But to see it every morning, every night, every time she went into her bedroom, would he have wanted *that*? Nick doubted it, but it did no good to say anything. Stella Androvich had a mind of her own, period. She wore the title of widow like a shield, barring entry to all but her children, and then, as time passed, her grandchildren, clutching the role of mother and grandmother, but never again woman, or even self. That part of her seemed to have faded with the much-laundered aprons she wore, washed each week for so many years, until the colors ran into one another and it was hard to remember what they had once looked like. That was his mother, blending into her children's lives, one washing at a time, a selfless person turned into a selfless woman.

Maybe it was the Androvich curse to end up alone. Uncle Frank had never even married, or been close to it, though there must have been someone, somewhere, in his almost sixty-four years of life. Maybe the Androvichs just didn't have it in them to love, or to open their hearts more than once. One time, that was it. Look at him, and Michael . . . perfect examples. Gracie was the only exception . . . so far. Maybe his kid sister would beat the odds, defy the curse; maybe she'd live happily ever after five doors down with her husband and children. Maybe . . .

And maybe, just maybe, with a little help and a lot of luck, times would change for the rest of them. That's why he'd invited Elise to Uncle Frank's party. She would be good for Michael, tone down his temper, keep him even-paced, make him think about something other than his next six-pack. Maybe he'd even remember he had two kids.

"Nick? Is that you?"

His mother's voice reached him from the other side of

the screen door. She was in the kitchen, baking bread from the smell of it. "Hey, Ma." He stepped inside. "My favorite cook." He walked over to her, gave her a peck on the cheek.

"Not from what I can see," she said, eying the pie in his left hand. "You've been to see Agnes Graeber again, haven't you?"

"How'd you know?"

She sniffed. "Simple. Who's the only woman, other than me, who makes you pie? Cherry, to boot?"

Nick grinned, put his arm around his mother. "So, Stella's got a little competition, eh?"

She let out a huff. "I could bake circles around that woman. I think she only makes you those pies because she thinks you'll ask her daughter out."

"Gloria?" Thirty-six-year-old, face-in-a-book, sit-in-a-corner, only-wear-black, mumbling Gloria? "I . . . don't think so, Mom." God, could it be true? Could Mrs. Graeber have been exaggerating the pain in her right foot, the one that *made it just impossible for her to climb the steps to his office*?

"I know that woman." She wagged a finger under his nose. "She's been trying to get that daughter of hers married off for years." She wiped her hands on her apron, a pinkish-green tulip pattern, grabbed a quilted mitt, and opened the oven door. "And you'd be the perfect catch. Ah," she breathed, closing her eyes, "now this is real baking." Nick watched her slide the rack out, lift a loaf of bread with one mitted hand, flip it upside down, and tap it three times with the tip of her fingers. *A dull thud means it's not done.* The loaf was golden, glistening with butter rubbed all over. Four more loaves and twelve more taps before she closed the door and said, "Another ten minutes."

Nick headed for the fridge, peeked inside. "What'd you have for dinner?"

"Your favorite. Stuffed peppers with parsley-buttered

potatoes.'' She smiled, ran a hand through her hair. It was
cut just above her shoulders, dark brown streaked with gray,
like a copse of pine trees topped with snow. ''I fixed you
a dish to take home.''

''Thanks, Mom.'' At sixty-three, she was still a handsome
woman, tall and slender, her movements measured and
graceful . . .

''Don't think Gloria Graeber has ever stepped foot in a
kitchen.''

. . . with an opinion about everything. ''I'll keep that in
mind.''

''You do that.'' Her dark brown eyes narrowed on him.
''And the same goes for that rent-a-heart doctor you've been
flitting around with lately. She strikes me as a take-out kind
of lady.''

Lisa . . . She was talking about Lisa. How had his mother
found out about *her*?

''And that's no way to raise a child. Justin would hate it.
You remember that.'' She *tsk-tsked* at him. ''No way at
all,'' she said under her breath.

''Lisa cooks.'' He paused, added, ''Some.''

''Oh.'' She waved a wooden spoon at him. ''Her name's
Lisa. I see.'' She tapped the spoon against the palm of her
hand. ''And what did this Lisa cook for you, Nick?''

How had they gotten into this conversation? He wished
he could stop it, right now, yank the words back, start again.
He'd shut up this time.

''Nick?''

He shrugged, jammed his hands in his pockets. ''I don't
know. Some kind of hors d'oeuvres with spinach and crab.''
They were pretty tasty, too. ''And shrimp cocktail.''

His mother nodded her head, a knowing smile spreading
over her face. ''I know what you're talking about. Sure do.''
Her head bobbed up and down. ''The hors d'oeuvres come
twenty-four in a box at the Market Basket.'' She tilted her

head in his direction, lowered her voice. "In the frozen-food section."

Nick wasn't going to let on that she'd gotten to him. "Hmm. Maybe I'll buy you a box sometime, see how you like 'em." So what if Lisa couldn't cook? The woman was a doctor, not a culinary expert for Chrissake. And it was just a few dates, a diversion, that's all. Lisa Kinkaid, staff cardiologist for North West Pennsylvania Cardiologists' Group, was a city girl, addicted to Saks, the theater, five-star restaurants, and sushi bars, none of which could be found in Restalline.

"Yes, let's do that, Nicholas. And you'll have to invite Lisa so I can meet her."

He smiled. "Sure, Mom. I'll have her check her schedule." No sense telling her Lisa wouldn't be back for another month.

"Well, I'm glad that's settled." She pushed her hair behind her ears and turned back to the oven. "I'll just get these loaves out and you can take one home with you."

"Thanks." Nick grabbed a fork from the silverware drawer, lifted up the tin foil on the glass casserole dish. "Where's Justin?" he asked, digging out a chunk of stuffed pepper.

"He's out back. Come to think of it, he's been there for quite a while. Maybe he wandered over to Frank's workshop."

Nick took another bite of pepper, set his fork down. "I'll go find him." He went out the back door, down the steps, and looked around, raising a hand against the sun. The memories came rushing back, crowding his senses, like they always did when he looked out over the land, acres and acres of it, some treed, some fields, but Androvich land, all of it. His chest still swelled with an indescribable feeling when he gazed out over it. There were a lot of memories here, most good, some bad. He and Michael used to climb the maple tree to his right, shimmy up fifteen feet in the air, arms hardly able to circle the thick branches, skinny legs dangling. It was just the two of them then, Gracie was still a baby. And Nick Androvich Sr. was so proud of his sons, Nicholas and Michael, heirs to thirteen hundred fifty acres of land and Androvich Lumber. *This will all be yours one day, boys. Yours and Gracie's.* They'd been standing in the middle of a field, knee-high in clover, the sun fading to pale orange as it drifted behind a blanket of trees. *It's part of you . . . this land . . . Can't you feel it pumping in your blood? It's part of you. . . .*

Nick and Michael had stood side-by-side, solemn, watching the sun inch below the trees, the bond between them tightening. Nothing would ever come between them, nothing. Not until Caroline . . .

"Dad?"

Nick blinked, blinked again. "Justin? Where'd you come from? I came out to look for you."

"I was here. Behind that tree." He looked up, squinted. "Are you okay? You looked kind of weird, like you were gonna throw up or something."

Nick cleared his throat, put an arm around his son. "I'm fine. What are you doing out here all alone?"

Justin's shoulders slumped forward a little. "Nothing." His voice drooped. "Just sittin'." His gaze shifted to his sneakers.

"Grandma says you've been out here for a while."

"I guess."

"Justin—"

His son looked up, and Nick saw tears in his blue eyes. Caroline's eyes. "What is it, Justin? What's the matter?"

"They said"—tears started streaming down his face—"they said Mom killed herself. That she burned to a crisp, like a marshmallow"—he hiccupped—"all black, and that her skin sizzled like bacon." He buried his face against

Nick's shirt, grief moving through him with the rise and fall of his tiny shoulders.

Jesus! "Who said that, Justin? Who?" Nick gripped his son's shoulders, forced him to look up. "Who, Son?" He gentled his tone, tried to keep the rage inside. Eight years old was too young for such hard truths. But then, so was thirty-eight.

"Jerry Toranchi."

Figures. The undertaker's kid. "Well, you ignore him, do you hear me? Just ignore him."

Justin swiped a hand over both eyes, sniffed and nodded. "Uh-huh." His voice wobbled.

"Good." Nick put his arm around his son, pulled him to his side. "That's my boy."

"Dad?"

"Hmmm?"

Justin looked away, past the field, out toward the trees, to the place where sky and land met, blended, joined. "Did she?"

Nick tensed, forced the word out. "What?"

"Did she"—his voice fell to a whisper—"kill herself?"

I can't do this anymore, Nicky. I can't do it. I'm falling apart. Caroline's words filled his head, threatened to make it explode. Nick squeezed his eyes shut, pressed two fingers against his lids. "No, Justin. She didn't kill herself."

The boy let out a long breath, as though he were holding it, waiting. "I knew that." He sounded relieved, almost happy. "Tell me the story about Mom again." Justin looked up at his father, gave him a timid half smile, just enough to show the space where his left front tooth belonged.

Nick drew in a deep breath. "Let's go sit under the tree." They took the few short steps to the maple, plunked down, let the bark scratch at them through their shirts. Justin wanted the story, *his* story, again, the one that Nick had been telling him since he was three and realized that Gracie wasn't his mother and neither was Grandma Stella. It was a beautiful story actually, a fairy tale, embellished with details and happenings that would have pleased even The Brothers Grimm.

"Once upon a time—"

"Not 'Once upon a time,' " Justin cut in. "That's for little kids, remember?"

"Oh, right. When you're eight, it can't start that way anymore." Nick cleared his throat. "Here goes. This is the story of Caroline Ann Kraziak and Nicholas Anthony Androvich. Caroline was a beautiful girl, sixteen when she met Nick, with long blond hair the color of corn silk, and eyes so blue they reminded him of a cloudless July sky."

"My eyes," Justin piped in, sitting up. "They're like my eyes."

Nick nodded. "She was in eleventh grade when she met him, after a Friday-night football game against the Elston Wildcats. Nick threw four touchdown passes that night, clinched the division title. Afterward, a bunch of kids went to Hot Ed's—that was the hangout back then, and that's where he met Caroline."

You're Nicky Androvich. She'd smiled, a perfect smile that lit up her heart-shaped face.

I am. He'd stared at her, taken in by her soft voice and blue eyes.

She'd held out her hand, so small, dainty, and he'd taken it in his own, mindless of his jammed finger and swollen knuckles. *I'm Caroline Kraziak. I'm just a junior so you probably don't know me.* Her skin was so soft, like baby powder.

You're Norman Kraziak's daughter, he'd said. *Our fathers do business together.* He'd stumbled over his next words, stuck between awe and disbelief. *I . . . I don't know how I never noticed you before.*

She'd laughed then, a tinkling sound that made him laugh

too. *How can you see anything past that flock of girls that surrounds you all the time?*

I want to, he'd blurted out. *See you, I mean.*

Caroline had taken a step closer, her eyes shining, and whispered, *I want to see you, too, Nicky Androvich.*

"So, Nick and Caroline started dating, and then he went to college."

"And she wrote to him every day because she missed him so much," Justin said.

"That's right." *Oh, Nicky, I can't stand being away from you. It's like a piece of me is missing. I love you . . . I love you . . .* "Caroline went to Midtown Community College to study business and she also worked part-time as a secretary at her father's sawmill."

"And she was real smart, too, wasn't she, Dad?" Justin leaned over, peered at Nick. "Smart as you."

"Yeah." He nodded. "Smart as me." *Who cares about silly old accounting? Who cares about school?* She'd snuggled up next to him, buried her hand under his shirt. *I just want to be your wife, Nicky, have your babies, make you happy. . . .*

"And you got married right after you finished your first year of medical school, and she moved to the city with you. Philadelphia. But you bought a house here, our house, for when you were done with school, 'cause you were coming back here to live."

Nick nodded, pinched the bridge of his nose. "That was the plan." He squeezed his eyes shut, but the memories were still there, waiting. *I can't take it anymore, Nicky. I can't. I'm afraid . . . all the time . . . of everything . . . can't even go outside. . . .* She'd covered her bulging stomach with both hands. *I want to go back home, Nicky, home to Restalline.*

Six months, honey, just six more months and then we'll go home. He'd pulled her into his arms, kissed her soft hair.

Okay? Just a little longer. But it hadn't been okay; nothing had been okay.

"And then I was born early."

"And then you were born early." *Caroline, don't you want to walk down and see the baby? He's in the incubator, but he's doing fine. You can put your finger through the opening and touch him. Caroline? Caroline?*

Justin smiled, inched closer to his father. "And she loved me more than anything in the world."

"More than anything." *He's your son, goddamn it, and you've only been down to see him once in three days. What's wrong with you? Can't you walk twenty steps to the nursery to look at him?* She'd been huddled on her left side, facing the wall, the white cotton blanket pulled to her chin, eyes closed. *Caroline? Caroline?* Her eyes fluttered open, then drifted closed. There was a bottle of seconal in her bedside stand, top drawer, red pills, hidden behind a bottle of Lubriderm. The pills had helped lull her to sleep the year before the baby, when Nick was working a lot of nights. She'd quit when she found out she was pregnant, but she hadn't forgotten about them. He wondered how many other expectant mothers packed sleeping pills in their hospital bags.

"And"—Justin sucked in a deep breath—"when the fire started, the smoke"—he faltered—"the smoke . . ."

Nick laid a hand on his son's knee. "The smoke had already made her breathing stop." So much smoke . . .

"And they put the fire out before it reached the bedroom."

We're sorry, Mr. Androvich, the body was burned beyond recognition. "She looked like she was asleep."

"Just as beautiful as the day you met her."

"Just as beautiful." Nick put his arm around Justin. "She's watching you, son. From up there." He pointed skyward. "Just like Grandma says. And she loves you, just as much as I do." That part, at least, he believed to be true.

"Yeah, I know." Justin looked up at the sky, raised his hands, and waved. "I love you, too, Mom." Then he turned to his father and said, "Thanks Dad, that was a great story."

Nick nodded. "It *was* a great story." A wonderful, fantastic, *great* story. Unfortunately, it was just that . . . a story.

Chapter 3

The sign read: RESTALLINE, 3 MILES.

Finally.

Alex maneuvered the Saab along the winding road, dodging potholes and an occasional squirrel, excitement mounting as she closed the gap between a dot on the map and the town itself. Soon, very soon, she'd be there, and then the real challenge would begin.

She wondered about the residents of Restalline. Would they be like those in the other towns she'd been to over the last seven years? Simple, honest people with pickup trucks and recipes for homemade applesauce, who took a person at their word, especially one who said she'd come to research their town, gather information for a documentary on small-town life? The way they'd puff out their chests and offer tidbits about their home, their land, their history, sometimes made Alex feel like she was stealing from them, snatching their lives in mid sentence, pushing a pen and paper in front of them before they realized what was happening. But she wasn't—she wasn't taking anything that she didn't give back . . . tenfold.

Opportunity, that's what she was really giving them. A way out, a chance to escape the drudgery of small-town life. Who would really want to can their own tomatoes when you could buy them in the supermarket any way you like? On the vine, in the can, diced, whole, pureed, peeled, crushed. Better yet, why buy them at all? Why not just eat out and let the restaurant take care of the details, *and* the cleanup? And why would a person want to spend hours on a riding mower, cutting acres of grass? That's what lawn services were for, though city life, or rather *suburban* life, didn't allow for acres of anything, except housing developments and shopping plazas. With the money WEC Management signed over on every deal, people could ditch the canning apparatus, sell the riding lawn mower, load up, and trek off to Suburbia, U.S.A.

They could move into the twenty-first century, all with the help of Alex and WEC Management. This town should be no different. She'd convince them that there was a better life to be had on the outskirts of Restalline. Some of them probably already knew that, knew that they didn't have to settle for three-year-old fashions from the only ladies' clothing store in town, not when they could move closer to a mall, shop at JCPenney or Sears, buy their swimsuits and dishes at the same store. Opportunity, that's all many of them needed. A glimmer of what could be, and they'd sell out.

So, they give up a chunk of land? So, their parents wouldn't be living three doors down anymore? And if grown siblings separated, only saw each other on holidays and vacations? So? Alex had grown up alone. No brother or sister, not even a mother or father, not really, though Uncle

Walter and Aunt Helen had done their best to fill in the gap
when her parents died. But there had always been something
missing, an intangible need that gripped her middle when
she saw a family together, one that told her Uncle Walter
and Aunt Helen hadn't quite gotten it right, not really. And
all of the instructions in etiquette, the piano lessons, the
European vacations, the private schools, the colleges, hadn't
replaced the longing for her parents, though she'd kept it
hidden away, even from herself.

Alex glanced at her briefcase on the front seat, caught a
glint of red sparkling against the sun. *Ruby. Red is ruby.*
She remembered the words, but not the voice, or the face,
though she knew it was her father's. The stone wasn't really
a ruby at all, it wasn't even a stone, but a piece of colored
glass, embedded in a wooden mirror that had been painted
green and blue and decorated with an assortment of colored
glass: topaz, turquoise, emerald, garnet. Even after all these
years, she still remembered the first time she saw it, the first
time she held it in her hands, staring at the jewels, watching
them wink back at her. *The true jewel is in the mirror*, the
voice had said. *Look into it, child. Look into it and see the
jewel.* She'd stared, squinted, turned the mirror upside-down,
hunting for a big gem, but she saw nothing in the mirror,
nothing except her own sunburned face looking back at her.
Alex had once asked Uncle Walter to help her find the jewel
in the mirror, but he'd only shook his head and told her to
stop her fancifulness. Aunt Helen's reaction had been quite
different. She'd dragged Alex by the hand into the big room
with the shiny bedspread where she slept all by herself,
opened several velvet boxes, and pointed a long red finger-
nail at them. *These are jewels, young lady. Real jewels.
Rubies, sapphires, emeralds.* She'd laughed then, a funny
kind of sound, and flipped open a blue velvet box. *And in
here*—she'd fingered the sparkling necklace—*these are a
girl's best friend.*

Alex had kept the mirror hidden in a bottom drawer after that, tucked behind her turtleneck sweaters. She didn't know why, but she didn't want her aunt or uncle to see it again, tell her it was nothing but a silly mirror with glass beads glued around the edges. It was more than that, much more. It was the only link Alex had to her mother and father, Peter and Nadia. She knew their names, knew their occupations. Her father had been a painter, her mother a ballerina and then a jewelry designer. And she knew that her parents had given her the mirror the day before . . . before they went to the ocean for the last time. *The ocean is heaven, Alexandra,* her father had said. *A pure, joyous slice of the divine.*

And then they were gone, taking the memories, the years, the life she had known, wiping it out with the force of high tide leveling her sand castles. No trace. At first, Alex had cried and asked Uncle Walter and Aunt Helen for pictures of her parents, wedding, high school, baby, *anything. There's nothing here,* her uncle had told her. *Your father and I weren't . . . in touch.* Alex had even scavenged in her uncle's study one afternoon, hoping she might find something, *something.*

But her uncle was right. There wasn't even a hint of her father or mother in the big brick house on Canterberry Road in Arlington, Virginia. Nothing. Just the blue-and-green hand mirror, embedded with glass beads with a chipped handle from the time Alex had pounded it against the bathroom tile in a fit of rage. She'd been so angry with her parents for deserting her. Why? Why did they have to leave her? Didn't they love her enough? Didn't they know she didn't want to be here, with these strangers who called themselves aunt and uncle? She'd pounded the mirror against the white tile, hard, harder, until a chunk of greenish-blue wood hit the toilet. She'd stopped then, swiping the tears from her cheeks. The handle on the mirror was chipped, a wedge of bare wood exposed. *I'm sorry. I'm sorry, Mommy and Daddy.*

I'm sorry. She'd clutched the mirror to her, close, closer, against her heart. *I'm sorry, I'm sorry, I'm sorry.*

From that day on, the mirror stayed close to her, accompanying her to summer camps in the Catskills and on Cape Cod, to France, Italy, and fifteen states, then it was off to college in a backpack, and later still, on trips across the country, even her honeymoon in Tahiti. It became a talisman of sorts, a link to past and present, a calming source that grounded her, soothed her.

And now, it was riding on the front seat of her Saab as she drove into Restalline, Pennsylvania, population 6,393, nestled in the mountains of northwestern Pennsylvania. Alex spotted a blue-and-white sign that read DOWNTOWN, with an arrow pointing straight ahead. *Lodging comes first, exploration second*, she told herself. The AAA book had listed the names of two hotels, Flying Fancy and The Juniper, both about a half mile from downtown. Unfortunately, both had "No Vacancy" signs flashing in their windows.

Great. Now what? Might as well head into town and see if I can find somebody who knows somebody who might want to rent out a room. Downtown Restalline was an odd mix of old and new, shingled one-story buildings with green-and-white-striped awnings, schoolhouse redbrick two-stories trimmed in white, tan cinder block edged in gray, and a handful of ultra-modern designs in sleek black tile. Signs jutted out from several storefronts, McCrory's five and dime, Able's Goods & Gifts, Buddy's Burger Bonanza, Baby's Boutique, Shoe Biz.

Alex pulled into a parking spot beside a restaurant with a red blinking marquee that read "Hot Ed's." Maybe Hot Ed would be able to tell her where to find a room. She stepped out of her car, rummaged in her purse for a quarter, and deposited it in the parking meter. Three cars down, a short, round policeman with thick black sideburns stuck a ticket under the windshield of a Buick. He shook his head, hiked up his pants, and then proceeded to the next vehicle, a Honda Accord. Seemed like the lawmen of Restalline took their jobs seriously. Alex stuck another nickel in the meter, just in case, and headed into Hot Ed's.

It was empty inside, nothing but the searing voice of Elvis singing "Love Me Tender." *Another greasy spoon*, she thought, as she worked her way to the counter in search of Hot Ed. How many places just like this had she been to— the Formica tables chipped and carved up with initials of high-school sweethearts, girls in pink sweaters and boys with Old Spice aftershave slapped on their cheeks, feeding each other french fries and promising to love one another forever? And the jukebox in the corner? There was always one of those, blasting out songs like "You've Lost That Lovin' Feelin' " or "Hang on Sloopy." The counter would be high, usually white, with waitresses only—sex discrimination was definitely practiced in these parts—and the owner would be big and burly, wearing an apron splattered with grease and God knew what else. And the grease, ugh, the grease in the air could fry a pound of chicken, maybe two.

Alex rang the bell next to the register.

"Hold on, hold on." It was a man's voice, low, raspy, and irritated. "Nice 'n easy, Alice. Nice 'n easy. Like this." The music stopped and Alex heard the sizzle of food— peppers and onions?—on the griddle. "Slow, slow . . . nice 'n easy or they'll burn, and then you're gonna have to tell the customers why their sausage sub's got no peppers and onions."

"Chill, Bernie, just chill." This must have been Alice. "I got it."

"Hmmm," he grumbled. "Be right back. Don't burn 'em." The saloon-style kitchen doors swung open and a man stood staring at her. He was in his late fifties, no more than five feet six or seven, wiry build, with a pack of cigarettes rolled up in his left shirtsleeve. "What can I do for you?'' He lifted a finger, stroked his handlebar mustache, waited.

"Hi. I'm looking for a place to stay." She gave him a half smile, shrugged. "Looks like the only two hotels in town are full and I was hoping someone might know of something . . ." She let the words trail off.

"Hah!" he laughed. "The Juniper and Flying Fancy have been closed goin' on a year now. Renovations. Hah!" He laughed again. "The old biddies who own 'em are too busy playing cinch at the senior center to worry about runnin' 'em."

"I really need a place to stay. Isn't there anything? A room, perhaps?"

"Hmmm." He stroked his mustache, scratched his frizzy gray head. "Might be. Depends on how long you're stayin', who's with you, what you're doin' here."

Nosy man. Alex cleared her throat, forced another smile. "Well, I was planning to stay about eight weeks, give or take a few. It would just be for me, the room, I mean, or . . . whatever is available."

"And what are you planning on doing in Restalline?" He took a step closer, crossed his arms, waited.

Here goes. "Well, I'm collecting data, information actually, on small towns. I'm going to do a documentary on small-town life, so I've been traveling all over the country, living in the towns, talking to the people, getting a feel for what it's like."

"Hmmm."

"So . . . do you know of any place?"

"Hmmm," he said again, twisting his mustache. "Where you from?"

"Virginia. Arlington."

"Hmm."

"Edna and Chuck Lubovich could let her use Tracy's place," Alice called from the kitchen.

"Don't burn those peppers and onions," Bernie hollered back.

Alice ignored him. "564 Abbington. White house, green trim."

"Alice!" Silence. Bernie turned back to Alex. "564 Abbington. Go through town, turn left on Center, stay straight for two blocks until you see it. Tell Edna Bernie sent you."

Alex held out her hand. "Thank you. Thank you, Bernie."

Bernie looked at her outstretched hand, examined it, then clasped it between his own rough ones. "Soft life, huh?"

"Excuse me?"

He released his grasp, turned her hand over, palm facing upward, and pointed. "No calluses, no blisters. Not even a mark. Soft hands, soft life, eh?"

Alex pulled her hand away, buried it in her pocket.

Bernie laughed. "How about a sausage sub? Best in town. Smothered with peppers and onions . . . if Alice didn't burn 'em all."

"No, thank you, I just ate a little while ago." *Half a Nutri-Grain bar—blueberry—and a raspberry yogurt.*

"Come back another time."

"I will, Bernie. Tell Hot Ed, I will."

He laughed then, a roar that seemed at odds with his size. "Tell Hot Ed! Did you hear that Alice? Tell Hot Ed!" He slapped a hand against the counter, threw his head back, laughed again. "That was a good one. Yesssirree!"

What had she said? What was so damned funny?

"I'll tell Hot Ed, all right. I sure will." He swiped at his eyes, wet with tears. "Better yet, you tell Hot Ed. Okay? Hold on, just a sec. Alice? Get Hot Ed!"

If she could have snuck out of there right then without appearing rude, Alex would have done just that. But good manners and etiquette forced her to stand her ground and bear the brunt of Bernie's humor. He returned in a few seconds, holding a big fat sub in his hands.

"This," he said, "is Hot Ed." A plump, shiny sausage glistened in a white sub roll, resting on a bed of peppers and onions, sautéed to near transparency.

And the smell . . . it reminded Alex of the only carnival she'd ever been to. She'd been thirteen and her friend's cousins had been visiting from Upstate New York. There was a carnival about ten miles away in a neighboring town and she'd gone with them, tagged along actually, so eager to join in, be a part of something other than Uncle Walter's and Aunt Helen's golf lunches at the country club and Saturday-afternoon museum tours. She'd snuck away just after lunch, told Aunt Helen she was going to play tennis with Eileen and would be back by dinnertime. And she would have, too, if the car Eileen's cousin was driving hadn't blown a tire. Unfortunately for Alex, it had also blown her cover. Uncle Walter was waiting for her in his black Mercedes when they rolled into Eileen's driveway two hours late.

It was the last time Alex did anything that might disappoint her uncle. It was also the last time she had a sausage sub smothered in peppers and onions.

"So, should I wrap it up for you? It's a real treat. Let me tell you, one bite and you'll be back for more." Bernie held it a little closer.

Alex took a step back, shook her head. "Later. I'll have one later. Right now I have to find the Lubovichs. 564 Abbington," she repeated, getting the address in her head. "Through town, left on Center, two blocks straight. Chuck and Edna." She waved, started to leave. "Thanks, Bernie. Thanks, Alice."

She was halfway out the door when Bernie called to her. "Hey!"

Alex turned around, waited.

"What's your name?"

"Alex. Alex Chamberlain."

Abbington Road was a cozy street, small and cluttered with trees stretching their limbs into neighbors' yards, shrubs and bushes poking out in all directions, bullying for the number-one position. The homes were all shingled two-stories with side porches and planters bulging with petunias, geraniums, and impatiens. Most of the driveways had been poured with cement, a few were blacktopped, none graveled.

The Lubovichs' house sat on the right side of Abbington Road, halfway down, between a dark green one and a canary-yellow one. Their home was white with green trim and in bad need of a coat of paint, perhaps two or three coats, but not until after someone, or rather, several someones, scraped the chipped and peeling remnants from the two-story dwelling. Alex pulled her car into the driveway behind a Chevrolet Caprice Classic, green, with a bumper sticker that read "In God We Trust."

There were two pots of fuchsia and white petunias, and a pot of red geraniums sitting at the foot of the steps. Alex climbed two wide steps to the front door. A gold cross hung several inches above the doorbell. She pressed the bell and waited.

So far, this was pretty much what she encountered in small-town life. There was always a person like Bernie, a place like Hot Ed's, even a behind-the-scenes woman like Alice. And the streets were the same, too. Small houses, tucked away, partially hidden behind foliage, trees, bushes, shrubs, all green, all dense, all the same.

Alex took a deep breath, pressed the bell again. Restalline was just another small town; she would not let it intimidate her just because she needed this deal to restore her uncle's faith in her abilities. She'd get him to believe in her again, get him to acknowledge her skill and talent. All she needed to do was convince the people of this town that life was better, sweeter, richer outside of Restalline.

And from what she'd seen so far, could it really be that difficult?

The front door squeaked open and a woman in a yellow housedress smeared with bright red poppies stood in the opening. She was in her late fifties, perhaps even sixty, it was hard to tell with the quarter-inch eyeliner and red lipstick she wore. Her hair, what was visible of it beneath the yellow kerchief and pink rollers, was red, the bottled version, and her cheeks were two circles, same shade as her lipstick. And her eyebrows, well . . . they were there, sort of, drawn in with a dark brown pencil.

"Hello?" She slid on a pair of red half glasses hanging from a crystal chain around her neck. "Do I know you?" She squinted, adjusted the glasses. "Are you Rita's daughter, the one from Albuquerque?"

"No. No, I'm not, Mrs. Lubovich. My name is Alex Chamberlain. I just got into town." Alex held out a hand, waited for the older woman to take it. "I'm looking for a place to stay and Bernie from Hot Ed's gave me your address."

"Oh, he did, did he?" Mrs. Lubovich's hand inched out of her pocket.

Alex nodded. "Actually, it was Alice who mentioned you first."

That made her smile. Then she threw back her head, laughed, exposing a mouthful of bridgework. "Alice runs the show, she does. Bernie's nothing but hot air, and a lot of it." She laughed again, grabbed Alex's hand, squeezed it hard. "Come on in, Alex Chamberlain. Let me get you a cup of coffee and I'll show you around."

This was not the time to tell Mrs. Lubovich that she only drank coffee before 7 A.M. and after 7 P.M. "I'd love some," she said, and followed the older woman inside. They passed through a narrow hallway, dimly lit, with pictures covering large sections of pink rose wallpaper. Black-and-white photographs, touched-up portraits with painted lips and soft white skin, snapshots, family gatherings, all set in gold, antique white, and brass frames. The kitchen was beyond the hallway, a tiny nook of cabinets and clutter, and ... yellow. Yellow cabinets, yellow curtains, yellow Formica table tucked in the corner, yellow cushions on the wooden chairs, yellow ceramic canisters with white lettering, yellow wastebasket ... even a yellow water dish in the corner. Cat or dog? A flash of tan and white with black paws flashed through her mind. Daisy. She'd loved that cat, dressed it up, talked to it, slept with it, and then it was gone, taken away from her ... just like her parents.

"This is the kitchen." Edna took a coffee mug from the cupboard, yellow, of course.

"It's ... very bright."

"Didn't used to be." Edna poured a cup of coffee from an electric percolator. "Three years ago it was dark and dingy." She handed Alex the cup, pointed to a bowl of sugar and a can of condensed milk. "Then Chuck had his heart attack." Her voice lowered, quivered on the last word. "He almost didn't make it. If it wasn't for Dr. Nick, he would have met the Good Lord, right there on the floor of NK Manufacturing."

Alex held up a hand. "I'm sorry, Mrs. Lubovich, I didn't mean to get you upset."

The older woman sniffed. "Edna, dear. Call me Edna."

"Edna."

"Talking about Chuck's heart attack just makes me remember how lucky we were, how lucky I am." She pulled a wad of Kleenex out of her pocket. "You know, sometimes you forget, especially when your husband does something that drives you crazy. Then, you forget about him lying in the hospital with tubes sticking out of everywhere and machines beeping, buzzing.''

Alex sipped her coffee, said nothing. Death had come to her three times, twice when she was only eight, and then three years ago, when Aunt Helen lost her battle to the god she worshiped most, nicotine. But there had been time to prepare for the inevitable, time to adjust to the sight of tubes in her nose, the way her skin turned gray when she couldn't get enough oxygen, the fits of wheezing, gasps for air. It was a horrible thing to witness, but at least it was there, in front of their faces, no denying or pretending it would dissolve with a few pills or treatments. It even had a name, emphysema, and it plagued her for six years, forcing her in and out of the hospital, fighting for every breath, until one day she sucked in her last gulp and closed her eyes forever. It was a sad but anticipated ending, and in Aunt Helen's last month she became almost . . . what was the word Alex wanted? Approachable, that was it. Almost, but not quite.

And the other two deaths, her parents', well, they still left her cold, empty. They'd gone for a morning swim and never come back; their bodies had, of course, days later, but they were just shells, bloated and deformed receptacles of Peter and Nadia Chamberlain. Her parents were gone, their souls swept up by a wave and carried out to the ocean, together, without even a good-bye.

''How long are you staying? And why are you here anyway?''

It was so typical of small-towners to just accept, and question later. Edna Lubovich knew less than nothing about her and yet she was already spilling half her life story over a cup of coffee and Alice's say-so. ''I'll be here about two months, I think. I've been traveling around the country, researching small-town life for a documentary I'm doing.''

''For television?''

''Possibly.'' It might be a lie, but it was only a half lie.

If she really were doing a documentary, then it *would* be for television.

"Well, honey, you've come to the right place. I can tell you anything you want to know about living in a small town." She lowered her voice, "And everything you want to know about *this* town." She set her coffee cup down, smoothed both hands over her yellow kerchief. "Been here thirty-nine years in September. Moved to Restalline right after Chuck and I got married."

Alex nodded. Now this was someone who could help her, give her the background information she needed to find out who the powerhouses were behind the community, and who could be persuaded to sell. "You must know everyone."

"Sure do." A quick smile spread over Edna's long face. "Everybody and everything."

"Edna! Edna!" It was a man's voice, booming from another part of the house.

Edna Lubovich shook her head. "That's Chuck." Then she raised her voice several decibels to match his. "What?!"

"Where'd you put my slippers?"

"Check behind the bathroom door! And don't come down in your underwear. We've got company!"

"Who?"

She turned to Alex. "He's as bad as our Tracy used to be, yelling from all over the house."

"Who?" Chuck Lubovich shouted again.

"Never you mind," Edna yelled back. "You'll see when you get down here."

"I hope your husband doesn't mind my staying here," Alex said, wondering if the next two months would be a barrage of shouting matches between her landlords.

"Nah, Chuck don't care." Edna took out another cup from the cupboard, set it next to the coffeepot. "It's just his way sometimes, that's all." Her voice softened, dipped. "We been together a long time, been through a lot." She paused, spooned a teaspoon of sugar into the empty cup. "You married, Alex?"

"No." *Not anymore.*

She poured a generous amount of milk over the sugar and began stirring. "Hmmm. Marriage teaches you a lot about a person; teaches you a lot about yourself, too. Chuck always puts his milk and sugar in first before he pours his coffee; been doing that for as long as I can remember."

Alex sipped her own coffee, thinking about how nice it was that Edna Lubovich fixed her husband's coffee for him, just the way he liked it. No one did things like that for Alex, mostly because she wouldn't let them; it made her too uncomfortable, too out of control. But watching Edna stir sugar and milk for her husband made her think that once in a while it might be nice to share something like that with someone.

She was still thinking about Edna and Chuck's coffee when the door separating the kitchen and the living room opened and Chuck Lubovich walked in. He must have taken Edna's words to heart because he was wearing a tan short-sleeved shirt, tucked in, with a brown belt and brown pants. There was a pair of brown corduroy slippers on his feet, probably the ones from behind the bathroom door. For all of the noise he'd made yelling to Edna, Chuck was a small man, standing no more than an inch or two taller than his wife. His build was medium to slight, maybe leaning a little more on the slight side, and his coloring was pale as if he hadn't seen the sun in a long time. His gray hair was slicked back, thinning on top, and he wore thick black glasses that distorted his eyes, making it difficult to tell what color they were.

"So, you're the visitor," he said to Alex, looking her up and down.

"Nice to meet you Mr. Lubovich," Alex said, walking toward him, hand extended.

"Mr. Lubovich was my father," he said, his voice deep, "and he's been dead over twenty years." He held out a hand, grasped Alex's. "I'm Chuck."

Alex smiled. "Chuck. Pleased to meet you."

He ignored the pleasantry. "What brings you to Restalline?"

Edna interrupted. "She's writing a documentary on small towns. It might be on TV."

"Oh?"

Alex worked her lips into a smile, the same one she used every time she gave this pitch. *Make them believe, make them believe. It's for their own good. Nobody wants to be stuck in a town that doesn't even have a mall. And I need this project. I really, really need it.* "Yes, that's right," she said. It had all been said so many times before that it almost sounded natural, true. "I've been traveling around visiting small towns, trying to get the feel of them, find out what makes people want to live there, stay there, sometimes from generation to generation." This part *was* true.

"That's Restalline, all right." Chuck rubbed his jaw, nodded. "We got a lot of families like that. Androvichs for one. Dr. Nick was the only one who left, but he came back."

Edna made the sign of the cross. "Thank God for that." She turned to Alex. "He's the one who saved Chuck's life."

"Damn right he did. Best thing that ever happened to the town was when he came back."

Androvich? Alex listened with heightened interest. Androvich was the name of the people who owned the lumber business and a substantial amount of land in the town. And there was a doctor? He'd obviously gone away to school, lived in or near a city, maybe come back more out of duty than desire. She needed to meet him, talk to him, maybe work through him to persuade the rest of the family that they could cash out of Restalline, buy a condo in the suburbs, drive a Volvo. But he'd come back? Why?

"The . . . Androvichs, is it? They've been around a long time?"

"They practically started the town," Chuck said, moving across the room to take the cup Edna held out to him. He took a drink. "Ahhh . . . perfect."

"She wants to know about Nick Senior and Stella," Edna said, like a child ready to blurt out information her parents don't know.

Chuck Lubovich held up a hand to still his wife, took another sip of coffee. "Restalline was nothing but a clump of dirt until the Androvichs came here with their saws and buckets of sweat. They started with less than a hundred acres . . . worked from dawn to dusk, cutting, hauling, selling, buying more land, bit by bit. Hard workers, all of them . . . not afraid to get their hands dirty." He scratched the back of his head. "That's what brought old man Kraziak here."

"And the furniture company where Chuck worked since the day he came home from the service." Edna beamed, pleased with her little offering.

"Kraziak started a lumber processing factory, took all the Androvich lumber and treated it, turned it into boards and the like, then shipped it all over the coast. Anybody who wanted a job had one."

Edna nodded. "They're good people, the Kraziaks. Good people." Her voice dipped. She made the sign of the cross. "Why such a tragedy should happen to good people like that—"

"Edna!"

She shrugged, pursed her red lips. "It *is* a tragedy, Chuck. And I think Dr. Nick still blames himself for it."

"It's not our business." He gave his wife a look that told her the discussion was closed.

But Edna Lubovich either didn't notice or didn't care. "Pshaw! Business. We've known him since he was a boy. He deserves to be happy."

"Just because he doesn't bring a girl to Sunday dinner, doesn't mean he isn't happy," Chuck said, an edge to his voice, "or that there isn't a girl waiting at home for him. Trust me."

"Don't you dare talk that way about Dr. Nick." Edna shook a finger at him. "He saved your life."

"And I'm trying to save his from a busybody senior citizen who's trying to butt into his business."

"Hmmmph."

"Excuse me." As much as Alex wanted to find out about the Kraziaks' tragedy and Dr. Nick's guilt, she didn't want to be embroiled in the Lubovichs' marital spat. Confrontation made her uncomfortable. No, that wasn't quite true; it wasn't the confrontation itself that made her uncomfortable, it was all of the emotions tied up in them, tight, coiled, choking out rational thought. That's what made her fidget, *avoid if possible, run away if necessary*. Like right now. Now was the perfect time to make an escape, and with what better reason than to tell the Lubovichs that she'd like to see her new room? Maybe that would sidetrack them long enough for her to get out of there.

"Excuse me." She cleared her throat. "Do you think I could see the room?"

"She's staying?" Chuck looked confused.

"She's staying." Edna set her coffee cup in the sink, moved to the door, eyes straight ahead. "For two months."

"Good. Good. Now Tracy won't be able to run home to Mama the next time she has a fight with Ted." He raised his voice as Edna turned her back to him and walked out the door. "She'll have to stay home and work it out!"

"Old fuddy-duddy," Edna said under her breath. "Come on."

Alex followed her up the narrow staircase. Uncle Walter and Aunt Helen had never raised their voices in front of her. Ever. Their tones were always well-modulated, quiet, respectful. Passionless. No emotions thrumming at the surface, threatening to explode in anger . . . or joy, not when it came to each other. It had all been the same, even when Aunt Helen died, Uncle Walter didn't cry, didn't grow hoarse with grief when he talked about his dead wife. He *referred* to her. *My wife loved to play bridge. My wife was an excellent golfer. My wife was president of the Garden Club.* My wife, my wife, my wife, rarely Helen. And never anything as personal as *I miss Helen. I miss her so much, some days I wake up and see her side of the bed is empty, and just for a moment, I think she's already downstairs, reading the paper, having her first cup of coffee.* Of course, he never said that. How could he? He and Aunt Helen had never shared the same room, let alone the same bed.

"Chuck and I finished this place off for Tracy when she graduated from high school." A wooden sign with the name TRACY painted in pink hung from the door. "She still comes here sometimes"—Edna turned the knob—"mostly when she and Ted have a little disagreement, you know, married kind of stuff, nothing serious."

No, Alex didn't know. The one and only disagreement she and Eric had ever had ended in divorce.

"They're getting along fine now." Edna opened the door, stepped inside. "I just talked to her this morning."

As long as she gets along for the next two months, Alex thought, taking in the living room. Pink. Very pink.

Edna pushed back a pink ruffled curtain, opened a window. "She lives just across town. I'm sure you'll meet her."

"That would be nice." Alex was too caught up with the room to say anything else. Good God, Edna's daughter had actually *lived* in this place? There was a pale pink sofa pushed against the wall, six hot-pink pillows—three round, three square—lining the back of it, a pink coffee table, pink lampshade, pink picture frames displaying pink carnations, petunias, and roses, a pink carpet. Pink carpet? Alex blinked.

Yes, a pink carpet. Even a pink trash can tucked next to a pink rocking chair.

"Isn't this room just precious?" Edna beamed. "Tracy did it all herself, wanted to make sure everything matched."

"Wow." It matched, all right.

"She loves pink." Edna pulled an afghan—pink of course—off the back of the rocker, refolded it, put it back.

"I guess she does." Alex wondered what Tracy looked like. Was she pink, too? Pink hair, pink makeup, pink clothes?

"You've got to see the bedroom. It's even better than this." Edna motioned for Alex to follow. Eight steps forward and three to the left, they entered Tracy's bedroom. It was covered in pink, starting from the ceiling and stretching to the rose wallpaper, wrapping itself around the teddy bear sitting in the middle of the satin bedspread and ending with three ceramic vases of silk roses tucked in the corner. Pink, pink, *pink*.

Edna leaned toward Alex, lowered her voice as though there were another person in the room, "I think she has a real knack for decorating, don't you?"

"Hmmm. She certainly knows how to carry a color theme." *To an extreme.* Alex spotted the pink knitted Kleenex box on the nightstand next to the pink alarm clock. At least at night she wouldn't be able to see anything but black, thank goodness. "I'd like to pay you by the week if that's all right with you." She'd didn't need to see any more, didn't want to see anything else that would make her feel as though she were being swallowed up by a giant gob of cotton candy.

"But I haven't even showed you the kitchen." Edna's red lips pulled into a frown. "Or the bathroom. Tracy has the most adorable soaps in there, shaped like baby lambs and kittens." Her voice drooped, fell, stilled.

"Of course, I want to see all of it," Alex lied. "Every

inch. But I just thought we could get business out of the way, and then''—she paused, forcing an extra eagerness to her voice—"I could just enjoy Tracy's talents.''

That made Edna smile wide, revealing a metal bracket of bridgework on her back teeth. "Okay, then. What about one hundred a week?''

One hundred a week? Alex was used to the ridiculous prices small-towners threw out for lodging, eyes darting around the room, hoping to earn a little extra for their wish lists: self-propelled lawn mowers, dirt bikes for the kids, dishwashers, air-conditioning window units, linoleum floors. It was obvious few of them traveled to the city, where one hundred *a night* was acceptable, even common. So, she paid her twenty-nine dollars a night at The Gazebo or whatever the place was, and let them think they'd gotten the better part of the deal.

But this? One hundred dollars a week? What was that? Fourteen dollars a day? Even for an apartment decked out in pink confection that was cheap, too cheap. Alex wanted to earn Edna and Chuck's trust, convince them to sell out, but she wasn't trying to rip them off.

"Is that too much?'' Edna pressed her hands together, bit her bottom lip. "I could go seventy-five. How's that? Seventy-five plus a meal a day.''

"Edna, please.'' Alex held up a hand, smiled. "I think it's not *enough*. I was thinking two hundred a week.''

"Oh, no!'' She flung a hand over her heart. "Too much. Way too much.''

Alex hoped it would be this easy negotiating for the Lubovichs' land. "Not really. Listen, Edna. You're paying all of the utilities, did you think of that? Water, electric, gas? I shower at least once a day, flush the toilet more than that, and I'll probably watch a little television, listen to the radio, maybe even cook once in a while. That all uses up utilities. It's only fair.''

"I'm an honest woman, Alex." Edna patted her yellow kerchief, squared her bony shoulders. "I don't take nothin' from anybody unless I earn it."

"Neither do I." That was true enough. "You're going to be my landlady, Edna." Good Lord, was it really going to be this easy to buy up the town? "You have something I want. I'm willing to pay for it, and even though you think it's a lot of money, it still isn't even fair market value, which means a reasonable price. So, we're really both making out. You're happy, I'm happy. You make more money than you counted on, I pay less money than I counted on." Alex held out her hand. "It's called business, Edna. Pure and simple business."

Edna clasped Alex's hand with both of hers. "It's a deal. But I'm still going to fix you one meal a day. You choose. Stuffed cabbage or chicken paprikash?"

"Can't say that I've had either." Alex subscribed to the grilled chicken, steamed broccoli, no salt regime.

"Really? Well, you'll just have to try them both. The only person in town who can even come close to my stuffed cabbage and chicken paprikash is Stella Androvich."

There was that name again. Androvich, Androvich. And here was an opportunity. "Well, then, I'd like to meet her sometime."

"Sure." Edna paused. "Why not tonight? There's a big party for Frank Androvich, Stella's brother-in-law, over at her house. It's his sixty-fourth birthday. Chuck and I are going. You come with us, meet people, talk to them about Restalline."

"But I haven't been invited."

"Oh, go on, don't worry about that. I'll call Stella, tell her we're bringing you with us."

"She won't mind?"

Edna waved a hand at her. "Nah. Stella won't mind a

bit. Especially when I tell her I've got somebody I want Dr. Nick to meet.''

"Me? Why?"

"Why not? You're young, pretty, smart—"

"Oh, no, Edna. I'm sure he's a very nice man, and I do want to meet him, but I'm really not interested . . . not that way." *Really* not interested. The last thing she needed was to get involved with someone whose property she was looking to buy up and flatten.

The older woman smiled. "You will be, trust me, Alex."

"Edna—"

She was already turning away, heading toward the door, her yellow slippers flapping across the linoleum. "I've got to go think about what I'm going to wear tonight," she went on. "You think about it, too. Dr. Nick likes blue, anything blue. See you around seven."

The door clicked and Alex was alone, caught in the middle of a pink nightmare. *Dr. Nick, Dr. Nick, Dr. Nick Androvich.* He was educated, city-schooled, descendant of a family who owned half the town. *He was the one*, the one she might convince to sell his land, the one who would then convince the others to sell theirs.

Chapter 4

He saw her the minute she walked through the door. Tall, graceful, blond, beautiful, reminding him of a present. One whose wrapping is so elegant, so exquisite, so fine, that the receiver almost dares not open it, choosing instead to admire the outer trappings, delighting in the beauty of the presentation, all but forgetting about the contents within.

Nick tried not to stare. He took a swig of beer, then another. His gaze shot back to the woman. She seemed to be with Chuck and Edna Lubovich, moving through the crowd of well-wishers at Uncle Frank's party, stopping when they stopped, smiling, holding out her hand. Who *was* she? A relative? One of Edna's sister's children? He doubted it. This one had too much class to be part of the Lubovich clan, he could see it in the way she held herself, head high, shoulders back, chin up.

"Nick," his mother's voice interrupted his assessment of

the mystery woman, "would you be a dear and carry out the stuffed cabbage and lasagna for me?"

"Sure." He straightened himself away from the doorway, leaving the woman behind, and followed his mother into the kitchen. "What would the old man say if he knew you were serving stuffed cabbage *and* lasagna to the guests?"

His mother smiled, pulled open the oven door. "He'd say the Italian in me was trying to drive out the Czech in me." She stuck her right hand in an oven mitt. "And then he'd snarl and say that all these years of marriage to him hadn't taught me 'one damn thing.' And *then* he'd probably insist on setting the Italian food on one table, way in the back, behind a table covered with Czech food. No pizzelles mixing with nut bread or pasta with cabbage rolls." She looked up at him, her face red with the heat from the oven. "Your father had very particular opinions about things."

"Except where a half-Italian, half-Czech girl from Restalline was concerned." Nick took the mitt from her, grabbed another pot holder, and lifted the tray of lasagna from the oven. They'd all heard the stories of how Nick Sr.'s parents forbade him to marry a woman with Italian blood, even if part of her was Czech, and how his mother had cried for a week when she learned her son had asked Stella Collianni to be his wife. Only Uncle Frank had stood by their side, telling Nick and Stella that *love goes where it's sent.*

"I was his one exception." Her voice fell low, almost blanked out by the polka music in the next room.

"I know." Nick lowered his voice, too. Even now, after all these years without him, he still heard the sadness in her voice. She missed the old man, *really missed him*, like a chunk of her life got torn away when he died. Did Nick's voice sound like that when he talked about Caroline, like there was a gaping hole right in the middle of his heart, open, bleeding? Probably not. How could there be? He'd mourned her more when she was alive than when she was dead. He'd lost his wife long before the smoke from the fire sucked out her last breath. And that's where the guilt crept in, housed itself in the corner of his conscience, pricked at him, tortured him.

A good husband would have been able to keep his wife happy. A better husband would have kept her safe. Obviously, Nick had been neither.

"Who's the woman with Chuck and Edna?" he asked, curious once again about the mystery woman.

"Woman?" His mother lifted a ladle, spooned sauce over the lasagna. "Oh. Edna called and asked if she could bring her new tenant with her."

"Relative of hers? Niece?"

She shook her head. "No, just someone passing through. Doing some kind of research on the town or something like that."

Research? The last time someone came under the guise of research, two years ago, Nick had booted him out when he discovered the man was only interested in gathering data to try and undermine the lumber company. "She better not be another one of those 'Save the Trees' people." Every year, Androvich Lumber received letters from different factions, protesting the cutting of trees. And every year, the company issued a statement regarding their conservation of natural resources policy—how they selected sites to be cut, the need to thin areas to permit maximum growth, alternating sites, replanting programs, and a general education pamphlet. And then, last year, three people showed up with signs that read, "We Are the Trees", "Save Mother Tree", and "Treed No More," and camped out in front of Androvich Lumber for three days. The whole town talked about them, two men and a woman, with ponytails and white robes, carrying signs and chanting. Nick tried to talk with them, get them to understand the company's position on supporting conservation. Michael was less diplomatic; he threatened to drag them out of Restalline by their ponytails. In the end, their own indiscretions got them booted out of town with the threat of jail if they ever came back. They'd been caught rolling joints, offering them to fifteen- and sixteen-year-old girls, and trying to persuade the same girls to "explore the group's bodies and get in touch with their emotions." In other words, sex. Nick and Michael had intervened, and the trio was gone in forty-five minutes, tent dismantled, pulled up by the stakes, and tossed into a beat-up Ford. "Save the Trees" posters were broken and thrown in the fire, weed confiscated and burned, the girls delivered to their homes. Nice, neat, complete, without raising a voice. Michael, being Michael, couldn't let them leave without what he considered to be a proper farewell, fitting the occasion: he punched the leader in the jaw and bloodied the other man's nose. *Take that you sonofabitchin' pervert.*

That was last summer. Nothing since. There had only been one other time when an outsider threatened the quiet existence of Restalline. Her name was Eve. She just showed up in town one day, about a year after Caroline's death, said she was looking to relax, unwind from the frantic life in the city. Her hair was the same pale gold as Caroline's and her eyes the same blue. But she wasn't interested in relaxing or anything else, except a story; a story of how the wife of a medical student burned to death in her home while her husband put in yet another shift at the hospital. The questions were subtle at first, casual. *I heard your wife died last year. How tragic that you have a baby son to raise, alone.* And then, *Do you want to talk about it? I'm a great listener. Was it an accident? Do you think*—just the right amount of hesitancy here—*that it could have been prevented? It wasn't . . . it wasn't . . . intentional, was it?* At this point, the real Eve surfaced and he knew, *knew* she hadn't picked Restalline by coincidence. *You worked so many hours, maybe she was depressed being alone so much of the time. Doctors are never home, are they? Maybe it was just too much for her? Maybe she took something to help her sleep and couldn't get out? Or maybe, just maybe, she just didn't want to wake up? Could that have been it, Nick? Could it have been that?*

Who are you? What the hell do you think you're doing, here, in my house, digging around in my past? Who the hell do you think you are? She'd looked at the floor, the table, the clock, everywhere but at him. *Tell me. Tell me now, goddamn it!* It all spilled out then, how she was collecting data for her master's thesis on depression and suicide in partners of medical students, and Nick's name and Caroline's death had surfaced in several discussion groups on campus. What better way to understand the dynamics behind the tragedy than to talk to the family firsthand? *I just want to ask a few questions,* she'd said. *That's all.* He'd taken her arm, dragged her to the back door. *Leave now, tonight, and forget you ever heard my name. If I see your car in the morning, I'll call the dean and report you for unethical behavior.*

In the morning, Eve was gone. *Family emergency,* he'd said, and nothing, not even his mother's persuasiveness could get him to talk about her again.

And now there was another mystery woman in his mother's living room, popped in out of nowhere. He'd be damned if he'd be taken in by this one. Nick tensed, forced himself to relax. Michael was the radical one with the quick temper, not him; he was cool, methodical, objective. That was him, all right. So why the hell was he getting all fired up, making suppositions about something he knew nothing about?

"Why's she here?" *Damn.* He'd find out right now.

"Nick?" His mother looked up at him, frowned. "Settle down. She's doing some sort of research on the town."

"On Restalline? What kind of research?" *It's about the trees, she's here about the trees.* He'd bet his last dollar.

Anger surged through him; he wanted to go out there and drag her out of town by her pale blonde hair.

His mother lifted her shoulders, shrugged. "Edna said she wanted to compare small towns, write a documentary about life here."

"Life *here?* In Restalline? Population 6,393?"

She eyed him. "Now don't go getting all in a huff, Nick. If she says she's writing a story about small towns, she's writing a story about small towns. Period."

"Did you see the pearls around her neck? The way she wears her hair? The pale blue sweater she's got on? She's a city girl, Ma, I've seen enough of them to know."

"So? Lisa is a city girl too, and you're not scrutinizing her."

Nick's gaze narrowed on his mother. "Lisa's not pretending to be somebody she's not."

"That's debatable." She scooped more sauce over the lasagna. "Have a little faith. At least be polite to her and listen to what she has to say." She *tsk-tsked*. "For heaven's sake, Nicholas, it isn't like you to be so judgmental."

"It's not just her. It's the whole damn thing." He dragged both hands over his face. "I don't want to have to deal with this tree issue again. All I want to do is take care of my patients, do the best I can, save some lives, hopefully, make a difference. And be a good father to Justin. Is that too much to ask?"

"No, of course not." His mother's tone gentled, her brown eyes grew soft. "And you're doing a wonderful job, sweetheart."

"So let me do my job and make Michael do his. Make him straighten up and run the company. For Chrissake, he knows it a hell of a lot better than I do."

"How?" She lifted her hands, palms up. "How can I make Michael do anything, Nick? You know how he is, the way he acts, like a bomb ready to explode."

Oh, he knew all right, only too well. "He's thirty-six years old, Ma. When are you going to stop protecting him? Do you think he's ever going to accept his responsibility when you're always there to pick up the pieces?"

"He tries—"

"Does he? Is that what you call getting into a brawl every other week at Cody's just because he thinks somebody looked at him the wrong way? Or not coming home most nights until Kevin and Sara are already in bed? Is that being responsible?" Jesus, he was so tired of Michael and his excuses.

"He's had a tough time, you know that."

"We've all had a tough time. That's just life. Besides, most of Michael's troubles were his own making."

"Damn that woman for leaving them." His mother poked a stuffed cabbage, hard. A squirt of sauce landed on her arm.

"Betsy was all wrong for him, you know that. He only married her because he got her pregnant. She hated Restalline, always had. If it wouldn't have been that pharmaceutical salesman from Buffalo, it would have been somebody else, a truck driver from Chicago or Detroit. She just wanted out and we both know it."

There were tears in her eyes now. "You're the strong one, Nick. You. Don't give up on Michael; help him."

You don't know what you're asking me, Ma. You don't know.

"Nick?" She looked up at him, touched his chin. "Please?"

He doesn't want my help, he doesn't want anything from me. He made that clear a long time ago. "I'll try."

"I always know I can count on you."

Damn. He leaned over, gave her a kiss on the cheek. "Let's get this food out there before it gets cold."

* * *

"And so Dr. Nick says, if I want to make Marie's wedding next month, I better shape up. So I went right home and threw out the pack of Reese's cups I had hidden in my workshop. And then I ate an apple. Swear to God, I did." Harry Lendergin raised a hand and made a quick sign of the cross.

Alex listened, nodded with the rest of the group. Harry Lendergin, recurrent gallbladder attacks, Ida Sellone, high blood pressure, Chuck Lubovich, recovering heart attack, Edgar Malowski, chronic backache. This was the fourth "testimonial" she'd heard to Dr. Nick Androvich's medical expertise and she and the Lubovichs had only arrived ten minutes ago. Had the good doctor invited all of his patients or were all the residents of Restalline his patients? She was curious to meet the man. Besides the fact that she wanted his property and his recommendation to the rest of the town, she wondered what type of person commanded such respect, almost awe. In business, it was always the go-getter, the one who sold the most, made the most money, had the most contacts. But here, in this tiny town, what was the deciding factor? How many patients he saw in his office? How many strep cases he diagnosed? Urinary tract infections? What? What was it?

And where was he? There were a lot of people crowded into the old farmhouse, many of them past fifty, several past sixty, though she'd seen a handful of children snaking in and out through the front door. And there were younger people there, but they were gathered in small groups, clusters of men and women scattered around the room, spilling onto the front porch.

So, where was he? *Where was Nicholas Androvich?*

"Alex, this is Stella." Edna Lubovich touched Alex's

shoulder, raised her voice above the polka music. "Stella Androvich."

Alex turned toward the woman next to Edna. She was tall, with brownish hair, wavy, cut just above the shoulders with streaks of gray that looked as though someone had taken a brush and painted them on. Her skin was tanned from hours in the sun, perhaps from tending the vegetable garden Alex had seen on the side of the house, or some other type of chore, no doubt. She was smiling, a big smile, and her brown eyes were warm, generous, inviting. "Mrs. Androvich, it's a pleasure to meet you." Alex took her hand, felt the chapped roughness of the other woman's.

"And it's a pleasure to meet you too, dear." Her smile deepened. "But we're quite informal around here. I'd prefer you call me Stella."

"Stella, then." There was a genuineness to this woman, a softness that made Alex picture her as a young mother, cuddling her children in her lap, reading them a fairy tale as they snuggled against her, the feel of flannel and a warm bath making them drowsy. This woman was a mother, a caretaker, a giver. A deep longing gnawed inside Alex. What must it have been like to be loved just for the sake of oneself? To not have to prove, achieve, *do* anything, other than exist? And to know the honest touch of a mother, a protector, a *giver,* who expects nothing in return? Aunt Helen had permitted kisses on the cheek and quick hugs when she wasn't wearing silk or linen. She had never been a giver, or much of a caretaker, and though she'd tried in her own way, she didn't have it in her to be a mother. But she and Uncle Walter had made it up to Alex in other ways, hadn't they? Tennis lessons, shopping trips to FAO Schwarz, and when she got older, Bloomingdale's and Saks. And wasn't she the only person in her seventh-grade class to go on a cruise? Including the teacher?

"Edna tells me you're doing research about small towns."

"Yes. I'm collecting information for a documentary."
*Actually, the information I'm collecting isn't for a documen-
tary at all. It's to decide if we want to flatten your houses
and put a resort on it.*

"Well, that's exciting." Stella smiled again. Alex looked
away, busied herself with her watch, adjusting, readjusting
the band. "Let me know if there's any way I can help."

Edna spoke up. "I thought you might introduce Alex to
Dr. Nick. Maybe he could show her around." She nudged
Stella with her elbow. "You know, they seem to be about
the same age, maybe he'd enjoy it."

"Edna, what did I tell you—"

"I think it's a perfect idea," Stella said, cutting off Chuck
Lubovich mid sentence. "Nick loves Restalline, and he
knows it as well as I do, probably better. When he was
younger, he and Michael used to go exploring, hills, paths,
in the woods." She let out a laugh. "Once they even got
lost for ten hours. Half the town was out looking for them,
and when they finally came out the woods, Nick held up
his compass and shouted, 'It worked! It worked!' " She
shook her head. "Needless to say, neither one of the boys
was allowed off the property for a month."

"If you think he wouldn't mind." *Finally.*

"Mind?" Stella looked her over, nodded. "Oh, no. To
tell you the truth, I think it's exactly what he needs."

Edna nodded, her red curls bobbing up and down.
"Exactly," she agreed.

Good. What better way to learn the land and who owned
what than to get a personal tour from someone who really
knew the terrain? She looked up, saw a man leaning against
the far wall, beer in one hand, having a conversation with
two older women. But his eyes weren't on them. *They
were on her.* He was tall, with dark hair, dark skin, big
forearms . . .

Stella followed her gaze. "There he is." She waved to

the man. "That's Nick. Come on, Alex, I'm sure you two will have a lot to talk about."

"I'm sure of it," Edna chimed in.

"Edna—"

Chuck's voice faded as Alex and Stella moved through the crowd, heading toward Nick Androvich. *God, he's still watching me. Why? Can he tell I'm fake? Does he sense it?*

"Nick, I want you to meet someone," Stella said, laying her hand on Alex's shoulder. They were close now, too close. Alex could see the fine wrinkles around his eyes and mouth, the wave in his dark brown hair, the patch of hair sticking out of the neck of his red shirt. But most of all, from this proximity, she could see his eyes. Deep, dark, with flecks of gold, mesmerizing eyes, the kind that pulled you in, held you, forced you to give up your secrets.

Alex looked away, cleared her throat, looked back. So, he was watching her? He didn't know, couldn't know anything about her or the real reason she was here.

"Nick?" His mother squeezed her shoulder. "This is Alex Chamberlain. Alex, this is my eldest son, Nick."

He nodded, held out a hand. "Alex." His smile was stiff, forced, much the same as hers. She placed her hand in his, felt the warmth of his grasp, quick, sure, and then he was loosening his grip and dropping his hand to his side.

"Alex, tell Nick about the project you're working on. I'm sure he'll want to hear all about it." Stella nodded, looking at both of them as though it was their first date and she was the chaperon.

"It's too loud in here," Nick said before Alex had a chance to respond. "Let's go outside where we don't have to shout to have a conversation." He motioned toward the kitchen door, placing a hand on the small of her back.

"I think that's an excellent idea," Stella said, her lips spreading into a wide smile. "And Nick, if you see Uncle

Frank wandering around out there, please try to coax him in.''

"Will do.'' Nick and Alex passed through the kitchen, the aroma of spicy sauce and peppers filling their senses. "This way.'' He opened the back door and Alex stepped into another galaxy. Night, black and velvety, sucked them in. There was a sliver of moon, high in the sky, buried behind a moving cluster of clouds that cast an occasional flicker of light at them. And the sounds, chirping, crackling, howling. Night sounds. The closest she'd come to hearing anything like this was when she pressed the buttons on the sound therapy machine at the Bed, Bath & Beyond store last Christmas. Crickets, rain, water, crickets, rain, water. These were crickets.

Nick took her arm. "Come with me.''

"I . . . I can't see anything out here.''

"You don't need to. The swing's ten steps to your right, then three to the left.''

She counted in her head, shortened her steps.

"I meant adult steps, not baby ones,'' he said, and she couldn't tell if he was amused or annoyed.

"Sorry.'' Alex took a bigger step, grabbed his arm.

"Relax.'' He stopped, waited for her to take another step. "Trust me, okay?''

Trust. He threw the word out with such ease. "Okay.''

Four steps later, they turned left and took three more before Nick stopped, placed both hands on her shoulders. "Now, turn around and sit.'' Alex reached behind her, felt the wooden slats of the swing before she sat down.

Nick followed. "Nobody has blind faith anymore, did you ever notice that?''

"What do you mean?'' She'd just followed a stranger in the dark, for heaven's sake.

He pushed the swing with his feet. "When I told you to

sit, you wouldn't, not until you could feel the wood behind you, check it out for yourself.''

"So?''

"So, that's what I mean. Nobody has blind faith anymore.''

"First of all, what do you call following a complete stranger in the dark, other than stupid?''

"Good point.'' The swing creaked as they rocked back and forth in the dark. "So, tell me why you're here in Restalline.''

Thank God for the night. At least he couldn't see her face, couldn't analyze her expression. "I thought your mother would have told you.'' Stall, breathe, breathe. "I'm doing a documentary on small-town life in the United States. I'm traveling all over the country, gathering information, talking to people, finding out what makes them come to a small town, what makes them stay there.''

"Where are you from?'' It was a simple question, straightforward, inquisitive.

"Northern Virginia.''

"Is there a particular place you call home, or do you just travel the entire terrain and set up camp as you go?''

There it was again, sarcasm or humor, hard to tell which. "No, of course not. I live in Arlington.''

"Uh-huh. Alex from Arlington. City girl.''

A frog or toad or something croaked in the background. "Well, yes, I guess you could say that.''

"Ever lived in a small town?''

"No.''

"So why the interest in them? If you haven't lived in one how can you possibly understand one?''

She heard the edge in his voice, had to fight hard to keep one out of hers. "That's why I'm *here*. So I can learn about them, see what brings people here, keeps them here.''

"That's easy,'' he said. "I'll tell you now, save you

months of research. People want to be more than just 'the man in 1A' or 'the woman with the red Porsche.' They want to be a name, a face, a . . . a person.'' He paused a second, went on. ''They want to be seen, understood, respected. Cities don't do that, they don't respect people. They beat them up, wear them out, put them under pressure, enormous pressure, always to be faster, faster, better, best. And the people lose themselves, fall apart somewhere between the espresso machine and the dry cleaner. So, they find a place like Restalline, and they take a deep breath, and then another and another, and they like it, away from the craziness but still close enough that they can get back on the track every now and then, run full out at the malls and the theaters, and then find their way back home. And they realize that they like having their neighbor know their first *and* last name, even their kids' names. They like being a person, being respected.'' He blew out a long breath. ''That's why they come and that's why they stay.''

Alex thought about the man beside her. Was he talking about himself? Had he been beaten up, worn out, in need of refuge?

''What's your neighbor's name?'' he asked.

''What?''

''Your neighbor's name? What is it?''

''Well, I live in a condo. I have lots of neighbors.'' Who was that lady with the Pomeranian next door to her? Esther? Ellen?

''Okay. Name one.''

Elaine? Eleanor? ''I've only been there a year.'' She'd bought the place right after she moved out of the six-bedroom colonial she and Eric had shared.

''Only a year?'' That was definite sarcasm. ''Case in point. You can't name any of them, can you? First or last name.''

''Of course I can. The woman to my right is Elaine. Yes,

Elaine." Or was it Eleanor? "And she has a little Pomeranian named Jessica."

"You sound more sure of the dog's name than you do of the woman's."

"Well, maybe because the *dog* is more friendly than the woman." Elaine, with her ash-colored hair and long red nails, saved her attention for the men at Chase Point.

That made him laugh. It was a nice sound, deep, rich, rolling over her like a fleece blanket on a winter night.

"You're probably one of those people I'm talking about. Running, running, running, from your meditation class to your aerobics session to your feng shui seminar. Boom, boom, boom, always in motion."

How had he known about the feng shui seminar? "I lead a very active life."

"I'm sure you do."

"*Because* I happen to enjoy it."

"Great. Then my meandering observations don't apply to you."

"Right. They don't." Elaine. Her name *was* Elaine.

He sighed. "If you really want to get a handle on life in this town, I'll take you around, show you the sights."

"You sound as though you're about to go before a firing squad."

He let out a short laugh. "Well, if you're going to draw a conclusion, I want it to be the right one."

"A spin doctor in Restalline. And here I thought you were a people doctor."

"Depends on the occasion," he said. "I've been known to be both."

"Too bad, Snow White, seems like you lose again."

Elise Pentani swung around. Michael Androvich came

toward her from the darkness, saluting her with his bottle of beer.

"You're late."

"I know." She just wanted to get inside, find Nick, apologize for not getting there sooner. Why did her father have to pick tonight to deliver two hundred rolls and five dozen cupcakes for her little cousin Gloria's communion party? It wasn't until tomorrow afternoon and Elise had promised to get up at 7:00 A.M., load them all herself, set them up in Aunt Jenny's kitchen. But no, Angelo Pentani wanted it done *pronto*, tonight, and he wanted Elise's help. What choice did she have? Tell him that the man she was in love with had finally, *finally* noticed her? No, Angelo would never understand that. If her mother were still alive, she'd have raised one dark eyebrow at her husband and Elise would have been getting dressed for the party.

But at least she was here. Finally. Now she just had to find Nick.

"Too late, Snow White. You're too late." Michael tipped the bottle to his lips, took a long swig. "He's gone."

"What?" Gone. Nick was gone?

"Yup. Gone." He smiled then, a lopsided twist that showed off his dimples. "Sorry you wasted all that perfume."

"Michael, will you for once just talk some sense?" He was no different than when he was in high school, still the same old, surly pain in the butt who used to hang around with her brother, Jack. Michael Androvich was a broader, more sun-beaten version of his older brother, with brown hair that curled behind his ears and around his thick neck. Untamed. Undisciplined. Uncontrollable. That was Michael.

"Just what I said. He's gone." He climbed the steps, stood next to her. Somewhere, buried underneath all that gruffness and stubble, there was a decent-looking guy, probably even handsome, but who would know with the three-day's growth on his face, the too-long hair, and over-faded jeans? And his eyes . . . she hated it when she couldn't see a person's eyes, but the Androvich Lumber cap he always wore was pulled low over his forehead, obscuring the top part of his face. Cheekbones and a nose that crooked to the left, that's what she saw.

"Who are you talking about? Uncle Frank?" *He knew! Michael knew!*

"Come on, Snow White, give me more credit than that. The whole family thinks I'm stupid, not you, too."

"Michael—"

He chuckled, held out his bottle to her. "Want a sip?"

She swatted it away. "You've had too much to drink and you're not making any sense. I'm going inside."

He grabbed her arm. "Nick's not in there." His voice was low, all traces of his earlier jovialness gone.

Elise clutched the railing. "Where . . . where is he?"

"Took off with Goldilocks about twenty minutes ago." *Goldilocks?* "Lisa?"

"No, not the doctor broad. This one's a real cool cookie. She's new."

"But . . ." Nick had asked *her* to come. He had. She'd memorized every word, clung to them like the lilac body splash she wore. *Elise, what are you doing Saturday night? . . . We're having a birthday party at the house for Uncle Frank. . . . Why don't you come? Why don't you come? Why don't you come?*

"Sorry, kiddo." Michael touched her shoulder. "I just didn't want you to hold out waiting for him. It's not going to happen between you two. You know that, don't you?"

No, she didn't know that. She lowered her head, squeezed her eyes shut. She didn't want to hear this.

Michael took her hand, pulled her into the shadows of the porch. "You've been working for him for two years. It would've happened by now."

She shook her head, willed the tears back. He was wrong. A little more time, that's what Nick needed. Then he'd notice her.

"I saw the way he was looking at this new one. He's a goner."

Elise stiffened, pinched the bridge of her nose, hard. Enough, she'd heard enough. "I ... I don't feel well. If anybody asks ..."

"Sure, Snow White, sure. I'll cover for you. Go home."

She turned and ran then, fast, down the steps to her silver Honda Civic, the tears burning her eyes, smearing her makeup, pouring the grief from her soul. And not until she was home, burrowed in her bed with the sheet pulled to her chin, did she realize that she'd learned something new tonight. Beneath the rudeness, the insults, the cockiness, the jesting, Michael Androvich kept a well-hidden secret: he had a heart.

Chapter 5

"Dr. Nick! Come. Come, come inside," Edna Lubovich held the screen door wide. She was wearing a white-and-black polka-dot blouse with black stretch pants and satin slippers. Her red hair was piled high, topped off with a little black bow tucked in the center like a baby bird in a nest. When she smiled at him, a smudge of red lipstick smeared her right front tooth.

"Hello, Edna." He stared at the shiny, black ball earrings dangling from her small lobes. "Don't you look fancy."

"Just got back from Mass." She patted her hair. "Alex went with me." She smiled again. The lipstick mark had turned to pink. "She's not Catholic but she followed right along in the missalette. I told her a lot of Protestants convert, especially when they get married and start having kids."

Nick hid a smile. "I'm sure she was glad to hear that."

"Said she'd keep it in mind." Edna lowered her voice, "She's Lutheran, you know, but not a practicing one."

Nick lowered his voice to match hers, "Oh. No, I didn't know."

"Well, now you do and *you* should keep that in mind. Anxious to see her again, aren't you?" Edna winked, didn't wait for an answer before she went on. "I can see why, I certainly can. She's a looker. Walks around like a princess, head up high, shoulders back. And she's got class, loads of it, smothered on thick, not the kind you get out of a tube or on a clothes rack." She leaned toward him, pointed at her chest. "She's got it from the inside out, don't you think?"

"Edna—"

She waved a hand at him. "Pshaw, Dr. Nick. Don't be embarrassed about falling for her. I was watching both of you last night; you two make the perfect pair. I was saying so to Chuck." She patted his cheek, grabbed his hand. "Just perfect. Now, why don't you come in and I'll fix you a cup of coffee while you wait."

"Actually, I've already had three cups. But thanks. I think I'll just see if she's ready if you don't mind."

She squeezed his hand. "You are anxious, aren't you? I know, I know. Stella's thrilled. It's been so long . . . after Caroline and all, God rest her soul." She made a quick sign of the cross, clutched the gold medal hanging around her neck. "Your mother thinks this just might be the one to bring you a little happiness."

"My mother said that?" *Good God*, how desperate could they be, matching him up with a woman they'd known for less than twenty-four hours?

Edna nodded. "She liked Alex. A lot."

"She knows nothing about the woman." This was ridiculous.

"Said you offered to show Alex around town, take her

on a personal tour.'' She raised a penciled brow, dared him to deny it.

What could he say? The truth? *I only offered to escort the damn woman around Restalline because I want to find out if she's one of those "Save the Trees" people in disguise and this is the only way I can do it?* No, he couldn't be that honest. Edna would be shocked that he could be so distrusting, and his mother, well, he could hear her now— *Nick, you need to have more faith in the goodness of others, especially strangers. You're such a doubting Thomas.*

He'd just play along for now, keep his mouth shut, much easier that way. ''Do you think she's ready, Edna?''

She shrugged, gave him a half smile. ''One way to find out, Dr. Nick. Only one way.''

Okay, so she was nice-looking . . . maybe a little more than nice-looking, maybe . . . pretty. Correction. Very pretty. But she wasn't beautiful. Her eyes were too wide-set, her forehead too high, her jaw too angular, her mouth . . . he glanced sideways, his eyes darting over her lips, full, soft-looking, moist. He swung his gaze back to the road, clutched the steering wheel. Her mouth was fine.

''Androvich Lumber has a very extensive conservation program.'' Might as well give her the spiel before they got there. ''Replanting, site selection, land rotation, education. They're all part of what keeps the company going, and''— if she was a ''Save the Tree-er,'' she'd like this one— ''*protects* the environment. We believe in giving back what we take. Always have.''

She shifted in her seat. ''Good. That's very . . . noble of you.''

Was she being sarcastic? Did she think their efforts were inadequate? ''If we didn't cut any trees, they'd all be scrawny, choking each other out, fighting for a ray of sunlight. And over half the town would be unemployed." Why was he trying to justify his family's livelihood? "If Androvich Lumber doesn't produce, then Restalline Millworks and NK Manufacturing go out of business."

"So, the town depends on these three businesses for its livelihood."

Now she was getting it. "Damn right it does."

"And it needs Androvich Lumber to supply materials to the other two companies."

"You got it."

"What happens if Androvich Lumber goes away?" She turned toward him. "Not that it ever would, but what would happen then? Could they get their wood from somewhere else?"

Shit. What was she trying to pull? An environmentalist wouldn't want wood taken from anywhere. Who the hell was this woman and what was she after? "They could, but it would cost them, probably almost double, and Norman Kraziak's a businessman, not a nonprofit organization."

"I see."

He doubted it. "Why all the questions, Alex? It's simple enough to understand. We've got three main companies that pump life into Restalline, keep it alive. Each of these companies work together, depend on the other, for material or orders. Norman's companies make up seventy-five percent of our business, and we make up one hundred percent of his. *We need each other.*"

"Kind of like interdependence," she said.

"Exactly." He saw the quarter-mile sign for Androvich Lumber. "Now you've got it."

She nodded. "Yes, yes, I think I do."

"Good. Then you think about that while I'm showing you around." He flicked his left turn signal on, maneuvered into the turning lane. "This afternoon, I'll take you to meet Norman and *then* you'll really understand."

* * *

Alex took great pride in knowing the difference between a desk constructed of cherry and one made of mahogany. She preferred the deeper, richer tones of cherry. Oak was too coarse a wood for her taste, poplar too indistinguishable, pine too cheap. But it was one thing to walk into a showroom, run your fingers along the polished, buffed-out grain, and claim yourself knowledgeable of finer woods, and quite another to be standing in a forest, surrounded by acres of trees, and still possess the ability to differentiate the cherry from its counterparts.

He'd shown her the trees, so many of them, as far as she could see, brown and green, packed together, woven to form a backdrop for ground and sky. And then he'd pointed out the trucks that hauled them, the words *Androvich Lumber* scrawled in faded white lettering across the sides of each dull-red cab, all lined up in one neat row—large ones with chains thrown over their beds and tires half as tall as Alex and several times wider. Lastly, were the men, sun-weathered and sweaty, some shaved, some bearded, in T-shirts and jeans, with dirt caked on their worn boots. When they saw Nick, they called out or raised a hand, their eyes slowly shifting to Alex, then back to Nick. Most smiled, a few did not.

Guilt pricked her conscience. If they only knew why she was really here, they'd be chasing after her, chain saws revving.

"You see this tree?" Nick said, interrupting her thoughts. He was pointing to a large tree in front of them. "This is a white oak." He ran his hand along the bark. "Put your hand here. Feel it."

She followed his instructions, the rough edges of the ash-gray bark beneath her fingers. "White oak has small scaly plates like this one. It's a dead giveaway."

"Maybe for somebody who's lived in the forest all of his life." Alex backed away, stared up at the tree's leaves. "So, you just look at the bark and you know what kind of tree you have?"

He wiped his hands on his jeans. "Pretty much, but there are other ways to tell. Look at the leaves. I know you did at least one leaf project in grade school. Remember, find the leaf, flatten it under a dictionary for a week, glue it down, and label it?" He laughed. "Half the class paid me a buck each to find them leaves. But Uncle Frank's the real master. He can walk through a forest and tell the type of tree just by looking at it. My dad used to be like that, too. When we were kids, we'd run around, pointing at trees and seeing how fast he could name them." He shook his head, rubbed the back of his neck. "Michael's probably the only one around these days who can still tell a tree just by eyeballing it."

"Michael's your younger brother."

"Right."

"I didn't see him."

"You won't."

"Oh. Why not?"

There was a short pause. "He stays in the woods. Cuts trees. Hauls lumber."

"He doesn't run the company?" It seemed like someone who could walk into the woods and identify every tree should be doing more than cutting and hauling. Especially if his last name was Androvich.

"No." There was an edge to his voice.

"Oh."

"How about some lunch? I'm starved."

"Sure," Alex said. He'd slammed the subject closed, right in her face. Something was going on between Nick and his brother. Rivalry? Jealousy? What? She'd find out; she was very good at ferreting around for information. Uncle

Walter always said that the more one knew about one's opponents, *and everyone's an opponent, in one way or another,* he'd told her often enough, the better equipped one would be to handle situations that presented themselves. *That's how we make opportunity, Alex. Out of situations.* There was a situation here with the Androvich brothers, and she full well intended to turn it into an opportunity.

Nick was quiet on the trip back to the car. She walked beside him, taking in the dense trees, shielding all but slivers of sun like a curtain, the dark earth moist and rich under her feet. Sound was everywhere: chirps, buzzes, hums, drones, crackles. Perhaps they should consider a nature trail here, maybe slice a ribbon right through the heart of the land, dump a ton of gravel for a path, hang up birdhouses, construct a rabbit warren. It would be a nice complement to a summer resort that offered swimming, tennis, golf, the usual. She made a mental note to explore this option further.

"There's a lake about two miles from here, on the outskirts of town," Nick said, hopping into the silver Navigator. "Lunch is in that picnic basket back there."

"Oh." That surprised her. "How thoughtful of you."

He shrugged. "It was my mother's idea. I don't even know what's in there."

Typical man. "Well, whatever it is, I'm sure it will be delicious."

"My mother's a great cook, but sometimes you're better off just eating it and not asking what it is." He threw her a sideways glance. "Ever had tripe?"

She shook her head.

"Liver?"

"Once."

"Sweetbread?"

Another no. "I guess I'm more of a conventional chicken and occasional pork kind of person."

"So cow's tongue and calf's thymus gland don't interest you?"

She stared at him. "No, not really."

He grinned. "Like I said, with my mother, it's better to just eat it and not ask."

Alex turned around, eyed the wicker basket lying on the backseat. "Any idea what *might* be in there?" A Hot Ed's sausage sub sounded awfully good right now, especially next to a tongue and some kind of gland.

"No, but I think she'll go easy on you. Probably save the good stuff for when she knows you better." He turned off the main road and onto a narrow side road surrounded by trees and grasses, so thick that they made it impossible to see into the woods. Alex felt like she was traveling in a tunnel of foliage. *Maybe this could be another nature trail,* she thought.

"We're very ethnic people," Nick said. "It's how we were raised. Liver, cabbage, cow's tongue." He laughed. "Not that we actually dug into it or fought for seconds, but at least we were exposed to it. How about you? Got any delicacies that you remember from childhood?"

Should she tell him about the time she spit out a mouthful of caviar at Uncle Walter's and Aunt Helen's annual Christmas party? She'd believed the old blue-haired woman who told her the little black balls in the crystal dish were better than candy, so she'd stuck a big spoonful on a cracker and stuffed it in her mouth. A half second later, she'd spewed it all over her red velvet dress and the white carpet. That was twenty-four years ago and it was the last time she'd tasted caviar. "No, not really."

"Nothing? No soups or stews or other family recipes that get passed down?"

"We were pretty traditional." She looked out the window, stared at the mesh of green blending together as they drove by. Family recipes? Aunt Helen left the recipes to *Bon Appetit* and the cooking to Rosa.

"What nationality are you?"

"Excuse me? Oh." She was remembering Rosa's chateau briand. "My father was English and my mother was Russian."

"Was?"

What was he doing, taking a history, like she was one of his patients? Alex prided herself on keeping her personal life just that, personal. She pressed her shoulders into the back of the seat, kept her head turned. "They died when I was eight. I was raised by my aunt and uncle."

"No brothers or sisters?"

She shook her head. "Just me."

"I'm sorry."

"Why?" She looked at him, forced a smile. "I never had to share a thing. I always got first choice, second too. My aunt and uncle gave me everything," her voice got louder, "everything I ever wanted."

He didn't look at her when he answered, didn't change the tone of his voice, just let it roll out in a matter-of-fact statement. "Like I said, I'm sorry."

"I hate pity."

"So do I."

She should just let it go, not push it. After all, she needed him on her side if she was going to convince him to sell. But she hated it when anybody felt sorry for her; she didn't need or want sympathy. Sympathy made people weak, made them powerless, made them think things. . . . *I'm sorry about your parents . . . Didn't they love you enough to avoid such a risk? . . . I'm sorry you don't have any brothers or sisters . . . Didn't your parents love you enough to want more than one child? . . . I'm sorry about your husband . . . Didn't he love you enough to stay faithful? . . . sorry, sorry . . . sorry* . . . She squeezed her eyes shut, willed the words from her

brain. It had taken a long time, a very long time, years, to
fight the belief that her parents had died because she wasn't
good enough, wasn't loveable enough, wasn't ... *enough*.
But she'd figured it out, all by herself, through reason and
intellect, that she wasn't responsible for their deaths any
more than she was responsible for her husband hopping into
bed with a Playboy Bunny. She was a good person, a *loveable* person. *She was*.

"So, what do you think of it?" Nick's voice reached her,
soft, low, perhaps a bit apologetic. Alex opened her eyes.
There, in front of them, sat a huge lake, blue and sparkling
like a jewel, surrounded by the rich foliage of trees and
shrubs and wildflowers.

"Beautiful," she breathed. *This is it*. As long as she didn't
have to get any closer, she could think of it as a backdrop,
a setting on a stage, and she'd be fine. Her pulse kicked in
an extra few beats the way it did when she saw bodies of
water larger than a Jacuzzi. *We need this*, she told herself,
it's perfect. You don't have to go near it, you can just look
from here. She forced her breathing to even out, as she
pictured a few small boats rowing toward the middle of the
lake, the women wearing broad straw hats and sundresses,
the men, polos and walking shorts. And there'd be a pier
off to the right, and a gazebo just past the left bank. There.
She took a deep breath through her nose, held it, let it ease
out past her lips. *I'm okay, I'm okay*.

"This is Sapphire Lake."

Perfect. *Perfect*.

"Let's eat and you can get a closer look."

"Sure." Alex had no intention of getting any closer. The
fear that crawled in her gut every time she saw lakes or
rivers or oceans might be ridiculous, but it was real. Years
of forced swimming lessons—*You will do this Alex*, Uncle
Walter had said. *Your parents' deaths were a fluke, an accident. There's nothing to fear in the water, nothing*—had

culminated in one last attempt to embrace the water: scuba lessons. Her hatred of defeat and desire to please her uncle had pushed her on, plummeted her in the water, dive after dive, until the final test, when she had to actually *put on* her gear at the bottom of a quarry. She could still feel it, clawing at the water as she fought her way to the surface, harder, harder, panic chasing her. *I'm going to die*, she'd thought . . . *I'm going to die. Out*, she had to get *out* or she wouldn't make it; she'd die, die, *die,* just like them.

Uncle Walter had never talked about that day, when the instructor dove in and pulled her out of the water, thrashing and hysterical. Nor had she mentioned it. There was no need to: fear had won. But each resort she worked on had either a natural lake or a manmade one in her plans. Perhaps it was a perverse method of facing her demons, indirect and remote as it might be, or maybe it was her subconscious attempt to appease her uncle for failing him. Either way, the inclusion of a lake in her resort plans added to the beauty of the land and made Uncle Walter very happy. He'd be thrilled with this lake. Not only would it save the cost and aggravation of installing a manmade one as they'd done on the last two projects, but this one had the mark and elegance of natural beauty that was often hard to duplicate.

"How about over here?"

"That's fine," she said, following Nick to a shaded spot underneath a big tree. Walnut? Chestnut? Oak? What had he told her about the bark? And the leaves? Who knew? Her excitement mounted as she envisioned sharing these wonderful findings with her uncle.

Nick spread out a quilt, red and white, with a circle of blue stars in the center. He placed the picnic basket between them and eased himself onto the ground. "So, what'll it be"—he flipped open the basket—"tripe and liver, or a sweetbread sandwich?"

"Uh—"

He laughed. "Just kidding. Looks like ham and Swiss on wheat, or"—he fished around, uncovered part of another sandwich—"turkey and Swiss on rye. You pick."

"They both sound good. I'll take whichever one you don't want."

"Alex, I'm eating both of them. My mother packed two for each of us; can't have anybody going hungry, or even think about *getting* hungry."

"Then I'll take a turkey and Swiss." There was more than just sandwiches packed away in the picnic basket. Stella Androvich had sent potato salad, sugar cookies, and lemonade, all homemade. And all delicious. Quite a departure from the raspberry yogurt Alex usually ate at her desk every day. The company wasn't bad, either, or maybe it was just easier on the digestive tract to hear about deer and rabbits feeding around the lake than it was reading about Wall Street's futile efforts to rally. Nick stretched out his legs, ate his sandwich, and told her about growing up in Restalline.

"Did you always want to be a doctor?"

"No. I thought about becoming an anthropologist, studying the history of man, where he came from, how he evolved. I used to go out in the woods and dig around looking for fossils, anything to tie in preexisting life. I'd spend hours on my knees with a shovel." He stopped speaking, took a drink of lemonade. "But then my dad died and everything changed."

"Do you have any regrets?"

He raised a brow, looked her square in the eye. "Everybody has regrets, Alex. But if you're asking me do I regret becoming a doctor, then no, I don't. I was fifteen when they carried my father's body out of the woods, and I swore I'd do everything possible to prevent that kind of thing from happening to somebody else."

"You were close to your father?"

He nodded. "It was a tough time. Thank God for Uncle Frank."

"The uncle who doesn't come to his own birthday parties," Alex said, recalling the guest of honor's absence at his own party last night. She'd inquired about him, curious to meet another Androvich, but Edna had only laughed and Nick's mother had shaken her head in disgust. *Who knows when that ornery old cuss will show up?* she'd said. *Maybe an hour from now, maybe two, maybe not at all. Never you mind, Alex, you just enjoy yourself. And eat as much food as you like, especially the stuffed peppers. They're his favorite. Serve him right if we leave him an empty dish.*

"That's Uncle Frank. He doesn't like big displays, never has, even less so since the accident two years ago. Anybody tell you about it?"

She shook her head.

"Here's a man who practically grew up with a chain saw in his hand, and one day he goes out in the woods, just like he's done ten thousand times before, but this time is different. This time, he hits a tough knot, he miscalculates by an eighth of an inch, whatever it is, he can't remember much right before it happened. Anyway, the saw kicks back and rips half his face off." He met her gaze. "Literally. He's got scars down one side of his face and a pocket where his left eye used to be."

"Oh, my God."

"Yeah. God was with him all right or he'd have bled to death."

Alex tried to picture the grotesqueness that Nick was describing. "Couldn't he . . . couldn't he have some type of reconstructive surgery done? Something to help him?"

"Of course he could, but you don't know Uncle Frank. He got fitted for a glass eye and it sits in his bathroom in a denture cup. He doesn't care what people think, just like he doesn't care about birthday parties. All he wants to do is stay in his workshop.''

"What does he make?"

"Anything with wood. He's an excellent woodworker, a real craftsman, the best in the area. People see the bowls he turns and they want to buy them, and the boxes he makes, they're incredible. A man even came from Pittsburgh last year, some big buyer for a specialty store. Told him he wanted to commission some of Uncle Frank's work. He wouldn't do it, said he wasn't interested in turning himself into a machine. He only gives them as gifts, didn't want to hear anymore about it.''

"But if he'd have taken that deal, shown some of his work in the city, do you have any idea how much exposure he could've gotten?'' *How much money he could be making?* The man might be an excellent craftsman, but he certainly wasn't a very good businessman.

"He's not interested.''

Alex fished a sugar cookie out of a plastic baggie. It had pink icing with pink and white sprinkles. She pictured Stella Androvich in her kitchen, dipping a spatula into pink icing, her silver-brown hair tucked behind her ears. Alex took a bite of cookie and a pang of feeling that could only be described as an emptiness spread through her. Never, not in all her years with Uncle Walter and Aunt Helen, had anyone ever made her sugar cookies. And even if they had, she was certain they wouldn't have been iced and sprinkled. She laid the half-eaten cookie on the blanket beside her. "Well, maybe your uncle just doesn't understand the value of what he's making.'' Business, that was a safe topic. She understood it, excelled at it, thrived on it. It was much easier than dealing with old emotions that could serve no purpose. Past was past.

"He understands it,'' Nick said, taking two sugar cookies.

"Well, maybe not. Some people don't, you know. They're

the true artists, they don't want to muddy their creative waters with something as obscene as money.'' That was probably it. Frank Androvich was an eccentric recluse who created for the sake of creating. "He might just need a manager, you know, somebody to handle the financial end of things for him, get him set up, advertise, take orders.

"You sound like a representative from S.B.A."

She shrugged. "I just don't like to see potential go to waste."

"You mean, you don't like to see the chance to make a dollar go to waste." He was watching her, his expression a mixture of disbelief and dislike.

"No, that's not it at all." But in a way, it was.

"You see that lake out there, Alex?" He pointed to the calm blue waters of Sapphire Lake. "Do you have any idea how it got its name?"

Sapphire Lake. Blue. Shiny. The lake was blue and shiny like a sapphire. "My guess would be that it was named after a sapphire because it sparkles like one and has the same blue color."

He shook his head. "That's not it at all, though most people would think that if they didn't know the truth." He picked up a blade of grass, ran his fingers down the middle. "Just goes to show you that appearances can be deceiving. You just never know."

"So, are you going to tell me or do I keep guessing?" Was he testing her, challenging her in some obscure way? She wasn't used to being cast into the role of quiet servitude.

He flung the grass in the air. "When my great-grandfather settled in Restalline, all he wanted to do was buy up land and start a lumber mill. That's it. So, for three years he worked hard, night and day, trying to raise enough money for a down payment." He rubbed his jaw, kept his gaze on the lake. "But the kids started coming along and they could never seem to scrape enough together. He became discouraged, disillusioned that he'd never realize his big dream. Then one day my great-grandmother went to town and when she came back, she had enough money to buy fifty acres of land and put a down payment on a lumber mill.'' His lips curved into a slow smile. ''She'd sold her mother's sapphire earrings, the only keepsake she had.'' There was a gentleness in his next words that reminded Alex of a summer's breeze blowing over bare shoulders.

''My great-grandfather was so moved, he named the lake in her honor. And the story goes that every time he came here and looked at the water, he didn't see jewels or sparkling gems—he saw love, and sacrifice, and hope. Simple riches. As for my great-grandmother, she didn't think about the earrings or what she gave up. She thought instead of what she'd given: a dream to her husband, and a cherished memory to her children, and her children's children, down through the years, so much more valuable than a pair of sapphire earrings.''

Alex listened, thinking of the velvet-lined boxes that had become hers when Aunt Helen died. Pearls, rubies, diamonds. Sapphires. Her aunt would never have given them up, any of them, ever, not for love or friendship or the realization of a dream. It was her legacy to Alex, but perhaps moreso to herself: a mark left behind weighed in carats and clarity, not compassion and consideration. Alex reached up, fingered the single strand of pearls she wore. Had anyone asked her, given her the choice, she, too, would have selected the memories, the stories of love and sacrifice, handed down from generation to generation rather than a glittering accumulation of meaningless jewels. She, too, would have chosen the simple riches. But no one had asked.

''That's a very touching story,'' she said, her gaze fixed on the calm blueness of the lake. ''Your great-grandmother must have been quite a woman.''

"She was. The Androvich women are all strong, deter-mined, single-minded."

"Not even a weak-kneed one in the bunch? One that's just a little off center maybe?" It had been meant as a joke, to lighten the uncomfortable inadequacy Alex felt when Nick talked about his family and their commitment to one another. Uncle Walter cared about her, loved her, and even Aunt Helen had in her own way, though not with words or actions. *Alex, my lipstick, please. Watch those sticky fingers. Not on my Armani.* Affection was foreign, unfamiliar, and uncomfortable.

But Nick didn't like her attempt at humor. Her words had him jerking his head around as though she'd slapped him. "Why'd you really come to Restalline, Alex?" There was a hard edge to his voice this time, no pretense of politeness.

"What?"

"Why? I want the truth."

"I told you—"

He slashed a hand in the air, cutting her off. "At first, I thought you might be one of those 'Save the Trees' people, but you don't know a tree from a piece of particle board. And it was obvious by the way you stayed right on the path this morning, never touched a thing, not even a piece of moss, unless I told you to, that you didn't belong in the woods, so I doubt you're one of those environmentalist crazies who's fighting for a bat's right to live there. So what is it?" His gaze narrowed on her. "Why are you really here?"

Alex cleared her throat, looked at the lake, tried to think. What to say? *You're right there, Nick Androvich, I'm not one of those environmentalist crazies. I'm not trying to save your trees. As a matter of fact, I was calculating a way to clear out more trees, except for a certain amount that would enhance the value of the area, and then I'd have you haul the lumber at cost, maybe involve Norman Kraziak, too. You see, Nick, the only thing I'm thinking about here is getting this land and saving money. Oh, didn't I tell you? That's why I'm really here, to buy up your town. That means the lumber mill, too. And then I'm going to flatten it and build a beautiful resort with this magnificent lake as a backdrop. That's why I'm really here, Nick.*

"I told you—" she tried again.

"Bullshit." He grabbed her wrist. "Look at me, damn it." She met his gaze, saw the clenched jaw, the flared nostrils . . . the eyes, dark, burning into her, branding her a liar. He released her wrist, and when he spoke again, his voice was calm, even, but just as threatening, perhaps even moreso because of the absence of emotion there. "What was that smart-ass comment about off center? Is this about Caroline?"

"Caroline?" She'd heard that name before. Edna had mentioned a Caroline, said something about the Kraziaks and a tragedy, a tragedy that Nick still blamed himself for. *Had she been one of his patients? Had she died and he'd felt responsible for her death?*

"If you're another grad student coming to prey on the misfortune of others for your research material, you can just pack your bags and head out of here. I mean it. I won't be so easy this time."

"What are you talking about?"

He eyed her. "Don't lie to me. Are you trying to cozy up to the town so you can find out about Caroline? Find out if I was responsible for her death?" His voice dropped, came out hard, low. "If it was my fault?"

"Nick! What are you talking about? And who's Caroline?" She didn't like the way he was looking at her, as though he wanted to reach down her throat and drag the truth from her, one syllable at a time.

He turned away, stared at the lake, saying nothing, his breathing hard, uneven, his right fist clenched. "Caroline is dead. Nothing will bring her back.'' His next words were precise, measured, cold. ''And I will not let you or anyone else desecrate her name or dredge up the past. Do you understand?''

Alex didn't answer. She had too many questions of her own pounding in her head, the first and foremost, crowding out the rest. *''Who is Caroline?''*

As much as she wanted to know, she almost wished she hadn't asked. His gaze moved over her, in slow motion, reel by reel, like the film on a projector, boring into her, through her, stopping, starting again, his face a distorted mask of pain. She wished she could fast-forward through this moment, but it went on and on until finally, his lips thinned out into a flat line and he spoke. ''Caroline was my wife.''

Chapter 6

There was something about her that reminded him of his daughter. He couldn't say exactly what it was. Perhaps it was the light shining on her blonde head, transforming each strand into pale gold, like whipped butter. Or maybe it was no more than the small smile she gave him, just a faint turn of the lips, when she caught him watching her. Or, worst of all, but quite plausible, it was nothing more than his own pitiful hope and longing wrapped up in despair so great, for a daughter whose death had left him hollowed out, alone.

Norman Kraziak wasn't disappointed when Nick beat such a hasty retreat a little while ago, saying he'd check in later in the afternoon. Norman understood the important position his son-in-law held in this town. A doctor had responsibilities, duties to his patients, his community, his profession. Besides, Norman was secretly pleased to have this time alone with the young woman standing next to him examining a piece of wood. Alex Chamberlain was young and fresh and filled with questions and curiosity. He blinked hard, rubbed his chin with the back of his hand. *And she was alive.*

"Mr. Kraziak, this is such an incredible process." Alex spread her arms wide. "The wood . . . there's so much of it."

"Don't start with that Mr. Kraziak baloney. It's Norman, just Norman." He clasped his hands over the slight paunch resting just above his belt. "I'm proud of this company, proud, too, of the men and women who work here. Never had a union, or a strike. They're good, solid people."

"You must treat them well."

"I treat them fair. That's all anybody can expect in this world anyway: to be treated fair."

"I guess you're right."

He scratched his head, thought a minute. "You seen enough, here? Long and short of it is that Nick's company supplies us with all of our wood. We cut it, plane it, process it, and ship it out all over the country. Nice, simple, honest." She smiled at him and damn if there wasn't that something that tore at his gut, reminded him of his baby girl. *Caroline, oh, Caroline, I miss you, Princess. Not a day goes by that I don't think of you, wish you back, right here with your daddy.*

"Is something wrong, Norman?"

"Huh?" He blinked. She was watching him, concern in her pale blue eyes. Caroline's eyes had been blue, a few shades darker, like a cloudless summer sky. "No. No, I'm fine." He shook his head, pinched the bridge of his nose. "If you've seen enough of this place, I'd like to take you across town and show you my real baby."

"Sure."

"I'll just call Nick and let him know where we'll be."

"No. I mean, that's not necessary. He's taken enough

time out of his busy schedule to escort me around, I really don't want to bother him anymore."

"Suit yourself. I'll be happy to drop you off at Edna and Chuck's. But I don't think Nick minded that much''—he chuckled, winked at her—"not with a girl as pretty as you."

She turned a dull pink. "He didn't have much choice. His mother kind of volunteered his services."

"That's Stella. She's a tough old bird." He shook his head, rubbed his belly with his right hand. Damn, he'd have to stop eating at Hot Ed's. Those sausage subs were doing him in. "Well, let's go before it's quitting time and you miss all the activity."

If she was impressed with the sawmill, Norman couldn't wait to see what she'd say about NK Manufacturing. The company didn't bring in a quarter of the revenue that the mill did, but he considered it one of his greatest sources of pride and accomplishment. "I'm taking you to NK Manufacturing," he told Alex as they headed toward the outskirts of town in his black Lincoln Town Car. "We make custom rocking chairs there from a lot of the hardwoods, especially red oak and cherry." He lowered his voice in reverence to the man who'd been father, companion, mentor, and friend. "It started years ago, when my father, Norman Kraziak Senior, came from his native Czechoslovakia to the United States with nothing more than a carving knife and an idea. Within five years, he was handcrafting rocking chairs out of the abundance of hardwood he found in the area: maple, poplar, red oak. Within ten, he'd set enough money aside to quit his job in the tannery and start his own company. He taught me everything I know about wood carving and furniture crafting, by hand, long before the introduction of the machines we have today." *Working with your hands, making something, one shaving at a time, that's an art,* his father had said. *Nobody wants to do it anymore. Press a button, that's what they want to do. Press a button.*

"I come to the shop sometimes at night, just to smell the wood and think." He didn't mention that he'd been doing it almost every night since Caroline's death eight years ago.

"You must feel a great sense of accomplishment," Alex said, "to have achieved such success, have a product you're proud of. Not a lot of people can say that."

"Too many people want to tear things down, Alex, just rip up the old and replace it with something new. These rockers are meant to last. The wood is hard, durable, and can be refinished eventually, even painted, though I personally believe that's a sacrilege. Who would want to paint over the grain of an oak or cover up the two-tone quality of cherry?" He shook his head. "Only a fool who can't appreciate the beauty of nature would do that."

"Do a lot of people in Restalline own your rockers?" Alex asked.

Norman inhaled, held it, exhaled, and flashed her a huge grin. "Damn straight, they do. Gave 'em away at cost to whoever brought me lumber. You know how many orders I took?" He didn't wait for her to answer. "Five hundred twenty-two. Not bad for a town this size, eh?"

He caught her staring at him. "That was very . . . generous of you." She sounded like she thought he was more crazy than generous. Maybe he was, but what the hell? It was only money, and you could only take it so far. The Good Lord wasn't going to let him pack up his IRAs or GE stock and take it with him, so he might as well unload some of it now. Besides, there was just him and Ruth and their grandson, Justin. How much would any of them ever need? It felt good and right to share, to donate to the less fortunate, to give in Caroline's name.

It was an hour until quitting time when they arrived at the brick storefront of NK Manufacturing. Norman pulled into the spot to the right of the main door. It was reserved for him, had been his father's before that, and in the early days, Norman had hopes that one day a son or perhaps even a daughter would park in that space. But three miscarriages and five years brought him no sons and only one daughter. Caroline Ann Kraziak came into her father's life, not with a wail, but a delicate whimper, as though she hadn't wanted to disturb anyone and was apologizing for making such an untimely appearance at 10:05 P.M. The moment he held his baby daughter in his arms, the years of anguish and disappointment fell away, leaving in its stead a love so great, so powerful, it made his body quiver. He had plans for his little girl, big plans, and he told them to her every night, in great detail. She would go to college, anywhere in the country, money was of no consequence, and then if she wanted, she would work in the business and one day take over. Or, if she chose another profession or business, he'd finance the start-up costs. The choice was hers, and there were many choices, as countless as the stars at night but much more attainable, he would see to that. *The world is yours Caroline*, he'd say. *Anything you want can be yours, will be yours. Anything.*

It had frustrated him at first, when he told her this and she'd only smile, throw her arms around his neck, and tell him she wanted nothing more than what she already had. Oh, there was the occasional toy or new dress, and one time she'd asked for a stereo, but it was always tangible objects, accessible incidentals. Norman wanted her to consider possibilities and potential. But, either she would not or could not. The largest commitment she'd ever made toward a goal was telling him she wanted a family. *I'm going to have lots of kids, Daddy*, she'd said when she was eight. *Six or seven at least. And I think I'll get a husband, too.*

Then one day, when she was sixteen, she came home after a football game, all flushed and breathless, her blue eyes shining. *I know what I want, Daddy. I know.* She'd twirled around and around, laughing and looking suddenly more woman than child. *Finally, finally, I really know.* Her laughter stopped, she reached for his hand. *More than anything, anything in the world, I want Nick Androvich. I want to marry him, have his children. That's what I want, Daddy.*

Alex followed Norman through the plant as he pointed out spindles, backs, legs, seats, all the necessary parts that went into making a Kraziak rocker. When he touched a piece of wood, held it in his hands, there was a reverence, a pure joy, on his face and in his voice. There'd been a few times, when she was asking him questions, or commenting about a particular process in the plant, that she'd caught him watching her, his blue eyes unusually bright, a shadow falling over his otherwise agreeable features.

What was it? Why was he doing that? Why was he looking at her that way? Did she remind him of someone, his daughter, Caroline?

When they reached his office, Norman led her inside and spread a hand wide. "Have a seat, Alex. I just need to collect a few papers and then I'll get you back to Chuck and Edna's."

She sank into a maple rocker, ran her fingers along the smooth surface, placed her hands on the armrests. Now she could try out one for herself. It looked comfortable; maybe she'd order one for her office. Cherry. She was just ready to start rocking when she looked up and saw a huge portrait of a young woman in the far corner of the office. Caroline. It had to be her. Norman's daughter. Nick's wife. The woman had long, flowing golden-blonde hair, with soft curls falling to the sides and back, framing part of her heart-shaped face. Her eyes were a brilliant blue, wide, reserved, shy. Or was it hesitancy Alex saw, as though the woman might not be certain she wanted to join in? The rest of her was straightforward, beautiful: nose, small and compact;

complexion, fair, perhaps light freckles, too hard to tell from this vantage point; chin, pointed, slight cleft; lips, full, parted in a glimpse of a smile.

Norman saw her studying the portrait. "That's Caroline."

Alex nodded, wondering if he was aware that he'd used the present tense. "Very beautiful." She kept her reply simple in order to avoid both present and past tenses.

"The light of my life," he replied, looking at the portrait of his daughter. "A thousand times more beautiful than any picture. She—" His voice wobbled, stopped. "She—" he tried again.

"I know," Alex found herself saying. "I know, Norman. I'm so sorry."

He nodded, cleared his throat. When he looked at her, his eyes were wet. "When you came in the door today, just the second before Nick introduced you, there was something about your hair that reminded me of her. I know you don't even have the same color or style, hers was much longer and more golden, but with the light on it, for just a second, it could have been hers. And then when you laughed"— he wiped a hand over his eyes—"it was her laugh." His shoulders slumped forward. "I'm sorry, Alex. I'm rambling; ignore me. Maybe it's all in my imagination." He lifted his white head and his eyes were red. "You're a beautiful woman. She was, too. Let's just leave it at that."

Alex walked around the desk, touched Norman's shoulder. "I'm so sorry, Norman. I know you must miss her terribly."

He laughed, a hollow sound that fizzled out. "Terribly. That's the word. She's dead, I know that, and nothing is going to bring her back. But I'd sell my soul to the devil himself for just one more day with her." His gaze moved over the portrait in a slow, soft caress. "Her birthday was the fifteenth, and I can't stop thinking about it. She would have been thirty-six." He closed his eyes, dragged his hands over his face. "Ahhh, you didn't come here to hear an old man tell you his troubles."

His pain was so real, so visceral, that Alex wondered if all parents suffered like this when they lost a child. Is it the same pain children feel when they lose a parent? She wished she knew. In the distant part of her memory, she saw Uncle Walter standing in a church, tall and erect in his suit and tie. Aunt Helen was there too, dressed in black with a big, floppy hat that bumped Alex's head whenever her aunt turned to whisper something to her. Alex was pinned between them, the new, shiny black shoes killing her feet. She was wearing a dress, navy blue with pink flowers; she still remembered it because it was the first one she ever owned. And it was uncomfortable and she hated it and the slip inside made her itch. Aunt Helen had bent over in her floppy hat, twice, and pinched her. *Show some respect for the dead,* she'd said. *Those are your parents up there in those coffins, young lady. Now sit still and do what's expected of you.*

"You know, I think Nick still blames himself, but he shouldn't." Norman rubbed his eyes, shook his head. "Caroline was having a tough time, we all knew that. And then the baby came—" He stopped, took a deep breath. "It wasn't his fault."

What? What wasn't his fault? Alex wanted to ask, but couldn't. Apparently, Norman thought she knew, but why would he think that? His next words told her exactly why he thought what he did. "If you and Nick," he started, fiddled with a paperweight. "What I mean is"—he cleared his throat—"well, it's okay with me."

"Norman? What are you talking about?"

He looked up at her, his blue eyes bright. "Nick needs to move on, find somebody to care about. He's too young to be alone."

"Why would you think he's alone?" She thought of

Chuck Lubovich's sage comment about Nick's prowess. *Just because he doesn't bring a girl to Sunday dinner, doesn't mean he isn't happy . . . or that there isn't a girl waiting at home for him.*

"There's alone and then there's alone," Norman said. "The one alone means you don't have anybody, period, just yourself, maybe family, but not that special someone." He rubbed his stomach in a wide circle, leaned against the edge of his desk. "The other kind of alone is worse. You might *be* with somebody, people might actually think you're a couple, hell, *you* might even think you're a couple." He pointed a finger at her. "But you're not, you're still alone. And that's the worst kind."

She couldn't help but ask, "Is that what you think Nick's doing? Being alone with somebody?" He didn't seem lonely; on the contrary, he seemed content, happy.

"Nah. Not really. But if he hooks up with that rent a doc he sure as hell will be." He pursed his thin lips together. "I think she's trying her damnedest to snag him; brings him some fancy new fishing pole from Pittsburgh, and a new watch, very expensive, which he never wears, sweaters, cologne." He leaned toward her, lowered his voice, "Doesn't do any good."

"How do you know all this?" She couldn't imagine discussing her love life with her ex-father-in-law, or Uncle Walter, for that matter. "Does he tell you?"

"Nope, not really. Doesn't have to." He lifted his left hand, moved his wrist around. The bright face of a watch shone under the fluorescent lights. Then he pointed to a far wall where a fishing pole lay propped in the corner.

Alex burst out laughing. "You're going to be awfully sad when he breaks up with this girl. No more presents."

Norman grinned. "I'll take 'em while I can." His smile faded. "I like you, Alex. I like what you're trying to do. You're going to tell people about this town, show them that everybody doesn't need to crowd into a city to survive, show them that there are places like Restalline all over the country, places where you can raise a family, start a business, be happy. That's the key, here. Be happy. I want to help, any way I can.'' He paused, took a deep breath. ''Caroline loved this town. In a way, it would be like honoring her.''

Blood rushed to Alex's head, so fast and hard she felt dizzy. *God, please stop, Norman. I don't want to hear anymore. I'm not your friend. If you only knew . . .*

''. . . so if something were to happen between you and Nick, I would be the first to congratulate both of you.''

No, no you wouldn't. She pressed her fingertips against her temples. ''We've only just met . . . we hardly know each other.'' *And he's already suspicious of me. Besides, the last thing I need in my life right now is a man.*

''I met my wife on a Thursday and proposed the next Wednesday.''

''Are you talking about me again, Norman?'' A woman stood in the doorway, her small frame swallowed up by the loose dress she wore. It was at least two sizes too big, the short sleeves cupping her elbows, the hem dipping to mid calf. Her gray-brown hair was pulled into a tight bun, stretching her nose, cheeks, eyes, across her face. She wore no makeup or lipstick, no adornments of any kind.

''Ruth.'' There was a note of surprise, and something else in Norman's voice. ''What . . . what are you doing here?''

The woman eyed Alex, took a step forward, then another. She was wearing white slippers, stained around the toes. ''Am I not allowed to visit my husband?'' she asked, her brown eyes darting from him to Alex. ''Is he too busy to see me?''

''No, dear, of course not.'' Norman rushed forward, kissed her on the cheek. ''I'm just . . . surprised.'' He lowered his voice. ''How did you get here?''

"How else?" She whisked past him, plopped herself into the overstuffed chair behind his desk.

"You . . . drove?" It was part question, part dread.

She burst out laughing then, a loud, rude sound that bounced between them. "Of course, I drove. Do you think I could walk the three miles into town?" She shook her head, tapped her slippered foot against the linoleum floor.

Norman's face turned a dull red. He cast a quick glance in Alex's direction, started to speak, hesitated, then pushed on. "You know Nick said you shouldn't be driving."

"And why in heaven's name not?" she shot back.

"Ruth," Norman gentled his tone. "You know why."

She started to crumble, right before Alex's eyes. Her lower lip quivered, her shoulders sagged forward in pitiful defeat, head bent forward. "It's that damnable medicine, isn't it?"

Norman came to her, placed a hand on her back, moving it in small, even circles. "It's okay, Ruth, it's okay."

"But I think I'm getting better. Really, I do, Norman." She lifted her head, eyes wet, tears streaming down her face, to plead with her husband. "Don't you think so? Don't you think I am?" It was the voice of a child, afraid and uncertain, seeking help, shelter, love.

He stroked the side of her face, trailing his fingers over her hair. It was a gesture, so tender, so personal, too personal. Alex looked away. "Let me take you home," he said. "I'll fix you a cup of chamomile tea. Would you like that?"

"Yes. Yes, I could use a cup."

"Good. That's very good."

"Who's the lady?"

"That's Alex. Alex Chamberlain. She's come to write about our town."

"Oh." Silence. And then she spoke again, and Alex understood why Norman had hesitated when he'd seen her standing in the doorway, understood why he was stroking her face and hair as though she were a child. With one sentence, she understood it all.

"Maybe Caroline will come today, Norman. Maybe today will be the day and then she can meet this young woman and tell her how wonderful this town is and just how much she's missed Restalline."

"She's loony, poor thing." Edna shook her head, lowered her voice. "He can't even trust her to go to the grocery store by herself." She clucked her tongue. "All that money, that beautiful house, and for what? Nothing will bring Caroline back, not all the money in the world."

"Edna, tell me about Caroline. What really happened to her?" Alex couldn't get the sight of Norman Kraziak or his wife out of her mind. She'd tried, but Ruth Kraziak's pathetic words kept coming back to her. *But I think I'm getting better. Really, I do, Norman. Don't you think so?* And then, the shocker. *Maybe Caroline will come today, Norman. Maybe today will be the day and then she can meet this young woman and tell her how wonderful this town is and just how much she's missed Restalline.*

Edna pushed back her chair. "Hold on a sec." She pulled back a yellow curtain, peeked out the window. "He's out back, trimming the hedges. It's safe for a little while. Chuck says I need to mind my own business, not talk about other people." She waved a hand in the air. "Says it's gossiping. I say, heck no, it's not, it's just transferring information, like the newspaper does, no difference. Right?" She looked at Alex, hands on hips. "Right?"

"Right."

"That's what I tell him, but you know men," she said, moving to the stove and lifting the lid off of a big pot, "they don't listen." She stirred the contents of the pot. "You ever hear them talking about their male parts the way we women talk about our female parts?'' Edna shook her head and the yellow bow in the back bounced up and down. ''Never. Don't talk about the fights they have with their wives or girlfriends, either.'' She grabbed a teaspoon from the drawer, dipped it in the pot, tasted it. ''Mmmm. Beef stroganoff tonight, Alex. Needs caraway, maybe a little more pepper.''

''I don't want to cause a problem between you and Chuck—''

''Pshaw! Don't you worry about Chuck; I know about Chuck.'' Edna sank back onto the yellow cushion, lowered her voice. ''Somebody should tell you about Caroline . . . and Dr. Nick. Who's gonna do that if I don't?''

''Thank you, Edna.'' Edna Lubovich was proving to be Restalline's version of Dear Abby. The woman knew everything about everyone.

''No problem. It'll help your documentary, right?'' She stirred her tea. ''No way to say it except to say it. Caroline died in a fire when Dr. Nick was finishing medical school. It's been almost eight years now, hard to believe it. She'd just had Justin. It was her first night home, and thank God the baby had to stay in the hospital. Dr. Nick was working. The fire started and she . . . she never made it out.''

''Oh, my God, how horrible.''

''You can't imagine this town, the way it grieved. Or Dr. Nick. He blamed himself, thought he should have been able to do something to help her.''

''What happened? How?''

Edna took a sip of tea, set the cup down. ''There was talk,'' she said, her voice falling to a hint above a whisper, ''a lot of it.''

''What kind of talk?''

She shrugged. ''People said Caroline took a bottle of pills, that she was depressed, that things weren't so good between her and Dr. Nick.''

''Do you think that's true?''

"Some of it. Dr. Nick never talked about it, still won't. And poor Ruth, she just fell apart, like a pumpkin smashed on the road, splattering everywhere. She lost it, couldn't accept that her baby was gone, that she'd died such a horrible death. So she started to pretend. At first, we were all sympathetic, didn't say nothing, just acted like we didn't hear her when she talked about Caroline coming home. But it got worse; she used to go sit at the bus stop every day, waiting. Now she only goes once a week. And she'd go to the grocery store and buy up all of Caroline's favorite foods: canned peaches and pears—cases of the fruit—cottage cheese, strawberry ice cream—gallons of it. Poor Norman. He finally had to take her to see Dr. Endson, the psychiatrist two towns over, and get her on some medication."

"Has it helped?" Alex thought of the thin woman in the oversized dress and stained slippers standing in the doorway of Norman Kraziak's office.

"Some. She gets out a little, not much. Dr. Nick keeps an eye on her, goes to visit her once a week, sometimes more. Stella says he's always torn up when he comes back. She hates what it does to him."

"What about the boy? Justin."

"He's a good boy. He'll be eight, let's see, July twenty-second. Dr. Nick's done a fine job, but he's had a lot of help from the rest of the family—Stella, Frank, Gracie, even Michael."

Alex didn't know who Gracie was, maybe Nick's sister or an aunt, but she had heard of Stella, Michael, and Frank. Definitely, Frank. "Is Frank, Uncle Frank? The man who didn't show up for his own birthday party?"

Edna threw back her head and laughed, showing a row of bridgework. "That's Frank. He's really an old softy, loves the kids, and they love him."

"Aren't they . . . afraid of him?"

"Because of his face? Nah. They're used to him. Anyway,

they're too busy listening to his stories and watching him make things to think about being afraid. You know, he made the kids a tree house with two ladders, a trapdoor, and windows with shutters. Half the town wants to buy one for their kids, but Frank's not interested.''

How could he not be interested? How? Alex would love to meet him, ask him how he could turn away business opportunities for his wood work when it was obvious there was a demand for it. Didn't he know about supply and demand? He could name his own price. People were always willing to pay exorbitant amounts for their children's pleasures. ''Seems like he's sitting on a gold mine and all he has to do is dig at it a little.''

''Maybe. That's just not Frank's way.''

''I'd like to meet him.''

''You will. Soon enough.''

Chapter 7

"Alex! Where've you been?"

"Hi, Uncle Walter."

"I've been worried about you, for God's sake."

She traced the edges of the glass jewels on the hand mirror. The colors were still bright, vibrant. "I left a message on your machine."

"That was five days ago, young lady." He sighed. "And there was no phone number, no way to get in touch with you. I told Eric if I didn't hear from you by tomorrow, I was coming to look for you."

The thought of Uncle Walter driving into Restalline in his navy Audi and Armani suit unsettled her. "No," she said, a little too quickly. "I'm fine. Really. I've just been very busy."

That seemed to calm him down. "Oh? What'd you find out?" There was an eagerness in his voice, the kind that always crept in when they were discussing acquisitions or new ventures.

"I think you'll be pleased. Very pleased. The backdrop is perfect, lots and lots of trees, and there's the lake I told you about, Sapphire Lake. I thought it could be a focal point of the resort, maybe we could build a lodge or a club close by, or a restaurant overlooking the lake."

"I like the restaurant idea. What about the skiing?"

"I think it'll work. It looks to have the same land slope as the one in New York."

"Good. Good." He paused. "And the people? Do you think they'll be amenable?"

"Of course." The mirror winked against the light when she turned it in her hand, as though it had spotted her for the lies she was about to tell. Alex thought of Nick Androvich, whom she hadn't seen since he'd dumped her at the Restalline Millworks. And then there was Norman Kraziak. . . . The poor man hadn't even been able to make eye contact with her after his wife promised to invite her over when Caroline got in.

So, there were a few hurdles, nothing insurmountable, and certainly nothing Uncle Walter needed to hear about. She'd handle it.

"How're the two principles? Kraziak and . . . what's the other man's name? Androski?"

"Androvich." *Nick.*

"That's right. Androvich," he corrected himself. "How are they?"

"Fine. They're fine." That wasn't quite true. Nick Androvich was avoiding her and no matter what his nurse said, Alex knew that he couldn't possibly be with a patient *every* time she called. And Norman . . . Well, Norman was battling the humiliation that an outsider knew about his wife and her problems. Maybe if they moved away, left the reminders behind, it would help Ruth Kraziak deal with her pain, get on with her life. It could be a very good thing for them, very good indeed. They might actually welcome an opportunity to leave Restalline behind.

As for Nick, from what she'd seen so far, he was a die-hard with his feet buried in Restalline soil like all of his ancestors before him. Persuading him to sell might be more difficult than moving Mount Saint Helens.

"You know I really want this deal," Uncle Walter said. "The whole thing, Alex. Can you get it for me?"

There was a ring of challenge in his voice. "I'll get it," she promised, clutching the mirror. *One way or another, I'll get it.*

"Who's coming to dinner tonight, Grandma? Who's the lady?" Justin pulled the salt and pepper shakers out of the corner cupboard and waited.

"Curious little bugger, aren't you?" Stella Androvich laughed, stirred the pot of pierogies she'd made that morning, potato and onion, Nick's favorite. "Her name's Alex."

"Huh?" He scrunched up his nose. "That's a boy's name."

"It's really Alexandra, but people call her Alex for short."

"Oh. Does she look like a boy?"

"No." Stella laughed. The boy asked more questions than any other child she knew. Michael's kids only talked when someone asked them a direct question, and then it was iffy whether or not they'd answer. Of course, what could anyone expect from children whose mother had run off to Buffalo with a pharmaceutical salesman, leaving them with a father who was too angry and sometimes too caught up in self-pity to notice they hadn't changed their shirts in two days? And Gracie's crew, Cecily and Sophia, well they just talked all the time, words flying out of their mouths, one trying to outdo the other, so loud and fast that nothing made sense.

Stella pushed back a lock of hair. Children were a blessing; she'd felt that since the second she held Nick in her arms, beet red and wailing louder than an Indian chief, thirty-eight years ago. She'd wanted to keep her babies young forever, their boundaries clear, their home secure. Safe. That's what she'd prayed to the Blessed Mother for every night. *Keep my children safe. Safe from bullets and knives, speeding cars, and cancer, safe from people who will use them and mistreat them and break their hearts. Please, please, please, take my happiness, but keep them safe.* She knew better than to use prayer as a bargaining tool, but these were her *children;* she had no choice. And just when she thought the Blessed Mother had heard her prayers and granted them, Caroline had died. And then Michael's wife ran out on him, and he started drinking. And then Nick and Michael had a horrible argument. . . . It went on and on; the worrying never stopped. She'd gone to church today and lit another candle. This one for Nick, asking the Blessed Mother to help him find his way, see more clearly. Give Alex Chamberlain a chance. She seemed like a nice girl. Nick and Michael needed to settle down, find women to care about them—women who weren't their mother.

And that's why Stella had taken it upon herself to invite Alex to dinner, tonight. Nick wasn't responding to his mother's innocent promptings that maybe he should invite that nice young girl to dinner, and didn't he think she was pretty? He'd done no more than shrug and change the subject.

"Grandma?" It was Justin again. "Does this Alex like to play baseball?"

Stella turned to her grandson, "Well, I don't know, Justin, but she might."

"Do you think I should ask her when she gets here?" His eyes were the color of a September sky, just like his mother's.

"I think that would be fine. All of you can play. Dad, Kevin, Sara, maybe even Uncle Michael, if he comes." Stella tried to keep her voice even. Michael had a habit of dropping Kevin and Sara off and then disappearing until their bedtime. When he came back, he was never full-blown drunk, just . . . loose, relaxed. And sometimes it seemed, well, she could swear he hadn't touched a drop, though she couldn't guess, or maybe she didn't want to guess, what he'd been doing for all those hours. Those were the nights he'd pull in the driveway, honk the horn, and yell, *Let's go! Now*. She'd tried to talk to him, as a mother, as a grandmother; so had Nick, and even Gracie, bless her naive soul.

But Michael wasn't interested in what any of them had to say. *If I want a sermon, I'll go to church,* he'd told them. There just was no give to the boy, at least not any that he was willing to let his family see. Somewhere deep inside him there was a pain that needed healing, a wound that kept opening, bleeding, threatening to spread. And the worst part of it all was that Stella could do nothing more than watch and pray.

But she could help her other son. Nick was more approachable, less antagonistic, more *likeable,* than his younger brother. Perhaps it was because he'd taken over when his father died, blamed no one for being the eldest of three children, and therefore, the figurehead, the one who must forge a plan, set an example. Nick had done what he'd needed to do, no apologies, no excuses. Stella put the colander in the sink, lifted the boiling pot from the stove. He deserved a little happiness. She poured the pierogies into the colander, the heat of the steam smacking her in the face. Alex was smart, pretty, and she was not *oohing* and *ahhing* all over Nick like a lot of other women did. That said something for her. The woman had spunk, and she had Stella Androvich and Edna Lubovich rooting for her.

* * *

"This is delicious." Alex forked a piece of pierogie. "What did you say was in this?"

"Onion and potato," Stella answered. "I made them this morning from scratch. You can buy them in the grocery store, in the frozen section where they sell other things like spinach-and-crab hors d'oeuvres and shrimp cocktail"— she threw Nick a pointed glance—"but there's nothing like homemade."

"Do you like to cook?" This from Gracie, innocent, unintentional.

Out of the corner of his eye, Nick saw Alex's left hand ball into a fist. She cleared her throat and said, "Uh, I don't get much of an opportunity, with traveling and all."

"So you probably depend on boxes and the freezer section?" He met his mother's brown gaze from across the table.

"Yes," Alex said, shrugging in half apology, "I do."

"Well, don't you worry, dear," Stella chimed in. "You'll be here plenty long enough for me to teach you a few things. We'll make bread; and every woman should know how to make pasta: long, short, stuffed—pierogies, too. And of course, stuffed cabbage and ba'bovka, our coffee cake." Her brown eyes lit up. "What are you doing tomorrow morning, say around nine?"

There was a breath of hesitation, then, "I don't have any plans. I'll be here."

"Good." Stella nodded. "Good." This with more force, as though they'd agreed on some heretofore unknown pact. "Isn't that great, Nick, that Alex is interested in learning to make things from scratch?"

Great. "That's great, Mom." Could she be any more obvious? Why not just grab his hand and put it on top of Alex's and tell them to go out on a date? Why not tell him to lean over and give her a kiss while she was at it? Wouldn't that be easier than all the innuendos, all the sly looks, the nudges under the table? God, but he hated this matchmaking his mother was hell-bent on. It wasn't enough that he'd had to hear about blasted Alex Chamberlain for the last few days, how intelligent, how sophisticated, how charming, even though his mother had come to that conclusion after a mere ten-minute conversation with the woman, but now he was face to face with her and it was so much worse. In truth, Nick hadn't wanted to see Alex Chamberlain again; there was something about her that bothered him, left him questioning himself, and her. He didn't know what it was, only that it rubbed him raw like a blister rips the flesh off a person's heels when they walk a mile in a new pair of shoes. He stuffed a whole pierogie in his mouth, chewed hard. The woman disturbed him, and the hell of it was, he couldn't even say why.

"Mom says you're from around D.C.," Gracie said, her brownish-gold eyes warm, welcoming. She reached over, wiped the apple juice dripping down four-year-old Sophia's mouth.

"Yes."

"Hmmm. I went there once when I was a senior in high school. It was our class trip. I've always wanted to go back." She turned, smiled at her husband, Rudy. "Maybe after the baby comes we can take a trip there."

Rudy lifted his crew-cut head, reached out and brushed a ham-sized hand over Gracie's hair. "Maybe after the baby comes, Stella will watch the kids and we can take a second honeymoon there."

"My grandbabies are welcome anytime." Stella smiled at the children seated around the table. "Each and everyone of you." She pointed to Sophia, who was stuffing a piece of bread in her mouth. "And that means you too, pumpkin."

Gracie picked up Cecily's empty glass, poured more milk into it. "Thanks, Mom."

"The more the merrier." Stella laughed. "I'd take another two, three, four grandchildren anytime, any way I can get them." She turned to Alex. "Are there any little people in your family, Alex?"

"No. I'm an only child."

"Oh." The clatter of silverware on dishes filled the room. "Well, all the more reason you should marry and have a big family yourself."

Nick coughed, cleared his throat. His mother could be about as blunt as a bulldozer in a flower patch. "Mom"—he shook his head—"I'm sure Alex can deal with her maternal needs by herself."

That didn't stop Stella from putting in another fifty-two cents. "I know that, Nick. I'm only reassuring her that just because she's an only child, it doesn't mean she won't be a good mother." She smiled at Alex, who was sitting like a deer frozen in headlights. "Meeting the right man, that's the key. If you do that, then the rest just comes naturally. Look at Gracie and Rudy. Married seven years, have Cecily, who's six, Sophia, who's four, and in two months there'll be another one. Girl or boy, who knows?" She shrugged. "Doesn't matter, so long as the partner's the right one."

"Mom, would you pass the stuffed cabbage?" God, he had to stop her.

"Alex, has Nick taken you to Sapphire Lake, yet?" Gracie's voice softened. "That's where Rudy proposed."

"I showed her the other day," Nick cut in. "She needed to see it for her research." He knew his family, knew how nosy they could be, straightforward when it came to family and family business. Nothing was private.

"Isn't it romantic?" Gracie said, her words gushing. "Oh, and have him take you to the Cliff." She and Rudy exchanged glances. "That's a perfect couples spot."

Alex nodded, dipped her head low, and stabbed at a pier-ogie.

"Thanks for the advice, Gracie." Nick narrowed his gaze on her. Kid sister or not, enough was enough.

Gracie shrugged, threw him a small smile.

"Alex, uh, do you know how to play baseball?" Justin hadn't said a word through dinner, but now he was eyeing their guest, pulling his lower lip through his teeth, once, twice, three times, waiting as though her answer would be the most important words he'd ever hear.

"I . . . I kind of know how. It's been a long time."

His shoulders drooped and he stared down at his plate.

"But," she went on, "they say it's like riding a bike. Once you learn how, you never forget." She spoke his name, then, soft, comforting, "Justin? Would you like to play baseball after dinner?"

His head shot up, and he nodded.

Nick watched the two of them, Justin with that stupid grin on his face, wide enough to show off the gap where his left front tooth had been, and Alex smiling, a real smile, not one of those polite shake-your-hand kind of smiles. She was being nice to Justin, and Nick appreciated that. When he got a chance, he'd tell her so. He hadn't pictured her for the kid type—not with the pearls and the Rolex and the Saab. That had translated into something more cosmopolitan, more chic, more self-centered.

Maybe he was wrong about Alex. Maybe he needed to back up and get a history on her, forget the initial impression. He pretended an intense preoccupation with the inside of a pierogie, separating potato from onion as though he were dissecting internal organs. Alex was still talking to Justin, and he was laughing, honest to God laughing.

"So, if the ladder wasn't tall enough, how'd you get the cat out of the tree?" he asked.

"Simple," Alex said. "I put on my old sneakers and

climbed it. Of course, at ten years old, I didn't think about how I was going to get down with a cat in my arms. I must've been up there two or three hours.''

''Weren't you scared?''

''No, not really. I had Daisy with me. We just sat there and I held her, pressing my cheek against her fur. She was tan and white, with black paws. To this day, I've never felt anything so soft.''

''Who found you?''

''My aunt.'' The lightness drained out of her voice. Nick set down his fork, looked up. She was staring at her glass but he knew she wasn't seeing it, knew she was miles away, years away, back in that tree.

''So, what happened next?'' Justin asked with the innocence of one anticipating a happy ending and wanting to hear every minute detail.

''Aunt Helen called the fire department and they brought their ladder and got us down.''

''Wow. That'd be so cool. Then what? Did Daisy stay out of that tree?''

There was a second's lapse, the briefest of moments when Alex's mouth clenched into a hard, fierce line. ''Yes, she stayed out of it. Aunt Helen gave her away two days later when I was at school. She said I was too young to care for Daisy; she'd be better off with another family, one who would be more responsible. Maybe in a couple of years, we'd try again.''

''Where'd she go? Do you know?''

''She went to the golf course to keep the area clean.''

''Huh?''

''To hunt mice,'' Alex said

''Did you ever go visit her?''

''Twice. One day she just disappeared, nobody knew where, and nobody went to look for her.'' She paused, then said, ''They just got another cat.''

* * *

"Thank you for playing ball with Justin."

"Oh, is that what I was doing?" She'd run, jumped, fallen, scraped her knees, and got hit in the shin several times in a weak imitation that didn't even vaguely resemble what she'd seen on a real baseball field.

"Sure was." She and Nick were sitting on the swing in Stella's backyard. The crickets were already filling the twilight with noisy cadence.

"Well, I couldn't tell him the only time I'd ever held a baseball was in a souvenir shop." She shrugged, thought of Justin's face when he'd asked her if she played baseball, so hopeful, innocent.

"I appreciate that. You know, no matter what we teach our kids, there are times when honesty really isn't the best policy."

Right. Like now, for instance. If I told you why I was really here, you'd be booting me out so fast my head would be spinning all the way back to Edna's. "You're right. There's a time when it's honorable to twist the facts."

"I've done it a time or two myself."

They were quiet after that, rocking back and forth on the old swing as it creaked and groaned with the weight of their bodies pressing against the boards. Justin and Kevin and Sara were on the front porch eating ice-cream sandwiches and trying to catch fireflies. Stella had herded them out of the backyard, waving the box of ice-cream sandwiches in the air like the Pied Piper of Hameln. She'd said nothing to Alex and Nick, merely turned and winked at them. Gracie and Rudy had packed up their brood an hour ago and headed home. *I'll see you tomorrow,* Gracie had said. *We'll make pasta together.* There was a genuineness about her, an open honesty that spread to everyone near her. Alex had never been like that; she'd always hidden her thoughts, huddled them close to her, careful not to show too much. It was the way she'd been raised. With reserve, dignity, poise. *Don't smile so wide,* Aunt Helen had told her when she was twelve. *You look like a horse. Practice. Practice in the mirror. Don't look so . . . happy. It's just so common. Elusive . . . that's what you want.*

"Are you still interested in showing me around town?"

He didn't answer at first. "My schedule's gotten really crazy—"

"That's okay." She cut him off. "You don't have to feel obligated." Why did she feel a pang of disappointment at his response? "I understand."

"It's just that—"

"Nick, forget it. I can't talk to one person that I don't hear about Dr. Nick and how he's fixed them up. I know you're busy." She paused. "It's just that I would have appreciated it if you would have returned my phone calls, told me yourself."

He stopped the swing, looked at her. "What phone calls?"

Alex shook her head, let out a sound that was half laugh, half aggravation. "Trying to *twist* the facts a little?"

"No." He touched her chin with the tips of his fingers. "Look at me. What phone calls, Alex?"

She turned, saw the confusion in his brown eyes. "I called your office a few times, but you were always busy. So after the fourth time, I got the message."

"I didn't."

"It doesn't matter."

"It does to me. If I'm going to tell you no, I'd like to know I'm doing it, not someone else." He rubbed the side of his face. "I wonder why Elise didn't tell me."

"You said you've been busy," Alex said, anxious to be done with the conversation. Even if he was telling the truth, and the look on his face told her he probably was, he'd just admitted he was too busy to show her around. Either way, it was a rejection and she wanted to be done with it.

"I am busy, so is Elise. But it's not like her to lose a message, or in this case, messages. I'm sorry."

"It's fine." She looked away as the last rays of light seeped through the branches. "Really." If there was one thing Uncle Walter and Aunt Helen had taught her, it was to never, ever be a burden to another person. Ever.

"Maybe I can take you around tomorrow night, say seven o'clock?"

She shook her head. "That's okay. Edna's offered; so has Gracie."

"Oh, God." He ran a hand over his face. His fingers were strong, tanned, capable. "Edna's a sweetheart, but you're going to hear about everything from Old Man Hatzinger's cat to Mrs. Glonski's pregnant niece from Schenectady. And Gracie'll drag you from Restalline to Clarkton looking for garage sales."

"Then I guess I'll include Edna's stories and Gracie's garage sales in my research. After all, it's small-town behavior that I'm researching." *And they won't think of me as an inconvenience.*

"I'll take you," he said, his voice firm, final. "Talk to them if you want. Listen to Edna tell you about the way Old Man Hatzinger dressed his cat and took him to church. Go with Gracie to fifteen zillion garage sales in search of the perfect pink tights for ten cents; but let me show you the land, the surroundings, the openness that's nothing like a city."

She hesitated a second, then nodded. "Okay."

"One more thing. We've got some eccentrics in this town, but they're ours. Good, honest, hardworking people. We take care of them and we care *about* them. I don't want you making fun of them for the sake of an interesting read."

"I wouldn't do that."

"Just remember that. They'll give you their trust, take what you say at face value and never think twice about it."

"But not you." The words fell out, cold, hard, wedged between them.

"I lived in the city, remember?" he said, avoiding a direct answer. "I know what preys there, what gobbles up other people, what can destroy them."

"Not everybody is Godzilla."

He didn't answer. "I'll help you, but just remember, you're writing about these people's lives, their families, the only town most of them have ever known."

"You really don't trust me, do you?" *Why don't you trust me? Why? You can't possibly know what I'm doing here.*

"I don't know you."

"Neither does your mother, but she trusts me."

"Yeah, well, she trusts everybody." He laughed then, and she did too.

I'll get you to trust me, you'll see. And then I'll convince you that life does exist elsewhere, maybe not in a big city, but a suburb. There are lots of hospitals in the suburbs, and they need someone like you, a doctor who cares about his patients, really cares. They'll pay you a lot of money, get you established, find Justin a good school. Suburbs have land, parks, grass, for God's sake, and theaters and ball games. You'll see, Nick Androvich, you'll see. I'll get you to trust me. I will. I know all about suburbs. I know a lot of people. I'll help you. I'll help them all. Trust me, trust me. We'll all be winners, every one of us.

"About my mother . . . ." He leaned his elbow on the back of the swing, balled his hand into a fist under his chin. "She's not the most . . . subtle person in the world."

"That's okay." She didn't want to hear this. Why couldn't they just ignore it?

"It's obvious what she's trying to do . . . what they're all trying to do."

Oh, no. Was he really going to talk about it? No, no he wasn't. "Why don't we just forget it?" She touched her throat, felt for her necklace, her thumb and forefinger grasping two pearls, turning them over and over, the soft, smooth feel of them calming her, reminding her who she was, where she'd come from. *Dignity, Alex,* her Aunt Helen had told her. *One must maintain dignity at all times.* "I really don't think we need to discuss it."

"Of course we need to discuss it." He sounded annoyed. "What are we going to do? Ignore it?"

"Well . . . yes." Her fingers worked the pearls, harder, faster.

"That's the most ridiculous thing I've ever heard. We have to at least address the issue . . . take a stand."

She shook her head. "I don't think so."

"You don't know my family." He blew out a long breath. "Next they'll be planning the—"

"If we just ignore it, eventually they'll stop."

"Is that how you deal with problems?" He was close, leaning toward her, his breath fanning her hair. "Just ignore them, wait for them to go away?"

Sometimes. She turned to face him, catching the last sliver of light on his face. He was close, so close. Alex inched back, felt the wood of the swing dig into her back. "Look, Nick, it's no big deal. Let's just forget it, okay?"

He ignored her. "I was just trying to apologize for them. Sometimes they don't know when to stop."

"Thank you." *Okay, now let's be done.*

"It's not as if . . . as though . . . you and I . . . we don't even . . ."

That was it. "I think I know what you're trying to say." She took a deep breath, straightened her shoulders, and stared at his face, half hidden in darkness and shadow. "You and I are not interested in one another in any capacity other than a strictly business one, in which you will act as a guide while I conduct my research in this town. There is not, nor will there ever be, even the merest hint of attraction to one another, and any attempt to enhance the relationship will be done so merely in the name of politeness.'' There. Let him think about that.

He did not respond at first, and she wondered if her words had been too harsh, too cruel. She'd spent so many years cocooning herself against others, burrowing under layers of aloofness that she didn't stop to consider whether that very thing that protected her, injured others. "I . . . I'm sorry."

The kiss came from nowhere, hard, powerful, consuming. He pulled her to him, his arms strong, protective, pressing her against his chest, hard planes to soft. She opened her mouth, let the feel of his tongue move over her, into her, through her. Heat pulsed deep inside, hot and wanting. Closer, she wanted to get closer. Her fingers found his hair, stroked its silkiness.

Then it was over and Nick was pulling away. His breathing was hard, heavy. Alex couldn't move, couldn't see his face in the darkness, couldn't see if it was filled with regret. He unwound her arms from around his neck, placed them in her lap, and stood. "I'm sorry, too, Alex." Then he turned and disappeared into the darkness.

Chapter 8

Alex sprinkled flour over the long strip of dough, flipped it over, and sprinkled the other side. Then she went to the next strip and the next until she had ten lined up. There had to be an easier way, there had to be. She was hot and sticky, the back of her neck was wet, even her bra clung to her. They'd been at it all morning, pouring flour from a twenty-five-pound bag of Robin Hood, mixing, kneading, cutting, flouring and—the fun part—running the flattened strips of dough through the pasta machine. Finally, they'd spread the noodles out on dowels, set up over the backs of eight chairs, in the dining room no less, with layers of newspaper covering the carpet. *They have to dry properly,* Stella had told her. *Air, that's what they need. Don't let them lump together, spread them around. In the old days, I didn't have dowels, so I used to cover the dining room table with paper towels and spread them out there.*

Alex tried to picture Aunt Helen's mahogany table covered with layers of Bounty and floured noodles. It was impossible, of course. *Furniture is to be respected,* she'd said, the one and only time Alex had left her algebra book on the table. *Do you have any idea what the value of this table is? What it's worth?*

But these people didn't seem to care. When Sophia spilled her cup of apple juice on the linoleum floor, Stella had just handed Gracie a rag and she'd cleaned it up. No fuss, no lecture, no warning that she was a disrespectful child.

"Alex? Ready to roll?" Gracie laughed, held out her hand for a strip of pasta. "Mom's grading you, you know."

Alex handed Gracie the pasta, waited for her to roll it through the machine twice, once to flatten it, and then a second time to cut it into wide noodles. She caught the noodles as they fell through the blades, then hurried to the dining room to lay them over a dowel.

"Stella," she said, after they'd finished another batch, "isn't there an easier way?"

The older woman looked up from the ball of dough in front of her. "What do you mean?" Her hands and fingers were crusted and caked with dough.

Alex wiped a hand over her forehead. "This is a lot of work! Isn't there an easier way to get it done? Automate it somehow?" She looked over at Gracie, who was smiling. "Buy it, maybe?"

"Buy it? *Buy it?* Why on earth would I want to buy someone else's noodles?"

Gracie laughed. "Bad words in this house."

Alex tried to explain. "Well, it'd be a lot easier and probably cheaper when you figured the time and effort you put into it."

"But, Alex, why would I do that? I'm making noodles because I enjoy it, that's half the reason for doing it. If I found a cheaper, faster way to do it, like those confounded bread machines they have out today, what would be the sense? Where's the feeling of accomplishment? Any imbecile can measure out flour and water, dump it in a machine, and press a button. It's the *knowing* that makes the difference, knowing the right ingredients by sight and feel, handed down through the family, working it in your hands. Creating something, that's what it is, Alex, and you can't buy that in a store or do it with a machine.''

"But you do use a machine for your noodles."

She nodded her head and a tangle of brown-gray hair fell forward. Stella pushed it back with her forearm. "My mother used to make it all by hand, on a big cutting board. She'd roll the dough into huge pieces—bigger than a pizza—and cut each noodle with a knife. When she got older, her fingers got gnarled with arthritis and she couldn't hold the knife. The boys, my brothers, bought her a pasta machine"—she patted the machine beside her—"this machine. And every time I use it, I think of her. That's why I don't cut the noodles by hand, and it's the only reason."

"Wait until you taste these, Alex," Gracie said from her spot on a kitchen chair. "They're to die for." She was resting her hands across her bulging stomach, occasionally massaging her fingers in small circles. She was her mother minus thirty years or so, with the same brown hair and eyes. They shared the same smile, and when they laughed, Alex had to look to see which one it was.

"We'll cook some of these up for lunch with a little oil and garlic," Stella said. "The kids can have butter if you want, Gracie, but I keep telling you it's time to introduce them to oil and garlic. We had to eat it when we were kids, and besides, it's much healthier."

Gracie rolled her eyes. "I know, I know."

"Okay, so you know, but I don't see you making it for them."

"I've just gotten Rudy used to it, Mom. Not everybody

wants to be Italian. You know he's Czech, and he eats all of your Czech food.''

Stella *tsk-tsked*, looked at Alex, who was playing with a few leftover dough crumbs. ''What about you, Alex? Do you like Italian?''

''Yes, as a matter of fact, I do.''

''Ask her if she likes Czech,'' Gracie said.

''What about Czech food? Do you like that?''

Alex thought of what Nick had said. *Thymus gland and cow's tongue.* ''Some.''

''See?'' Stella cast a triumphant look at her daughter. ''She's a good girl.''

''Come for cow's tongue tonight, Alex. We'll see how much you like it.'' Gracie grinned when she saw Alex pinch her lips together in disgust.

''How often do you make pasta?'' Alex asked, trying to steer the subject away from cow's tongue; next, they'd be talking about a thymus gland sandwich.

''Oh, not so much anymore, probably twice a month, unless someone gets sick or asks for it. When the kids were babies, I made noodles once a week, faithfully. Nick Senior loved them''—her voice fell an octave—''especially the thin ones; said that's really why he married me.'' She drew in a deep breath. ''When he died, I made them two, three times a week. It was my therapy.'' She shrugged. ''It helped me feel close to him. I gave most of them away, but I just kept making them.''

''And then everybody started asking for them,'' Gracie said, ''and they haven't stopped. You'd think she was a store, Alex. People call her up and ask her not only for the noodles, but for the chicken soup or sauce that goes with them. Do you believe it? And you know what? She does it! *Do you believe that?*''

''No, not really.'' How could somebody do that? Give everything away? Why? *Why would they do that?* ''If you lived in the city, someone would have snatched you up a long time ago, Stella, given you a trade name like Mama Stella's Cuisine, and marketed it in the gourmet section of the grocery store. You'd be rich.''

Stella met Alex's gaze, gave her a slow smile filled with a wisdom that only comes with living. "I already am, Alex."

"Yeah, well, I think what Alex is saying is that you'd have money too, Mom," Gracie said. "Not just kind words and thank yous, and 'oh, by the way, I'll take another pumpkin nut roll,' but cash. Dinero."

"You girls." Stella shook her head. "One day you'll understand."

"I know, I know, 'give and you shall receive' and all that." Gracie stood up, yawned.

"Gracie, speaking of giving, why don't you and Alex drop a bag off at Nick's and one at Michael's after lunch?"

Nick. Alex stared at the crumbs in front of her, tried to steady her breathing. In and out, in and out, *just breathe.* She'd been waiting for one of them to mention his name all morning, half hoping, half dreading that he would show up here in his mother's kitchen, explain why he'd kissed her, then said he was sorry, too. What had he meant? What? Was he sorry he'd kissed her? Sorry he felt the same way she did? Sorry for what? The kiss? *What?* She'd spent hours lying on Tracy's pink ruffled comforter, playing and replaying those five seconds in the dark, when life stood still and nothing existed but the feel of Nick, his lips, his tongue, his hands.

And then the other question, the one that had her tossing and turning the second half of the night. Was she sorry he'd kissed her? Well, was she? The truth, the honest truth, no twisting allowed, was yes . . . and no.

"I'm not very happy with either one of my brothers right now," Gracie said, grabbing a large pot from the bottom cupboard. "They both promised they'd stop in Clarkton at the flea market and look for an old cradle. You know, the kind with the base that's suspended in the air. I even sketched it out for them.'' She lifted the pot, put it on the stove. ''Last week.'' She carried the pot to the sink, turned on the faucet. ''I haven't heard a word about it, not a peep.''

''You know they've both been very busy.''

''Yeah, well, see if I make them brownies anytime soon.''

''Now Gracie—''

''And don't you go making them any either, especially not the ones with the double fudge. Busy or not, I'm their sister, their *only* sister. They could have found an hour in the last seven days to check it out.''

Stella sighed. ''Alex, see what having siblings does to a grown woman? It just makes her behave like a child sometimes.''

Gracie ignored her mother, turned to Alex. ''Respect and a little consideration, that's all I'm asking.''

''Maybe they're planning a big surprise for you,'' Stella said. ''Maybe you shouldn't ask so many questions or you'll ruin it.''

''But I need it now so Rudy can strip it and get it refinished before the baby comes, Mom. You know, seven weeks is right around the corner, and what if I'm early, like I was with Cecily? Then what?''

''Then you just relax and Rudy will set up the crib in the attic. Now hush before you spoil everything.''

A huge smile spread over Gracie's face, a mixture of pure joy and anticipation. ''They got it already, didn't they?''

Stella kept her eyes on the pasta board in front of her. ''I'm not saying anything else.'' She picked up a knife and started scraping dried dough from the wooden board.

''They did, didn't they, Mom?'' Gracie's voice squeaked with excitement.

''Gracie Ann, if you don't stop pestering me right now,

I'm going to tell your brothers, and then see if you get anything!''

Gracie laughed, rushed over to her mother—as fast as a seven-month's-pregnant woman could—and hugged her. ''Thanks, Mom. I won't say a word. Promise. And Alex and I will take the noodles *and* I'll make both of them a batch of brownies tonight.''

''I didn't say anything,'' Stella said, ''you just remember that.''

Alex watched the interaction between mother and daughter, her chest tightening with a pain she hadn't felt since she was in the eighth grade and the students put on a commemorative play to honor their mothers. Afterward, there was a reception with lemonade, and chocolate chip cookies baked in Home Economics. The mothers sat in folding chairs and drank from plastic cups. Each of the students wrote a note to their mother, thanking them for being so caring and generous with their time and their love. Alex wrote a note, too, filled with wonderful, sappy words, all for Aunt Helen: *I love you so much. You are such a wonderful person. Thank you for coming into my life.* And more than anything she wanted the words to be true, wanted to feel the love, the gratitude that flowed from those words, wanted Aunt Helen to be so moved that she'd pull Alex into her arms, mindless of the wrinkles it would put in the linen of her Chanel suit, and hold her tight, sobbing with joy and love. *Yes, Alex, yes I love you, child. I've always loved you. And now, now I'm going to show you.*

Alex had waited for those words with the innocence of one who believed that wishing hard enough could make the impossible come true. She remembered Aunt Helen's face with her smooth, perfect makeup as she scanned the note. *Thank you, Alex. That's very nice of you,* she'd said in the same tone she used when she told the gardener to clip a little more off the privet. And then she'd laid the note down, leaned over, and whispered in Alex's ear, *Can you believe they're using plastic glasses? For God's sake, plastic! And where are the table linens? You'd think they'd take a little more pride in presentation.* Alex knew then, as the pain gripped her chest, tore her hope apart, that Aunt Helen would never love her the way a mother loved a daughter.

Mothers were women like Stella Androvich.

"Alex, do you know what time Nick will be by?" Stella was at the sink, rinsing lettuce for lunch.

"No. I have no idea." The thought of seeing him again made her suck in a deep breath. Oh, God, what would she do when she saw him? Should she pretend nothing had happened? *Could* she pretend?

Stella looked over her shoulder, met Alex's eyes. "Oh. I was just wondering. You and Nick looked pretty cozy last night."

"We were just talking." It came out in a rush, the words all jumbled together. Had Stella seen Nick kiss her?

"Sure. I know. Talking." She turned back to the sink. "Just talking."

She loved to watch him.

The way he moved, the absent gesture when he rubbed his jaw, his smile, the left side of his mouth tilting up a fraction higher than the right, and his eyes, darker than bittersweet chocolate . . . He'd been up a good part of the night, called in during the early morning hours when Chuck Lubovich was rushed into the hospital, possible stroke. There was a dark shadow along his face and jawline, evidence that the electric razor he kept at the office couldn't compete with the razor he used at home. The tiny lines on the sides of his eyes and mouth were more pronounced today, etched in. He'd changed into one of the clean shirts he kept in his office, a blue-and-white pinstripe, same jeans. His eyes were closed, his head resting against the back of the leather chair.

She'd been waiting to talk to him for four days, waiting for just the right time to ask him why he'd invited her to his uncle's birthday party and then disappeared with another woman. Of course, she'd saved face, slipped away before anyone even saw her, except Michael. So, why had Nick left with *her*? He couldn't possibly know her, and she couldn't know him, not really. Did this woman, this Alex Chamberlain, know that Nick only ate the insides of éclairs? That he kept a stash of caramel corn in his bottom left drawer, in the back behind the Nutri-Grain bars? And that he hummed "You've Lost That Lovin' Feelin' " when he thought he was alone? Or that he'd shaved his head last year when Jenny Sanalucci started chemo and lost all her hair?

Did Alex Chamberlain know *any* of this? But more than anything, did she know, have even a speck of an idea, how much Elise Pentani loved him?

"Elise."

It was Nick. She loved when he spoke her name, longed to hear him whisper it in a soft caress. Someday . . . someday . . . She picked up the day's schedule. "Yes?"

"When's my last patient?" His eyes were still closed, head tilted back.

She scanned the sheet in her hand. "Four-fifteen. Mr. O'Shaunessy. Possible kidney stones."

"Okay. Call me when he gets here. I'm just going to rest my eyes."

"How's Mr. Lubovich doing?"

"I think he'll be okay. Looks like a midbrain stroke, and I guess if you have to have one, that would be the best choice. Edna's the one I'm really worried about, crying and screaming. The poor man was more upset about her than he was about the stroke." He paused, rubbed his eyes. "Thank God Alex was with her."

Alex? "You mean the woman reporter?"

"Yeah, I guess you could call her that. She's staying with Chuck and Edna. She's the one who called 911."

"Oh."

"Got Edna calmed down, took her to the chapel to pray, then home to bed."

"Where was Tracy? Didn't anybody call her?" Edna's daughter should be taking care of her mother; they didn't need an outsider, a stranger, to share their grief.

He blew out a long breath. "Edna said she and Ted went to Niagara Falls for a few days."

"They must be speaking to each other this week."

"I guess." Nick swung his chair around, opened his eyes. "Say, Elise, Alex Chamberlain said she tried to call me a few days ago, three or four times, but I never got the messages."

"Oh." She had called, four times to be exact, but Nick had been with patients, and then, well, then Elise had decided if the woman really wanted to talk with him, she'd find a way, which obviously she had, and if not, then maybe Alex Chamberlain would just go away. "Yes, she did call, but it was busy and—"

He waved a hand in the air. "I understand, don't worry about it. I told her it wasn't like you to forget messages but we'd been very busy so it probably just got pushed aside."

Elise attempted a half laugh. "It has been crazy." Her voice dipped. "I'm sorry."

Nick smiled, his left upper lip rising a bit higher than his right. "Don't worry about it."

"Nick?" Now. She was going to ask him now. "About the other night, the party?"

"Yeah, I'm sorry you couldn't make it. I was there until around ten o'clock or so and then I left."

I know, Michael told me. "I got tied up with my dad, getting ready for Gloria's communion party. Two hundred rolls and five dozen cupcakes, frosted and delivered."

"That's okay. No big deal."

That's what you think. It was a big deal, Nick, a very big deal. "Maybe . . . maybe you can invite me another time?"

"Sure. There's always some kind of Androvich get-together."

He ran a hand through his hair, thick, with just a hint of wave, perfect for a woman to run her hands through . . . She swallowed. "Sounds great." *But it would sound better if you and I could get together, alone, without fifty of your closest relatives.*

"I'm sorry you didn't see Michael."

That got her attention. Her smile faltered, faded. Had that little skunk squealed on her? Had he? "Why . . . why do you say that?" She should have known better than to trust him, should have known that he didn't know anything about honor, or trust. Damn, but she'd been a fool.

Nick shrugged. "No reason. I just thought maybe the two of you might enjoy each other's company."

"Michael and I?" She laughed. Michael hadn't betrayed her. It was worse, much worse. The man she was in love with was trying to fix her up with his *brother*. That was so bizarre, so ludicrous, it was funny.

"I happen to think you'd make a great couple. Have you ever thought about it?"

"No. Never."

"Michael just needs somebody to care about him, who'll make a commitment and won't run out when things get tough. You wouldn't do that, Elise. You'd hang in there, you'd make it work."

You're right, I would. So why won't you give me a chance? Let me show you that I care, that I can commit, that I can and do love you. "Nick—"

"I know he can be a bear, and he's having a tough time right now. Hell, I want to strangle him myself half the time. But if he had a good woman beside him, he'd straighten up, quit the bars, stay home."

"Nick—"

"Just think about it, okay?"

"I really don't—"

The office door opened, cutting off the rest of what she was about to say. Elise turned, expecting to see Mr. O'Shaunessy for his four-fifteen appointment. She did not expect to see Michael Androvich standing there, in jeans and a T-shirt, bronzed and grimy from the woods, *Androvich Lumber* ball cap pulled low over his head. His two children, Kevin and Sara, trailed behind, with Sara clutching his left pant leg.

"Elise." His lips curved up in what might have been taken for a smile had she not heard the mockery in his voice. "Did I interrupt something?"

"No. Nick and I were just finishing."

"Michael? Is that you?"

"Uncle Nick, Uncle Nick!" Kevin and Sara broke loose and ran into Nick's office.

"Hey, kiddos!" He scooped them up in his arms. "How are my two favorite rugrats?"

Sara wound her arms around his neck, kissed his cheek. "Scratchy."

Kevin rubbed his fingers over Nick's cheek. "Double scratchy."

Nick laughed, let them down, and pointed to the jar filled with Jolly Ranchers on his desk. "One."

Elise watched him as he held the jar open. He needed more children—two or three—she could give them to him . . .

Michael leaned against the doorway watching her, his eyes hidden under the bill of that stupid baseball cap. She wondered what his face looked like these days since she never saw more than cheekbones, nose, jaw, and a tangled mass of longish hair curling down his neck and around his ears. "I got the cradle."

"Great," Nick said. "Will you"—he paused, went on—"have time to refinish it?"

Elise knew why he'd paused, knew what it meant. Michael had nothing but time, but he wasted it in Cody's bar or God-knew-wherever-else he disappeared to, probably some woman's bed. There'd been a lot of talk about a year ago that he'd taken up with Trudy, the bartender at Cody's. Did he wear his *Androvich Lumber* cap when he was in bed with her? Oh, God, what was she thinking! Elise pushed the thought of a naked Michael Androvich as far out of her consciousness as she could get it.

"It's done," Michael answered, a hint of challenge in his voice.

They were talking, they were being civil, that was good; not like it used to be, *before,* but at least it was better. There was a time when Nick and Michael were inseparable. She remembered seeing them as a young girl, dark heads bent toward each other, talking, whispering, laughing. And then it all changed, because of *her,* because of Caroline, because one brother married her and another brother still loved her.

"Thanks." Nick nodded, crossed his arms. "I appreciate it."

"No big deal."

"Did you get it in Clarkton?"

Michael shook his head. "I found a better place, just kind of picked it up one day. It's at the house if you want to stop by."

"I will. We've still got a few weeks before the shower."

"Mom says Gracie's been nosing around."

"Figures."

"Yeah." Then Michael turned to her. "Hey, Elise, I've got a really big favor to ask you."

A favor? Michael Androvich needed a favor? Was this a form of blackmail for not telling anyone she'd shown up at his uncle's birthday party? "What?" The word came out harsh, defensive.

He smiled. "I have a few things to take care of this afternoon. Do you think you could watch Kevin and Sara, when you're through here? Say until six-thirty?"

"I . . ." she stumbled around. Why was he asking *her?*

"I'm really in a bind. Mom's got a meeting at the church and Gracie's got her hands full already."

"I . . ."

"We can all go out for pizza afterward. How about it?"

Say no, say no. You do not want to start doing this man any favors. He'd never be back by six-thirty, more like nine-thirty or ten-thirty. Say no.

She opened her mouth to speak.

"I'd really appreciate it . . . Elise." He tipped back his hat, just a fraction, but it was enough for her to see his eyes . . . a soft whiskey color with gold. Beautiful eyes. And then he smiled.

"Yes." The words fell out before she realized she'd spoken them.

Chapter 9

Alex sat in the living room of her condo, her fingers running over the smooth satin of a cream-colored pillow. This one had tassels, elegant combinations of cream and white woven together. Soft, rich, very expensive. She tossed it aside, watched it land on the floor, and picked up the blue-and-green hand mirror beside her. *The true jewel is in the mirror.* Her father's words surrounded her. *Look into it, child. Look into it and see the jewel.* It would be four weeks tomorrow since she'd packed up and headed home from Restalline, but it felt like much longer—months, years, light years.

She was a stranger in her own home, surrounded by order and quiet, with the exception of an occasional yap from Jessica, the Pomeranian next door. Her owner's name *was* Elaine; she'd checked the mailbox on the way in.

Alex brought the mirror closer, stared into it, through it.

Who was the stranger looking back at her? Where had she come from? Why wouldn't she go away? It was like this every time, right before a deal went through, she'd be plagued with guilt and indecision. Should WEC Management have such power over another person's life? The questions went on and on, but eventually she'd convince herself once again that growth was good, expansion was necessary, and individual prosperity was to be applauded, not condemned.

But this time, it felt different. This time people's faces were crowding out the logic: Stella Androvich, making noodles and sharing her recipes for cucumber salad and bread dumplings, a smile on her weathered face; Edna Lubovich, eyes swollen with tears, clutching a rosary in one hand, and Alex's fingers in the other, praying for her husband; Norman Kraziak, smiling at her through misty eyes as he talked about his dead daughter; Gracie, coaxing Alex's hand over her belly as the baby inside her kicked and moved; Justin, running after a baseball, grit and determination on his small face.

And Nick. *Oh, God, Nick.* She'd seen him; they'd spent the last few weeks together, but never alone, not since the night he'd kissed her and knocked her world off its comfortable, logical axis. He showed her the town, from his perspective, in between office hours and emergency calls, with Justin between them most days or running off ahead, an unknowing chaperon, a protector of propriety and inhibitor of male-female emotions.

Alex had hiked the backwoods trails behind Restalline, crossed three creeks, climbed a tree with Justin, picnicked once again on the banks of Sapphire Lake—careful not to get too near, despite his pleas that she kick off her shoes and run in—and helped build a campfire next to Androvich Lumber, where all the Androvich grandchildren congregated to roast marshmallows and tell ghost stories. It was what she'd always imagined families doing, and for the first time since she was eight years old, she almost felt like she was part of it, part of a real family.

Nick had given her all the tools to take the town away from its people; he'd shown her everything, with honesty and pride. Restalline would be the perfect summer/winter resort, ten times better than the one in New York. There were natural slopes for ski trails, paths for hiking and wilderness exploring, a cool, temperate climate, two or three fresh springs . . . and Sapphire Lake. It was all there, in a natural wooded area, nothing prefabricated or contrived. And that meant big money.

But if she used that information to make her pitch to Uncle Walter, would that be betraying Nick? If she could get the town twice fair market value, because the return on investment would be triple that, would *that* be betraying Nick? What if she could convince Uncle Walter to let Nick stay on as a consultant of sorts, maybe to oversee the development of the project, insure that wherever possible trees were left standing, what then? *Would that be betraying Nick?* And the rest of the town, what about them? Would Edna and Chuck Lubovich pack up their yellow kitchen and call her a traitor? Would Chuck have another stroke when he found out Alex's real purpose for coming to Restalline? And Gracie? Would she still tell her she wished Alex were her sister? And Stella? Would she smile and make little comments about how Nick needed a good woman?

And what about Norman Kraziak? What would *he* do? She'd dropped in to see him her last week there, sat in his office across from the portrait of Caroline, and asked him if he'd ever thought of moving away. There'd been no mention of Ruth or the fact that she needed professional help; they'd both carefully skirted the issue. Norman had rubbed his chin, pulled off his black reading glasses, and tossed them on the desk. He'd turned his chair just enough to see Caroline's portrait. When he spoke, it was the voice of a man who was tired, defeated. This had been Caroline's legacy, he'd said, and one day it would be Justin's. But the boy already had Androvich Lumber in his blood. So, if Norman could cash out, he'd rather give his grandson a huge trust fund as opposed to a sawmill and a furniture factory, but only if the price was right, better than right, say, three times fair market value. Then he'd give selling some serious consideration.

What would Uncle Walter say to three times fair market value? He'd refuse at first, that was expected, but once the annoyance settled, then what? Would he consider it? Possibly agree to it? With slight modifications? He was a great believer in addendums. And then what? If Norman Kraziak sold both of his companies, Restalline Millworks and NK Manufacturing, hundreds of people would be out of work, they'd sell out, and Androvich Lumber would be forced to close its doors.

Alex's stomach churned. And what about Nick? What would he say? Something was happening between them, she could feel it when he looked at her, his gaze moving over her with slow, careful precision, dissecting her every move. The sound of his voice ignited her like liquid fire.

It had never been this way before, ever, not even with Eric. Nick could strip away the walls she'd so carefully constructed with nothing more than a look, a word. He questioned her logic, made her question it herself. *Why can't you take a walk in the woods or just sit by the lake without telling me how much people would pay to be near all of this? They don't have to pay anything, Alex. Don't you get it? It's not for sale. It's free.*

What was he doing to her? What?

* * *

Alex pulled the photos out of her handbag and passed them to her uncle. "I think you'll like what you see," she said, leaning over his desk so she could give him a narrative of what he was viewing.

Uncle Walter lifted the pictures from the packet, slid his reading glasses onto his nose. "Hmmm."

"The town is surrounded with pockets of wood just like these." Alex pointed to the clusters of maple and oak. A few weeks ago she'd barely been able to tell a maple from a pine. Her uncle flipped to the next photo. "Those are the natural springs. There are two of them on the outskirts of town. Kids love them. Tourists would be very intrigued." She remembered the day Justin took her to one of the springs and showed her how to get a drink by putting her mouth just below the tip of the rock and catching the water as it trickled over. There were more photos too, of back roads, trails, huge trees, hills, and finally . . . Sapphire Lake.

"Beautiful," Uncle Walter murmured.

"It is, isn't it?" Looking at it reminded her of the first time she'd seen it . . . with Nick.

"It's perfect." He rubbed his jaw, his gaze fixed on the blue water.

"It's even more beautiful in person."

He laid the photo of Sapphire Lake aside. "I've studied the reports you sent in great detail. You've done a good job, very informative."

"Thank you."

"But you haven't indicated your recommendation yet." His gaze shot to the picture, then settled on her. "What will it be, Alex? Are you advocating we purchase this land, turn it into our next resort?"

"I don't know," she said, her voice falling. "Maybe, but

I need more time. There are still too many things to consider." That was the honest truth.

"I see."

She could tell from the tone of his voice that he didn't like her answer, expected something much more definitive, and she couldn't blame him. It wasn't like her to exhibit such uncertainty. She was usually straightforward, self-assured, certain.

"What's this?" Uncle Walter asked, holding up the next picture. "A farmhouse?"

"Actually, that's Stella Androvich's house. It's got a lot of character." She pointed to the right side of the photo. "There's a small stone pathway that leads to the backyard. She's got a magnificent garden, with tomatoes, peppers, zucchini, cucumbers, everything. And there's an old tree house, and a swing . . ." . . . *where Nick Androvich kissed me.*

He flipped the photo face down on his desk. "Alex?"

"What?"

"Forget the house, it doesn't matter. You know there's no sense getting attached to it or the owners." He leaned back in his leather chair, steepled his fingers under his chin. "If we buy the place, we're only going to flatten it."

She looked at him, trying to find the words to tell him that it *did* matter, it did.

Something was wrong. He'd sensed it the minute she'd walked through the door. And now she was telling him that if they did decide to go ahead with the project, they should offer two times fair market value for each house. What in the hell was she thinking? It was absurd. Ludicrous.

"I'm a businessman, Alex," Walter said. "Not a charitable organization."

"I know, I know." She leaned forward in her chair, turned her hands over, palms up. "But the lake is already there, the slopes too, once you clear out the trees. It wouldn't require extensive manmade duplications." Her voice lowered. "Did you review the plans and diagrams I sent you detailing the rest of the town? I think it *might* be what you're looking for . . . what you want . . ."

"So why should we pay double for it?" Alex reminded Walter of her father right now, filled with some ridiculous notion of paying double for something he could get for less than half. It wasn't like her to let her emotions get in the way of cold logic and common sense.

"They love their town," Alex went on. "Everybody I've met has a story, a history . . . It's hard to put a price tag on that kind of thing." She paused. "If we offer them an extraordinary amount up front, I think it may help assuage any guilt or feelings of uncertainty."

"For whom? Them or you?" *What was going on here?* "You make it sound like this is the first time you've done this, Alex. Good God, you've been going to small towns for seven years. You know the routine: you go in, you look around, if it meets our requirements, we make a deal, and everybody's happy."

"We also debilitate the town by buying out the industry that supports them, which forces the people to unload their property for well below market value."

He leaned back in his chair, rubbed his jaw. "And? Didn't they teach you at Wharton that that's known as good business?"

She studied her hands. "I just think if we decide to go ahead with the deal, we should consider offering them a hefty price up front."

"Alex? What's wrong with you? That's totally unreasonable. Why would we do that? We're in this business to make a profit, not give handouts." *What was she thinking?* "What about the businesses? Kraziak and Androvich? Any thoughts on either of them?''

"Well . . . yes, maybe. Norman Kraziak indicated he might consider selling . . . if the price were right."

"How much?"

She met his gaze, held it. "Three times market value."

"Three? Are you serious?"

"Very. And I think he might be, too, given the right incentives." She paused, pushed back a lock of hair. "His businesses are his life . . . he lost his only daughter several years ago, and his wife . . . well, she's . . . not well."

"Alex, this is absurd. Do you know what you're asking here? You want me to ignore every business principal I've ever learned, and offer this man three times what his business, no, businesses, are worth? I'd be a fool to do that."

"You'd get your money back."

He raised a brow. "I'm disappointed in you, Alex. You know better."

"It may be the only way he'll sell."

"There's never just one way." He paused, said, "What about Androvich? What kind of prospect is he?"

She looked away. "He isn't."

"Oh?"

"At least not yet . . . but . . . I'm working on him."

"Oh?"

She nodded. "I need some time."

"Maybe I should send Eric—"

"No!"

His gaze narrowed on her.

"This is my project. I'll get it done. Just give me a little more time."

"One month. You've got one more month to get this project, these people, in place. If we're going to do it, we're going to do it then. Understand?"

"Yes."

"Good. I'll expect you to call me every few days, give me feedback, no more of this disappearing and forgetting to call."

"But I—"

He held up a hand, cut her off. "Communication, Alex, that's the key. I need to know where you are, what you're up to. Understand?"

She nodded.

"Good. And work on this Androvich. As for the other, I'll be damned if I'll pay three times market value for anything." His lips curved into a faint smile. "I'll have Sylvia make reservations at Emilio's. I'll pick you up at seven-thirty."

Alex left a few minutes later. Walter picked up the phone, buzzed Sylvia and said, "Tell Eric I want to see him. Now."

Beethoven's "Moonlight Sonata" filled the air, swirling over tables draped in stiff white linen, with delicate gatherings of pale pink orchids spilling out of Waterford crystal like a gentle waterfall. The waiters wore black tuxedos with crisp white shirts and solemn expressions. They knew each patron by name, first as well as last, knew also their spouse's name, perhaps even their mistress'. Filet mignon, veal Oscar, chicken Florentine; these were not just meals, they were presentations, productions served with great fanfare and flowers. Emilio's prided itself on its food, its elegance, and its exclusiveness.

And Alex would have given just about anything right now to be back in Stella Androvich's cozy kitchen with its wrought-iron roosters, sipping Maxwell House coffee, and eating bread dumplings and stuffed cabbage.

"Madame?"

She looked up at the waiter, wondered if he waxed his thin mustache to make it curl up at the ends. "Yes?"

"More wine, madame?"

She shook her head, glanced at her half-filled glass. "No. No, thank you." Stella would like this wine, she thought. Cabernet 1962. Perhaps she should bring her a bottle, maybe some crystal glasses, too.

"So, Alex, tell the truth, isn't it great to be back in civilization again?" Eric leaned closer, his smooth voice rolling over her skin, lifting the tiny hairs on her forearms.

"Restalline isn't exactly the Stone Age," she said.

He laughed, laid a hand over hers. "No, that's true. The Beverly Hillbillies would be my guess."

She didn't like his tone or his words. "They're very nice people, Eric, with successful businesses, families, lives that fulfill them."

"So I hear." He glanced at Uncle Walter. "Who's this doctor? Androvich?"

Her pulse kicked in an extra beat. Alex slipped her hand out from under Eric's. "His name is Nick Androvich, and yes, he's a doctor, family medicine."

Eric straightened in his chair, picked up his wineglass. "Probably went to some school in East Podunk, U.S.A., graduating last in his class."

"Actually, no." This would kill Eric and his self-importance. He thought he was one of the only ones who was gifted with supreme intelligence. "His mother said he was in the top tenth of his graduating class from Hahnemann and even received a fellowship to study Family Practice. And of course, he's board certified."

"So, what's the catch?"

"What do you mean?"

"What's wrong with the guy?" He pushed up his wire-rimmed glasses. ''I mean, if the guy's such a brain, why isn't he at Johns Hopkins? Or the Mayo Clinic or the Cleveland Clinic? Why's he in some little no-name community hospital in the middle of nowhere?''

''Maybe that's where he's needed most.'' She thought of all the people she'd met over the past few weeks: Harry Lendergin and his gallbladder, Ida Sellone and her high blood pressure, Chuck Lubovich and his heart, and Edgar Malowski and his chronic back pain. A person couldn't cross the street without hearing praise for Dr. Nick. How many other doctors still made house calls? And how many accepted roast chickens and cherry pie as payment? Of course, Eric would never understand that.

''Or maybe''—he took a long sip of wine—''maybe that's the only place he could get a job.''

''Eric.'' Uncle Walter's voice held the hint of quiet authority that had gained him praise throughout the boardrooms of Northern Virginia. ''Androvich's medical abilities aren't in question here. I'm more concerned with his ability and desire to take the deal we're offering him, should we decide we want the town.''

''Of course.'' Eric paused. ''I just don't want Alex getting all friendly with these people and losing her focus on why she's there.''

''I'm not losing my focus—''

''I didn't say—''

''Alex. Eric.'' Uncle Walter gave them both a hard look. ''This isn't a competition between you two.''

''She's losing her edge, Walter. I can hear it in the way she talks about these people, like she wants to be their best friend, for God's sake. And what about the money, huh? What's with this two and three times fair market value? Why not just give them a blank check, let them fill in the zeros.''

"You're being ridiculous, Eric."

"I'm being practical. I can't go in and negotiate if you're opening up the checkbook. I'll look like an ineffectual ass."

"It's always about you and what you'll look like, isn't it?" Anger, hot, burning, seethed through her. "You don't give a damn about what's the right thing to do, the fair thing, do you?"

"Fair for whom? Right for whom?" He frowned. "We've got a business to run here, Alex, and I'm hired to make sure we see a profit. You're supposed to be doing the same thing."

"I am."

"Well, well," Uncle Walter said, "at least I can be assured WEC Management has two dedicated employees, eager to do right by it, albeit perhaps in different manners. Why don't you two settle your differences and let's enjoy our meal?"

Alex and Eric stared at one another, neither willing to concede defeat.

Eric straightened his pale blue silk tie, met his employer's gaze. "I think I should go back with Alex, Walter. See what's going on, make sure she's on the right track."

"I'm not a child. I know my job."

They both looked at her. Finally, her uncle spoke. "Very well, then, Alex. Four weeks. You've got four weeks to prove it and then I'm sending Eric."

"Why are you doubting me?" She stared at her uncle, hurt and anger pulsing through her words. "This may not even be the right location. It may all turn out to be nothing."

When he spoke, his voice was calm, even, matter-of-fact. "But that's not what you really think, is it, Alex?"

She couldn't lie. "No. No, it's not."

"Deep down, you think this could be the greatest resort WEC Management has ever built, don't you?"

She met his gaze, looked into those pale blue eyes, the color of ice melting on a lake . . . and nodded.

"Then do this, Alex"—his eyes burned with a look of power—"get them to sell, and I'll make you president of WEC Management."

Chapter 10

"Isn't she beautiful?" Stella Androvich leaned over, whispered to Nick.

Beautiful. She was beautiful, all right, but it was more than that. He kept his eyes on her, the slight tilt of her head, the sway of her hair, her bare arms, her hips, her legs . . .

"Yes, she is." His voice sounded horse, unnatural, as though he'd pulled an all-nighter and then downed three shots of Jack Daniel's. But he'd done neither.

"She looks like an angel, doesn't she?" His mother clutched his forearm, squeezed. "Doesn't she, Nick?"

He nodded, watching the full pink lips move as she smiled . . .

"She's the perfect bride."

He tore his gaze away, stared down at his mother. "Bride?" What was she talking about?

"Marie, the bride, Nick." His mother frowned at him. "Who did you think I was talking about all this time?"

"Oh, right, Marie. Of course, I knew." He yanked at the collar of his shirt. It was getting damn hot in here. "She is beautiful, Mom. Kenny's a lucky guy."

His mother, the spy, was already scanning the floor, widening the perimeter where Marie stood. Her gaze stopped when it hit her target: Alex Chamberlain. She was standing a little to the left of the bride, talking with Gracie. She was wearing a pale pink sleeveless dress, cut a few inches above the knees, with panty hose that shimmered when she walked, and, of course, pearls.

"Ah, I see."

"What?"

"Nick." There she went with that patronizing voice. "I'm your mother." She smiled up at him, patted his arm. "You're smitten, admit it."

"Of all the ridiculous—"

"I knew it. Gracie thinks she's smitten with you, too." If her smile got any wider her face would crack.

She did? Why would Gracie think that? Had Alex said something? He wanted to know, but he'd cut out his tongue before he'd ask his mother. She'd pester him to death, interrogate him, badger if necessary, and enlist accomplices to ferret out information. Anyway, so what if he admitted Alex Chamberlain was beautiful? So what? It didn't mean anything, not a thing. So what if he'd called Edna Lubovich the last three days, asked about Chuck, and then, so very casually, inquired if Alex had returned from her trip yet?

In truth, he doubted Edna was fooled. She was probably in cahoots with his mother; maybe they'd compared notes and conversations over coffee, tried to decipher what was happening.

What *was* happening? Damned if he knew, but he'd been restless since Alex'd left, had driven past the Lubovich's five times looking for her Saab. He missed her, wanted her to come back, and yet, he hated admitting it to anyone, especially himself.

He should never have kissed her, damn it. He should have kept the relationship simple, platonic, but he couldn't have prevented himself from tasting her any more than Adam could've refused the apple in Eve's hand. It was done, fait accompli. *Now,* was what mattered, now. He just couldn't do it again, right? Hadn't he behaved in an exemplary manner after that night, kept everything cool, detached, impersonal? Of course, he'd kept Justin wedged between them, reminding Nick that there was no room in his life for a personal involvement with Alex Chamberlain. She was a short-timer, heading back to the city for good in a month or less, and he didn't want a serious relationship anyway. *Did he?* Of course not.

When, Nick? When are you ever going to settle down again, love again? He heard his mother's words floating around in his mind, loose, unfettered, the same words he heard every six months filled with the same sadness, the same desperate need to help. She was a fixer, all right, but not this time.

Love? He always gave her the same answer. *What are you talking about? I love you, I love Justin—*

A woman, Nick. A woman. When are you going to love a woman again?

Loving a woman is like having your wisdom teeth, impacted ones, pulled out with a pair of pliers and no anesthetic.

Why, then, had the blood rushed to his head, and his penis, when he saw Alex Chamberlain walk into the community hall a little while ago with Gracie? And when she'd met his gaze, held it, then looked away, why had he felt a stab of disappointment?

"Nick?" His mother tapped him on the shoulder. "Go talk to her." She gave him a little shove. "Go."

"Stop it, Mom. I'm not sixteen." *I feel like it, though.*

"Didn't say you were. But you two have been eyeing each other for the past ten minutes. Nonstop." She crossed her arms under her chest. "Any fool can see you've got some things that need to be said. Or done." A small smile crept over her lined face. "Why don't I take Justin tonight? You relax, go have some fun."

Nick stared at his mother. "It's not what you think—"

"I know, I know. Didn't say it was, did I? Justin and I have a score to settle. He's beating me by fifty points in rummy and I need a chance to catch up."

He paused, nodded. "All right."

"So, go talk to her. If it's nothing but friendly conversation, what are you worried about?"

"What's everybody doing?" The music had stopped and the deejay was holding two cream-colored satin pillows edged in lace and ribbon in his hands.

"It's the pillow dance!" Gracie said in a gush of excitement.

"The what?"

"The pillow dance. It's tradition." She lowered her voice. "The first time Rudy kissed me was during a pillow dance. The Jawkowski wedding. I hardly knew him, but when somebody puts a pillow in front of you, what choice do you have? You kiss them. Not that I minded, but I thought it was awfully bold of him." She sighed, smiled. "Awfully bold."

"Gracie? What's the pillow dance?" *Kissing?* Nick was here; she'd seen him. Oh, God. *Kissing?*

"It's one of the fifteen million traditions we Czechs have, been doing it for as long as I can remember. See those pillows?" She pointed to the deejay. "Everyone forms a circle around the bride and her father, like they're doing now—come on, Alex, you too—and then they'll start the dance, first a polka, then a waltz. When that's through, Harry and Tilly, his wife, will join hands. Marie will take the pillow and place it on the floor next to Kenny. They'll both kneel on it and kiss. Then it's their turn to do a polka and a waltz. Follow me, so far? Okay, when all of that's done, Kenny will throw the pillow at one of the ladies forming the circle, go over, kneel, kiss, and dance with her. When they're finished the lady tosses the pillow to a man, they kneel, kiss, yada, yada. Oh, and the guys have to put money in a cigar box every time they dance. Don't ask me why it's a cigar box and not a velvet-lined wooden box or something fancy like that. It's always been a cigar box. . . . And Alex,'' she said, raising a dark brow, ''you have to kiss the person who puts the pillow in front of you.''

''Sounds awfully . . . invasive,'' Alex said, thinking of all the men, young, old, in-between, forming the circle.

''Oh, come on, don't be such an old fuddy-duddy.''

''I . . .'' Her gaze met Nick's from across the room. She had to avoid him until she could sort out the feelings that made her jumpy whenever he was within fifty yards of her. She was here on a mission. Her uncle's words filled her head. . . . *get them to sell, and I'll make you president of WEC Management . . . president of WEC Management.* It would be the ultimate act of faith on her uncle's part. Finally, after all these years, she'd have earned his trust and his faith. She had to do this . . . she had to . . .

''Come on scaredy-cat.'' Gracie pulled her along. ''Who knows, you might get lucky. Nick might kiss you.''

Alex whipped around. ''I—''

''Yeah, I know,'' she cut her off, inched her way between a heavy-set woman with red curls in a matching red polka-dot dress, and a tall thin man with thick black glasses and a green-silk striped vest. ''You two are friends, *just* friends.''

''Right.'' *Had Nick said that?* ''That's right.'' And if he had, had he believed it? She hadn't spoken to him since she'd gotten back in town late last evening and he hadn't been at the wedding ceremony, some emergency, Stella said. Twenty minutes ago was the first she'd seen him, when she'd looked up and caught him watching her. Waiting? For what? For her to smile and beckon him forward? She hadn't; she'd stared back and then looked away, pretending she didn't want to see him, speak with him, be with him. And she didn't, she *couldn't*, not until her brain could take charge of her emotions, make them settle down, stay focused. That was the plan, but it had been much easier to formulate and anticipate executing when Nick Androvich was hundreds of miles away instead of just across the room.

The music started, the "Tanta Anna Polka", and with hands clasped tight, the crowd began its slow, rhythmic circling of Marie and her father. Harry smiled down at his daughter, pride and love etched on his face. *This is love*, Alex thought, *the love of a father for his daughter.* Her chest tightened as Harry whirled Marie around, her satin skirts swirling. *And this is love,* her heart told her, when Kenny took Marie's hand and pulled her into his embrace. They twirled and danced, eyes shining, hearts pounding with love and promise, as the ribbons of the small satin pillows floated around them.

"God, just look at them. They're so much in love," Gracie said.

Alex nodded. What would it be like to have such commitment, such devotion? She and Eric had never had that. They'd said all the right words, gone through the motions, the proper ones, the expected ones, had a most elaborate wedding, one that could have been replicated in *Bride* magazine. And the gifts, so many of them, expensive, unique, no Correlle everyday dishes at this union. Everything had been perfect, perfect, from the Sterling roses and white orchids in Waterford crystal vases to the three-carat diamond ring from Cartier shining on Alex's third finger. Bright, bold, noteworthy. In all of the grandness of planning, they'd only neglected one thing; not the prenuptial agreement—that had been their first consideration. No, the only area lacking, with an emptiness so vast it could not remain hidden for long, was commitment.

Eric and Alex committed to *things*; a prenuptial agreement, of course, a lease on a condo, a pension plan, even an extended, first-anniversary trip to Hawaii, but they did not commit to each other. Ever. Marie and Kenny had made that commitment; it was in their eyes, bright, shining, their movements, soft, cherished, their kiss, filled with love, hope, promise. They were thrilled with their honeymoon trip to the Poconos, the matching Penn State sweatshirts, the Black & Decker coffeepot, the cork coasters. The gifts didn't seem to matter; it was the sharing, the commitment to each other that made them smile, even cry.

So, why were they so happy? How? Marie worked in the kitchen of the local hospital, went to school three nights a week at Midland Community College, twenty miles away. She wanted to be a nutritionist, but it would take her three, four, maybe five years to finish, if she didn't get pregnant first. And Kenny, he worked for Norman at the Restalline Millworks. *How could they be happy?* How? Did they want to live in a two-bedroom box for the rest of their lives, with peeling paint and a wrought-iron front railing that wobbled when you touched it? The heck of it was, it didn't seem to bother them at all.

Did happiness only elude people like Alex? The well-educated overachievers who doubted anything that wasn't fact-based, who depended on no one but themselves for solutions and resolutions, who pushed and pushed until the enjoyment and the desire behind the original goal was beaten into the ground, stamped out, and all that remained was bitter resolve to see the job done because no one else could be trusted to do it? What? What was it?

Had her parents been this way? Had they pushed forward, determined, eyes always on the next goal, never savoring the present achievement? Bigger, bigger, better, better? She thought of the hand mirror, the time and care that had gone into creating it. And love. There had been love in the working of that mirror, she felt it, knew it. Perhaps her parents had been like Marie and Kenny, committed and loving, to Alex, to each other. Perhaps they had intended for their daughter to be that way, too. If so, they would be very disappointed.

"Get ready, Alex," Gracie said. "George Konklin's heading straight toward you."

Alex stared at the wiry little man moving in her direction. How many turns had they taken? She'd been so caught up in her own thoughts, she hadn't noticed. Her gaze swept the circle. Nick wasn't there.

"Keep your lips closed tight," Gracie said in a loud whisper, "or he'll try to slip his tongue in your mouth."

"Thanks for the warning."

"He's gross, lives with his mother, but you should see the magazines he buys. A regular skin collection. Pervert."

George Konklin dropped the pillow in front of Alex. She stared at his tongue, thick, fleshy, protruding, as it inched out to run over his thick lips, leaving them wet, shiny, coated with saliva. *Oh, God, I'm going to be sick.* He started to kneel. Alex stared at the floor, blinked twice, hard. When she looked up, Nick was kneeling in front of her, his tanned face hard, unsmiling. George Konklin was nowhere in sight. Nick reached out, took her hand, and pulled her to him. The music, the people, all of it faded away, everything but this man, this moment. She knelt, whether by the pressure of his hand or her own volition, she couldn't say, didn't care. Closer, closer, her gaze locked with his. *The mission! The mission!* a tiny voice screamed. *Stop. Stop, now, before it's too late!* Her eyes fluttered closed, their lips met. *It's already too late. It's always been too late.* The kiss was long and slow, her mouth opening, inviting, his tongue searching, mating, her fingers buried in the nape of his hair, his hand pressing her against his chest.

She felt his heart pounding, or was it hers? The feel of him, the smell of him, she wanted more, more, *more*. Then it was over and he was pulling away, his breathing hard, choppy, his gaze dark, unreadable. They stared at each other, Alex looking up at him, confused, floundering . . . mortified . . . by what she'd just done in front of a room full of people, what she'd just admitted, to them . . . and to *him*. She tried to turn away, to get out before she humiliated herself any further, but Nick grabbed her arm, stopped her. He flung the pillow into the crowd and said, "Let's get out of here."

Alex followed him outside, taking two steps for his every one. Was he angry? Upset? And if he was, with whom? Himself or her?

It was late afternoon and the sun slid over the trees, filtering through, scattering a dancing pattern of light on the back of Nick's head, making his brown hair shimmer with auburn as he moved in front of her. When they reached the silver Navigator, he opened the passenger door and she climbed in.

"I'm sorry." They were the first words he'd spoken since they'd left the hall. Alex glanced at him. He was staring straight ahead, hands gripping the steering wheel, knuckles white.

Sorry. "For the kiss? Or the display?"

"The display. The kiss." He shook his head. "Both." He swung around, looked at her. "Jesus, Alex, I don't know what the hell I'm sorry for."

"Are you . . . sorry that you kissed me, Nick, or sorry that you did it in front of half the town?" *Don't be sorry for the kiss, please, don't be sorry for the kiss.*

"I couldn't let that weasel slobber all over you," he said, ignoring her question.

She turned away, focused on a huge maple tree, its dark red leaves a brilliant backdrop against the green lawn. *I wanted you to kiss me, Nick. I wanted you to, even when I knew it was the last thing you should do, even when I knew it wasn't logical, or sensible.*

"Alex?" He said her name with hesitancy, concern.

"It's okay, Nick. I'm sorry, too."

They sat in silence, the threads of polka music and laughter spilling out of the hall. "It's not okay," his words filled the space between them. "Look at me." She turned slowly, met his gaze. He had the most beautiful dark brown eyes, like bittersweet chocolate. "I lied." He rubbed a hand over his jaw. "I'm not sorry I kissed you. Jesus, I haven't been able to stop thinking about kissing you since that night on the swing, even before that. Every time I looked at you, I thought about how you tasted, and I wanted more, but I kept telling myself it was crazy, I'd be a fool to get involved with somebody like you." His words were coming out in a rush, as though he had to get them all out now or they'd be gone forever. "That's why I dragged Justin everywhere we went. I didn't trust myself, didn't trust the way I was feeling. And then you left." He ran a hand through his hair, let out a long sigh. "I missed you." It was a confession, one that didn't seem to please him.

"Nick—"

He held up a hand. "I wanted you to come back, and when I saw you today, the only thing I could think about was touching you, but you avoided me. You feel something for me, too. I know it, Alex, whether you admit it to yourself or not, you can't kiss me like that and pretend it's nothing."

"I know." The words were a whisper.

"And sooner or later you're going to have to admit that

there's a chemistry going on here—'' He stared at her. ''What did you just say?''

''I said, I know. I know I have to admit I have feelings for you.''

''So are you?''

Alex twisted her hands in her lap. It was one thing to harbor secret feelings for Nick Androvich, but to make them public, to tell the man himself, that was quite another, and yet, what choice did she have? Her heart was battling with her brain, and for once, *for once,* it was winning.

''Alex?'' He laid his hand over both of hers, stopped her fidgeting. ''Answer me, damn it.''

''Yes,'' she breathed. ''Yes, I have feelings for you, but—''

She got no further. Nick pulled her to him, half lifting her over the gearshift column to sit in his lap. His hands framed her face, his lips moved over hers, hard, possessive, desperate, tongue plunging inside, taking, taking. Alex moaned, wrapped her arms around his neck, pulling him closer, the taste of whiskey filling her senses. She wanted to get closer, *needed* to get closer. Nick's fingers worked their way down her neck to her breast, molding it with his palm, massaging her nipple through the soft fabric.

''Oh, God, Alex,'' he whispered, ''I dreamed this a thousand times.''

She moaned against his lips, too shaken to respond.

''I can't get enough of you,'' he said, trailing his tongue along the side of her neck, sucking gently. ''I want you . . .'' He slid a hand between her legs, parting them, pressed a finger against her heat, ''. . . all of you.'' Alex thrust her hips against his finger, once, twice, three times.

He let out a laugh, deep in his throat. ''Come to me, Alex. Come to me.'' He stroked her through the silk of her panties, worked small circles over the sensitive flesh, sending shocks of sensation through her body. He kissed her again, drawing her tongue into his mouth, sucking, tasting, and all the time moving those magical fingers between her legs. It was too much; it wasn't enough; she wanted more, more. She jerked against his touch, harder, faster, as he played her like a pianist honoring his masterpiece. And when at last he slipped a finger beneath her panties, and stroked bare flesh, she fell apart, one chord at a time, splitting into a thousand melodies, grasping for that one final note.

Nick pulled her limp body to him, cradling her in his arms, protecting, perhaps, for the briefest of moments, even cherishing. He brushed the hair from her face, planted a soft kiss on her temple. "I've been wanting to do that for weeks."

She buried her face against the solid wall of his chest, inhaled. He smelled of starch and whiskey and Davidoff Cool Water, scents that would be ingrained in her memory forever, as would this man, this place, this coming together.

"Alex?" His voice was low, gentle. "Are you okay?" He stroked her hair, once, twice, the softest of gestures, born of caring, pure and honest, and it was this touch, this gentleness, that made her eyes burn, her throat swell.

She nodded, trying to blink away the tears. *God,* what was wrong with her?

He pulled her closer, whispered, "Let's go to my place. It's a little less cramped and a lot more private."

"I . . ." She swallowed. *Follow your heart, for once, for once, follow your heart.* "Yes. Yes, Nick." She pressed her lips against his shirt. His heart beat steady, strong. "I want to be with you."

Michael watched them leave. Any man with half a gonad would know what came next. Nick was taking Alex home to fuck her brains out. Correction. "Have sex," "get together," "be intimate." *Fuck* was too crude a word for Nick and his sexual relationships with women. Fuck was

Michael's word; it's what *he* did with a woman. Fucked, screwed, banged. *Shit*, he was getting hard just thinking about fucking.

"Daddy, Daddy, there's Elise." He followed his daughter's finger and indeed, there she was, all decked out in some sleeveless blue concoction, moving around in the circle of the pillow dance. Her black hair was all piled up on her head and he could see a lot of neck and shoulders. Smooth, dark. His penis jerked. *Fuck!* He looked away.

"Let's go see Grandma," he said, moving toward one of the long tables at the edge of the room.

"Dance, Daddy," Sara said. "Dance with Elise."

He should never have come. He hated weddings, hated watching the goo-goo-eyed bride and groom pledging their hearts, their love, their fidelity, and every other bullshit imaginable to one another. How about the T-Fal frying pan? Why not pledge that, too? It was all fake, a lie, a scam. The groom was probably wondering what it would be like to jump the maid of honor's bones, and if he were honest with himself, really honest, he'd be awfully depressed, if not downright pissed, that he'd pledged himself to one pussy for the rest of his life.

It was such a bunch of shit. Michael pulled at his collar. This monkey suit was choking him. By the time he left, he'd be dead from strangulation if the bullshit in this place didn't suffocate him first. He would've stayed home and watched the Pirates if his mother hadn't begged him to come. *Those children need to see you among people, Michael. You're always alone. For heaven's sake, can't you take a few hours and show them you can act normal?*

Normal? You mean like Nick, don't you, Ma?

No. I mean normal. Like a human being, interacting with people, with your children. Then she'd looked at him and there'd been tears in her eyes, his mother, who rarely cried. *They need a father, Michael. You. They need you, not me,*

*or Elise, or anybody else who watches them while you run
off to do God knows what.*

He'd said nothing; what could he say? *I got nothing to
give them, Ma, I'm sucked dry?*

"C'mon, Daddy. Let's go." Sara tugged his arm, pulling
him toward the wide circle.

"Michael?" It was his mother, eyes bright and shining.
"You came." She said it like she'd known he would, spoken
as statement, fact. How could she have known when he
hadn't known himself?

"Yeah, we made it." He slid a finger underneath his shirt
collar, tried to loosen it.

"I was looking for you at church."

He shrugged. "One miracle at a time."

She turned her attention to the children. "Hello, sweethearts." She bent down, drew them into her arms for a big
hug. "Sara, you look beautiful. Kevin, quite handsome. Just
like your father."

Michael felt the heat crawl up his neck. Damn this monkey
suit. He'd give half a week's pay for his jeans and ball cap.
"How's the food?"

"Delicious. Stuffed cabbage, kielbasa, parsley-buttered
potatoes, chicken paprikash, and your favorite, beef stroganoff."

"Lead the way."

"Dance first, Daddy."

"Sara—"

"Go, Michael. Elise Pentani's out there."

"So?"

"Dance, Daddy, dance." Sara swung his arm back and
forth. "Please?"

"She asked if you were coming."

*Yeah, so she can tell me how much time I'm not spending
with my kids.* "Oh, for Christ's sake—"

"Go." His mother motioned for Sara and Kevin to come with her. "We'll watch Daddy, okay kids?"

"Yeah. Dance with Elise, Daddy." This, from Kevin.

"Traitor." He pointed at Kevin. "One dance, that's it. Just one." He threw them all a disgusted look and headed for the wide circle of bodies moving slowly to the music. Elise was wedged between Hot Ed's proprietors, Bernie and Alice. Her gaze was fixed on the floor, her mouth pinched shut as though she were in pain, and maybe she was. It must be a bitch to watch somebody you loved sucking face with somebody else. He wouldn't know, he'd never loved Betsy, she was more of an obligation, an oops-I-screwed-up-and-got-you-pregnant kind of commitment, though he'd been pissed when she up and left, more from a bruised ego than a bruised heart.

And Caroline, well she'd been a dream, a surreal desire to be cherished, a woman in need of being rescued. *Help me, Michael, help me. I hate it there, I don't want to go back. Nick's deserted me.... I never see him ... I'm all alone ... help me ...* He'd listened to her, allowed himself to believe that his brother, his best friend, was mistreating his wife, ignoring her, abandoning her, and he, Michael Androvich, was the only one who could save her. She'd needed and needed and needed in a sick way, deep down Michael knew that, and yet he couldn't turn her away, couldn't find the words to shut her down, send her back to Philly, because for once in his life, someone was turning to him, to *him,* not his older brother. *Stay here,* he'd told her the last time he saw her. *With me. I'll help you raise the baby, here in Restalline. I ... I love you, Caroline.* Her big blue eyes had filled with tears. She'd touched his cheek, her lips trembling as she smiled. *Oh, Michael, don't you see? I can't. I can't. I love Nick. I've always loved him. Always.*

And then she was dead, and Michael felt both betrayer and betrayed. He'd loved his brother's wife, a woman who'd come to him, cried to him, left him. How could he ever forgive himself for what he had been ready to do? He couldn't, so he kept away from Nick as much as possible, sheltered with guilt and bad memories and an occasional fifth of Jack Daniel's.

But he'd be damned if he'd ever, ever fall in love again. He'd rot in hell first.

"Michael! Come on." A tall, busty brunette yanked his hand forward and drew him into the circle. Cynthia Collichetti. Big tits. He'd felt her up a few weeks ago in the back room of Cody's. "You were supposed to call me."

"Yeah, well, I've been busy." What the hell! Why couldn't she just take the hint? Nick wasn't interested. Elise was still staring at the floor. His eyes moved from her blue shoes to her tanned legs, all the way up, up, up to her thighs, her stomach, stopped at her breasts. Perfect. More than a mouthful's just a waste. *Shit!* What was the matter with him? He was drooling over Elise Pentani, for Chrissake.

"I'm free every night after nine, except Thursdays," Cynthia said. "Thursdays I bartend at Jasper's until eleven."

"Okay." "Beautiful Brown Eyes" drifted from the sound system.

"Call me."

"Sure."

She leaned over, kissed his ear. "You won't be disappointed."

The crowd stopped, and Janice, the waitress at Hot Ed's, knelt before him. She wore a hot-pink dress that looked like it had been painted on her body, one stroke at a time. She licked her lips, grabbed his forearms with two-inch hot-pink nails, and kissed him, thrusting her tongue deep in his mouth. He jerked back, his gaze riveting involuntarily to Elise, who stared at him in surprise and shock. Janice pulled him onto the dance floor and spent the next thirty seconds rubbing her body against his. When the dance was over he snatched the pillow from her hand and sucked in air.

His feet began moving before his head registered where he was going. He placed the pillow at Elise Pentani's shiny, pale blue shoes and knelt down. Their gazes locked, she moved forward.

"I . . . I don't remember seeing you without your ball cap."

"Yeah, well, guess it doesn't go with the suit."

"You're very nice-looking, Michael." She sounded surprised.

"Even dogs take a bath once in a while."

She inched closer, touched his cheek. "So smooth. And your eyes . . . like honey and brown sugar."

Shit! He was hard and ready. What was wrong with him? "Stop it, Elise. Nick's gone. I'm not his substitute."

She jerked back as though he'd slapped her.

"Kiss her! Kiss her!" the crowd shouted.

Michael pulled her toward him, determined to show her, teach her so she'd never confuse the two brothers again. Her lips parted, full, pink lips, moist with anticipation. Her eyes fluttered shut. *Who the fuck was he kidding?* He couldn't kiss her, couldn't taste those lips, because once would never be enough. And she was in love with his brother. Michael brushed his lips against the side of her mouth, stood up, and headed for the bar.

Chapter 11

Nick turned the wheel with one hand, winding along the back roads toward home. His other hand held Alex's, clutched tight, in case she had second thoughts—not that he thought she would or that he would force her to stay if she did . . . hell, he didn't know what he thought right now. All he did know was that his erection was throbbing hard and heavy against his zipper and he wanted her . . . *now*.

They hadn't spoken much since he'd turned the key in the ignition ten minutes ago. One last kiss, then she'd eased away from him and fastened her seat belt. She seemed almost shy, timid, as though she weren't used to or comfortable with the emotion they'd shared. Was she? He knew very little about her personal life other than the fact that she was an only child, an orphan, who'd been raised by her aunt and uncle. What else? *What else?* That was all he knew, and now was sure as hell not the time to go digging around asking questions about her past relationships with men. Later, he'd find out later. All that mattered right now was that she wanted to be with him.

"It's just around the bend, another mile," he said as they passed his mother's house.

Alex nodded. "Justin showed me one day. He pointed it out when we were on our way to buy corn."

"You should've stopped."

"You weren't home."

Hmmm. Maybe she'd thought about it. "Well, next time you can stop whether I'm home or not." He paused, squeezed her hand. "And if I'm not, maybe you can wait for me to come home."

"Maybe."

Maybe. There were a lot of maybes floating around between them. "Here we are," he said, turning down the wide road that led to his house.

"It's . . . so you," Alex said, her eyes fixed on the white farmhouse with the wraparound front porch.

Nick scanned the house and surrounding area: white, neat, clipped, with a comfortable old glider on the front porch and a barn in the back. His mother had spread her green thumb to his yard with three pots of impatiens and six hanging ferns. "It's me, all right," he said, hopping out of the Navigator and hurrying to the other side. He opened the door, pulled her to him. "You can see anything you want later." His lips brushed over hers, his fingers inching her pale pink dress up her thighs. "Right now, there's only one thing I want to see . . . you . . . naked in my bed."

She moaned into his mouth, flung her arms around his neck, and melted against him. He let out a groan of need and want, lifted her into his arms, and carried her to the house, his lips never leaving hers. God, but he couldn't wait to taste the rest of her . . . he climbed the last stair, headed toward his room ... couldn't wait to sink himself deep inside, deep, so deep.

"Nick?" She broke the kiss, breathless.

He laid her on his bed, sat down beside her, placed a hand on her thigh. "Yes?" Her skin was pale, almost a pink blush against his dark fingers.

"I ... I ..." She pulled her bottom lip through her teeth. "There's so much we don't know about each other ... maybe ... maybe we should talk ..."

He laughed, ran the palm of his hand under her dress. Higher, higher ... She caught her breath, held it. Alex wanted to talk about as much as he did right now. "I've got a better idea," he said, finding the silk scrap of panty wedged between her legs. "Let's practice the Braille method, huh?" He flicked his thumb against her panties. "Talk through touch. How about that?"

Her lips parted, her eyes grew wide, serious. "Nick ..."

"Just say yes." It was as close to a plea as he'd ever come.

She hesitated, just a second, then said, "Yes. Yes, Nick."

He reached for her, a pulsing mass of heat and need, pulling her to him with an urgency that surprised him. His lips were everywhere, her throat, her breasts, the tip of her hipbone. He slid his hands up her thighs, reached for her panties, and yanked them off. "God, but you're so soft," he whispered, planting a kiss on the inside of her thigh. She clung to him, her fingers buried in his hair, a low moan on her lips. He lifted his head, watched her.

"Open your eyes, Alex. Look at me."

She met his gaze, her blue eyes bright. "Nick ... Nick, I ..."

"Shhhhh." He stroked her cheek, ran a finger over her lips. "No words. Not now. Okay?"

She nodded, reaching for him. And then there were no more words as he flung aside her dress, her bra, her reserve,

reveling in the touch and feel of her, the way she fumbled
over his belt buckle, shy yet determined, yanking his pants
off, clinging to him, mouth open, welcoming his tongue,
gasping in frustration when she couldn't get close enough.
He wanted her and she wanted him. The need was there
too, throbbing between them as though it had a life of its
own, demanding, reaching, pleading for union, for complete-
ness, for the desperateness of this moment to end. Her whole
body trembled when he entered her, shook and vibrated as
he moved inside her, gasps of pleasure on her lips. She
wrapped her legs high over his back, pulling him closer,
tighter, bucking with him, against him, tearing at the tiny
scrap of control he had left. And when he knew he'd explode
if she moved one more time, she jerked and convulsed
against him, screaming out his name. It was too much; Nick
grabbed her buttocks, buried himself into her one final time,
deep, and let his release flow over him and into her, hot,
needy, exhausting.

Alex rolled over, wondering what time it was. Five? Six?
The last time she looked at the clock it was three-thirty and
Nick had just—her whole body throbbed with the thought—
turned her onto her stomach, spread her legs, and slipped
inside. She'd been asleep, or half asleep, until his hardness
invaded every pore in her body.

She was exhausted, sore . . . sticky. . . . Nick. They'd made
love three times, each different, equally explosive, totally
possessive. The first had been filled with a clinging neediness, a fear that the moment would slip from their grasp if
they didn't take their fill from each other, drink, hard, fast,
greedy. The second was a leisurely exploration of touch
and sensation, a promise of heightened pleasure and hidden
passion. And the third, the three-thirty wake-up call, well,

that was a new familiarity based on desire and need, base need, pure and elemental.

Last night, no, it had started long before last night. Nick had stripped away her layers of cool reserve, the self-possessed attitude that had taken Uncle Walter and Aunt Helen years to teach. *There's no room for blatant displays of affection,* Aunt Helen had told her over and over. *Base emotions are crass and unsophisticated. Remember that, Alex, always remember that.* Had she remembered *too* well, believed *too* much, lived *too* much of the disjointed, separate-bedroom relationship her aunt and uncle shared? Was that why her earlier relationships with men had failed? Why no man had been interested enough to push past the aloofness, the distancing, why they gave up long before they got to *her,* the real Alex Chamberlain, crouched in a corner like a lost child, hidden somewhere beneath advanced education and impervious etiquette? Even Eric, when he was her husband, had not tried hard enough, with enough courage, determination, or sincerity to elicit any response stronger than tepid acquiescence.

But Nick Androvich had gotten to her, through sheer will, expectation, and honesty. She'd seen the truth on his face; he'd wanted *her,* Alex Chamberlain, the woman, not Alex Chamberlain the socialite, vice president of Development at WEC Management, the magna cum laude graduate of Wharton, the niece of Walter Chamberlain, the heir to her uncle's vast wealth. No, Nick had wanted none of that, he wasn't even aware that any of it existed.

Alex let out a slow breath. He'd made love to her and yet, he knew almost nothing about her. Her stomach clenched, twisted. What would he say if he found out she was planning to buy him out, flatten his house, his mother's, his sister's? *What would he say then?* Would he forgive her? Would he listen, even try to understand why she'd done it? Could she convince him that life in the suburbs, even in the city, really did have a lot to offer him and the people of Restalline? Or would he turn away, shun her, just when she might have found the one person who could make her feel something real? *Would he hate her?*

Alex's heart was pounding so hard in her chest that she never heard the footsteps coming toward her. It wasn't until an unfamiliar voice shot into the semidarkness that she realized someone else was in the room, a man, and it wasn't Nick.

"Well, well, if it isn't Goldilocks."

Her eyes flew open and she saw the shadowy cast of a man standing beside the bed, dressed in jeans and a dark T-shirt, a baseball cap pulled low over his eyes.

"Michael." Instinct told her that this was Michael Androvich, Nick's brother. He was taller and broader than Nick, with wide shoulders and muscled forearms. She pulled the sheet closer to her body, aware of her nakedness. Nick? Where was Nick?

"So you've heard about me?" He let out a hollow laugh that bounced off the walls. "I'm sure Nick had some interesting things to say."

The animosity in his voice was hard to miss. "Actually," Alex said, "he didn't seem to want to talk about you."

He laughed again. "That's called diplomacy."

"He isn't here."

"Obviously." He pulled up a chair, sat down. "No man with half a pulse would leave his bed with a beautiful woman in it unless he had no choice." He rubbed his jaw. "Nick's probably doing his doctor thing, you know, the patient comes first bullshit."

"I'll tell him you stopped by," she said. *Leave.* She wanted him to leave.

Michael touched the brim of his cap. "Appreciate it. Alex, isn't it?" He crossed his broad arms over his chest. "I've heard all about you, Alex. Everybody has. The whole town's talking. Some say you're one of those smart sophisticates from the city, who's come to write about the plight of the poor common folk.''

"That's not exactly—"

"Others say you like small towns, and you're traveling around, trying to promote them to your city publishers.'' He paused. ''And then there's a few that say you've got a whole different agenda, one that nobody's even thought about.''

Alex tried to remain calm, keep her voice even. "And you, Michael? What do you say?''

He leaned forward, placed his big hands on his knees. "Me? I say I don't care what in the hell you came to Restalline for, but don't screw with my brother.''

"I don't know what—"

"Save it, okay? I've seen the way he watches you, like you're all he can see. Shit, everybody saw him practically deep-throat you at the wedding yesterday. That's not Nick. He's never out of control, but you've done something to him.'' His tone was whisper soft, in total opposition to the menacing words coming out of his mouth. ''Nick and I don't see eye to eye on too much these days, but he's still my brother and I'll be damned if some short skirt is going to waltz into town and screw him over.'' His laugh was crude, raw. ''You can screw him all you want but you better not screw *with* him, you got that Goldilocks? I don't know what your game is, but I'll be watching you and I'm not the gentleman Nick is. I'm a street fighter.'' He jabbed his thumb at his chest. ''Don't mess with him, and I won't mess with you, you got that Goldilocks?''

She nodded once, unable to find the words to respond.

"Good.'' He stood up, tossed something on the bed. ''You dropped these.'' Then he turned and left.

Alex didn't move until she heard the sound of an engine outside. When she was sure he was gone, she looked down

at the objects Michael had thrown onto the bed. Three shiny
condom packets, ripped down the middle, lay on Nick's
pillow. *You can screw him all you want but you better not
screw with him, you got that Goldilocks? . . . I'll be watching you . . . I'll be watching you . . .*

She flung back the covers and raced to the bathroom,
crouched in front of the porcelain toilet. Her stomach heaved
and roiled, Michael's warning twisting her insides. . . . *I'll
be watching you . . .*

Alex almost drove right past the woman sitting on the
bench next to the Stop-n-Go. Actually, she had driven past
her, but the idea of a gray-haired woman in a floppy white
hat sitting on a beaten-up bench in her Sunday best on a
Wednesday afternoon, clutching a white purse with white-
gloved fingers, was so out of place that it made her do a
double take. It was the second take that made her gasp and
turn the car around.

What was Ruth Kraziak doing on the edge of town dressed
like she was going to church? It was the middle of the week
and St. Stanislas was five blocks away. Alex parked the car,
got out. Uncle Walter would have to wait another day for
the information and photos he'd requested because it didn't
look like Alex was going to make it to the post office today.

"Mrs. Kraziak?" she called, walking up to the older
woman. "Ruth?"

Ruth Kraziak blinked, turned toward Alex. "Oh. Hello."
She tilted her head and the hat flopped to one side. "You're
the young lady Norman introduced me to the other day."

"Yes. I'm Alex."

Her thin lips pulled into a frown. "Alex. That's a boy's
name."

"It's short for Alexandra."

"Alexandra." The name rolled off her lips. "Alexandra."

"May I sit down?"

Ruth Kraziak lifted a white-gloved hand, arced it in the air. "Sit down, Alexandra."

Alex slid onto the bench, folded her hands in her lap. *Did Norman know his wife was sitting on a bench in front of the Stop-n-Go?*

"I hope she makes it today," Ruth said, consulting the small gold watch on her left wrist.

"Who?"

A hint of a smile crossed the older woman's lips. "Caroline."

Caroline? Ruth's Caroline? "How did you get here, Mrs. Kraziak?"

"I drove, how else would I get here?"

"I guess it would be kind of far to walk from where you live." Hadn't Norman told her she wasn't supposed to be driving? Yes, yes, Alex remembered the scene in his office the first time she'd met Ruth, because she'd felt sorry for her, embarrassed, even. And hadn't Ruth acknowledged what he'd said, blamed it on some medicine she was taking?

"Indeed." Ruth slouched a little against the back of the bench. "Though I tried once or twice. Norman knows I come here every Wednesday. I've told him I want to be here when she gets off that bus but he keeps misplacing the extra set of keys." She leaned forward, whispered, "I think he may be getting a little . . . forgetful. You know"—she touched her hat—"light upstairs."

"Oh, no, I didn't know." She'd bet Norman had no idea Ruth was here.

She nodded. "He's a very proud man. I would never say anything; it would only make him feel worse. How do you tell a person you've been married to for forty-five years that his mind is out of focus?"

"I . . . I don't know."

"Neither do I. But yesterday, when he was at work, I

searched every drawer in the house, even the silverware ones, and found the extra keys.'' Her plain brown eyes lit up. ''They were in the bathroom, behind the Right Guard deodorant and Dr. Scholl's foot powder.''

''Does Norman know—'' She stopped, tried again. ''Are you here by yourself?''

''No. You're here, aren't you, Alexandra?'' She reached over, patted Alex's hand. ''I do hope Caroline comes today. I'd like you to meet her. Ah''—she smiled—''she's a mother's delight.''

''Why do you think she'll come today?'' *Or any day?*

The older woman pointed to the Greyhound sign on the edge of the Stop-n-Go building. ''See that sign? Nick couldn't bring her. She has to come by bus.''

''I see.''

''Have you met Nick, her husband? He's the doctor in town, takes care of most of the people who live here.''

Alex's chest tightened, her throat clogged up. She fought for air, tried to overcome the dizzying sensation that threatened to engulf her, suck her in. ''I . . .'' She forced the words out, ''I've met him.''

''He's wonderful. Isn't he wonderful, Alexandra? Imagine such a kind, caring person being married to my daughter.'' Her voice turned soft, melodic. ''It was a storybook romance, those two, since high school. Love at first sight. From the day they met, they've never looked at another person; it's always been Caroline and Nick. Isn't that wonderful, especially in our world today, when everybody's switching partners, hopping in and out of bed faster than grasshoppers?''

Alex thought she was going to be sick. She felt like an invader, a mistress, the other woman.

''Look, Alexandra, down there.'' Ruth pointed to the bus. ''It's coming. Oh, I do hope she's on it.''

They waited in silence as the bus pulled up to the stop, its gears shifting and grinding, exhaust fumes filling the air.

When the bus door opened, six people filed out, three white-haired women carrying shopping bags, one hunched-over balding man with a newspaper, and two teenage girls with backpacks slung over their shoulders. The bus driver got out and went into the store.

"I . . ." Ruth swallowed, look confused. "I thought she'd be on this bus."

"It doesn't look like she is." *She's not coming home, Ruth. Ever.* Alex would never say the words; they'd be too cruel, too painful, too hopeless, and Ruth needed something to hold on to. Maybe that hope, distorted and unreal as it was, got her through the day, pushed her to get up in the morning, breathe in, breathe out.

"Maybe"—she twisted her gloved hands in her lap—"maybe she fell asleep, maybe she's still on the bus."

No, Ruth, no, she's not on the bus. "Would you like me to check?"

Hope lit her eyes. "Would you?"

Alex gripped Ruth Kraziak's fingers, squeezed through the cotton fabric of her gloves. "I'll be right back." She made her way to the bus, hesitated the briefest of seconds, then climbed the steps to the tiny platform next to the bus driver's seat. A handful of people remained on the bus: a teenage boy and girl, brother and sister probably, with earphones in their ears, staring straight ahead, a large, middle-aged woman, head thrust back against the headrest, snoring, and way in the back, a twenty-something man with wire-rimmed glasses, reading the newspaper.

Alex turned around and headed down the steps. "I'm sorry, Ruth, she's not there."

The older woman's lower lip trembled. "I thought today . . . maybe today . . ." her words slid into silence.

Alex sat down next to Ruth. The Greyhound-bus driver came out of Stop-n-Go carrying a Biggie drink and a bag of potato chips. She waited until he pulled away from the curb, heading for Pittsburgh, before she said, "Do you want to go now?"

Ruth shook her head. "No." Her voice was small, fractured.

"Okay, I'll just sit with you a while, if that's okay with you." *How long had she been doing this, coming here, waiting for her daughter to step off the Greyhound bus? How old was Justin? Almost eight. Had Ruth been coming here for eight years? Hadn't anyone tried to help her? Norman? Nick?*

Seconds passed, then minutes, then a half hour, then three quarters of an hour, and still they sat, silent, waiting; for what, Alex had no idea, but the thought of this poor woman alone on this splintered park bench was too pathetic for her to consider, so she didn't, she just sat. Crazy thoughts rumbled through Alex's head, images of a woman, shadowed and indistinct, waiting for her, calling her name, missing her. And a man, reaching, reaching, swinging her into his arms, holding her tight.

The screech of tires yanked her back to the present. A black Lincoln Town Car pulled up to the curb and Norman Kraziak half fell out in his rush to get to them.

"Ruth! I was worried to death something happened to you." His gaze flew over Alex, rested on his wife. "I just stopped home to get my glasses, and you were gone. . . ."

"I thought she'd be here today." It was the softest of whispers.

Norman ran both hands over his face, drew in a deep breath, touched his wife's shoulder. "Come on, Ruth. It's time to go home."

Alex followed them in Ruth's car, stayed while Norman placed his wife's floppy white hat on the dresser and removed her shoes and gloves with the gentlest of care. Ruth Kraziak sat on the edge of the bed, half frozen, as though his ministrations were performed on someone else, not her. Alex watched as Norman eased his wife's head back onto the pillow and pulled the cream comforter around her small body. He didn't cry until they were downstairs, in the kitchen, drinking the iced tea Alex found in the fridge.

"I can't . . . I can't. . . ." He buried his head in his hands. "I don't know how much longer I can do this, Alex."

She stared at his shoulders heaving up and down, wanting to comfort him, to help, yet not knowing how. Such honest emotion had always been a stranger in her family, unwelcome, forbidden. It exposed too much, left open wounds, raw edges that couldn't be covered with makeup or fancy words. Avoidance. That was the tactic.

"Has she been going there since . . . the accident?"

He pinched the bridge of his nose. "Every July, the whole month if she can." His voice cracked. "That's the month . . . the month . . . it happened. Caroline sent her a letter and told her she'd be coming home on the Greyhound bus just as soon as the baby could travel. Nick couldn't come." He lifted his head; his eyes were red, swollen. "The bus only comes to Restalline on Wednesdays."

"Norman"—she laid a hand on his forearm—"have you ever considered getting help for Ruth?"

"That's all Nick used to say to me, 'Get help, get help.' How? How do you get a person help when they don't want it?" He blew out a long breath, scratched his head. "He finally convinced her to see Dr. Endson and take the pills he gave her to relax, be less jumpy."

"That's good." She hated the look on his face, tortured, helpless.

"I know I should make her go talk to somebody," his voice was small, barely audible, "but I can't bring myself to do it. I'm afraid, Alex, afraid of what they'll say. What if they took her away, put her in a home? I . . . I can't let them do that to her."

"What about you, Norman?"

"Me? I don't care about me, just Ruth and Justin. And Nick, of course. He's been like a son to me."

"Did you ever think about getting out of here, taking her away, maybe to a place where every inch of space didn't remind her of Caroline?"

"Hundreds of times. Even picked a spot in Arizona. Tempe."

"Then why don't you go, Norman? Take Ruth, start over. Try. She might still end up needing professional help, but at least you'd have tried."

"It's not that easy, Alex. I've got the businesses . . . they'll be Justin's one day. I've got to do right by him. . . ." He rubbed a hand over his jaw. "Who'd want to buy two businesses out in the middle of nowhere? Who, Alex?"

She'd been so immersed in Norman's grief, so torn by the sight of Ruth in her floppy white hat sitting on the bench waiting for a daughter who would never come, that she'd thought of nothing but helping the Kraziaks ease their pain. When she'd suggested leaving Restalline, there'd been no ulterior motive, no subterfuge; she'd wanted only to help them in the truest sense of the word.

But now, now Norman had confessed a deep longing to get away, somehow. Alex could help, she could, she could get him out of here, she knew how, she had the power. It would all be so easy now.

But what of the rest of them? The town, the people, the Androvich family? They would hate her, all of them, when they found out, especially Nick. He would hate her most of all.

Chapter 12

It was 11:50 P.M. The Lubovich house was dark. Edna and Chuck went to bed every night right after Jay Leno's monologue. Saturday and Sunday were exceptions, when they watched Turner Broadcast Classics until 1:00 or 2:00 A.M. Last weekend they'd seen *Casablanca* and *Twelve Angry Men*.

Alex let herself in the side door and flicked on the entry hall light. All she wanted to do was sink into bed, bury her head under the covers, and stay there. For a day, a week, as long as it took to sort out the mess she was in. Uncle Walter had called twice today, looking for reports, projections, specs, and most of all, her recommendation regarding the project. *What the hell's going on up there, Alex? What's slowing you down? This isn't like you to be dragging your feet so long. You usually know within forty-eight hours if a deal's a go or not. Do I need to come there myself to get the*

ball rolling? What about Kraziak? What about Androvich?
Have you sniffed them out, found their weak spots? What
the hell have you been doing up there?

Now, there was a question. She and Nick had taken Justin
to Mama Lina's for pizza tonight, but she'd barely been
able to finish her first piece. It wasn't the extra cheese or
pepperoni that did her in, it was the memory of Norman
Kraziak, hunched over and defeated, asking her who would
possibly be interested in buying his businesses. It had been
four days, but she could still see him, still hear the words.
Who'd want to buy two businesses out in the middle of
nowhere? Who, Alex? She hadn't told Uncle Walter about
the conversation she'd had with Norman, though she didn't
know why; there'd been plenty of opportunity. But it just
hadn't seemed right to capitalize on the man's pain in that
moment. Later, when Norman could think more clearly,
without emotion, without the image of Ruth sitting on the
bench waiting for a bus that would never come, then, she'd
tell her uncle.

And Nick. How could she tell him Ruth had said he and
Caroline were made for each other, a perfect match, so in
love that neither had looked at another person since the day
they met? How could she look at him and speak without
choking on the words, the images, the confusion running
through her brain? She couldn't, and so she said nothing.

Time and sleep, that's what she needed right now. Alex
pulled the key from her purse, looked, froze. *What the—*
There was a figure huddled against the door. In the faint
gleam of light she made out a pink sundress, pink sandals,
a pink crocheted handbag lying on the floor.

"Tracy?"

The woman, not more than a teenager really, with pigtails
and pink ribbons in her hair, raised her head. Black streaks
of mascara ran down a face swollen with tears. "Alex?"
Her lower lip quivered. "I . . . I'm sorry." Her shoulders

shook with each word. "I don't want Mom to know, not with Dad just getting out of the hospital and all. I . . . I had no place else to go." This last she finished with a low keening moan.

Alex knelt down beside the young woman, placed a hand over hers. "Why don't you come inside?"

"Thanks." She swiped a piece of blonde hair from her face. "You won't . . . you won't tell my mom, will you?"

"No." Alex stood up, helped Tracy to her feet, then slid the key in the lock.

Tracy stepped inside, sniffed. "I just knew from what Mom told me that I could count on you."

What had Edna said? Why? If she only knew . . . Guilt wedged in her throat, made the next words almost impossible to get out. "You *can* count on me."

The tears came then, heart-wrenching sobs of grief and pain. "I don't think he loves me anymore, Alex. I don't." The words slid to a whisper of despair. "Oh, God." Tracy buried her head in her hands, swayed, crumpled her small body against Alex.

"It's okay," Alex said words that needed saying. Right or wrong, they would give Tracy strength—she hoped. She guided the young woman into the living room, helped her to the couch, and flicked on a table lamp. The room lit up in soft shades of pink. "Why don't you tell me what happened." She felt like a mother or an older sister preparing to hear a tale of heartache, though she had no words of wisdom to share, and hoped she wouldn't be asked for any.

"He started on me the minute he got home from work. I don't know"—she shook her blonde head—"he thinks I'm his slave and I'm *not*. I told him I'm not his mother or my mother, I'm my own person." She jabbed her chest. "Me. And he can't force me to be something or somebody I'm not. That's right, isn't it, Alex? He can't force me to cook and clean and fold his clothes."

"No." *This was Edna's daughter?* She wondered what Tracy thought of her mother ironing her father's underwear and socks?

"Right. That's what I told him."

"But it would be nice if you could find a halfway point." A jar of Prego and an occasional spray of 409 might go a long way.

"He thinks I have nothing to do all day, says I should have had the decency to fix him a meal, even if it's a TV dinner. What do you think?"

What did Alex know about domestic expectations? Aunt Helen had always planned the week's menus and handed them over to Rosa. And with Eric it had been takeout or eat out. "Well, I don't know a lot about cooking, but I do know quite a bit about negotiations, and it sounds like that's what the two of you need to do."

"Huh?" Tracy sniffed.

"Well, negotiate. He wants a meal; what do you want? Cleanup? A picture hung? A garden bed dug out? A movie on Saturday night?"

"I don't know." She shrugged, smoothed her pink dress over her knees. "I just don't want him to *expect* me to do it, that's the thing, you know?"

"Then talk to him, Tracy. Negotiate what's important."

"Hmmm."

"Do you care about Ted?"

Her eyes filled with tears. "God, yes. I love him so much it hurts."

"Then stop coming here, to this apartment. Don't run away from your problems, stay there, fight, let him know you care and you're not giving up. Make him feel he's worth it, the relationship is worth it."

"You think so?"

"I do." God, she felt like such an imposter. When had she ever been able to commit, really commit to a relationship with a man? When hadn't she given up when they got too close, too personal, the situation too difficult? Would the same thing happen with Nick?

Tracy wiped her eyes, streaks of mascara smearing on her cheeks and fingers. "Thanks, Alex. Thanks a lot." She smiled then, looking so young, so vulnerable, making Alex feel so . . . old.

"You're welcome. I hope it helps."

"It does, definitely." Tracy pushed back a lock of hair, studied her. "No wonder you snagged Dr. Nick."

"What? I didn't—"

Tracy laughed. "Sure you did, Alex. The whole town's talking about it." Her voice turned serious. "I'm glad. He deserves to be happy." She grabbed her handbag, fished out her keys. "You take care of him. He was my first crush, did my mom tell you that? I never thought I'd get over him. God, but he's beautiful." She didn't seem to notice that Alex hadn't replied. "Oh, and thanks for not saying anything to my parents about this." Tracy gave her a quick hug. "I knew I could trust you, Alex, I just knew."

The night was hot, the air still. A slit of moon spilled over Sapphire Lake, casting it into luminescent calmness. *Breathe, just breathe*, it seemed to say as its waters lapped and fell upon each other in gentle repetition.

Alex stared, transfixed, lulled by the water and the aftermath of Nick's lovemaking. He lay beside her, naked, his hand resting on her hip, fingers stroking her flesh in slow, absentminded circles. She shivered. Silence, thick, heavy, pulsing with emotion, blanketed them, pulled them together. There were no words, there hadn't been since the moment Nick dropped the blanket on the ground and eased the tank top over her head. It had been only sensation then, pure, elemental, mixed with emotions too deep for words, too confusing for interpretation. It had been ten days since Marie Lendergin's wedding, and still their lovemaking was no less needy, no less consuming than it had been on the first day, or the third, the fifth, the seventh, the ninth. This wanting of another person, this passion that devoured waking moments was new and frightening for Alex, and yet . . . and yet . . . she craved it. But it wasn't only the physical union that left her breathless, it was the *being* together, and the quiet, the space between the words, like now.

People were talking about them. Alex saw them staring when she and Nick and Justin stopped at Hot Ed's for sausage subs or the Stop-n-Go for Justin's favorite, a raspberry Slurpee. Most smiled, nodded their approval, offered a few well-placed, if indirect, hints that they wouldn't mind seeing Alex in Restalline on a more permanent basis. The worst offender, and most blatant spokesperson, was Stella Androvich. *You've made Nick happy, Alex,* she'd said, tears in her brown eyes. *It's been a long time since he's smiled like that, a long time.* And then there was Gracie. *So, like, do you think you might find some reason to hang around, Alex? Huh? Like, for good?* Only one person's voice hung in the back of her mind, shifting to the forefront every night just as she was drifting to sleep. *You can screw him all you want but you better not screw with him, you got that Goldilocks? . . . I'll be watching you . . . I'll be watching you . . .* Michael Androvich. She hadn't seen him since that morning, though she'd looked for him everywhere, was always wondering if he was behind her, in front of her, watching . . .

She couldn't let this relationship develop any further without saying something to Nick. It was time. . . . Time to try before it was too late.

"What would you think," she began, "about getting away for a few days?"

His face was in profile, nose, mouth, chin, and she couldn't see his expression. When he spoke, his voice was slow, measured. "What did you have in mind?"

"I know this place in Upstate New York, quiet, secluded . . ." *If he sees Krystal Springs for himself, he'll fall in love with it. I know he will.*

Nick blew out a long breath. "I thought you were going to go metropolitan on me, New York City, D.C., population fifty gazillion."

She laughed. *Maybe this part will be easier than I thought.* "No, nothing like that. It's quiet, surrounded with trees and lakes, trails for horseback riding or backpacking."

"Sounds like my kind of place."

Much easier than I thought. Once he saw it, saw the magnitude of the operation, the beauty of it, maybe, just maybe, he'd seriously consider selling Androvich Lumber. Then, she could offer Norman a deal without feeling any guilt . . . and then . . . maybe Nick would consider setting up practice somewhere closer to her . . . much closer . . .

"I think you'd really like it."

He ran his hand up and down her back, long, slow strokes. "I like the quiet part."

"Can you take off a few days?" His fingers curved to the side of her breast. *Focus, focus, this is important.*

"I should be able to get coverage for three, four days. And Mom can watch Justin."

"I . . . I'd suggest taking him, but . . ." *Will I ever get tired of his touch?*

"Another time," he said. "I like the idea of sleeping in the same bed with you the whole night, not sneaking out at one or two in the morning."

"I do, too."

"Give me a day or two to get coverage and then we can set a date."

"Thanks, Nick."

He pulled her into his arms, kissed her forehead, the tip

of her nose, her mouth. "Yeah, well, you can thank me another way."

She laughed, fell back onto the blanket, his hard body covering hers. "So, what's the name of this great hideout?" he asked, planting kisses along her neck.

God, he was driving her crazy; she wanted him. *Again.* "Krystal Springs."

He was off of her and three feet away before her brain registered that something was wrong. Very wrong. "Krystal Springs? Please tell me you're joking." His words were angry, his body tense. "I wouldn't set foot in that place for a million dollars."

Alex scrambled to sit up, make sense of his reaction. "Why?" was all she could muster.

"Why? *Why?* How much do you know about that place?" His voice shook. "They flattened the town, Alex, the whole thing. They took people's lives, flattened them right out, and turned the town into a playground for the rich."

"No—"

"Yes. Yes, they did. They went in and tore up every house, every landmark, every sign of life as those people knew it."

No. He was making it sound so cruel, sinister, even. *It wasn't like that.* "Those people received money for their property, all of them."

"Jesus, Alex, is it always about money?" He yanked on his jeans. "Some fancy-talking attorney came to town with his right-hand man and convinced them it was the right thing to do."

"How"—she kept her voice even, kept the fear from surfacing in her words—"how do you know that, Nick?" *Eric had been the attorney and she . . . she had been the right-hand man.*

"One of my father's old friends lived there. We used to go fishing and camping up there when we were kids. There was nothing like it, it was so beautiful. Perfect, really. Crisp air, green all around, black dirt. You could see the mountains on a clear day. And then a big corporation came to town one day, started whacking away at the people, little by little, throwing dollar signs in front of their faces, convincing them that they'd be better off in the suburbs with central air-conditioning and two-car garages.''

"Maybe they are."

"Hell, no, they're not." He picked up a stone, skimmed it over the surface of the lake. It skipped eight times, disappeared. ''Not any more than the people in this town would be if somebody came and dumped a pile of money on their table and offered to buy them out.''

She couldn't breathe, couldn't get air . . .

"Leonard tried to hold on as long as he could, but he's an old man, his health is failing . . .''

"Leonard?" She knew, *knew* what he was going to say next.

"Leonard, my dad's friend. Leonard Oshanski. He sold out for his nieces and nephews; *he* didn't give a damn about the money. All he cared about was preserving a maple tree his father had planted on their land when his little sister died. I told him not to count on it staying, even if they'd promised; people break promises all the time. But he said, no, this one person, this woman had given her word. And he believed her.'' He let out a cold, hard laugh. ''What do you think, Alex? You think that maple's plowed ten feet under? I do, no doubt about it.''

"Are these absolutely delicious, or what?" Gracie spoke around a mouthful of Hot Ed's sausage, pepper, and onion.

"They're delicious," Alex said, taking a bite. She and Gracie had gone to the Market Basket to get a few things on Stella's list, and halfway out of town Gracie had had a sudden craving for a Hot Ed's sausage sub. And now, here they were.

"I really hope it's okay if you eat this thing."

Gracie grinned. "What's the worst that could happen? I might go into labor?" She dug out a french fry, dipped it in ketchup. "I'm thirty-seven weeks now, Alex, and big as a house. Besides, I haven't slept in over a month, or"—she leaned over, whispered—"had sex with Rudy." She laughed when Alex blushed. "I wouldn't mind going into labor now. As a matter of fact, if I thought the sub would do it, I'd eat another one."

"You know what Nick said—"

Gracie waved a hand at her. "Nick says a lot of things. That's what big brothers are for, right? Especially a big brother who's a doctor; he's really a pain, it's like having a watchdog with you 24-7."

"He just said be careful—"

"Yeah, yeah, yeah. I know. Don't go wandering around too far from home, bring a cell phone, take a nap, blah, blah, blah."

Alex smiled. "You are a very noncompliant patient."

"Hey, Nick's my brother, not my doctor."

"So, what did your doctor say?"

She gave her a sheepish grin. "Same thing."

"Eat your sub, Gracie."

"I will." She took another bite, leaned back in her chair, rubbed her belly with her left hand. "Oh, Alex, wait until you have kids one day. You'll learn all the joys of hemorrhoids, varicose veins, stretch marks, heartburn—" She stopped suddenly, clutched her belly. "Yow!"

"What? What is it, Gracie?"

The color drained from Gracie's face. "I . . . I . . . ." She massaged her fingers over her belly. "Oh, man!" She squeezed her eyes shut, took several quick little breaths. "It's either heartburn or . . . or I'm having a contraction."

"I'll call Nick." Alex reached in her purse, grabbed her cell phone.

"Wait." Gracie panted. "Just . . . wait. Don't want to overreact. She panted again, blinked hard. "I'm not sure."

"Well, how will you know? We can't just sit here, we need to get help."

"Alex. Stop. Sometimes things just happen on their own . . . in their own time. Relax. I . . . I want to go home, lie down."

"Okay, okay, I can get you there." Action, Alex wanted to do something, anything. She went around to Gracie's side, helped her to her feet. Gracie took a few steps, stopped, and said, "Forget home, take me to the hospital."

"Why? What's wrong?"

Gracie sucked in a breath, gritted her teeth. "My water just broke."

Alex couldn't remember much after that; just a blur of voices and figures moving around her, beside her, giving Gracie instructions, encouragement. Alice was the first, running out from the kitchen carrying a stack of white hand towels. She helped Gracie stand, piled them on the red vinyl seat, her blue-veined bony hands flattening the material. *Take it easy, Gracie,* Alex heard her say. *Little breaths, now, that's a girl. Okay, you're gonna be just fine, just fine.* She sat on a chair next to Gracie, held her hand. *I'll rub your back for you, Gracie, ease some of the pain. Hold on, hold on, that's a girl.*

Bernie called 911, then Nick, then Rudy, then Stella. Alex watched it all, a mere spectator, awed and . . . *afraid.* Yes, she had to admit it, she was afraid; afraid of the pain on her friend's usually jovial face, afraid of a circumstance that stripped control and relied on God and fate for the outcome, afraid of the emotions running through the small diner, so raw, so stripped, so real. She was afraid.

At one point, Gracie held out a hand. *Come here, Alex,*

help me. Alex grabbed a chair, thankful to be doing something, *anything,* and gripped Gracie's fingers. Alice helped Gracie breathe, pant, *he-he-he,* relax. This tiny speck of a woman who cooked sausages with peppers and onions fourteen hours a day showed both women what resolve and focus really meant. When the ambulance came and took Gracie, Alex turned and saw Alice staring at the red and white flashing lights, face pulled in pain, eyes bright, burning, haunted. Then Alice turned and disappeared into the kitchen. It wasn't until later that night, when Alex and Nick were lying in bed, recalling the very loud, very demanding entrance of Rudy Steven Romanski Jr. in the back of the ambulance, *he's got his mother's big mouth and his father's big feet,* Nick had said, that Alex thought of Alice, thought of her spirit, her take-charge attitude . . . her face when the ambulance pulled up.

"Alice really knows a lot about labor," she said.

Nick was silent for a few seconds, his hand trailing up and down her back in casual intimacy. Did he know even now, scant minutes after they'd made love, that the lightness of his half-distracted touch made her body tingle, made her want him again, close, closer, surpassing the desire for mere physical union?

"Yes," he answered, "Alice knows a lot about labor."

She saw Alice's face, leathery and lined. "How many children does she have?"

His fingers stilled. "She had three."

"Had? What happened to them?"

"The first child was stillborn, a little girl, Elizabeth Ann. And the second, John Henry, died of meningitis when he was about six."

Alex's chest tightened. "How tragic." She pictured Alice, her thin body bent over, rubbing Gracie's back. Had she done that with her little boy, rubbed his body, soothed him, watched him die?

"Samuel was the baby. Spoiled rotten. Bernie and Alice bought him a motorcycle for his sixteenth birthday, a Harley." He blew out a long breath. "He died two weeks later going around a bend on a rainy night."

"Oh, my God." The words reverberated through her body.

"Sometimes God has nothing to do with it."

Alex lifted her head, stared at him. The dim light filtered through the pink lamp shade on the bedside table, making his features dark, unreadable. "How can you say that? Don't you think He could have stopped those children from dying if He'd wanted to? Don't you think He should have?"

"There was a reason, it had to happen, I believe that. But God doesn't *make* bad things happen, or necessarily stop them from happening. What He does do is give us strength to understand and persevere, learn from and through the tragedy."

"You really believe that?"

He nodded. "I do."

Alex laid her head on his chest, the slow rhythmic beat of his heart flowing to her, through her. He believed his words, she could tell by the way he said them, with such conviction, such certainty. She and Nick were so different. Too different? Nick had family and faith and a town of people who knew him, trusted him, loved him, even. What did she have? An uncle who measured his love by her ability to close a deal, an ex-husband who only wanted her because he didn't have her, a wall filled with degrees and certificates instead of photographs, an apartment filled with glass and chrome? There were no brothers, no sisters . . . no parents, not even memories of parents.

Were she and Nick just too different to form any kind of a real, lasting relationship? Did she want one?

"Alex?"

Did she?

"Hey, are you sleeping?"

She shook her head. "No."

"You did a good job with Gracie tonight."

"Huh. I was petrified. All I did was hold her hand, try to give her support, but I think it was Gracie who was giving *me* support. Alice did everything."

"But you were there. Sometimes it's just being there that means the most, especially when you're scared."

"I felt so ... inadequate, I guess that's the word. And helpless."

"I know."

"I can't imagine you ever feeling that way, Nick."

He stroked her hair, said, "The last two years with Caroline, all I felt was inadequate and helpless." He stopped, as though thinking and rethinking his next words. "It was very difficult. I'm a doctor, I should have been able to help her and I couldn't. I could save other people but I couldn't save my own wife." His voice fell. "God, I tortured myself. I couldn't make her happy no matter what I did. She said she was alone all the time, said she had no friends, so on my nights off I'd sometimes arrange a get-together with a few colleagues, but she didn't like that because she said they were all city types, not like the people in Restalline. When I was working, she'd call the hospital three, four times a night to say she missed me or was scared. We moved to a suburb so it would be more like a small town, and still, it wasn't enough." He let out a long breath. "Nothing was enough. She came back to Restalline, spent weeks here, couldn't wait to move back for good when I got through with my residency. But that wouldn't have been enough, either. What she really wanted was to go back and have everything be the way it was before, when she was sixteen and we were dating and she had nothing more to think about than what to wear on Saturday night. If she'd have lived, this town wouldn't have made her happy; nothing would have."

Alex heard the frustration in his words, felt the pain in the spaces between. The idyllic union of Nick and Caroline had not been so idyllic after all. "But maybe," she said, "with Justin, things would have been different. She might have changed." She wanted to say "grown up," but didn't.

"Maybe, but she couldn't hold on long enough to get help. The fire started in the kitchen that night; she should've been able to get out, at least yell for help . . . unless she was so drugged up she couldn't wake up . . . or didn't want to."

"Oh, Nick—"

"I don't ever want Justin to know. He needs stories of his mother loving him, fighting the devil himself to stay alive. The hell of it is, all Caroline ever wanted to do was be a mother, more than anything . . . but after Justin was born, she barely wanted to look at him. I thought it might be postpartum depression, thought about having her see someone . . . but I wasn't quick enough. . . ."

"I'm sure you did everything—"

He cut her off. "Everything I could? That's the hell of it, Alex. I honestly don't know if I did everything I could. Maybe I never should've let her leave the hospital. Maybe I should've ignored her pleas, made her see somebody. Maybe then she'd still be alive."

Alex closed her eyes, tried to shut out the pain of those last words. And then he spoke again. "But if we were still together, it would have been out of guilt, not love. That's no way to raise a child, and it's no way to live a life." He tightened his hold on her. "And you, Alex Chamberlain, you would have been nothing more than a mere acquaintance, and that I would have regretted most of all."

Chapter 13

The scream, a sharp, piercing howl, resonated through the walls, jolting them awake. Alex jumped up first, grabbed a robe. "It's Edna. Something's wrong." She ran out of the bedroom, naked under the pink cotton, barefoot, hair flying.

Nick yanked on his jeans, pulled the polo over his head, and ran a hand through his hair. *Jesus,* he thought, *Chuck.* When he reached the bottom landing, Edna's howl had turned into a long, consistent wail mixed with a hiccup of barely intelligible words.

"Chuck. Chuck. No. No! Jesus, dear sweet God, no."

Nick hurried into the living room; Alex was calling 911, Edna was crumpled in the corner of the room, head bent, crying. Direct center, positioned six feet from the television was Chuck Lubovich in his green-and-gold Lay-Z-Boy, eyes wide open, head tilted to one side, mouth slack. His face was ashen, both arms dangling from the edge of the recliner.

He knew even before he felt the cold skin on the old man's neck that there would be no pulse. Chuck Lubovich was dead.

"Oh, Dr. Nick," Edna said, rising and half lunging at him, "thank God you're here. Help. Please, help Chuck."

He glanced up at Alex, saw the hint of understanding in her eyes before she put her arm around Edna and said, "He'll do whatever he can, Edna. You know that."

"I . . . can't lose him." She shook her red head, a bobby pin glinted in the light. "Not now . . . not yet. Oh, God, not yet."

"Let's go in the bedroom. Come on." Alex took her arm, led her away. "It's out of our hands. You know that, Edna. Now, it's God's will. We'll pray He gives you strength to understand . . . and persevere."

They were the very words Nick had spoken hours before. She'd challenged them then, and yet now she'd used them to ease Edna's grief. Would he ever truly understand Alex Chamberlain? No, he didn't think so. He folded Chuck's arms over his stomach, pulled up a chair, and sat down to wait for the ambulance.

Elise opened the back door of her Honda Civic and lifted out the box. Croissants, fresh from the bakery, stuffed with ham and cheese, grapes, juice boxes, and cream puffs for dessert. She hadn't planned on dropping off dinner at Michael Androvich's house, but Nick had mentioned his mother was going over to Gracie's to help her out with the baby, so Michael, or more correctly, Kevin and Sara, would probably be on their own for a meal tonight. They'd be lucky if they got Spaghettio's or leftover pizza.

Michael Androvich was not one of her favorite people right now, though she'd seen Kevin and Sara almost every day for the past two weeks at Stella's. They'd called her at work, begged her to come see them, play a game of Sorry or Uno, take them to the park, or her father's bakery. Stella had seemed pleased with the children's attention toward Elise, even encouraged them to go. Michael had said nothing; chances were he didn't even know about her visits. Ever since Marie Lendergin's wedding, he'd avoided her, pretending he didn't see her when she drove by downtown, turning his back, looking away. The few times he'd called Nick at the office, he'd been abrupt, almost angry. What was his problem? She'd done nothing, not a thing. Elise thought of Marie's wedding, thought of the pillow dance and Michael kneeling before her. Was this whole cold shoulder about *that?* About the split second before the kiss that almost happened when they'd looked into each other's eyes and . . . no! Of course it wasn't. What a ridiculous, silly notion. Lord knew, the man looked at lots of women, actually did a lot more than *look* at them. He probably didn't even remember the incident, he was most likely just ticked about something, who knew what, and was being his typical self: a jerk. So what if he was ignoring her? It wasn't as though they'd been good friends, or friends at all; they'd been more . . . acquaintances, people who shared mutual friends, that was all.

Oh, and there was the small fact that Elise was head over heels crazy in love with Michael's brother, and the two brothers were at odds with one another over heaven knew what, though deep down, Elise thought Michael might be jealous of Nick. Who really knew? The man infuriated her, period. He was arrogant, and willful, and sarcastic. And he saw more about her than she wanted him to see—like the fact that she was in love with a man who didn't know she existed in any capacity other than as his employee.

She walked up the stone pathway, shaking her head at

the mounds of weeds pushing out over the sides of the slabs. The house was a two-story log cabin made of rough-hewn logs, with wide windows and a front porch. If she owned it, she'd fill the wooden planters on either side of the steps with petunias and pansies, white, pink, and purple. She'd hang ferns from the rafters, and a grapevine wreath on the front door, layered in chrysanthemums and hyacinths. She'd give the children sunflower seeds and a trowel so they could plant them on the side of the house where the sun was brightest. She'd . . . *good God,* what was she thinking?

Elise rested the box on her knee, got ready to ring the doorbell. No! This was a mistake, a stupid mistake. She should never have come *here,* to his house. What was wrong with her? Kevin and Sara could survive one night of Spaghettio's or cold pizza. She'd just leave now. No one would ever have to know she'd had a momentary brain lapse. Elise hefted the box up higher to get a better grip.

The door flung open. "What the hell—"

She dropped the box, stared at Michael Androvich, bare-chested, fly half open, hair ruffled and unkempt. He looked like he'd been . . . like he'd been . . .

"What the hell are you doing here?" His brown eyes were almost black.

"I . . ." She tilted her head toward the box. "I brought the kids dinner."

"They're not here," he said. "And I'm not a damn charity case."

"Michael," a woman's voice came from inside, spilled over them, "who is it, sweetheart?"

"Is that . . . is that . . . ?"

He glared at her, stepped forward, and pulled the door shut. "None of your damn business who it is."

"It is, isn't it?" Cynthia Collichetti. Bartender at Cody's and town slut.

Michael ignored her. "Listen here, Snow White. Why don't you take that little Italian ass of yours out of here before those virgin eyes see something they shouldn't?"

"Cynthia Collichetti." Word had it she'd slept with men who were sixteen—which would make them boys in Elise's mind—and every age after that up to and including Mr. Simpson, a seventy-six-year-old widower who drove a black Cadillac and smoked thin cigars. "Cynthia Collichetti," she repeated again. "You're a pig."

He reached out, grabbed her arm. "Damn right I am, honey, and don't you forget it."

She tried to twist away, but he tightened his grip, took a step closer. He smelled of beer and too-sweet vanilla, probably from Cynthia Collichetti. "Let go, you're hurting me."

"Not as much as I'm going to if I catch you coming around here again." He pulled her to him, dark face inches from hers. "You come here again, Snow White, and I'm gonna think you're looking for something." He patted the front of his pants. "And I'm gonna give it to you."

Elise broke free, ran to her car, the sound of his laughter rolling over her as she flung open the car door. She stopped, turned slowly. Michael was laughing, his eyes on her, arms crossed over his chest like a giant statue, strong, powerful ... all alone. He might be a jerk, and she'd called him a pig, but he wouldn't hurt her, even with his threats. Deep inside, she felt that, *knew* it. And in that instant, she knew his bad-boy behavior was more contrived than real. Anger boiled inside, a slow, quiet rage that wanted to lash out, hurt.

"You don't scare me, Michael Androvich," she yelled at him. "You're the one who's scared!"

He started toward her, fists clenched. "You watch your mouth."

"What are you afraid of, Michael? Afraid if you act like a decent human being people will start to expect things from you? Maybe expect you to be responsible, carry your own weight?"

"Shut up."

"Oh, this way, who cares what you do, right?" Her voice trembled. "You order a pizza and sit in front of the television with Kevin and Sara while you eat, and that's considered dinner, right? And nobody says anything because at least you're feeding them, right?"

"I said, shut up." He was standing less than two feet from her.

"You're afraid to settle whatever it is between you and Nick because then you might have to actually be responsible for the business, and what if you screw up, make a mistake? Oh, my God, what then, Michael? So just let Nick handle it even though he doesn't know half as much as you do about the business and he's got a practice to run. That's it, isn't it? Just think of Michael, think about what Michael wants."

"You're fucked up."

"Maybe I am. Maybe I am . . . fucked up. But I'm not sleeping around because I'm afraid of a real relationship. And I'm not blaming my ex-wife for my *fucked up* life. And I'm not hanging out at Cody's and ignoring my kids because I think I've gotten a raw deal. I'm not doing any of those things. You are."

"Get the hell out of here. Now!"

"I'm going!" She got in her car, slammed the door. "For somebody so strong, you're the weakest man I ever met."

"And stay away from my kids!"

Elise started the engine. "How will you know if I come near them or not? Huh, Michael? How are you gonna know when you're never with them?"

"Fuck you!" he shouted. "They're my kids. Stay away from them."

She sucked in a breath. "Be a father, Michael. And if you won't"—she stared straight at him—"then fuck you, Michael Androvich. *Fuck you.*" Then she threw the car in reverse and tore out, leaving a trail of gravel and dust in her wake.

It wasn't until she was past his house, past the split-rail fence marking the edges of his property that she started shaking. And then the tears came, hard, fast, heavy, half blurring her vision, clogging her throat. She needed to talk to someone, confess what she'd done, get absolution. *She'd just told Michael Androvich to go fuck himself.* God, she hadn't said anything like that, ever. The closest she'd come was seventh grade English at St. Stanislas when Tommy O'Reilly said her parents needed to take an English class or get back on a boat to Italy. She'd turned around and told him to go to hell, right there in the classroom with Sister Winnifred standing at the head of the class pointing out prepositional phrases with her wooden ruler.

Stella Androvich. She would listen; she was the one Elise needed to talk to. Would she be back from Gracie's yet? Elise reached for a Kleenex, blew her nose, swiped at her cheeks. *No more tears*, she told herself. *No more.* By the time she reached Stella's driveway, she began to wonder if baring her soul to the mother of the two men who caused the most anguish in her life was such a wise idea. Maybe she should keep her own council, wait and see if Michael said anything. Of course, he wouldn't, she knew that.

The decision to blurt out her story or keep quiet was over the minute Stella opened the door and saw her standing in the doorway like a pathetic urchin. "Elise? What on earth is wrong, dear?"

No tears, no tears, no tears . . . But they came anyway,

choking out Elise's voice. She could do no more than shake her head.

"Elise! Elise! Wanna play on the tire swing?" Kevin came running toward her, with Sara two steps behind.

"Swing. Wheeeeee!" Sara ran up, hugged Elise's legs. She bent down and scooped up the little girl in her arms. She had her father's brown eyes . . . and his chin . . .

"Not now, children," Stella said, lifting Sara out of Elise's arms. "Elise and I have to talk. Why don't you two go outside and play?"

"Can I push Sara on the tire swing?"

"Can you be careful? Very careful?"

Kevin nodded his dark head, mouth flat, unsmiling, reminding her of his father in miniature. "I'm always careful, Grandma."

Stella ruffled his crew cut, smiled. "Then off with the two of you. I'll bring out your ice-cream sandwiches in a little while." When the screen door banged behind Kevin and Sara, she turned and said to Elise, "Sit down, child. Tell me what's on your mind."

Elise pulled out a chair, sat down at the kitchen table, bit the inside of her cheek, blinked hard.

"Cry, cry if you need to." The older woman reached out, took her hand.

"I . . . I . . . it's awful." Tears slid down Elise's face. "I did something really awful a little while ago, Stella."

"Elise Pentani, I've known you your whole life, known your father and your mother, God rest her soul. I don't think you're capable of doing anything 'really awful.'"

"I . . ."—she sniffed—"I did. Michael . . ."

"Oh, I see." She nodded, heaved a sigh. "Finally. This is about Michael."

"I thought I'd bring some food for the kids. Nick said you were going to Gracie's so I figured Michael would have them. Anyway, I got a box of their favorites together, ham and cheese croissants, cream puffs, juice boxes, and I went to deliver it.'' Her lip started to quiver. ''I didn't think . . . I thought Kevin and Sara would be there . . . not Cynthia Collichetti.''

''Oh, I see.''

Elise hung her head, let a heavy drape of hair fall in front of her face. ''That's not the worst of it. I went and confronted Michael about it. Told him he was hiding behind his irresponsible behavior because he's really afraid of making mistakes and . . . and commitment.''

''I'll bet he didn't like that much.'' There was humor in Stella's voice.

''Not at all. He told me . . . to . . . to . . .''

''Michael has a very colorful vocabulary. I can imagine what he said.''

Elise looked up, met the older woman's kind gaze. ''But I told him the same thing, Stella. I can't believe I said some of the things I did, but he made me so mad, I just couldn't control it. No, I didn't *want* to control it, *I wanted to say those things*, I wanted to hurt him.'' Her shoulders sagged. ''What's wrong with me? I'm a horrible, horrible person.''

''No, I'd say you're a normal person with normal human emotions. You were mad, you lashed out.''

''But what I said . . .''

''I love my son, but I'm sure he deserved it.''

Elise shrugged. ''I shouldn't have stooped to his level. He was just trying to scare me away. You know, Michael is more hot air than anything else. I mean, I think underneath all the tough guy stuff is a decent person. I think it's just an act . . . and I told him so.''

''Well, he wouldn't like that. He doesn't want to hear it from his mother or his brother, so I'm sure he wouldn't take too kindly to hearing it from someone outside the family.''

''No, he didn't.''

"But you told him anyway." Her lips curved upward in a hint of a smile.

"I couldn't help myself, he made me so angry."

Stella nodded, patted her hand. "Emotion, girl, honest emotion. You know, sometimes love and hate aren't really that different from each other."

"What?" What did love have to do with Michael Androvich?

"Well, both love and hate are very strong emotions, and sometimes people get confused between the two. They start out with this intense dislike, hate, if you will, and somewhere along the line it changes, and grows into another intense emotion, like love."

"Stella, I am not in love with Michael."

"I didn't say you were, just making a point."

"Michael *could* be a decent human being, and I know he's your son and *you* love him, but right now, he's still a jerk."

"I agree. Michael's a jerk, but I still love him. I can see the real person under all the huff and bluster. Maybe you're starting to see that person, too."

"I still see a jerk." But there had been a few times . . .

"It doesn't happen all at once." Stella got up, went to the sink, and brought back a colander of string beans and a glass bowl. She picked one up, snapped off the ends, and threw it in the bowl. "These things take time."

"What does, Stella?"

"You're not in love with Nick, even though you keep telling yourself you are." She paused. "You thought I didn't know? A mother always knows. It's not love; it's infatuation, with his skill as a doctor, the respect he gets from the town, the fact that he's a genuinely good man. That's not the foundation for love. Besides, he's found his match. He and Alex are perfect for each other, and look at how those two started out. Less than friendly, I'll tell you that. And now, well, now you can't turn around to see one that the other isn't close behind.''

Heat crept up Elise's neck, spread over her face. She grabbed a bean, snapped it, grabbed another. ''Well, I'm not in love with Michael nor do I intend to be, now or at any time in the future.''

''I know dear.'' She smiled. ''I know.''

Chapter 14

I'll miss you.
I'll miss you, too. . . . maybe I could change my schedule
. . . come with you.
No! No. It's only two days.
Sounds like two forevers.
I'll be back in time for Justin's birthday party. I promise.
He's counting on it. . . . I'm counting on it.
So am I.

Alex pushed the elevator button for the eleventh floor.
She glanced at her watch. One-fifteen P.M. Fifteen minutes
late. Uncle Walter would be pacing, despite her phone call
to tell him she was stuck in traffic. He'd thought her plan
to drive from Restalline to Arlington at 4:00 A.M. was ridiculous, had told her in numerous different ways, interrogated

her, asked her if she'd lost her mind *and* her focus. *What the hell is going on up there, young lady? Answer me. What's got a hold on you? Or is the question* who? *Is that it? Are you involved with someone? Good God, Alex, is that it? Are you involved with one of those . . . those . . . hillbillies?*

She'd denied every accusation, though the more he prodded, the weaker her response. And then the anger, a slow burn pulsing through her took over. So what if she was involved with someone? *So what?* Did he care, really care, or was he more concerned that she'd lost focus, as he'd put it, on the project?

Well, she hadn't lost focus. If anything, these last months in Restalline had *given* her focus, real focus, the kind that shapes lives, gives meaning to the insignificant, finds a purpose that's deeper, more valuable than a gold card or a seven-figure bank account. Simple riches, that's what Nick had said. Living, loving, family. The people of Restalline had community. When Chuck Lubovich died, St. Stanislas was packed for his funeral, and people were singing "Amazing Grace," really singing, not just half mouthing the words, and crying into big white handkerchiefs and wads of Kleenex. And the food, Edna had so much food: pumpkin rolls and banana breads, ba'bovka and stuffed cabbage, and chicken paprikash and stuffed dumplings. Yet, it didn't end there. Stella came the first night and stayed with Edna so she wouldn't be alone, and the next night, Elise Pentani, and then Alex found herself sitting by Edna's bed watching her toss and turn in restless slumber.

There was a beauty about this town that went much deeper than the grandness of a massive oak tree or the blueness of Sapphire Lake. It extended to the people themselves, to their selfless acts, to Nick, as he accepted a live chicken from Elmer Figgee as payment for office visits, to Alice at Hot Ed's as she helped Gracie through labor despite the loss of her own children, and to Edna and Chuck Lubovich when they opened their home to Alex, a stranger, never questioning, never doubting.

Alex owed it to these people, and to herself, to make the right decision, the only decision. *Restalline was not for sale*.

She stepped off the elevator and headed for her uncle's suite. His door was open, and as she'd guessed, he was pacing. "It's about time." His pale blue eyes took in her wrinkled suit. "Damn ridiculous idea you had, leaving at some unholy hour of the morning. Don't let it happen again."

"Hello, Uncle Walter." *Not even a hug*. "Nice to see you." She walked to the round table in the corner of the room, set down her briefcase. "I've got the proposals here."

"They were due yesterday."

"I know. I'm sorry." She didn't offer an excuse; he'd never understand Edna's need to visit Chuck at the cemetery for three hours yesterday, or Justin's surprise visit to her apartment . . . or the strength of Nick's arms protecting her, making her want to stay.

"What the devil is going on?" He closed the door, walked toward her.

"What do you mean?"

"This isn't like you, Alex. And it doesn't become you, not at all." He adjusted his gray silk tie, Armani, no doubt. "You don't return my phone calls, and when you do, you sound as though you're a thousand miles away and the last thing on your mind is the project. Eric never received the reports you were supposed to send last week." He tapped his well-manicured nails on the table. "Do you honestly think I can even consider the remote possibility of making you president with this kind of behavior?"

She said nothing.

"Do you?"

Alex shook her head. "No, no I don't."

That seemed to surprise him. His cool blue gaze narrowed

on her. "And that doesn't concern you? What have you been working for all these years, if not for that?"

She tried to find the words to tell him.

"Don't you care? Don't you want to be president of WEC Management?"

The truth lay there between them, cold, stark. "I . . . I . . . No, no, I don't think so."

The left side of his jaw twitched. "You have a chance to obtain a 200 percent increase in your salary and you *don't think so*? What does that mean, Alex? What, in the name of God, does that mean?"

She looked away. *Be strong, be strong.* "It means . . . just what I said. I've . . . done some thinking"—*tell him, tell him*—"and I don't think I want to be president."

"You don't think you want to be president? *What do you want to do, Alex?* Disappear into that hillbilly country and saw lumber for the rest of your life?"

She looked at him, saw the mottled color of his face. Rage. It was pure rage, but he controlled it so well. Her whole life she'd listened to him, followed him, worshiped him, even, desperate for his approval, hoping it would one day transform itself into an expression of love. That's all she'd ever really wanted from him: love. But seeing the people of Restalline, living with them, almost becoming a part of them, had shown her that her uncle wasn't capable of that kind of love—not the selfless, unconditional love of parent to child. He could give her money, education, position, any measure of material wealth, but he could not give her a piece of himself. Her eyes burned as she forced out the words, "I don't know what I want to do, Uncle Walter, but I can't continue to do something I no longer believe in."

"Oh? Oh. I see." He began pacing again. "And what is it that you no longer believe in, Alex? Is it making money?

Does that seem vulgar to you now? Who's changed your mind?''

"No one.'' *Everyone.*

"Do you object to creating, because that's what we're doing, creating vision.''

"But we're destroying beauty to create that vision. Is that right? Is it fair?''

He stared at her. "Stop this foolishness right now. You've been destroying beauty, as you call it, for seven years now. Don't tell me all of a sudden you don't have the stomach for it.'' He inclined his silver head toward her. "You're the best, Alex. The best.''

Two months ago, this dribble of praise would have made her redouble her efforts, work harder, longer, do whatever was necessary to gain another pat on the head. But not now; things were different now. *She* was different. "Restalline isn't for sale,'' she said, forcing herself to meet her uncle's steely gaze. "Even if I wanted to do the deal, you wouldn't get the support. Norman Kraziak is firmly entrenched in his businesses,'' she lied, "and Nick Androvich's company isn't open for discussion.''

Silence filled the room, stretching over her, heavy, suffocating. Could he tell she was lying about Norman? Is that why he was still staring at her, why he hadn't said a word, why his jaw twitched again? Alex glanced at the portfolio in front of her; it contained a twelve-page document citing numerous examples and conclusions refuting all previous support data she'd submitted regarding the development of Restalline, Pennsylvania, into a luxury resort.

Uncle Walter walked to his desk, picked up the phone. "Sylvia, send Eric in.'' She watched him, his movements calculated, precise.

"I'm sure,'' Alex started, anxious to break the silence, "you'll be able to find another location to develop, if that's what you're so inclined to do.''

"So inclined?" His lips curved up, froze. "Oh, yes, my dear, I'm so inclined."

The door opened and Eric appeared, looking very metropolitan in his navy pinstripe suit and red silk tie. Alex thought of Nick in his faded Levi's and polo shirt, and his smile, pure, genuine, not contrived and forced like Eric's.

"Alex! Glad you could make it back."

"Eric." She ignored the jab, her gaze flying to the file in his hand. *Now what?*

"Alex tells me that Restalline isn't for sale, Eric," Uncle Walter said, his voice calm, smooth. "She says the principals, Kraziak and Androvich, aren't interested, says that Kraziak is, what was the word you used, Alex, 'entrenched'? Yes, I think that was it. She says that Norman Kraziak is 'entrenched' in his businesses and"—he rubbed his jaw— "not willing to even consider selling."

"Really?" There was a split-second exchange between the two men, an almost imperceptible acknowledgment, before Eric's thin lips curved up into a smile.

"That's what she says. Right, Alex?"

"That's right." She crossed her arms over her chest, preparing for Eric's disappointment. He'd never liked the words *no* or *can't,* and his ruthlessness in the boardroom stretched throughout the business, making him a formidable opponent. But she was not prepared for the soft laughter that filled the room as he walked toward her, stopping less than a foot away.

"If that's the truth, then I'm confused," he said, flicking the file he held with his index finger.

"What do you mean?" She glanced at Eric, who had the look of a predator preparing for the kill, and then Uncle Walter, whose expression was cold, implacable.

"What Eric means," her uncle said, taking the file from Eric and flipping it open on the table in front of her, "is that he's talked to Norman Kraziak. And the man's more than willing to sell, isn't that right, Eric?''

''I just got off the phone with him. Of course, he was a little hesitant to speak with me at first, but once I told him who you were and why you were *really* there, he opened right up and practically begged us to buy him out.''

''No.'' She shook her head, stared at the file with Norman Arthur Kraziak, Restalline Millworks, and NK Manufacturing typed at the top of the page. ''No. You can't ... he can't ...''

''I don't know why you thought he wouldn't sell, maybe he just needed time,'' Eric went on as though she hadn't spoken. ''We owe it all to you, Alex. If Kraziak didn't trust you so much, he wouldn't have given me the time of day. Androvich will be squeezed out; he won't have a choice but to follow. And it's all because of you.'' He smiled, patted her on the back. ''You're the one who's making this happen, Alex. You. Because of you, we're going to turn this place into the most incredible resort in the country.''

''Eric's right,'' Uncle Walter said, watching her. ''It's all because of you. Now why don't you forget all that silliness about destroying and whatever other nonsense has been fluttering around in your head, and finish the deal?''

''Nick? Nick?''

''This is the residence of Dr. Nick Androvich. I'm sorry, I'm unable to come to the phone right now, but leave your name, number, and a brief message, and I'll get back to you as soon as possible.''

Click. Alex hung up the phone, dialed his office. She had to talk to him. *Now.*

''Dr. Androvich's office, may I help you?''

''Elise, this is Alex. Is Nick in?''

''He's on another line right now, may I take a message?''

Was he talking to Norman, was she too late? *Oh, God, no.* "I . . . it's kind of an emergency. I'm calling from Virginia."

Pause. "Hold on. I'll see if he can take your call."

The wait was less than a minute, but it seemed to drag on forever with Alex picturing Norman Kraziak on the other line, telling Nick the truth about her.

"Alex?" It was Nick, his voice filled with concern.

No, he didn't know yet. "Nick! Nick." She sucked in air. "I'm on my way back. I've got to see you."

"What's the matter? Are you all right?"

"I'm fine . . . I . . . need to talk to you. . . ."

"Relax. Tell me what's the matter. You sound like you're scared out of your mind."

"No, I'm fine, really." She took a deep breath. *Calm down, calm down.* "My meeting finished up early, so I thought I'd head back."

"Did they like your work?"

"Yes, yes they did." *Oh, yes, they liked it all right. As a matter of fact, they loved it. I sent them enough background information on Norman that they knew exactly how to get to him.*

"That's great. I'm sure you're proud."

Proud. "Uh-huh." She swallowed. "Have you talked to Norman lately?"

"No, why, am I supposed to?"

"No, he's just been on my mind."

"I guess I should give him a call—"

"No! I mean, why don't you wait until I get back and then we can go and see him together."

"Okay. Alex, are you sure you're all right?"

"I'm fine."

"Why don't you at least wait until morning? Rest up?"

"No." She had to get to him, talk to him, face-to-face, before anybody else did.

"I miss you, too, Alex," his voice dipped, "but I want you to be safe."

"I'm fine. Really. I'm already an hour on the road."

"Okay. Should I leave the door unlocked?"

"Yes, I need to see you tonight. . . . Nick, I have some things I need to say."

Pause. "I have some things I need to say, too, Alex . . . some things I want to say."

Her chest tightened. "I'll see you as soon as I can. Goodbye, Nick." *Click*.

She dialed Norman Kraziak's direct office line next. "Norman Kraziak speaking."

"Norman," she breathed, feeling a mixture of guilt and relief when she heard his voice.

"Alex? Is that you? I can hardly hear you," he half yelled.

"It's my cell phone. Look, Norman, did you talk to a man named Eric Haines?"

"I did. He said you worked for some big real estate development company in Virginia and you were looking to develop Restalline."

If there'd been any food in her stomach, she would have thrown up right then, all over the steering wheel. "Norman—"

"Is that true, Alex? Were you just using the documentary thing as a cover so you could get information about all of us, about our town, so we'd let down our guard and talk?"

It sounded so devious when he said it, so underhanded. "It wasn't . . . I never meant to . . ."

"It's okay, I still like you. Actually, I'm grateful you came. This Eric offered me a deal for both companies, Alex. Three times market value, can you believe it? Who would have thought?"

"Norman, do you really want to sell? Think about it; what would happen to the rest of the community? If Restalline

Millworks and NK Manufacturing are gone, what happens to the jobs, the people?'' *Nick?*

"Oh, well, your man told me they'd all be taken care of, offered a good deal, said a lot of people are just waiting for an opportunity to start over and your company was giving it to them. That's kind of how I'm looking at it, Alex. They'll all get a chance to start over, better themselves.''

"But Norman—''

"You're breaking up on me, Alex, I can't hear you very well.''

"Nick!'' she shouted. "Please don't tell Nick!''

"Ah, now that's a problem, you and Nick, isn't it? I'll tell you, he's not going to be happy when he finds out about this.''

"Please don't say anything to him, Norman. Please!''

"You want to tell him? Fine by me. I don't relish being in your shoes, Alex, not one bit.''

It was a little past two in the morning when Alex opened the back door. Nick had left the stove light on for her. She slipped off her shoes and moved to the staircase. *Home*, this place felt more like home to her than her condo in Virginia. Maybe it was the comfortable furniture, tweeds and oak, worn and slightly soiled around the arms with homemade afghans strewn about, that invited her to sit down, stretch out, relax. Or perhaps it was the photographs of Justin hanging on the walls as he progressed from infant to just shy of eight, at first toothless, then one, two, then two whole rows, then a missing one, two ... Or maybe this place felt like home because little by little she was shedding all the "musts and must nots'' that had molded her entire life, and finally, finally she was stretching ... stretching ... reaching out to Nick ... to Justin ... Stella ... Gracie ... Norman ... even to Ruth. ...

Alex climbed the stairs, opened Justin's door, listened. His quiet, steady breathing filled her ears, gripped her heart. She closed his door and moved down the hall to Nick's room. A sliver of moon slid through a gap in the curtains, casting a faint glow on the bed. He was asleep on his side, his back to her.

I need you, I need you now, Nick. . . . She pulled off her shirt, shrugged out of her shorts, panties, bra, letting them fall in a heap at her feet. *I'm sorry* . . . She approached the bed, eased under the covers, *I'm sorry* . . . She touched his hair, his neck . . . *I'm so sorry* . . . She leaned into him, let the heat of his body permeate hers . . . *I never meant to hurt you* . . . *I* . . . *I* . . . She wrapped her arm around him, pressed her hand against his heart . . . *never* . . . *I love you.*

"Alex." Her name came out on a half-mumbled sigh as he reached for her, pulled her on top of him. "Alex." This spoken with such tenderness, such raw emotion that her throat clogged up and she couldn't find the words to respond. She bent her head, brushed her lips over his mouth, once, twice, until he tightened his grip and deepened the kiss, his tongue mating with hers in soft, almost reverent, gentleness.

I'm sorry . . . *I love you* . . . *I'm sorry* . . . *I love you* . . . "Nick," she began, "I . . . need to talk to you—"

"I need to talk to you, too," he murmured against her mouth, his fingers sifting through her hair, dragging down her spine. "Later."

"But—"

He flipped her onto her back, nudged her legs open, and entered her with one swift thrust. Heat, incredible heat surged through her. "Didn't you ever learn, Alex"—he stroked her cheek, pushed a lock of hair from her face—"that there's a time to talk and a time"—he moved inside her, slow, long, deep—"not to?"

Chapter 15

"Happy birthday to you, happy birthday to you, happy birthday dear Justin, happy birthday to you!"

Justin sucked in a deep breath, then blew out the candles, all eight of them, with one big whoosh of air. He beamed, a half-toothed grin on his face. "I made my wish, Dad," he said.

"Oh?" Nick nodded, acting as though he had no idea what that wish could possibly be. But anyone who had even a remote acquaintance with Justin knew the boy had been begging for the same thing for three years now. Man's best friend, a four-legged little creature who would learn how to catch a Frisbee, fetch sticks from the lake, run the fields with him, sleep at the foot of his bed on a blue-and-red rug, be his pal.

"What did you wish for, Justie?" This from Gracie, standing at the foot of the table, holding Rudy Jr.

"Yeah, what?" Kevin leaned forward, peeked around the chocolate sheet cake.

Justin grinned, nodded. "You all know. Well, maybe the only one who doesn't is Alex." He looked at her. "Dad said when I was eight I could get a dog."

"I said when you were eight we could *talk* about getting a dog because you'd be older and more responsible." Nick winked at Alex.

"Right." Justin fidgeted in his chair, half stood, sat back down. "Well, am I?"

"Are you what?"

"Geez, Dad." He rolled his eyes, blew out a long breath. "Older and more responsible?"

Nick scratched his chin, rubbed his jaw. He was probably as excited about the bundle of fur in the box on the front porch as Justin . . . a black Lab, seven weeks old. Nick couldn't wait to see the look on his son's face when he opened the box, held the pup in his arms. "Hmmm. Grandma? What do you think?"

Stella laughed, folded her arms across her chest. "I think if you don't stop tormenting this boy soon, he's going to fly out of his seat."

"Justin," Nick tried to sound stern, but the gentleness in his voice slipped out. "There's a box for you on the front porch."

Justin tore out of his chair, almost toppling it over, ran to the front door, swung it open, and let out a hoot. Nick, Alex, Stella, Gracie, and the rest of the family followed. "Look at him," Justin squealed, lifting the pup out of the box. "He's so black, and . . . furry."

"What are you gonna call him?" Kevin asked, inching forward.

"Jet."

"Jet," Stella repeated. "As in jet black."

"Yeah, Grandma, Jet Black. Cool, huh? That's his name,

Jet Black Androvich.'' Justin buried his face against the puppy's neck, rubbed his cheek along its coat.

''Well, why don't we bring Jet Black Androvich inside, in his box?'' Nick said, ''so we can finish this party. I want a piece of Grandma's chocolate cake.'' For all the years to come, this would most likely be Justin's most remembered gift.

''Okay. Let's go, Jet.'' Justin looked the puppy in the eye. ''We'll get you some water and food. Dad? Did you get food, too?''

''What do you think?'' Nick asked, pointing to a corner of the porch. ''I've never met a baby, human or otherwise, that didn't want to eat.''

''Can I—''

''After. Let's go.'' Nick started to head back inside, reached for Alex's hand, pulled her to him. ''I did good, didn't I?''

She smiled. ''You did good.''

''Do you remember your first pet?''

Alex nodded, avoided his gaze. ''It was Daisy. First and last.''

''Oh.'' *Oh.* The cat that climbed a tree and got farmed out to a golf course. ''Nothing else? Not even a fish?''

''No.''

Oh. The more time he spent with her, the more snippets of information slipped out here and there, telling him more than she probably wanted him to know. A child who was forced to give up her pet because . . . why? *Why, other than the fact that it was probably an inconvenience for the aunt?* And who was this uncle she refused to talk about, never even called him by his first name, just said, *my uncle?* What was his deal? And the aunt? No cousins, no mother, no father? He'd tried to ask her about it once, but she'd clammed up, said her parents were both dead and her aunt and uncle were her only family. The Androvich clan must be a shock to her, an adjustment to say the least, though she seemed to like being around his mother and Gracie, and didn't seem as terrified of the new baby this week as she had the last. Tonight, she'd actually held Rudy Jr., just for a few minutes, but still . . .

Alex Chamberlain was in his blood, pulsing through his veins with a life of its own. He wanted to be near her, touch her, talk to her, learn everything about her, gain her trust, her friendship, her love. *Yes, damn it.* He tightened his hold on her hand; he wanted her love.

Was he crazy? She was a difficult, reclusive woman who might give her body to him but certainly hadn't opened up her heart or her past to him. He knew bits and pieces about her: she was well-educated, she lived in Virginia, drove a Saab, so what? He knew more about his neighbors and he hadn't slept with any of them.

And she was leaving in a few weeks, wasn't she? And then what? A long-distance romance relegated to weekends or off-call schedules? How long would that last? Hell, he was only kidding himself. He didn't want her to leave, he wanted her to stay here, be with him . . . love him. Alex was a city girl, she liked fine things, any woman who wore pearls with jeans wouldn't understand a man who accepted food and repairs to his home in exchange for medical care. Apple pies didn't buy diamonds. And she'd expect diamonds.

Nick's hand slipped away.

"Nick?" Alex's voice was soft, low. The buzz of his family faded into the background.

He looked down at her, said nothing. The pearls around her neck glowed in the soft light.

She smiled, a small, hesitant smile. "I . . . I wonder what Justin will think of that doghouse you're going to build for Jet."

"I don't know." How the hell could she think of a dog-house right now when he was so agitated, so miserable?

"I'd love to see his face when you tell him how elaborate it's going to be."

He shrugged. "I'm not going to tell him until I can start on it, and that's a good two, maybe three months off, probably late fall."

"I know, you already told me." She paused, reached for his hand, her gaze meeting his. "I'd still love to be here when you tell him."

"What are you saying, Alex? Huh? I'm not in the mood for you to wax rhetoric on me." God, she was torturing him. "I'm sure you'd love to be here but the truth is, we both know you won't be, so let's stop pretending. You'll be long gone by then."

"I . . ." Her eyes grew bright. "I don't want to leave, Nick."

They stood there in the corner of the room, locked in their own world, oblivious to the laughter and the chatter that flowed around them as Justin ripped open one present after another, with Jet in his box by his side. "What?" He couldn't have heard her right.

"I don't want to leave." Her face turned a dull red. "I mean"—she looked away—"if you want me to stay, see how things work out . . ." She glanced back at him.

"Alex, I don't live the kind of life you're used to . . . it's not me."

Her lips trembled when she spoke. "It's not me anymore, either."

Nick pulled her to him, kissed her, long, hard, deep. "Stay, Alex," he breathed against her lips, "stay."

In the middle of the room, Stella Androvich watched her son and Alex. "She's the one, Gracie. I told you, she's the one."

"What do you think, Mom? Three months? Four before he proposes?"

Stella smiled, wiped her hands on her apron. "Months? I'd say more like days."

Alex would always remember Justin's eighth birthday. It was the day his wish came true: he got Jet. It was also the day Nick asked her to stay in Restalline . . . be a part of his life. There was so much to talk about, so much for her to explain, but he'd been called away on an emergency and she'd ended up taking Justin and Jet home, then lying on Nick's couch, listening to the clock on the mantel tick away the minutes, waiting with Jet sleeping in his box by her side. At 12:15 A.M. Nick had called to say Harry Lendergin was having emergency gallbladder surgery.

I might be a while, why don't you get some rest?

I can't sleep . . . there are things I have to tell you . . . explain to you . . . that I should have said before.

I know. Me, too. We'll talk in the morning, okay?

I . . . okay.

Click.

Sleep had come sometime after 3:00 A.M., a restless slumber haunted with visions of Nick, first laughing, holding her hand, kissing her, then jerking back, his face dark, his body tense, then turning away and leaving . . . leaving . . . *Nick! Nick! I'm sorry . . . I'm sorry . . . I was going to tell you . . .*

Alex jerked awake.

"Hey, Alex." Justin sat on the floor beside her, dressed in a Nike T-shirt and boxers. "You okay?"

She sat up, rubbed both hands over her face. God, she was shaking.

"Alex?"

"I'm fine, Justin. Just a bad dream."

"About what?"

About your father finding out I lied to him. "Huh?" She couldn't wait any longer, she had to find Nick, tell him the truth . . . and pray he'd still want her to stay.

"What was the bad dream about?" He leaned closer, his blue eyes intent on her.

She shrugged. "Some guy was chasing me." *What was one more lie?*

"Do you ever dream about your parents?"

"I used to; not anymore."

"Did you"—his gaze fixed on his fingers, he picked at a piece of skin—"ever dream about how they died? Like, you know, wonder about it, try to picture it?" He shot a quick glance in her direction, then dodged back down to his fingers.

"I . . ." Suddenly, she was eight again, staring out through the big window, waiting for her mother and father to come home . . . only they never did. "I used to."

He nodded, scratched at his nail. "Me, too." Pause. "Dad says the smoke got her, put her to sleep before . . . before . . . you know." He pulled his teeth over his lower lip. "Are you afraid of water 'cause . . . 'cause, you know, 'cause of what happened to them?"

If he could be so honest, so could she. "Yes."

He jerked his head up, stared at her. "Really?"

"I'm petrified, actually." She ran her hands over the wrinkles in her pants, tried to smooth them out. "Haven't been in the water for ten years." Not since the failed scuba certification Uncle Walter had persuaded her to undertake. He'd been convinced from the outset that if she faced her fears she would defeat them. Alex had been enrolled in every swimming program available, starting the month after the accident. Scuba diving was the final step in her uncle's attempt to prove to her that water was not to be feared. But she'd choked fifteen feet down, with the mask in her hand, filling with water as she kicked and flailed her arms, the air piece falling out of her mouth. It chilled her still to remember the seconds before her instructor pulled her out, when she thought she would die, meet the same demise as her parents.

"Really? But, you go to the lake with Dad all the time."

"But I don't go in, and never too near. If I'm far enough away, I can pretend it's not real, that it's just scenery, you know, background, like in a movie."

"And it can't hurt you?"

"Right." Why was he asking so many questions? Was he afraid of something? Fire? Fire killed his mother, was that it? "Are you . . . are you afraid of something?"

"Nah, not me." He peeked at her, shrugged. "Well, I'm not too crazy about fire." He paused, his blue eyes narrowing. "Dad knows, and Grandma, and the rest of the family, but nobody else. Well, now you know"—he scratched his chin—"but you're kind of like family, so I guess it's okay if you know."

"Thank you."

"So, are you gonna marry my Dad, or what?"

It was almost noon when Alex dropped Justin and Jet off at Stella's.

"Come, have a bowl of goulash." Stella was standing at the stove, stirring a big pot with a wooden spoon. "Fresh bread, too, not out of the oven twenty minutes. Stay."

"I'm sorry, Stella, I can't. Not today."

"Oh? Got a better invitation?" She raised a brow, waited.

"Nick called. He has a little free time."

"Oh."

"I . . . I need to talk to him."

"I see." She smiled, shook her head. A twist of gray-brown hair fell across her cheek. "There's nothing like new love. Everything is so right, so fresh, so . . . so urgent." Her voice swayed, dipped. "The trick is keeping the love when the mystery fades and you've seen him in his dirty socks and underwear with a fever and a foul temper. The real person has a way of sneaking out, warts and all, and that's the person you need to love. He's the truth. Nothing's cute then, believe me, and he'll want to swat you away if you flit over him trying to get him this or that. You'll drive each other crazy, wonder how you ever thought you'd want to spend the rest of your life with such a miserable, ungrateful person." She looked up, met Alex's eyes, and there were tears in her own. "But then you remember. And when you look at him again, it's not the speck of drool on his pillow you see or the way his belly hangs over his pants a lot more than it used to. What you see, deep down, is the love, and the memories, and the hope. That's what makes everything worthwhile."

"You still miss your husband, don't you?" The words wobbled, fell flat on a heavy sigh. She'd never seen such a display of emotion when Uncle Walter talked about Aunt Helen. As a matter of fact, there had been no emotion at all, just cold precision.

Stella squeezed her eyes shut, opened them. "God, but I do," she breathed. "I miss him every day. There were so many things I wanted to tell him, needed to tell him. I thought there was time. . . . I didn't know that day when he went into the woods . . . I'd never see him again. I didn't know. . . ." She swiped a hand over her face, sniffed. "You and Nick, you care about each other. I see it"—her lips pulled into a sad smile—"a mother knows. . . . a mother always knows."

"I—"Alex started.

"I'm happy, Alex. Nick deserves to be happy. Make him happy." She waved a hand, dismissing her. "Go. He'll be waiting for you."

"I . . ." She had to say this, now, to his mother. "I do

care about Nick. I don't want to hurt him, ever.'' *God, but I think I already have.*

"Then don't.''

Alex left then, Stella's words pounding in her brain. *Nick.* He needed to know the truth, all of it. What would he say? Would he even listen, or would he be so angry, so hurt, that he'd shut her out of his heart, his life?

She had to make him see, make him understand that she'd just been doing her job when she'd come to his town, that she'd had no intention of befriending the people of Restalline, of meeting someone like him, falling in love. But she had, and now things were different; everything was different because Alex had seen too much, felt even more. There were visions of Ruth Kraziak sitting at the bus stop, waiting for a daughter who would never come; Edna Lubovich clutching the casket of her dead husband; Justin Androvich asking her if she ever thought about the way her parents died. And Nick. Nick looking at her, trusting her enough to tell her that the love for his wife had died long before she had. Alex knew he had never spoken those words aloud before.

She had seen the pain, etched on all of their faces, taut and unsmiling, heard it in their voices, faint and distant, sensed it in the movements of their bodies, rigid, lifeless, but mostly, she'd felt their pain, *felt it so deeply in her soul that it became her pain, her misery, her loss.*

It was this need for unity, this quest for oneness, neighbor to neighbor, friend to friend, that gave her clarity, made her truly see that Restalline was more than just a town, more than acres of land to be excavated and recreated in a broader, more commercial manner that would generate enormous sums of money. Restalline was a true community, a gathering place . . . a home.

Alex turned the corner, saw the white sign with black lettering hanging on a post in front of Nick's office.

NICHOLAS A. ANDROVICH, M.D. She sucked in a deep breath, flicked on her turn signal, and pulled into the parking lot.

"Oh, my God." She slammed on the brakes, hands gripping the steering wheel. "Oh, my God." The words slipped past her lips, fell around her, choking out her next breath. There, right next to Nick's silver Navigator, partially hidden from view, was a shiny black Audi with a Virginia license plate.

Uncle Walter was here.

Chapter 16

"Nick?" No, no, *no*. She had to get to him. "Nick?"

Elise Pentani motioned toward the closed door. "He's in there. With a man who says he's your uncle."

Alex flew past her. Maybe she could cut Uncle Walter off before he did too much damage, before he exposed her. . . . She knocked on the door once, then barged in, the words falling out of her mouth in a breathless rush. "Nick, wait, I can explain."

"Hello, Alex." She jerked her head from Nick to Uncle Walter, who sat in a gray tweed chair, his long legs crossed, his arms folded in his lap. He wore a dark gray suit with a pale blue silk tie a shade lighter than his eyes. Cold eyes. His expression was calm, almost relaxed. "Nick and I were just having a friendly conversation, getting to know each other."

She forced her gaze back to Nick. He sat behind his desk,

hands clasped behind his head, looking very tired and in bad need of a shave, but not angry or—worse yet—filled with hatred. In fact, he actually seemed pleased to see her. Maybe, just maybe she'd gotten here in time. . . . Maybe it wasn't too late. Her chest tightened, her heart banged against her rib cage.

"Your uncle was just telling me about all of your brilliant accomplishments," he said, smiling at her.

"He was?" Her gaze shifted from her uncle to Nick, then back again.

"Of course. I told him all about Vassar and Wharton. It's quite an achievement, nothing to be shy about, Alex. You earned it; Nick realizes that."

"I . . ." She twisted her fingers, forced herself to remain calm. "I wish you would have told me you were coming."

His lips curved up in his version of a smile, a half twist of lips pulled over teeth. "And ruin the surprise? No, Alex, some things are best received with little preparation and no forethought."

That's how you squash your opponents; you get them when they least expect it.

"Well, I'm glad you're here," Nick said, leaning back in his chair. "I know you're Alex's only living relative." His gaze flitted over her, softened. "You two must be very close."

There was only the slightest hesitation, a half-second pause, maybe less. "Yes, yes we are."

"Uncle Walter, do you think I could speak with you for a moment? In private?" *Nick didn't know, not yet.* There was still time to tell him herself.

"Don't be so shy, Alex. I'm sure whatever you have to say, you can say in front of your young man." He rubbed his jaw, paused. "Unless it's something you'd rather he not hear."

"We don't have any secrets from each other," Nick said.

"Good. Very good."

"Uncle Walter—"

"Wasn't that clever of her to think of the documentary idea?"

"Nick—"

"Yes," Nick said, smiling at her. "I think writing a documentary about small-town life and its values is a great idea."

"Writing? Who's writing? Didn't she tell you the real reason she came to Restalline?"

She tried to speak, tried to stop what she knew was coming, but the words froze halfway past her throat.

"What are you talking about?"

"You really don't know, do you?"

"Nick, I can explain—"

"Somebody in the hell better explain what's going on here."

Tsk, tsk, tsk. "Alex, I'm disappointed in you." This from Uncle Walter.

She ignored him, rushed to Nick, touched his arm. "I can explain. I can explain everything."

"Don't be too harsh with her, Nick, she was only doing her job. She came here to research your town, and if conditions were right, lay the groundwork for us to come in and turn it into the biggest resort in the country."

Nick jerked his arm away. "Who the hell are you?"

It was a blanket question, directed at Uncle Walter, but she felt the bite of his words aimed at her, too.

"I'm Walter Chamberlain, CEO of WEC Management. We're a real estate development company based in Arlington, Virginia. We buy up property, usually small towns that possess keen aesthetic appeal with mass-market potential and convert them into resorts. Perhaps you've heard of the Krystal Springs resort in Upstate New York? That was our project. Alex spearheaded it. She's excellent at spotting locations, weighing the value of the land and the monetary potential that can be extracted from it.'' He leaned forward, his lips tilting into a semi smile. ''She's vice president of acquisitions, but when she wraps up this one, she'll be made president of the company.''

Nick sat perfectly still. When he spoke, there was no emotion, not even anger in his voice. ''So, it was all a lie.''

''No! No, Nick. I was going to tell you.''

''A story. A fabrication.''

''Think of it as a means to an end,'' Uncle Walter said.

''Right.'' Nick laughed, harsh, cold. ''A means to an end. Do whatever it takes.''

''But it's not that way.'' Alex planted her hands on his desk, leaned closer. ''Well, maybe at first it was, but before this town, I always believed the people would be better off selling, getting out, taking their cash and moving to the suburbs. I couldn't imagine anyone actually wanting to live in these little godforsaken places, but this time I got to know the people . . . got to see how much they cared, and what they cared about . . . and then I met you . . .''

''Right, you met me.''

''Don't do this, Nick. Listen to me. I made a mistake . . . a horrible one. I realized that and that's why I went back to Virginia last week, to tell my uncle that Restalline wasn't for sale.'' She looked up, met her uncle's cool gaze. ''Tell him, Uncle Walter, tell him what I told you.''

If Alex ever wondered about her uncle's love, his next words killed any hope she had that he cared for her as more than a vehicle for economic benefit and advancement. ''She's right, Nick. Alex did come back spouting off all sorts of nonsense about Restalline not being for sale. She said the two major parties''—he nodded toward Nick— ''you and a Norman Kraziak, weren't interested in selling.''

''That's right. Nothing's for sale, not the town or the people.''

"Ah, spoken like a true idealist." His smile faded. "Don't underestimate the value of the dollar."

"And don't you underestimate the power of unity." Nick straightened in his chair, crossed his arms over his chest. "We're not pawns on a chessboard that can be moved around at will."

"But don't you see, in a manner of speaking, you are exactly that. Pawns. And I would never underestimate the power of unity; that's why I've seen to it that unity will not be established. You see, Nick, I'm a businessman, and when I sensed Alex was teetering toward loyalty to a man and a town versus loyalty to me and the company, I had to hedge my bets, insure that if we wanted the town, we'd get it."

"What are you talking about?" Alex stared at her uncle. *He'd been plotting something behind her back?*

"Don't trouble yourself, Alex. I did what any other businessman would do when faced with a similar predicament." He leaned back in his chair, steepled his long fingers under his chin. "I found the weakest link. Thanks to you and your excellent research, Norman Kraziak has agreed to sell his companies and his interests to WEC Management." And then, in a gesture so unlike him that she could do no more than stare, he winked. "Well done, Alex. Well done."

"Norman is confused right now, he doesn't know what he wants." She held up her hands. "He needs time. Please, don't push him."

He ignored her, glanced at his watch. "It's later than I thought. I need to catch up with Eric, finalize a few details of the sale." He stood up, brushed his hands over his suit jacket. "We're staying about ten miles from here, at the Glendover Manor. This area is certainly not known for its overnight accommodations is it? Alex, I'd like you to have dinner with us tonight." He looked at Nick. "Of course, you're invited as well, though it might be a bit awkward with Eric there." He paused. "She did tell you about Eric,

didn't she, Nick? No? He's the head of WEC's legal counsel
. . . he's also Alex's ex-husband.''

Nick dug his fingers into the hard plastic on the rounded
edge of the chair. He watched Walter Chamberlain leave,
his erect, designer-suit-covered frame moving with distinc-
tion and authority. The soft click of the door closing filled
the room.

How could he have been so stupid, so naive, so ridicu-
lously gullible? Alex had played him for a fool. Instinct had
warned him to question her, but he'd been hunting the wrong
animal, traveling down a path in search of answers when
there would be none. She hadn't been out to save the trees
or uncover a story. Her goal was more insidious, more lethal
by mere definition: she'd wanted to flatten the town, uproot
the people, build a playground for the wealthy. God, it made
him sick.

"Nick."

She was still here. He rubbed his hands over his face,
tried to focus, keep his voice calm as rage replaced the first
waves of shock. "You betrayed us, Alex, all of us."

"No." She shook her head, panic filtering through her
usually clear voice. "No, Nick. I didn't betray you. I
wouldn't do that."

"Everyone trusted you. *I* trusted you." She reached out,
tried to touch him. "Don't." He jerked away.

"Listen to me, Nick. Please. I can fix this, I can make it
right, I know I can."

"How?" He turned to her, stared at her pale golden hair,
her slender neck, and saw nothing but betrayal, felt nothing
but rage. "How are you going to do that, Alex? Huh? Are
you going to try and persuade Eric, the ex-husband I knew
nothing about, to forget the whole thing?" He slammed his
fist on his desk, made her jump back. "What else don't I

know? What other secrets have you got locked away, waiting for the right moment to pounce on me?''

"Nothing. I'm telling you the truth, Nick. Honest.''

"The truth? Honest? You don't know the meaning of those words.''

There were tears in her eyes, running down her face. So what? He should be the one crying, he'd been the one who was betrayed. "Just tell me one thing, Alex. Was fucking me part of this whole scheme?''

"Stop it.''

"Was it? Did you and your uncle plan it all out, maybe even old Eric? 'Fuck him and weaken his reserve, get him to do anything you want,' is that it?''

"That's sick.''

The tears were really coming now.

"Right. You'd never stoop so low, is that what you're thinking?'' Her eyes widened, in what? What was it? Shock, disbelief? Disgust? That made two of them. "What if it meant a promotion to president of the company?'' The words kept coming; he couldn't seem to stop himself. Hurt, that's what he wanted to do to her. Hurt her as much as she'd hurt him. He ignored the tears, the quiet sniffling. "Would you fuck somebody for that?''

"Stop it! Stop it!'' She turned away, shrank into the chair her uncle had vacated moments before. Her head was bent forward so he couldn't see her face.

"I can't stop this, Alex. You started it and now I've got to finish it.'' There was raw pain in his voice, visceral, palpable. "I trusted you. I trusted you, Alex, and you lied to me.''

"Yes, damn it, yes, I did.'' She lifted her head, her eyes bright, filled with emotion. "I came here to buy up a town, build a beautiful resort with Sapphire Lake as a prime attraction.'' Her voice rose, steadied. "I did that, I'll admit it, Nick. I wasn't interested in anything or anybody but getting the deal." She gripped the edges of the chair. "But then I met Edna and Chuck Lubovich, and Ruth and Norman Kraziak, and Bernie and Alice, and Stella and Justin, and Gracie." She paused, drew in a deep breath. "And then I met you, Nick. Then I met you."

"Yeah, and then you met me."

"It doesn't have to be like this. I'll talk to Norman, get him to change his mind, make him realize what he'd be giving up." Her eyes teared up again. "I can do that because I can see it all so clearly now and I couldn't before. Do you understand what I'm saying? I realize what he'd be giving up, what the whole town would lose if he sold out, because finally, *finally* I know in here"—she laid a hand against her heart—"and I know one more thing." She held his gaze, her voice trembling when she spoke. "I love you, Nick Androvich. I love you."

"Don't." He held up a hand, tried to fend off the words that pierced his soul, made his heart bleed. "Just . . . don't."

"But I—"

He shook his head. "It's over. It's over, Alex. Go home. I want to forget I ever met you."

Small towns have a way of spreading information faster than a wildfire in California brush country. One word, a few poignant phrases, a well-placed pause, and the whole town starts talking, drawing conclusions, formulating opinions.

Stella Androvich didn't think much when Gracie stopped by to see her that afternoon and told her about the handsome silver-haired gentleman in the dark gray suit she'd seen coming out of Nick's office earlier.

"Probably an insurance salesman," Stella had said.

"He was driving an Audi."

"And you wonder why doctors pay so much for malpractice insurance?"

Gracie had shrugged, pulled a diaper out of her bag, and proceeded to change little Rudy. The discussion ended there, with Stella busying herself at the table, cleaning the last of the strawberries. Maybe she'd make a strawberry pie tonight, send it over to Nick. It was one of his favorites. She'd have to remember to give the recipe to Alex. Future mothers-in-law were supposed to give subtle hints regarding their children's likes and dislikes, weren't they? And there was no doubt in Stella's mind that Alex would be her daughter-in-law. Of course, no one had said anything yet, not even a hint, but a mother could tell when her son was heading toward commitment. And it was about time. Nick needed a wife, Justin needed a mother, and Stella, well, she needed to see her children settled. Now if Michael and Elise would only realize they were meant to be together. . . .

When the phone rang, Stella put down her pairing knife and answered it. "Hello."

"Stella? This is Elise."

Speak of the devil. "Elise. What a surprise." She'd probably been thinking about the conversation they'd had the other day. Maybe she was finally going to admit she had feelings for Michael, maybe . . .

"It's Nick. Something's happened."

"What? Is he okay?" Panic gripped her, choked the breath from her lungs. She was a strong woman: she'd buried a husband, raised three children on her own, but Jesus God, she would not be able to handle it if something happened to one of her children.

"Yes. No. I mean nothing's wrong with him physically"—pause—"it's Alex."

"Alex?"

And then the story came spilling out about Alex's real reason for coming to Restalline and how it had nothing to do with a documentary at all; how she was some big-wig with a development company and she'd been sent to do research so her firm could buy up the town, drive everyone out; how Norman Kraziak was ready to accept their offer, how the man with the Audi was her uncle.

Stella sucked in a breath of air, feeling winded and light-headed, as though she'd just run a mile uphill. "Who told you all of this?"

"Nick."

"Maybe . . . maybe he's wrong." *Dear God, let him be wrong.*

"I don't know. Alex was very upset when she left, crying and all. And Nick, well, he was in pretty bad shape, too."

"Is he still there?"

"No, he left, didn't say where he was going." Pause. "Stella? You know I wasn't crazy about Alex, and you know why, but I think she really loves him . . . and I think he really loves her, too."

"So do I." She sighed, tried to massage the pounding pain in her right temple. "Let's just hope it's strong enough to get them through this." Stella said good-bye and clicked the phone off, then she sat there, staring at the mound of strawberries in the stainless steel bowl she'd been using for the past thirty years. There were a few dents on the sides, and hundreds of scratches worn into the metal, but it was still sturdy, still functional. It had withstood the raising of three children, the death of a husband, the birth of six grand-children, and thousands upon thousands of potatoes, straw-berries, green beans, blueberries, broccoli. A tear slipped down her cheek.

Surely Nick and Alex's love for each other was stronger than a silly stainless-steel bowl, more durable, able to weather hardship? Surely, it must be so.

"Mom? Mom?" It was Gracie, her soft brown eyes filled with concern.

It all just poured out—the phone conversation with Elise, what Nick had said, what Alex was supposed to have done.

When Stella told her the part about Nick calling himself a fool for trusting Alex, Gracie's eyes were wet, her gaze fixed and staring.

"Hey, who died?" The screen door slammed and Michael strolled into the kitchen.

"You tell him, Gracie. I'm tired of talking."

It was Gracie's turn to relay Elise's phone conversation. When she was finished, Michael flicked the bill of his cap up, met his mother's teary gaze. "I knew she was no good." He blew out a long, disgusted breath. "Didn't I tell you she was no good? Nothing but trouble."

"Michael, stop." This from Gracie. "You don't even know her."

"I know about her and that's more than enough."

"Well, I like her and so does Mom."

"How? How can you like a person who came to this town to destroy it? Do you think she cares about any of us? Do you think she's not going to get a six-figure salary and a bonus on top of that if she lands this deal? She's interested in money, not people; she couldn't give a shit about any of us." He yanked off his cap, ran a hand through his wavy hair. "And what the hell's wrong with Norman? Has his crazy wife made him go loony, too? How could he even consider selling out?"

"We don't know, Michael. We have to wait for Nick." Stella dug out another hull, tossed a strawberry in the bowl. "He's the only one who can tell us what really happened."

"Right. You think he's gonna tell you he was played for a sucker? I doubt it." He picked up a strawberry, popped it into his mouth.

"Michael, can you just stop with the comments, huh?" Gracie glared at him from across the table. "Can't you just this once act like the human being that I know is hiding under all those smart-ass remarks?"

He shrugged. "Just calling it as I see it."

"Well, don't."

"You know, there may be another way to find out the truth." Stella set down her paring knife, looked at her children. "Actually, it might be the only way we'll really know what happened."

"What are you gonna do, Ma, go see the woman yourself, ask her if she was trying to screw us the whole time she was here, while she was eating our food, sitting at our table?"

"Yes, that's exactly what I'm going to do."

Why did she always have to lose the people she loved? Why?

Alex sped along the country road, mindless of the mossy, green trees and vibrant foliage reaching out to her from the sides of the road. There were wildflowers, bright yellow, and tiny white ones growing in clusters along the guardrails. Huge gray rocks jutted out along the east side, surrounded with a brush of thick limbs and leaves of varying shapes and sizes. Maples, oaks, cherries, pine.

But Alex saw none of it. Her mind and her heart were focused on reaching Glendover Manor and confronting her uncle. Every mile took her closer to the answers she sought. How could he have come here, confronted Nick, deliberately destroyed the fragile love that was emerging between them? And it was love, for Nick, too, she was sure of it. But all of that was gone now, torn in two by an uncle who cared more about controlling her than seeing her happy.

It had always been about control with Uncle Walter. As long as she did what he wanted, what he expected, sometimes even demanded, and as long as she thought about his needs first, his expectations, and buried her own under the desperate desire to please, then he bestowed a token show of affection, a well-earned nod of pleasure in her direction.

But this time would be different. This time she would not quietly acquiesce, no, not this time. The tears had dried up miles ago, and all that was left was a heavy emptiness and the need to put things right, say what needed to be said, face-to-face, Uncle Walter on one side, Alex on the other.

Had her father and Uncle Walter been on opposites sides? Was that why her uncle never spoke of her father? Offered no childhood memories, no details, no pictures? Nothing? Alex glanced at the green-and-blue jeweled hand mirror resting on the passenger seat, glinting in the sunlight. *The true jewel is in the mirror. Look into it, child. Look into it and see the jewel.* Finally, *finally*, for good, for bad, she *was* finding herself; she just hoped she could live with the person she uncovered.

When she reached Glendover Manor, an elderly woman with blue-white hair and red lipstick told her that Walter Chamberlain was expecting his niece and could be found on the back veranda.

He was sitting there, under the shade of a patio awning, reading the *Wall Street Journal*. His only concession to the humid heat of the July afternoon was his suit jacket resting on the wrought-iron chair beside him and a very fine film of perspiration clinging to his upper lip, barely detectable. That was it.

"Alex," he said as she approached him, "I've been expecting you."

"Why'd you do it, Uncle Walter?"

He ignored the question. "Sit down, dear. Would you like a glass of lemonade? The surroundings are a bit anti-quated, but the service is adequate."

"I don't want anything . . . except answers."

She saw the way he raised his brow, a hint of surprise passing over his features. "I should be the one expecting answers from you." He lifted his glass, sipped at his lem-onade.

"How could you do it? How? Was it so important to teach me a lesson, show me that you could do whatever you wanted, that you had to come here, to Nick?" Her voice wobbled and she cleared her throat, pushing the words out. "What was it really about, Uncle Walter? You wanted a summer and winter resort, but it didn't have to be Restalline. I'd only invested two months of research into it; you couldn't just have accepted that, pulled out, and gone on to your next choice?"

"I wanted Restalline." His voice was calm, matter-of-fact.

"But why? Was it because I'd told you 'no,' this wasn't the right place? Or maybe because you sensed this place meant more to me than just another small town? Was that it? Did you want to show me that you could control me, take something I wanted?"

"I have no idea what you're talking about." He undid the top button of his shirt, loosened his tie.

"Just tell me the truth. For once in my life, tell me the truth." Her voice rose with the pitch of her emotions. "Did you just want to win, because you knew you could, no matter who got hurt, even me?"

"Of course not. What's wrong with—"

She cut him off. "I love Nick. Do you hear me? I love him. And I was going to tell him everything, beg him to forgive me for lying to him, for taking advantage of all the people in this town who trusted me." Her next words fell flat, low. "I was going to stay here, with him and his son, hopefully have a life together. But don't worry about that now, Uncle Walter, you've taken care of everything, just like you always do. He hates me, can't look at me without thinking about how I betrayed him, and I owe it all to you."

"You don't belong here. You're too good for this. You deserve better. My God, this town isn't much better than a cow patch."

"I loved it here."

"And what? You didn't like it in Virginia?"

"I didn't belong there, not really."

"Don't!" The word flew out like a steeled command. "Don't start this, Alex." He cleared his throat, shifted in his chair. When he spoke again, he sounded like the uncle she was used to, poised, unemotional. "We'll go back tomorrow, all of us. We can draw up the papers and you won't have to see any of these people, ever again. Eric can take care of the rest of the negotiations. Once Kraziak signs it'll only be a matter of time before the rest of the town follows."

"Haven't you listened to anything I've said? I love Nick Androvich, real love, not the *Bride* magazine, Tiffany kind, but the honest, dirty laundry, 'till death do us part' kind. I didn't want this town to change. I wanted to belong here, more than anything"—she blinked hard, forced the rest of the words out—"but now I'll never belong. I have to leave and I've got nowhere to go."

"That's the most ridiculous thing I've ever heard. You were born and raised in Virginia, you belong there."

"No"—she shook her head—"I don't. I don't belong anywhere." The tears were coming, she felt them, threatening to blur her vision, blind her with their intensity. She blinked several more times, afraid that if she started crying she'd never be able to stop.

"Stop being so damn dramatic, you sound just like your father, turning his nose up at everything I offered him, ranting on and on about not belonging. Goddamn it, he was a Chamberlain, he didn't belong with that Russian woman."

"My mother?" Never had he ever spoken of her mother and father before.

"Hell, yes, your mother. Damn gypsy Russian ballerina. He had to have her, had to marry her no less, give her his name." He ran a hand over his face. "He could've had anything and he gave it all up for her. Jesus, to live the life of a nomad, travel up and down the coast painting and making jewelry. A Chamberlain,'' he spat out, ''painting and making jewelry and living in . . . in filth.''

''He must have loved her very much.''

''Love?'' His pale blue eyes chilled her with their intensity. ''Yes, he was foolish enough to love her. And what did that love get him? I'll tell you''—he leaned forward, his nostrils flaring—''it got him killed. He could've had everything, money, power, prestige, but he walked away from it all. I made a vow the first time I laid eyes on you sitting in the corner of that hovel you called home, your hair ratty, your feet covered in sand, that you would have everything your father rejected, the wealth, the money, the power and prestige that came with being a Chamberlain. I would see that you had it all, Alex, and I have.''

Chapter 17

Nick sat at the kitchen table waiting for Justin to finish washing his hands for dinner. Tonight was goulash, compliments of his mother, with extra paprika and black pepper, just the way he liked it. He opened his right hand, stared at the crumpled-up piece of paper in his palm. He'd committed every word she'd written to memory hours ago, even down to the squiggle on the smiley face at the bottom of the page:

I'm taking Justin to your mother's, then off to the grocery store. He wants pizza for dinner—he and I are going to try to make it together from one of your mom's recipes. That should be interesting! See you tonight. We have to talk, no more diversions.

Love, Alex

We have to talk . . . Had she planned to tell him tonight? Heat rolled through his body, intense, angry, pounding into his brain, circling his chest. What was she going to say? *I'm sorry I was planning to screw you and your town, but it was just business? I didn't really mean it? Can we just forget it, pretend it never happened? Oh, and by the way, you know you can trust me, don't you?*

Shit. He wished he'd never met Alex Chamberlain.

"Hey, Dad, what's wrong? Your face is all weird-looking."

Justin stood in front of him, hair slicked back, hands still damp, his own features pulled with worry.

Nick dragged a hand over his face, rubbed his temple. "I'm fine, just tired. That's what happens when you're a doctor, you know. You can forget about sleeping like normal people."

Justin pulled out a chair, sat down. "Are you gonna tell me where Alex is? She said we were making pizza tonight." His lower lip puckered out. "She promised."

Damn the woman, damn her, damn her. His son was going to be hurt, another victim caught up in her web of lies. "Alex," he started, forcing himself to say her name, "isn't coming tonight."

Justin rolled his eyes. "I know that, Dad. *But where is she?*" He crossed his arms over his chest. "When I see her again, I'm going to tell her—"

"She's gone."

"Huh?"

Here it comes, might as well get used to it. He'd have to repeat variations of the story for days, first to his family—his mother, sister, even his brother—then friends, patients, probably most of the town. "Alex," he started again, "will be leaving Restalline very soon, if she hasn't already. She'll be going back to Virginia." His chest tightened with each word until he felt pain, real pain.

"Why? I thought she was going to stay . . . be with us

... like a family. I thought you two might get married. Grandma says she thought you would.''

"No.'' Nick shook his head. "No, Justin, we're not going to get married.''

"But ... why?'' There were tears in his eyes now, a fine trembling in his voice.

"It's ... complicated. Adult stuff.'' *How could he tell his son that they'd both fallen for a liar?* "Alex is gone.''

Gone. Alex is gone. He heard the shakiness of his own voice; he'd have to practice those words before he said them again. Maybe after a hundred, no, five hundred times, the reality of it all wouldn't hurt so much and he'd be able to glide right through it as though he were talking about a change in the forecast.

A tear spilled down Justin's cheek, first one, then another, until his face was wet and he was sniffing. "How could you let her go, Dad? Can't you bring her back?'' And then, the words that sent his world crashing, "We love her, Dad, both of us. We love her, don't we?''

It was almost 7:00 P.M. when Alex finally made it to Norman Kraziak's house. She was hot and sticky and exhausted but she had to see Norman, had to convince him he was about to make the worst mistake of his life.

Bright light spilled out of almost every window in the Kraziaks' two-story brick home. Alex rang the doorbell and waited. *Norman, don't do it!* The words pounded in her head. *Don't listen to them! Eric Haines is a conniving manipulator who'll promise anything to get a deal. Tell him no. . . .*

"Alex.'' It was Norman, standing before her in a short-sleeved plaid shirt and brown pants, his white hair slightly ruffled, his reading glasses dangling from a black nylon cord around his neck. "I've been expecting you.''

She nodded, unsmiling, and followed him into his study.

"Norman! Is that Alexandra?" Ruth Kraziak appeared in the doorway, her small frame covered in a blue cotton dress that hung well below her knees. "Alexandra." She smiled a wide, bright smile. "Have you come to take me to the bus stop? Is it time? I'll just grab my purse—"

"Ruth." Alex didn't miss the tired resignation in Norman's voice. "She hasn't come for that."

"It's only Sunday, Ruth," Alex said. "We go on Wednesday, remember?" She'd taken her to the bus stop the past two Wednesdays, sat with her for two hours while Ruth waited for her daughter to arrive. When the last bus pulled in and she saw that Caroline wasn't on it, she'd get up, adjust her hat, and announce that she must have been mistaken, Caroline must be coming in next week. Then they'd get into Alex's Saab and drive to Hot Ed's for a cup of his specialty brew coffee.

What would happen when Alex was gone? Who would see that Ruth got to the bus station? Would she attempt to go herself? If Norman did sell out, and move away as he'd talked about, then what? *Then what?*

Ruth wrung her hands in front of her. "Oh. My mistake." She patted the side of her brownish-gray hair. "I seem to be so forgetful lately." She looked at them, her eyes bright. "But I don't want to forget Caroline. How would it look if she got off the bus and no one was there to greet her? A mother never forgets her child." Her voice faded, fell to a soft, reverent whisper, spoken in a tone that made Alex wonder if somewhere, deep inside Ruth's brain, she knew her daughter would never be on any bus. "Well, I'll leave you two to your business. Wednesday, I'll see you on Wednesday, Alexandra."

"Wednesday," Alex repeated as the door closed, leaving her and Norman alone.

He let out a long sigh, sank into his black leather chair.

"I want to thank you, Alex, for . . . for spending time with Ruth. . . ."

"Sure. I . . . I don't mind, really."

He nodded, waited.

"You must know why I've come."

"I think I do." He picked up a paperweight. It was molded in the shape of a golden rocker, the symbol for NK Manufacturing.

"You know I didn't come to Restalline to do a documentary on small-town life." When he nodded, she continued. "And you also know that I was sent here to investigate the town . . . see if we wanted to buy it up, turn it into an exclusive resort."

"I know." He turned the paperweight over in his hand, once, twice, three times.

"Then you should also know that somewhere along the way, I changed my mind about . . . about everything." She toyed with the tassel on her skirt. "I've been doing this for seven years, Norman, and this is the first time the town got to me . . . the first time I really saw the people, their way of life . . ."

"And Nick."

She swallowed, forced herself to keep her voice even. "And Nick."

"I'm selling the companies, Alex. I spoke with your lawyer"—he set the paperweight on the desk, pushed it away—"he's getting everything in order."

"Norman, you can't do this." She leaned forward, gripped the edge of his desk. "Think of the town, it'll be destroyed. If they get you to sell out, it'll only be a matter of time before Androvich Lumber is forced out, too."

"They?" He lifted a brow. "I thought you were 'they'."

She felt the heat crawl up her neck. "I was, but not anymore. I quit."

"I see."

"Norman, please, I feel responsible. I'm the one who put the idea in your head. I gave them the information they needed to make you an offer." She swallowed, held his gaze. "I told them if they offered you three times market value that you'd most likely take it, that you wanted to get out."

"You told them the truth."

"But I shouldn't have. I shouldn't have given them that power. *I* picked Restalline, I told them how wonderful it was here, the land, the trees, the lake. It was me," Alex said, pointing at herself. "It's on my head and . . . and I have to make it right."

"For Nick?"

"For Nick, for Justin, for you, for everyone."

"I like you, Alex," he said, his thick fingers toying with the paperweight again. The golden rocker moved, back and forth, under his index finger. "And I'd like to help, but I'm tired. I was thinking that maybe if Ruth were in a different location, maybe in Arizona or somewhere, she'd do better."

"She needs help, Norman. That's the only way she'll get better."

He shrugged. "She takes her medicine and I take care of her. Maybe if we go where there aren't so many memories . . ."

"And what about Justin? You're just going to leave him?"

"He's part of the reason I'm doing this. Don't you see?" His eyes grew bright. "They've promised me three times market value and it's all for Justin."

"It's only money, Norman, a child doesn't understand that." *How well she knew.* "He needs grandparents right now more than he needs money. And he needs to feel safe. He lost his mother when he was a baby, he shouldn't have to lose his grandparents and his town, too. Do you really want to take away everything that's familiar to him? Restalline is all Justin's ever known. And what about you and Ruth?

You'll move away, just leave him?'' Panic gripped her. She knew about being left behind. How could Norman even consider such a thing?

"Justin will adjust, children always do. And Ruth and I will visit and he can visit us, too."

She shook her head. "Don't, Norman. He'll never forgive you if you do this."

"The lawyer promised to name the resort after Caroline." A faint smile played over his lips. "What do you think of that? A town named after my baby girl."

"Norman, listen to me. Caroline's dead. You can't bring her back no matter how much you stare at her portrait or how many promises they make you." Her voice dipped, smoothed out to a low plea. "But Justin's alive. The town is alive. Everyone needs you. Please, *please* reconsider."

He looked at her, through her, his eyes glistening, his words earnest, reverent. "They told me they'll rename the lake after her, too. Isn't that wonderful, Alex? Sapphire Lake, the most beautiful body of water in the area is going to be renamed Lake Caroline ... for the most beautiful woman in this world ... and the next."

There were no words left to describe the sad despair clinging to Alex as she climbed the stairs to her apartment. She'd gone to Norman's, spoken with her heart, tried to reason with him, and still, still he'd vowed to sell Restalline Millworks and NK Manufacturing.

So this was what it felt like to be on the receiving end of the firing squad, blindfolded and waiting for the first bullet. That was the only one that mattered. The spray of shrapnel that followed would be no more than an inconsequential barrage. It was the first bullet, the one that set the mark, that tore into the captive, made him realize there was no way out. That's what Alex's conversation with Norman had felt like: a bullet fired straight at her heart.

She'd thought she could convince him to change his mind, consider his grandson, his wife, his responsibility to his town. But Norman couldn't see past Eric's promise to name the resort and the lake after Caroline. Alex had tried to tell him that even if that did happen, even if the resort carried his daughter's name, it wouldn't matter, guests wouldn't know or care who Caroline was. The only people who cared aside from Norman and his family, were the people of Restalline. They would remember with fondness, with sympathy, with heavy hearts. But Norman hadn't heard her words, none of them. He was selling his businesses and Caroline was getting a resort and a lake named after her.

Alex slipped the key in the lock, turned the knob. By tomorrow the whole town would know of her duplicity. They'd hate her, all of them . . . Justin, Stella, Gracie, Edna. . . . They wouldn't care that she'd tried to fix things, make them right. She'd failed. They would never forgive her for what she'd done; Alex doubted she'd ever forgive herself.

She couldn't stay here, but she had nowhere to go. Arlington wasn't her home, not now, not anymore. Maybe she'd pack up her car and just start driving, look for another town . . . another Restalline . . .

She was so caught up in her own thoughts that she almost didn't notice the light in the living room . . . or the circle of women sitting there.

"It's about time." Stella Androvich rose, walked toward her. "We thought you'd never get home." Her words were soft, gentle, there was a faint smile on her weathered face.

Alex backed up, felt the hard edge of the stove digging into her back. In the other room she saw Gracie with Rudy Jr., sitting in the rocker, Edna on the pink couch, Tracy perched nearby. And Elise Pentani, on a stool in the corner. They were all staring at her, waiting. Why? Why were they here? They didn't know yet, did they? No, they couldn't. If they did, they wouldn't be here. Stella wouldn't be smiling.

"I . . ." Alex didn't know what to say, where to begin. *I've betrayed you, all of you. Forgive me, forgive me.*

Stella reached out, touched Alex's arm. "It's okay, Alex."

Alex shook her head. "No, no it's not." It came out in a low, tortured moan. "You . . . you don't know . . ." her words fizzled, died.

"We do know," Stella said, taking a step forward and holding out her arms. "We know everything."

There was a second's hesitation, then Alex crumbled into Stella's arms, sobbing with grief and remorse. "I . . . I . . . sorry . . . so sorry."

"Shhhhh." Stella stroked her hair, held her close. "It'll be okay."

Alex didn't know how long they stood there, with her clutching the woman who'd become like a mother to her, or exactly how they made it to the couch, or when Tracy stuffed a handful of Kleenex in her hand and smiled at her through wet eyes and said, "Hey, Alex."

"We've heard some other versions of what's happened," Stella said, "but we'd like to hear yours."

The whole story poured out then, beginning with Alex's intrigue over the specs on a little town in Restalline, Pennsylvania, and ending with her meeting at Norman Kraziak's house tonight.

"Damn it, Alex, why didn't you tell me? I thought we were friends." This from Gracie, who sat across the room, one foot pushing off on the rocker, her mouth stretched in a straight line.

"We were . . . we are," Alex said. "But I couldn't tell you, I . . . I didn't understand it all myself, and once I did,

I thought I could just go back to my uncle and tell him it wouldn't work, that Restalline wouldn't be a good location to build on.'' She pressed her fingertips to her temples. ''I never dreamed he'd take on the project himself. I . . . I'm so sorry, Gracie.''

Gracie stared at her, said nothing. There was hurt in her eyes, hurt and betrayal.

''I wish you would've talked to us, but we probably wouldn't have listened.'' Edna Lubovich reached for her hand, squeezed it. ''I know Chuck wouldn't have.'' Her eyes glistened with tears. ''Oh, no, not my Chuck. He would have called you ten kinds of a traitor, made you leave.''

''But you fell in love with the town, didn't you, Alex?'' Tracy sat beside her mother, sounding so much older than she had a few weeks ago. ''And the people. The way you talked to me, like you really cared. That wasn't fake, I know it wasn't. I don't care how or why you came to Restalline, what matters to me is that you came and you cared, cared about us.''

''You became one of us,'' Stella said.

''And you fell in love with one of ours,'' Gracie whispered.

''And he fell in love with you,'' Elise Pentani spoke. She'd said nothing since Alex arrived, but now the power of her words filled the room.

''No.'' Alex shook her head. ''He . . . doesn't love me . . . he . . . can't even look at me.''

''Time. Time heals all.'' Stella put her arm around Alex, pulled her close. ''You'll see.''

In the whole town of Restalline, Michael Androvich was the last person Alex would have called on to help her. She'd only seen him a handful of times, only spoken with him once, when he'd come to Nick's and found her in his bed and given her a warning that she'd better not hurt his brother. Well, she'd done that, and quite openly, not only hurt him, but in his eyes, made a fool of him, too. But Stella had insisted, as had the rest of the women last night, that Michael might just be the only person, as odd as it sounded, to get Nick to listen, get him to help Alex in her attempt to thwart her uncle.

After hours of talking, two pots of coffee, and a pot of chamomile tea, they'd decided on a plan to "save" the town. It could be done, Stella insisted, with stick-to-it drive, prayer, and a little luck. Alex knew her uncle and Eric would launch an all-out campaign on the townspeople, try to win them over, force Nick and Androvich Lumber out. They'd plan a forum, call a town meeting, but if Nick were there, backing her, she could get the people to listen to the other side, make them see that fancy words and vague promises didn't build dreams or raise families or foster goodwill in communities. Maybe she could make them understand what she had not: that small towns have an intangible, intrinsic value, and it's the people caring about, and for, one another that makes the difference, instills the hope, creates the faith, builds the trust for the future.

But she needed Nick's help. The people wouldn't listen to her without his backing. And why should they? She'd lied to them once already, taken their trust and abused it. They would only expect her to do the same a second time. It was senseless to even try to approach Nick. He wouldn't talk to her, wouldn't trust her enough to help her even if it helped the town. Unless someone he did trust convinced him.

That someone was Michael. Stella insisted that for all of their differences, for all of Michael's sullenness, his short temper, and escapades, and for all of Nick's critical demeanor toward his younger brother, they were still close. Michael could make him listen.

Alex headed down the grassy path behind Michael's house. There was a large shed a few hundred feet from the two-story log cabin. He was in there, she could tell by the loud humming sound coming from the shed that reminded her of some type of saw. No one had ever mentioned he had an interest in making or repairing anything. Her curiosity drove her to peek in the window of the shed, see what Michael Androvich did in his off-hours besides carouse around.

He was bent over some type of machine, wearing goggles, his muscles bulging under a dark T-shirt as he steadied a long instrument against a block of wood that turned around on the machine. Alex watched, mesmerized, as the wood hollowed out in the middle and took the shape of a bowl. After a few more minutes, he cut the power and the bowl stopped spinning. He lifted it off of the machine, held it up.

"Nice. Very nice, Michael." An old man with a long white-and-gray beard moved into Alex's line of vision. He was shorter than Michael by two or three inches, solid, still well-muscled. When he turned his head, Alex bit the inside of her cheek. There was a scar slashing half of his face, a pocket of skin where his left eye should be, stretched and pulled to just below the left nostril.

Uncle Frank.

Michael turned his head, just a fraction, spotted her staring at them through the window. His expression turned mean, dark. "Get the hell out of here!" he yelled at her.

The older man, Uncle Frank, turned, looked at her with his good eye. Alex held his gaze, unable to look away.

"I'll get rid of her," Michael said.

Uncle Frank stopped him. "No. Bring her here."

Alex turned away from the window, worked her way to the door.

"What the hell are you doing here?"

"Hello, Michael, nice to see you, too."

"Cut the bullshit. Why are you spying on us?"

"I wasn't spying. I needed to talk to you."

"Talk? To me? Haven't you done enough damage in this town already? They should've booted you out of here last night."

"I . . ." Why did he make her so uneasy? Maybe because he did nothing to hide his contempt for her. "I need your help."

That made him laugh. "You need my help?" He laughed again, stopped abruptly. "I'll give you my help, Alex Chamberlain, vice president of WEC Management. Leave town now and I won't let them drag you out by your hair."

"Michael." It was Uncle Frank. "Forgive my nephew, Alexandra. He forgets his manners."

Alex tried to focus on his good eye, a piercing brown-black, tried not to look at the jagged, ugly flesh that stretched over the left half of his face. "You must be Uncle Frank."

He smiled. "I am. Come." He held out his hand. Alex took it and followed him into the shed. There were two chairs tucked in the corner of the room. "Sit."

"She shouldn't be here." Michael followed them inside, his longish hair plastered to his neck, the sides of his face.

"It's all right, Michael. I've been looking forward to meeting Alexandra." He turned to her, patted her hand. "Stella has told me much about you. Thank you for coming to my birthday party."

"You're welcome," she managed, wondering if he ever attended any of his parties.

"I understand"—he drew in a deep breath and stroked his beard—"that you are having a difficulty, a problem—"

"She's a liar and she got caught." It was Michael, staring at her, with eyes so like his brother's . . . eyes filled with hate . . .

"This is true?"

Alex dropped her head, nodded. "I thought I was doing

the right thing, just doing my job, what I'd been trained to do, but it was wrong, all wrong, and when I tried to fix it," her voice dipped to a whisper, "it was too late."

"Hmmm."

"And my uncle"—she shrugged—"he wouldn't let me fix it. He insisted we go through with it, but I couldn't, so I left."

"Left? What did you leave, Alexandra?"

His voice was so soft, his words so soothing, that her shoulders started to shake, the last remains of her resolve to crumble. "I left my job and . . . and my uncle. I left them both. He wouldn't understand, didn't want to . . . he only cared about . . . about getting this place. That's all he's ever cared about . . . the winning . . . not me. He's never cared about me . . . not unless I brought him a prize . . . or became the prize."

"Now what will you do?" Uncle Frank asked. "Where will you go?"

"I don't know where I'll go yet, but I know I have to make things right before I leave." She lifted her head, sought out Michael. "That's why I came here, Michael. I need your help. I . . . need you to talk to him."

"You lied to the whole town." He glared at her. "Why should anybody care about what you have to say? You're a liar and you lied to my brother . . . probably about *every-thing*."

He meant her relationship with Nick, her love for him . . . "No." She shook her head. "Not everything."

"Michael, listen to yourself. Think of what you are saying. Have we not lied to the whole town these past years? Have we not deceived our friends, even our family?"

"No, Uncle Frank. That's different."

"Is it?" The old man stroked his full beard, held his

nephew's gaze. "I don't think so. We did what we thought was right. Me, to protect a tradition, and you, well, you to protect an old man's pride."

"But—"

"Did you know, Alex, that I once made bowls and boxes carved from the most beautiful wood in Pennsylvania? Cherry, oak, red maple. And did you know that men traveled from all over the country, trying to get me to sell my things, but I refused? Nothing was for sale. They could only be given as gifts."

"I've seen your work. It's magnificent."

"And did you also know that since the accident that took half my face off, I have not been able to make one box or bowl?"

"Uncle Frank—"

Alex shook her head, puzzled. "But Stella told me—"

"Yes, she did. Stella still believes I make all of these beautiful things. But I don't. It's all a lie, no different than yours, maybe worse." He patted her hand. "Michael; he's the one."

"Michael?" She wouldn't have thought him capable of creating a bowl made of Popsicle sticks let alone such fine wood.

"He makes the bowls, the boxes, I only observe. So, you see, a lie. Michael lets people think he runs around, acts like a hoodlum, when much of the time, he's right here, in this shed with me, working."

"But why?" This addressed to Michael.

He shrugged, looked away.

"For Michael, it is easy to have people think this way of him. That way they will never be disappointed. But one day he must learn that in the end, he will be the one who is most disappointed. I think," he said, tilting his head to get a better look at his nephew, "that it is time for honesty, time to let the town know that Michael Androvich is the creator of such beauty, and also a man of honor, and integrity.''

Michael shoved his hands in the back pockets of his jeans, said nothing.

"Now, Alexandra, how can my nephew help you?"

Chapter 18

Michael let himself into the house, headed for the refrigerator. Miller Lite, Lipton Brisk Iced Tea. Miller Lite, Lipton Brisk Iced Tea. *Ah, what the hell.* He grabbed the can of iced tea and popped the top.

Nick should be home any minute now, and then they could have their *talk.* He'd had to bullshit him a little, tell him something was up with Uncle Frank that needed discussing right away. Hell, if he had so much as breathed *her* name, Nick would have clammed up, told him to go to hell. At least that's what Elise told him last night when she'd called his house to beg him to talk to Nick. What the hell, they must have all held a big pow-wow, decided to gang up on the men, get them to work on Nick. First it had been Alex, then his mother, then Elise.

Elise. *Shit.* He was thinking about her too much lately. Last night when she'd called him, he'd been lying in bed, and just for a split second, he'd thought, hoped, she'd just wanted to talk to him, Michael, but the first words out of her mouth had been Nick. She still didn't get it, did she? Nick was off-limits to her, he loved Alex, even though right now he might hate her, and if things didn't work out between them, he'd be through with women for a while. Caroline had done that to Nick, too, purged his heart of feeling for a long time. And then, Alex Chamberlain had driven into town in her black Saab with her fifty-dollar haircut and fancy pearls and he was a goner.

Until she fed him the big lie. But the bitch of it was, and he hated to admit it, she really did seem to love him. He almost felt sorry for her yesterday, crying on Uncle Frank's shoulder, her little nose red and puffy. Almost. He was here because he'd promised his uncle he'd do this and that was the only reason. Elise Pentani had nothing to do with it, either. So what if she was disappointed in him? *So what?*

He took a gulp of iced tea, sank into the recliner, and fished around for the remote. He'd just found an old rerun of *Gunsmoke* when the screen door banged open.

"Michael. Is that you?"

"In here."

Nick walked in carrying a Miller Lite. "What's up with Uncle Frank?" He sat down on the couch, kicked up his feet on the oak coffee table.

"He wanted me to tell you . . . Shit, I don't know how to say this."

"Then just say it."

Michael flipped his cap up, scratched his forehead. "You know those bowls and boxes he makes?"

"The ones everybody begs for? The ones the company from New York wanted to market last year? Yeah, I know those boxes."

"Yeah, well, he hasn't made a box or a bowl since his accident."

Nick laughed, took a swig of beer. "Funny, Michael. I'm not in the mood for jokes. His accident was two years ago."

"Right."

"So, if Uncle Frank isn't doing the woodwork, who the hell is, huh? Santa Claus?"

"No." Michael fidgeted in the recliner, tried to get comfortable. "I am."

"You?" Nick laughed again, this time louder.

"That's right. Me."

"Come on, Michael, that kind of work requires hours of concentration, skill, dedication . . ."

"And I'm not capable of anything like that, right?" He was getting pissed. "Why? Because I'm the screw up in the family? Because I could never be responsible for anything worthwhile? Right? Is that what you're thinking?" *Shit*, now he was really pissed.

"Hey, settle down. That's not what I meant. I guess you're capable, I just never thought of you as doing anything like that." He took another drink. "So what's the real story? Why's Uncle Frank pretending he's not making the stuff?"

Michael gave him a surly look. "Because he's not."

The room fell silent. Nick was the first to speak. "You're really making the bowls? And the boxes? Even the ones carved out of cherry with the scrollwork?"

"That was my design."

"Hell, do you realize what kind of business you could have? How much money you could make? Shit, Michael, you could name your own price!"

Michael shook his head. "They're not for sale."

"But—"

"Not everything's for sale, Nick. You should know that better than anybody. I'm doing it because I love the feel of wood in my hands, love to create something with it."

"Then at least come out of the woods, give that up."

"How? How can I give up the smell of pine, the leaves,

the earth? There's nothing like it after a rain. I can't give that up, Nick. It's a part of me. I might as well cut my hand off.''

''I've been waiting, hoping you'd run the business, give me a break, let me just concentrate on the hospital.''

Michael rubbed his jaw. ''I might help out . . . to help you . . . but I don't think either one of us wants to run the business. We'd suffocate. Why not turn it over to Rudy? He's grown up with wood just like us.''

''You really don't want it?''

''No.''

''Okay, then. Rudy. Hmmm.''

''Or Gracie,'' Michael said. ''She's a tough-ass kind of broad. She'd keep the guys in shape.''

''Gracie,'' Nick said. ''I like that. Gracie Ann Androvich Romanski, CEO of Androvich Lumber.''

''Yeah, print that on her diaper bag.'' Both men laughed.

''Thanks, Michael. I appreciate your help and I'm sorry if I misjudged you.''

Michael lifted his iced tea, saluted his brother. ''It's okay, really. I know I can be a real asshole sometimes.'' He cleared his throat. ''That thing about Caroline . . . I never should have doubted you. You're my brother, I should have trusted you more.''

''It's over, Michael. It's been over a long time now,'' Nick said. ''Let it go, okay?''

Michael nodded. ''Consider it done.''

''Good.'' Nick tipped his head back, finished his beer, and crunched the can with his fingers. ''That wasn't as bad as I thought it would be. When you said you needed to talk to me I had no idea what you needed to tell me.'' He laughed. ''This was nothing.''

Michael cleared his throat. ''Actually, there is one other thing.''

''Oh?''

"Uncle Frank wanted me to talk to you about it. It's coming straight from him."

"Sure. Anything for the old man. What is it?"

"He wants you to talk to Alex."

That stopped him. His eyes got real narrow and he cleared his throat—twice. "How does he know about her?"

"She came to see him, I mean me, and he was there. There was this instant connection between them, she cried on his shoulder, told him what a bad girl she was and how sorry she was for all of it and, well, you know Uncle Frank. He tried to make her feel better, told her you'd meet with her, help her persuade the town to stand firm and fight her uncle."

"Jesus." Nick rubbed a hand over his face. "How could he do this to me?"

"The hell of it was, she seemed so damn sincere, especially the part where she told him she loved you." He eyed his brother, saw the involuntary jerk of his shoulders. "Yeah, it was probably all a scam, but I saw her face, it looked damn sincere."

"She's a good actress."

There was pain in those words, deep, gut wrenching. "Maybe she's not acting." Did Michael believe that, or was he just saying it to make Nick feel better? No, he believed it.

"Hell, what do you know about it? You've got Elise Pentani so confused and mixed up, she can't think of anything but telling me what a worthless piece of scum you are."

"Elise?" *She's in love with* you, *fool, not me. She can't stand me.* "Elise and I don't exactly see eye to eye."

"You could do worse than settle down with Elise, you know."

"I'm not settling down with anybody. Besides, she hates my guts."

"If she hates your guts so much then why was she so upset when she found Cynthia Collichetti half naked at your house? Huh? Oh, didn't think I knew about that? Elise told me all about it . . . several times."

She was upset? How upset? Of course she'd be upset, she thought he was worthless, a reptile of the lowest form. "This isn't about me," Michael said, changing the subject. "Alex's uncle is holding some kind of town meeting tomorrow night to try to persuade the rest of the town to sell out so he can build that rich-bitch resort of his. She's going to try and talk people out of it, tell them the downside of selling out and all that, but she doesn't think anybody will listen"— he scratched his chin—"unless you give her your stamp of approval." He downed the rest of his iced tea, burped, and said, "So don't be such a chickenshit, talk to her, will ya?"

Nick turned the phone over in his hands. Once, twice, three times. Michael was right. He really was a chickenshit. But damn it, he didn't want to talk to her, to hear her voice, to see her in his mind. He wanted to forget her, be done with it, over, *now*, not tomorrow or the next day or next week; but how the hell was he going to do that when he had to have a goddamned conversation with her that was only going to start the remembering all over again?

Hadn't he promised himself after Caroline that he was never going to let himself get into that kind of situation again, where you gave your heart, your soul, your trust, where everything *mattered so damn much*? Lisa hadn't mattered, much to his mother's pleasure, neither had the ones before that. Until Alex. She mattered.

Shit.

This one was going to be a long, slow death, the kind that sucked you dry, left you hollowed out and decaying, half insane with remembering, filled with bitterness and longing that you'd deny to your grave.

Goddamn it.

It hadn't been that way with Caroline. Her death was merely the culmination of a tortured relationship gone bad. He'd loved his wife, loved her with every part of his being, but he couldn't save her, couldn't stop her from suffocating their marriage with her insecurities, her neediness, her paranoid reactions to life. She'd died long before they pulled her charred body from the second-story bedroom on Freeman Avenue. If he were honest with himself, he'd have to admit that the Caroline he knew and loved had died the day she left Restalline, withering a little more each year, like a flower without water, until the essence had disappeared, crowded out by insecurity and clumps of neediness, burying all indication of what had been.

Nick flipped the phone from hand to hand. He'd promised Michael he'd call. Uncle Frank was expecting him to do this—so was his mother, his sister, hell, who else thought he ought to call her? Fine, so he'd do it and be done. He picked up the phone, punched out her number.

"Hello."

It was her. "It's me, Nick."

"Nick."

He didn't like the way she said his name, like she was sucking in oxygen. "Michael said you came to see him."

Silence. "Yes. Yes, I did."

Why was she so hesitant? Where was the take-charge, ball-busting Alex he knew? Was she trying to be demure, hesitant, so he'd feel sorry for her? Too late, she'd get no sympathy from him. "He said your uncle's holding a meeting tomorrow night at seven."

"Yes." Pause. "Can you be there? I . . . I wouldn't ask if I didn't need your help."

"What, you mean you blew your credibility?" He knew he was being an asshole, but he didn't care.

"If you called to make me feel worse, that's not possible. So, are you going to put aside our differences and try to make these people see sense or not?"

There was a trace of the old Alex. "Seven o'clock. I'll be there."

"Thank you. Do you think we should meet before that, try to come up with a plan?"

"How about something new and innovative, like the truth?"

"You're never going to let this go, are you?"

"Probably not."

"I'll see you tomorrow night."

"Right." *Click.* Nick set the phone down, rubbed his eyes. He had to get a grip, stop acting like a wounded animal ready to lash out, rip flesh from bone. She was only a woman . . . Jesus . . . one woman . . . and he was more than one kind of fool if he thought he could just blink twice and forget about her.

You've got Elise Pentani so confused and mixed up, she can't think of anything but telling me what a worthless piece of scum you are. . . .

You could do worse than settle down with Elise, you know. . . .

If she hates your guts so much then why was she so upset when she found Cynthia Collichetti half naked at your house? . . . Elise told me all about it . . . several times. . . .

It was early morning. The sun hadn't been up more than an hour and Michael was walking the trail, preparing to take down two big oaks that were wedged between a copse of cherry and walnut saplings. There was an art to felling them without disrupting the younger trees, but Michael would have the oaks on the ground before the rest of the crew showed up. Twenty minutes, tops. He set down his saw, sized up the first tree. It was a big mother, wide and burly, with branches that were themselves the size of trees and roots—thicker than both of Michael's legs—protruding from the ground.

Morning in the woods was his favorite time. That's when he could really think. . . . He touched the bark, felt the coarseness of the wood . . . his mind wandered . . .

Nick didn't know what the hell he was talking about. Elise wasn't in love with Michael. Hell, she couldn't stand his guts. She loved Nick, she'd always loved Nick. But if he were honest with himself, he'd have to admit that there'd been a time or two when he'd wondered what it would be like to nip at the soft spot just beneath her ear, trail his lips down her throat, hear her moan as his hand closed over one melon-sized breast. They were just fleeting thoughts, maybe dreams of some sort, coming to him right before he fell asleep at night, or at predawn, or, shit, coming to him once when he was banging Cynthia Collichetti. He'd felt like a real slime bucket after that. What kind of man bangs one woman while he's thinking about another one?

Elise Pentani wasn't interested in him and he wasn't interested in her. Michael swore under his breath, picked up the saw, pulled the cord. It ripped to life and he took the first cut, the same cut he'd made thousands of times before.

Even if for some crazy, ridiculous minute, he thought about wanting to be with her, it would never work between them. He made a second cut, angled the saw. *Never*. Just because she got along with his kids and they were always pestering him to see her, it didn't mean they'd make it as a couple. *Cut, cut, angle*. So, okay, he was attracted to her. So what? *So what?* She was repulsed by him, his language, his actions . . . everything. He'd seen it on her face, in her dark eyes. She'd never love him. She loved Nick. The tree hit the ground in one thundering whoosh, slicing a path between cherry and walnut.

Michael eyed the tree with the distracted disinterest of one who's performed the task so many times he's already five steps into the next process. He checked his watch. Ten minutes left before the first crew showed up and he still had one more tree to take down. The second oak was some fifty feet away, its path blocked by the branches of the one he'd just taken down. He revved his saw again, started cutting a trail.

If she hates your guts so much then why was she so upset when she found Cynthia Collichetti half naked at your house? . . . Elise told me all about it . . . several times. . . . Damn that woman! What he did was none of her business . . . none at all. *So why did it bother him so damn much that he'd hurt her?*

When the saw kicked against a knot and the blade ripped into his shirt, Michael jerked back, cut the motor, and stared at the bright red color seeping through the torn material of his shirt. *Shit!* He'd sliced himself. *Goddamn carelessness, that's what it had been.* He grabbed a handkerchief out of his back pocket, eased his shirt up over his forearm. *Goddamn!* The flesh was torn in a jagged line, ripped open, oozing blood. He managed to tie the handkerchief above the wound, then pressed his fingers against the area. *Shit, of all the stupid-ass things to do.* How many times had he told his men, *Never cut in the woods alone; things happen when you least expect them to.* And then the most basic rule of all: *Keep your mind on what you're doing. I don't want you thinking about anything but the tree in front of you, not the woman you screwed last night or the one you're gonna screw tonight. Understand?*

He felt dizzy, light-headed. Michael eased himself onto the fallen oak. His shirt was soaked with blood, his fingers wet and sticky. He closed his eyes and hoped the crew would be on time.

Elise hurried out of the elevator, rushed down the hall to the visitor's waiting room. Nick was sitting in a tan vinyl chair reading the paper. "Nick? Where is he? What happened? Can I see him?"

Nick looked up, set the paper aside. "Michael's fine. He came out of surgery a little while ago. Mom's with him right now."

"Oh, God." She sank into a chair beside him. "If the crew hadn't come along when they did . . . if they hadn't found him . . . he would've been out there all alone . . . he could have . . ." She pressed her fingertips against her temples. "Oh, God."

"Elise." Nick took her hand. "He's going to be okay. The doctor said he tore up his arm, but with therapy and time, eventually, he should regain full use."

"How much blood did he lose?"

"Enough. They gave him two units in surgery."

She shook her head, fought back tears. All these weeks and she could think of nothing but cursing Michael Androvich for the way he'd hurt her, been cruel, thoughtless, rude. The thought of *that woman* with him tortured her every night, deprived her of sleep and common sense. And then there were his taunts, pounding in her head, over and over, *You come here again, Snow White, and I'm gonna think you're looking for something . . . and I'm gonna give it to you.* Why did she care? Why?

The answer flowed through her, hard and steady, true; because somewhere underneath all of that hard, outward irascibility, that crude front, was a gentleness, a softness in hiding, too timid and unsure to emerge. She'd glimpsed it— at Marie Lendergin's wedding when he'd looked into her eyes and almost kissed her. And the first time, when she'd come to his uncle's birthday party and found out Nick had already left with Alex. Michael had saved her from humiliating herself with tears and disappointment. He'd told her to forget Nick, forget falling in love with him. How had he known when she'd kept it such a well-guarded secret from everyone else? How had he figured it out?

And then there was the electricity that flowed between them whenever they were in the same room. It was palpable, igniting them, a force pulling opposites together, overpowering with sheer magnetism. He had to feel it, *he had to*.

"Elise, stop crying. He's going to be okay."

She swiped at her cheeks, sniffed. "I have to see him, Nick. I have to see him."

"Okay. As soon as Mom comes out, I'll take you in. Okay?"

She managed to nod, clutched Nick's hand tight, and prayed to the Blessed Mother. *Please let him be all right, Most Holy Mother . . . please let me not be too late . . .*

Did Michael still think she was in love with Nick, or rather, did he still think she *thought* she was in love with Nick? He didn't, did he? Would it make a difference if he knew she had been merely infatuated with his older brother, admiring him for his deeds and his person, but love, *real love*? No, not real love. That emotion was reserved for someone else.

For him. Michael John Androvich. And she had to tell him, *now*, because she'd only just realized it herself. She would be good for him, she knew it, and if he let himself open up, he would be good for her, too.

She didn't hear Stella come out until she was standing in front of her. "Elise. I'm so glad you came."

Elise opened her eyes, not trying to disguise the anguish she felt. "You were right, Stella . . . about me . . . and Michael . . . about all of it. You were right."

The older woman leaned over, gave her a hug. "I know dear, I know. Now why don't you go tell my son so he knows, too?"

"Yes." Elise stood up, half dazed, suddenly afraid to see him, afraid not to. "I'll go and see him. Now." She turned, headed down the hall, past the double doors that led to his room.

Michael was in room 214. She slipped into the room, eased the door closed behind her. He was sleeping, his large frame filling up the bed, looking out of place and almost funny in the standard hospital blue-and-white gown. There was an I.V. in his right arm and his left was bandaged and propped up on a pillow. His curly brown hair was matted down, his jaw covered in dark stubble. His chest rose and fell in equal rhythm.

He looked wonderful. Elise stood there, watching his chest move up and down, assessing the quality, the quantity. He was alive . . . alive . . .

"You my private duty nurse?"

Her head snapped up. "Michael." She could barely speak.

"Yeah, what a screw up, huh?" His voice was groggy, slurred.

"No, it was an accident." She moved to his side, touched his hand. "Accidents happen. I'm just glad you're all right."

His dark eyes narrowed. "Are you, Snow White?"

"Of course, I am."

"Why? So you wouldn't have to come to my funeral and pretend you were going to miss me?" He tried to smile, but it ended in a grimace.

"Michael, stop. You shouldn't even be talking, you should be resting right now."

"Why, Elise? Why are you glad I'm all right? And don't play any of that 'nursey' stuff with me."

She swallowed. He'd called her Elise. "Because . . ." she

forced the words out, "because I don't want anything to happen to you." *I love you, you big, ridiculous idiot.*

"That's hard to believe. I haven't been exactly nice to you."

She'd been all prepared to bare her soul, tell him she loved him even if he didn't feel the same way about her. But now, standing next to him, feeling his eyes on her, she couldn't do it. "Michael, this isn't the time. Can't we discuss this later?"

"No, goddamn it, we cannot discuss this later." He winced, sucked in a breath. "Because I did something really stupid today and I still can't figure out why. You know what I did, Elise? You know why I had the accident?"

His voice was getting louder; he was agitated, maybe from the pain medication . . . probably because she was in the room. "Michael—"

"I'll tell you why." His fingers grasped hers. "Because I was thinking about you. *You*, Elise, like I've been doing for the past two months, and it's driving me crazy. You're driving me crazy. So, Jesus, will you put me out of my misery and just answer the fucking question?"

Laughter bubbled up inside her, spilled over, leaving her giddy. "Yes, you big oaf, I'll answer the question." She leaned over, planted a soft kiss on his lips, and said, "I cared because, fool that I am, I love you, Michael Androvich, with my whole heart."

Chapter 19

The manufacturers of central air-conditioning units did not make their livelihood in the hills of Restalline. No one, with the exception of perhaps five families and the hospital, had central air. The rest of the town used window units if they were fortunate, ceiling fans if they had a post-1980 home, or just plain box fans if they were normal folk. City Hall had four window units and several box fans, but in mid July with the night temperature hovering at 85 degrees and the room packed with two-hundred-plus bodies spilling out into the street, air circulation was minimal if not stagnant.

Walter Chamberlain wiped his fine linen handkerchief over his brow, stuffed it back into his pocket. He looked out at the crowd, a rather common lot: men in plaid shirts with sunburned faces and untrimmed hair, women looking wrinkled and unkempt in polyester-cotton blends, sans makeup, children, too, tanned and sneakered. Even a few wheelchairs, accommodating overweight women with sparse gray hair, wearing pastel housedresses. The town had indeed come out to hear about the proposal, or proposition, depending on how one chose to view the issue.

One thing was certain in Walter's mind. They would sell, all of them, given the right incentive, and he knew what that would be. *Money.* It always was; the only variable was the number. Would it take a little extra cash thrown their way or perhaps a fair amount? No matter, eventually they would sell; Walter would have his deal, his resort would become a reality.

He checked his watch, 6:45 P.M. Alex should be here soon. Eric was set up in the corner, dressed in white and gray striped poplin, looking cool and unruffled as he prepared documents for those parties interested in signing tonight. Walter almost smiled. That's what he admired most about Eric, that self-possessed air of one who is always in control, who never permits the opposition to see a hint of uncertainty cross his perfect features.

So unlike Nick Androvich, who'd shown several sides of himself yesterday: anger, disbelief, pain, betrayal. He and Alex didn't belong together, anyone could see that. Eric, he was the one for his niece, and when they got back home, Walter planned to have a serious discussion with Alex, set her straight on her behavior, make certain she understood that being a Chamberlain carried various duties and responsibilities that could not be ignored.

He supposed he'd forgive her for her outburst in Virginia and again yesterday. But he wasn't going to promote her to president of the company, not with the way she'd all but given up this project. No, he'd put Eric in charge of developing the Restalline resort, Alex could report to him. Maybe that would teach her about loyalty. She was becoming more like her father and his gypsy Russian wife every day, and it worried him. Perhaps he should pull her from this project altogether, give her something else to focus on, get her away from Nick Androvich and this town, these people who were making her question everything he'd taught her.

Alex arrived by the side door wearing a simple pink shift, sandals, and no pearls. *Where were her pearls?* She always wore them; they'd cost him a small fortune at Cartier when she graduated from Wharton. Yes, Walter decided, she'd been in this hillbilly town too long. He was ordering her back to Virginia in the morning.

"Hello, my dear," he said. "Interesting choice of clothing you've chosen for a business meeting." His gaze ran the length of her, not trying to hide the distaste he felt. *No hosiery, either.*

"Uncle Walter." She nodded at him.

"We should be able to conclude our business here this evening. At the most it might take a day or two for Eric to draw up the papers, but I want you back in Virginia tomorrow."

She looked at him but did not respond.

"I'll speak first, then you can apologize for not divulging the true nature of your business earlier, but tell everyone we wanted to be certain this was the location we wanted before we got everyone's hopes up that we'd buy them out." He leaned forward, lowered his voice. "Put a positive spin on it, Alex, you know how. Let them think we're doing them a favor by offering to cash them out of their homes, which we are, if you ask me."

There was a flurry of activity among the crowd. Walter looked up to see a short, squat man working his way up the aisle, shaking hands and smiling as he went. *The mayor,* Walter thought. *Mr. B.J. Huffington. Looks like an ineffectual bug that needs to be squashed.* A second wave of commotion rolled over the gathering as those crowded around the double doors moved and Nick Androvich entered and took a place along the back wall.

"Ladies and gentleman," the little bug of a man rapped a gavel against the heavy oak desk. "It's time to begin our meeting. Let me introduce Mr. Walter Chamberlain, CEO of WEC Management Company. Mr. Chamberlain is from Arlington, Virginia." He turned to Walter. "Mr. Chamberlain." Mr. Huffington clapped, followed by a weak response from the crowd.

"Thank you, Mr. Huffington," Walter said, turning to the crowd. "As you all know, we've asked you here tonight to discuss a very critical issue that could affect the future of your lives as well as your children's and your children's children. Tonight, you will make a decision that could afford you heretofore unimagined opportunities." He paused, gazed out at the group of people, careful to avoid eye contact with Nick Androvich. "I'm talking about selling your property to WEC Management and moving away, getting a fresh start. I know for many of you this may be a scary venture; you've lived here all of your lives, maybe you've never left this town. But I tell you today, that opportunity awaits you beyond the limits of Restalline. *Let us give you that opportunity, let us help you.*" He worked his lips into a smile.

"Many of you know this young woman, standing to my left." He pointed at Alex. "What you may not know or may have just learned is that she's my niece, Alexandra Nicole Chamberlain, vice president of WEC Management, future president. Alex came here to your town because she believed it could be the next location for one of the largest, grandest, summer-winter luxury resorts in the country. But she needed to research it, see the area firsthand, study it, then make her recommendation. Her intent was never to lie or deliberately withhold information as to the true nature of her visit, but we deemed it essential not to disclose anything unless a decision was made to go ahead with the project. Please understand, we kept quiet for your own good as well as the good of the project. We could not risk individuals approaching her with the intent to sell prior to our decision to purchase.'' He smiled again, held out his hands in an open embrace. ''But now, now that we have concluded Restalline would be a perfect location, we are most eager to begin negotiations with each and every one of you.''

A man with a baby in his arms stood up. ''Is it true that Norman Kraziak has already agreed to sell both of his companies to you?''

''We've been negotiating with Mr. Kraziak and yes, it would be fair to say we've agreed in principal and are working out the details.''

''What about Androvich Lumber?'' This from a middle-aged woman in a plaid housedress. ''Are you planning to buy them up, too?''

''That is open for negotiation, of course.''

''They won't sell.'' All eyes turned to Alex. Her eyes were on the back of the room, near Nick Androvich. ''They won't sell,'' she repeated in a louder voice, ''and you shouldn't either.''

''Alex, what is the meaning of this?'' Walter clenched his jaw, forced himself to remain calm.

''You've had your say, Uncle Walter, now let me have mine.'' She cleared her throat, straightened her shoulders. ''You should all know that what my uncle says about my coming here is true. I did come to Restalline to investigate a location for a luxury resort.'' She moved toward the crowd. ''And the intent was that if we chose this town, we'd flatten it and build a beautiful resort in its place.'' She paused. ''Have any of you ever seen one of our resorts? They're beautiful, truly superb. You could spend seven days there and never run out of entertainment or food . . . or activities. We cater to the wealthy and the wealthy have the money to pay and the power to spend.'' Her voice dipped. ''But for all of its manufactured beauty, nothing compares to the beauty of this town, as it stands, today, right now. I'm not talking about the trees or the winding roads or Sapphire Lake, though they in themselves are truly impressive. I'm talking about the people who make up this town ... the caring, the friendship, the openness that greeted me, and in some cases, even the love that pulled me into its embrace. I have lived my whole life raised in the lap of luxury and yet when I came to this town, I saw how truly devoid of wealth I was, how lacking.

"The beauty of this town is found in the beauty of each one of you: a kind word, a gesture to a stranger looking for a place to stay, homemade chicken soup sent to a sick friend, the outpouring of food and prayers when a neighbor dies, the pulling together, the love of a mother for all of her children, not just those who please her." Her voice cracked, wobbled. "And forgiveness for a person who's hurt others. This is true wealth, this fabric of life woven with both joy and sorrow that breathes through each of us. Simple riches, measured with heart and commitment, not bank accounts or property values. Don't give up the real wealth, don't do it. Please."

Walter couldn't speak at first, couldn't find the right phrases to discount Alex's words. Did she really feel she was lacking? Hadn't he given her everything? *Everything? Hadn't he?* When he looked up, she was gone.

The time had come to leave Restalline. When she said good-bye to Edna Lubovich for the last time, the older woman clung to her, tears and smudges of mascara streaming down her face. There was pain there—Alex saw it, felt it, compared it to her own that had transformed into a state of dry-eyed numbness over the last twenty-four hours.

It was time to leave; there was nothing more to stay for, no one holding her here. Of course, she could infringe upon the goodwill and hospitality of Stella Androvich and Gracie, and even Edna, but what would be the point? It would all have to end sooner or later. There was no reason to hold out any longer, hoping Nick would reconsider, change his mind and let her back into his life. Some things could not be forgiven, she understood that now, had learned it at great cost. There was nothing left to do for the town; now it was their decision, hold or sell, it was out of her hands.

She was going back to Arlington, the city where she'd lived for some twenty-five plus years. Odd, but she'd always thought of it as home until she arrived in Restalline and discovered the true meaning of home. What she'd witnessed these past few months was a place where memories were created, good and bad, love, feelings, tradition, even losses were shared. Restalline could have been her home . . . could have given her all of those things . . . if only. She wouldn't stay in Arlington, not for long, just enough days to pack up, close up, and move out, head down the road, maybe west, maybe to another small town . . .

As she pulled into the long driveway of the Androvich homestead, Alex thought of the first time she'd seen this place. It had called to her even then, reaching out in all of its earthy homeyness, pulling her into its bosom, welcoming her. She slowed the car, saw Justin run out, Jet tagging after him, barking.

"Alex," Justin said as she climbed out of the car, "do you have to go? Can't you stay? Please?" His expression was grave, his eyebrows pulled together, mouth unsmiling.

"I . . . I can't, Justin." What could she say? *I lied to your father; I destroyed the best thing that ever happened to me?*

"Why? Dad says the same thing. But why?" His blue eyes filled with tears. "Why can't you make up? I thought . . . I thought you cared about us"—his voice cracked— "about me."

She pulled him to her, stroked his soft hair. "I do care, very much."

"Then stay." He wrapped his arms around her middle, held tight.

Pain shot through her, a deep, hollowed-out grief, clutching her heart, squeezing.

"Will I see you again?" he mumbled into her shirt.

She could lie, tell him they'd meet again one day or keep in touch, but that wasn't true. Nick wouldn't want her corresponding with his son, and he certainly wouldn't permit her to visit him. That would be too awkward, too painful. It was time to tell the truth. "I don't think so." She felt his small body jerk toward her, then stiffen. He pulled away, swiped at his face.

"Wait, I have something I want to give you." She tried to smile but the attempt fell flat, lifeless between them. "Just wait." Alex reached into her car, pulled out the blue-and-green mirror her father had given her so many years ago. *The true jewel is in the mirror*, her father had said. *Look into it, child. Look into it and see the jewel.* It had taken years to understand what he meant, and even more years to actually find it, but she had. *Finally.* Finally, she had found the jewel: she'd found herself. Now, maybe she could pass it on to Justin and one day he, too, would make that same claim. "My father and mother gave this mirror to me," she said, holding it out so he could see the way the colored glass shone in the sun. "Right before they died." The reds and blues glinted. "And my father told me to look into it if I felt lost or confused, and keep looking into it until I found the jewel inside. 'The true jewel is in the mirror.' That's what he told me." She handed it to Justin who turned it right, left, over.

"The jewels are on the edges," he said. "I don't see any inside."

"You have to look very hard, Justin, and be patient, and one day you'll find it, right there, staring back at you."

"Huh." He held the mirror up to the sun, squinted. Then

he looked at Alex. "Can you . . . can you write to me and I'll write back?"

She should cut everything off now, make it easier on herself instead of dying a little more every time she opened her mailbox, but she couldn't. "If your father says it's okay."

The front door of the Androvich house opened and Gracie and Stella stepped outside, carrying shopping bags.

"Mom doesn't think they have food in Virginia, so she's making sure you don't starve."

"Stop, Gracie." Stella shook her head, smiled at Alex. "You can't tell me they make bread dumplings in Virginia; I won't believe it."

"No, they don't make bread dumplings," Alex said, thinking of the wonderful taste.

"Right. And you won't be getting ba'bovka or chicken paprikash, either." She pulled out a large Ziploc baggie. "Inside here"—she pointed to the baggie—"are a dozen or so recipes. How to make stuffed cabbage, chicken paprikash, goulash, homemade bread, noodles. What else? Oh, when you make the dumplings, don't forget, slice them with a thread. No knives."

Alex stared at the baggie. If Stella had given her a gift from Bloomingdale's it could not have touched her half as much as the recipes inside the baggie. She bit the inside of her cheek, trying to hold onto her composure. "Thank you, Stella," she said, her voice hoarse, cracking. "Thank you so much."

The older woman set the bags down, held out her arms. "I'm sure gonna miss you, child," she said, pulling her into her embrace. "I love all my children, but I'll be damned if I understand any of them."

Gracie was next. "Alex." They held each other, the ache and sadness flowing through their bodies. Gracie had been the closest she'd ever come to having a sister . . . or a best friend. "I . . . I really would have liked to have had you for a sister-in-law."

"I know."

"Maybe he'll—"

"No." Alex pulled away, met her gaze. "He won't."

Gracie nodded.

From the corner of her eye, Alex saw a flash of silver coming up the driveway. *Nick!* She hadn't expected to see him again. She wasn't ready, not now, not when her emotions were so raw, the wounds too open. He parked his Navigator behind her, got out.

"Hi, Nick," Gracie said. "Bye, Nick."

He didn't answer—his eyes were on Alex. Stella and Gracie disappeared into the house. Justin was nowhere in sight. Alex forced herself to plant her feet and stand firm when what she really wanted to do was get away, run, fast.

"Hello, Nick." Incredible that those were her words, her voice.

"You left last night before I could thank you for what you did." He shoved his hands into his pockets. "You gave a very convincing speech."

It wasn't a speech, it was the truth; did you hear it? Did you listen to any of it? "Thank you."

"Your uncle tried to discount most of what you said, but I don't think he was very effective. They're holding a vote today at one o'clock."

She nodded. "And Norman? What's his stand on all this?"

"Wavering a little, I think. He was there last night, did you know that? I guess what you said really tore him up, so, who knows? I'm going to see him when I leave here, maybe help change his mind."

"I hope it works out."

"Yeah, me too. At least that's something we can hope for."

"Nick . . . I . . ." There was so much she wanted to say, a lifetime wouldn't be long enough. "I . . ."

"Yeah." His eyes moved over her face, her body, back to her face. "Me too."

Then he was gone.

Sapphire Lake was the last stop before she left Restalline for good. It seemed only fitting that this place should be her last memory, her treasure to take away in her mind, her heart. Was it only two months ago that she and Nick had come here, shared their differing philosophies on beauty, wealth? He'd told her the story of his grandparents settling in Restalline and his grandmother who sold her sapphire earrings so her husband could purchase a tract of land. And his grandfather, so touched by what she'd done that he'd named a body of water after her selfless act.

Alex sat down on the bank, splayed her fingers in the soft grass. She closed her eyes, tilted her head to the sun, and let its rays wash over her, cleanse her, heal her. Nick. She loved him. She would always love him.

A car door slammed behind her, followed by the sound of footsteps and a dog yelping. Alex swung around, saw Justin heading toward her.

"Alex!" He was waving his arms.

"Justin! What are you doing?" Jet ran up to her, sniffed, ran away.

"I'm coming with you! Jet! Jet! Come back here!"

Alex scrambled to her feet. Justin had been hiding in her car? The little scamp! Now she'd have to take him back to his father's . . . have to see Nick again . . . Would it never end?

Jet tore off around the lake, zigzagging, barking, picking up sticks and tufts of grass along the way. Justin ran after him, yelling his name, exciting the dog with his high-pitched demands. Alex kept an eye on both boy and animal. "Justin! Come back here!" He was getting too close to the water. "Justin!"

What happened next was all a blur. There was a splash and Jet was in the water, his small body bobbing up and down after something only he could see. "He's going to drown! He's going to drown!" Justin jumped in after him, arms paddling, feet kicking wildly as he tried to close the distance between himself and the dog.

Alex watched, frozen. *Dear God, let them be okay, dear God, let them be okay.*

They were almost to the middle of the lake when Justin reached Jet, grabbed him by the collar, but the dog squirmed, got away. "Jet! Jet!" Suddenly, Justin let out a howl. "Alex! Help! My leg! It hurts. I can't move it!"

Fear, cold, brutal, ripped over her, tore at her. "Paddle, Justin, use your hands."

"My leg! My leg!"

She was running to the other side of the lake. "It's a cramp. Just try to relax . . . use your hands." Alex eyed the stretch of water, her heart pounding in her throat. She hadn't been in water other than to shower or bathe since the scuba diving debacle ten years ago. *Oh, God! Help me! Help me!*

"Alex—" Justin's head went under the water; he came up choking, gasping for air. "Alex—" He went under a second time, came back up, arms flailing, screaming. "Alex!"

There was no more time to think, to hesitate. If she didn't do something he wouldn't make it. "I'm coming, Justin." She flung off her shoes, stared one more time at the water, then focused on Justin's head. *Justin. Justin. Think of Justin.* Alex dove in, slicing through the chilly water, propelled past her fears through sheer will and need. He went down a third time when she was twenty feet away. This time he did not come up. She dove beneath the surface, desperate, frantic. *Jesus, God, where is he?* Then her hand brushed against his shoe and she latched on, pulled his small body up and out of the water. Justin emerged choking, coughing, eyes red, arms wound around her neck. Alex swam to shore, slowly, Justin shivering and clinging to her side. When they reached the bank, Jet ran up to them, a yelping scrap of wet black fur.

"See? He's fine," Alex said, collapsing on the grass. "You saved him, Justin."

"Yeah." He coughed again. "And you saved me." They lay on the ground, sucking in air, until eventually their breathing evened. "Alex?"

"Huh?"

"Aren't you ... aren't you"—he turned on his side, looked at her—"afraid of the water?"

"Uh-huh, I am." She met his gaze. "But sometimes there are things that are more important than what we're afraid of"—she touched his cheek—"like you. Sometimes we have to fight back those fears so we can help someone or do something important. Like now."

"Oh. So are you still afraid of the water?"

She nodded. "Yes."

"Oh." He looked away, looked back. "Because, you know that mirror you gave me, the one with all the jewels and the hidden one in the middle? I ... I had it in my back pocket ... and when I started sinking, I felt it fall out."

"Oh." *Oh.* She looked at the lake, so blue and quiet, yet so cold ... *sometimes there are things that are more important than what we're afraid of* ... She sat up. "I'll be right back."

Justin's face lit up. "Thanks, Alex."

She walked to the edge of the lake, closed her eyes, and dove in. When she reached the place where she thought Justin had gone under, she plunged beneath the surface, forced herself to the bottom, and began scouring the murky floor. Old pop bottles, a bicycle tire, rocks, a shoe, but no mirror. She swam up to the surface, sucked in air, and made three more attempts, all in vain. "I can't find it," she yelled to Justin, "I need a break, then I'll try again."

"Okay."

"Come to this side," she said, pointing to the west side of the bank. "It's a shorter swim."

"Alex! No!"

But she wasn't listening, all she wanted to do was get back on the ground and plunk her body on the grass. She was halfway between the middle of the lake and the shore when her leg caught on something. *What the!* It felt like a wire of some sort. She tried to kick her way out of it, but it only tightened. "Justin! I'm stuck!"

"Alex!" He was standing on the shore, his voice filled with panic. "I tried to tell you, I tried to tell you not to go there. There's a big wire"—he spread his arms out—"none of us kids are allowed to go on this side of the lake 'cause you can get caught in there."

Alex tried not to let him hear the terror creeping into her voice. "Well, I'm caught in there. Every time I move my leg, the wire gets tighter. I need you to get help. Go to my car, bring my cell phone . . . it's in my purse."

He stared at her, eyes wide, mouth trembling. "You aren't . . . you won't . . . you won't die, will you?"

"No." Her arms were already heavy as she paddled to keep herself afloat. "No, I won't die."

He ran then, fast, with Jet on his heels. It seemed like hours before he made it back, although it was only minutes. Amazing how time can dangle in infinity when you don't want it to, and then leap back through when you're hoping it will stop.

"Here it is." Justin held up her cell phone. "Now what?"

She didn't hesitate. "Call your dad. Then call 911." It took four attempts before Justin figured out how to get the call to go through. Alex tried not to think about the cold water sucking the energy from her body, tried not to focus on the cramp starting up her left leg. Her neck was stiff, the muscles in her arms aching from the continuous movement necessary to keep her afloat. She was cold, so cold. Her father's words floated to her. . . . *Next year, you can come with us and I'll show you what heaven looks like. Next year* . . . Was this to be her heaven? Was she going to die with the mirror of truth lying at the bottom of the lake? And then Justin's fearful words, swirling around her as cold gripped her, and she fought for consciousness . . . *You aren't . . . you won't . . . you won't die, will you?*

No, Justin, no, I won't die. . . . I won't die.

He came to her in a dream, his voice a soft, gentle rush of warmth covering her body, wrapping her in love and hope, keeping her safe, cherished.

I love you, Alex . . . I love you, Alex . . . I love you . . .

Over and over she heard the words, sometimes a mere whisper, other times a long, drawn-out sigh, and still others, a heart-wrenching cry. If this was heaven, she could ask for no more than to hear the man she had loved with her whole being speak endlessly of his love for her. If this was heaven . . . She felt a sharp pain in her left leg. If this was heaven, she'd feel no pain. Her eyes flew open.

Nick was leaning forward in a chair, his head in his hands. "I love you, Alex."

"I love you, too."

Slowly, he lifted his head, met her gaze. His eyes were bloodshot, his hair disheveled, his jaw unshaved. "Alex," he breathed, "thank God. *Thank God.*"

She lifted her hand and he took it, kissed her fingers, closed his eyes, and rubbed his cheek against her skin. "Forgive me for letting my pride get in the way, for not seeing how much I needed you until I almost lost you.''

"There's nothing to forgive, Nick. I just . . . I just want to put it behind us . . . start over.''

He leaned forward, kissed her lips. "I'll make you happy, I promise.''

"You already have.'' She touched his cheek, pulled him closer. "You've given me my very own slice of heaven.'' Her mouth brushed against his, once, twice, three times.

"Hey, break it up, break it up.'' The voice behind them could be none other than Michael Androvich. He stood there, grinning, one arm flung around Elise Pentani's shoulders. "Thank God, you're awake,'' he said to Alex. "This man's been a real maniac, driving us all crazy worrying about you.'' He turned to Nick. "Did you worry about me like that, your own brother, when I was lying half dead in the woods?''

Nick shook his head. "You're such an idiot, Michael.''

"Of course, *I'm* only his brother''—he looked at Alex—"and what are you to him, exactly?'' He scratched his head, rubbed his jaw. "Oh, yeah, that's right . . . his future wife.''

"Usually, it's the involved party who proposes not the involved party's brother,'' Nick said.

"I know, I know, but who knows how long it'll take you to get around to it? Alex, if he doesn't pop the question in three months, you come see me, I'll get him moving.''

Nick laughed, shook his head. "Speaking of popping the question? . . .''

"December twenty-fourth,'' Elise said, smiling.

"She won't live with me, so I have to marry her.''

"Michael—''

He turned to Elise, brushed his fingers over her cheek. "I *want* to marry her,'' his voice was low, husky, "the sooner the better.''

Alex couldn't believe the man standing at the foot of her

bed was Michael Androvich. He was gentle, clean shaven, sans ball cap or rude comments ... civilized, that's what he was, and it was very appealing.

"Shit!"

Well, almost civilized.

"I mean heck. Where'd I put that damn, I mean darn, bag?"

Elise held up a small brown bag. He smiled, kissed her on the mouth. "Thanks, babe." Then he turned to Alex. "Before I forget, Mom said to tell you Rudy found the mirror. Said you'd know what that meant." He cleared his throat, shifted from one foot to the other. "I know I haven't been exactly nice to you since you came—especially that first time"—he had the good grace to turn a dull shade of red—"but this is for you." He held out the bag.

"Thank you, Michael." She reached inside, pulled out a hard object covered with tissue paper. When she pushed the paper aside, she could barely see through the tears. It was a box, *one of Michael's boxes*, a beautiful, rich cherry. She ran her hands along the edges, lifted the lid to peer inside at the burgundy velvet. Michael had told her that his boxes weren't for sale; they would only be given as gifts.

And he'd done just that. He'd given her a gift: his friendship.

"Welcome to the family."

It was late. Nick had gone home a little while ago to get some sleep and reassure Justin and the rest of the Androvich family that Alex was going to be okay, and, equally important, that she was staying in Restalline.

Alex closed her eyes, happy yet exhausted. She'd fought two fears these last few days and battled her way through both to emerge the victor. The first was the water, the second, more treacherous, was almost losing Nick.

She didn't hear the man's footsteps as he entered her room, came to stand beside her bed. Not until he spoke, in a voice that she recognized as vaguely familiar but somehow different, did she realize that she was not alone.

"Alex?"

She opened her eyes, stared. "Uncle Walter?"

Of course it was Uncle Walter; she knew her uncle. But the man standing in front of her didn't look like the man she'd grown used to seeing for the past twenty-odd years. That Uncle Walter always wore a suit with a silk handkerchief tucked in the pocket, and fine, hand-tailored linen shirts. Even on Saturdays he donned gabardine or wool. And his face, always clean shaven, nails well-manicured, hair trimmed and re-trimmed. His voice was steady, sure, his words clipped, demanding. *Walter Chamberlain was power*.

The man before her was none of those. His shirt was wrinkled, sweat-stained under the arms, no tie, hair disheveled. But it was the way his shoulders slumped forward in obvious resignation, perhaps defeat, and the wavering in his voice that shocked her most, told her something was terribly wrong.

"Alex," he said again. "I came as soon as I could. I was on my way back home, thought I'd check in with Kraziak," his voice cracked. "He told me."

"I'm fine, really." *Why are you here?*

"Jesus, Alex, would you have risked your life for that ridiculous mirror your father gave you?" He ran a hand through his hair. "Would it have been worth it?"

She nodded. "Yes, yes it would have been."

"I see. What you said last night . . . about lacking in your life . . . did you mean it?"

Alex looked away. He'd never understand.

"Do you hate me so much?" The words were filled with agony. "So much that you can't credit me with one good thing in your life?"

She forced herself to meet his gaze. His face looked hollowed-out, a shadow of its former strength as though he were diminishing right before her. "I don't hate you, Uncle Walter. I loved . . . love you, but I can't live my life for you anymore." Tears filled her eyes. "Ever since I came to live with you, I've done nothing but try to please you, do what you and Aunt Helen wanted me to do, expected me to do. And do you know why? So I could get a small scrap of praise, a pat on the head or a nod. . . . I settled for that because what I really wanted, what I needed most of all, I knew I'd never get." She swiped at her cheeks. "Do you know what that was, Uncle Walter? Do you have any idea what I've been working for all these years? Do you?" Her voice cracked, dipped to a whisper. "All I ever wanted, ever, was your love."

A single tear fell down his cheek. "Why do you think I've worked so hard to protect you, educate you, see that you got the right start in life, made the right choices? I did it because I love you, Alex." Another tear fell. "I've always loved you."

"It didn't feel like love. It felt like possession."

He fell into a chair, buried his head in his hands. "I tried to shield you from your parents' nomadic ways. I didn't want you to end up like them." He shook his head. "All I wanted was for you to have what your father rejected, what was yours by birth."

"And all I wanted was your love."

He lifted his head, his eyes bloodshot. "My God, what have I done?" It was a moan, a supplication.

Alex reached out, hesitated, laid her fingers on his shoulder. He grasped her hand, clung to it as though it were a life source.

"I took every memory of your parents, the pictures, the letters, the artwork, and I hid it all, except for the mirror, and you only got to keep that because you slept with it under your pillow every night.'' His shoulders slumped forward. ''I was afraid for you . . . afraid for me . . . afraid I'd lose you . . . to their lifestyle . . . their memory. But I lost you anyway, didn't I?''

''No. No, Uncle Walter, you haven't lost me. But you have to love me, the real me that's inside, not the one you want me to be.'' She sucked in a deep breath. ''I'm staying in Restalline. I want to live here and love here and hopefully grow old here. But I can't if you take the town away. Please don't do that, Uncle Walter, please.''

''I pulled out the minute Norman Kraziak told me what had happened to you. I knew if there was any chance of repairing our differences, this place couldn't be an issue between us.''

''Thank you, Uncle Walter. Thank you.''

''I'm thinking about getting out of the development business, maybe concentrate on renovation instead. Preserve our history. What do you think?''

''I think that's a great idea.''

''I'm proud of you, Alex.''

''I'm proud of you, too, Uncle Walter.''

He smiled then, a real smile. ''Good.'' He clutched her hand in his, a sign of love, respect, and need. ''Good.''

Epilogue

"Are you sure you want to do this?" Nick pulled the silver Navigator in front of the small ranch-style home.

Alex nodded. "I'm sure."

He reached over, kissed her on the lips. "Let's go."

It would be a lie to say she wasn't afraid, that she didn't fear the owner would slam the door in her face. And who could blame him? She'd lied, not directly, but indirectly, as an accomplice—if not in the beginning, then down the road, after she'd learned the truth. Maybe if she'd taken a stand, spoken out, tried to fight, she could have made a difference. Maybe, but, she'd never know.

Now, she had to face Leonard Oshanski and tell him that his sister's tree, the one his father had planted in the name of his dead daughter, Emma, and entrusted to his sons to protect, the same one Alex promised would not be touched, had most likely been uprooted, plowed under, stripped, and hauled away with the first clearing of the lots.

Nick had told her he understood if she wanted to leave things alone. After all, his father and Leonard had been friends, both from the old school, where a man was only as good as his word. Leonard would not think too highly of a person, man or woman, who gave a promise and then broke it.

But Alex had insisted. Right was right and maybe one man's open mind could right a wrong. She pressed the doorbell, waited. *Right was right. Right was right.* The door opened.

"Yes?" There was a half inquisitive smile on Leonard Oshanski's face as he opened the door. Then he saw Alex. "Hello! Come in." He turned to Nick.

"Mr. Oshanski, my name is Nick Androvich, from Pennsylvania. I don't know if you remember me—"

The old man's eyes lit up. "Of course, I do. Nicholas Androvich. Your father was the best woodcutter in this part of the country." He looked from Nick to Alex, "You two, you are . . . together?"

Nick nodded. "We are."

"Good. Come in, come in." He shuffled into the small living room, leaning on his cane. "Would you like something to drink? Coffee? Tea? A shot of Johnny Walker?"

"No, nothing for me, thank you." This was not the greeting Alex had expected. She took a seat on a small, blue-plaid loveseat, swallowed. Did he think Emma's tree was still standing? Could he not know? Oh, God.

Nick sat down beside her, covered her hand with his. "Mr. Oshanski, Alex has something she wants to tell you, something she feels you should know."

Leonard Oshanski lowered himself onto his tweed recliner, smiled at her. "Your uncle's already been here."

"Uncle Walter? He has? Why?"

Mr. Oshanski rubbed his chin. "Probably the same reason you're here. He called me a few weeks ago, said he had something important to discuss. The next thing I know, he's here."

"What . . . what did he say?" *Uncle Walter had visited Mr. Oshanski?*

"He told me about Emma's tree, apologized for going back on his word and not saving it." He pulled out a white handkerchief, blew his nose. "Then he did the damndest thing. He showed me a piece of paper, all notarized and legal, renaming the winter part of that there resort you're building. And you know what the new name's gonna be?" He grinned. "Emma's Promise. How about that?" His voice tapered to a soft drawl. "Emma's Promise. I wonder what in the devil got into him to do such a thing."

"I think I know." Alex smiled at Nick, turned to Mr. Oshanski. "He found this wonderful place that changed his life. Maybe you've heard of it"—her fingers interlaced with Nick's—"it's called Restalline."

AUTHOR'S NOTE

I grew up in a small town in northwestern Pennsylvania, much like the one in *Simple Riches*. There were four of us kids—my two older brothers, me, and my younger sister— all of us born within 5½ years. There were no McDonalds in our town, no malls, no fancy movie theaters. I walked over a mile to school every day (yes, really!). Time was filled with little things, everyday life: weeding the flower beds and garden by hand and getting snail guts under my nails, holding the flashlight while my brothers caught night crawlers, helping my mother bake bread or hang sheets on the line so they could 'catch the fresh air,' huddling with my sister in bed on Easter Sunday before Mass, gorging on a milk chocolate baby doll, planting a maple tree, *my* maple tree, with my father in our backyard, listening to my grand-mother speak in broken English as she told stories of being a young girl in Italy and coming to America, getting ready to go out on Saturday nights and fighting over *one* shower and *one* hair dryer between the four of us.

Today, my brothers and sister and I live hundreds of miles away from that little town in Pennsylvania, but it is still part of us and always will be because that's where we learned the true meaning of family and friendship, and the importance of honoring your word.

So when I decided to write about a small town and its people with their traditions and values, I thought about my life as a child and as an adult, and this is the question that led to *Simple Riches*: What is real wealth? Is it a balanced stock portfolio and a seven-figure income? Or is it more elusive, intangible, something perhaps that cannot be measured or identified or even understood? Is real wealth that which reaches out to us, touches our hearts, our souls, filling us, yet leaving us longing for more? Is it a fall morning, crisp and clear, with tips of frost covering green, a smile, full and honest, a tradition handed down, a string of memories planted with a maple tree? . . .

About the Author

As a child, I can still remember crowding around our black-and-white television set with my brothers and sister, anxiously awaiting the annual presentation of *The Wizard of Oz*. I was petrified of the flying monkeys and the wicked witch's green face, and her voice, but I was perplexed when the narrator told viewers that the first half of the movie would "look" different than the second. Ours never did—not until our black-and-white television died and our parents bought a color set (after much deliberation, I must add!). Then I understood. And that's what writing has done for me: put the color in my life. I have always been grateful for my family: my husband, my children, stepchildren, mother, brothers, sister, and all of God's gifts to me, even the heartache along the way that has made me stronger. But writing is the gift I give myself, in full-blown color, and it is the gift I wish to share with you.

I live in Ohio with my husband, my three children, and two stepchildren (yes, that equals five!) and our resident queen, a six-year-old black lab named Molly.

I would love to hear from you, whether it's about my books or just to tell me what "colors" your life! My e-mail address is **mary@marycampisi.com** and my web site address is **www.marycampisi.com**. Snail mail should be directed to me at Zebra Books, 850 Third Ave., New York, NY 10022.

<u>BOOK YOUR PLACE ON OUR WEBSITE</u> <u>AND MAKE THE</u> <u>READING CONNECTION!</u>

We've created a customized website just for our very special readers, where you can get the inside scoop on everything that's going on with Zebra, Pinnacle and Kensington books.

When you come online, you'll have the exciting opportunity to:

- View covers of upcoming books
- Read sample chapters
- Learn about our future publishing schedule (listed by publication month *and author*)
- Find out when your favorite authors will be visiting a city near you
- Search for and order backlist books from our online catalog
- Check out author bios and background information
- Send e-mail to your favorite authors
- Meet the Kensington staff online
- Join us in weekly chats with authors, readers and other guests
- Get writing guidelines
- AND MUCH MORE!

Visit our website at
http://www.kensingtonbooks.com

Thrilling Romance from
Lisa Jackson

DO YOU HAVE THE
HOHL COLLECTION?